D1074069

THE PIANO MAN

St. Martin's Press

New York

THE PIANO MAN

Noreen Gilpatrick

 For information, address St. Martin's Press, 175 Fifth Avenue, New York, N.Y. 10010.

Design by Diane Stevenson/SNAP-HAUS GRAPHICS

Library of Congress Cataloging-in-Publication Data

Gilpatrick, Noreen.
The piano man / Noreen Gilpatrick.
p. cm.
ISBN 0-312-05492-0
I. Title.
PS3557.I4638P5 1991
813'.54—dc20 90-15536
CIP

10 9 8 7 6 5 4

Author's Note

The Island used as a setting in this story is based on a real Island located in Washington state, in the southern end of Puget Sound. To those familiar with the area, exactly which Island has been used will be plain. To those who aren't, go visit and explore . . . it's lovely there.

The reason the Island is not named in the book is that for purposes of the story line and the pace of the book, some parts of the Island that really do exist were never brought into play. For instance, there is no mention of either of the two lakes that provide so much pleasure for the Islanders, nor is the golf course development and surrounding community brought into the story at all. The roads, however, are real Island roads, properly named, as are Oro and Amsterdam bays, and the Island cemetery is as close to the real cemetery as the author's powers of description allowed. And yes, Lyle Point does exist in all its bluff-top splendor, as do the forests, choked with firs and alder, huckleberry thickets and salal.

The residences of the fictional Islanders are mixed. Some used in the book do not exist at all, and some that do exist on the Island have been altered or removed from the fictional landscape in order to simplify the telling of the tale. Though Ben Murdock's house is invented, the land used as its setting is real, a lovely sprawling farm at a bend in the road with an incredibly beautiful sweep of pasture running all the way down to the sea. Grace's house, the first one north of the ferry dock, is in reality a recently built cedar-sided home with a great-room concept, very open and modern, fronting on a quiet, deserted beach that runs along the Sound. Tom Ross's cabin, built on a western bluff with its magnificent views of water and the Olympic mountain range in the distance, is a prototype of many of the sturdy, rustic homes built throughout the Island. Old Jeb's farm never was, and probably never will be.

As for the Island General Store, it is real. Very real. Complete with deli, coffeepot and tables to gather 'round. The place is usually filled with a mixture of wonderfully contrary, cantankerous, outspoken, opinionated, individualistic people who make the Island such a warm, fascinating, and unique place to live. And since this book will provide speculation around that coffeepot for many a moon to come, it is important for the author to state categorically that under *no* circumstances is *any* character in the book based in *any* way on *any* real Islander, dead or alive. However, thanks do go to one infamous Islander for allowing the fictional Grace to use her real-life nickname, "Raunchy Red."

The Piano Coop? At the time the story was written, it really did exist, it really was a converted chicken coop, ninety feet long, and it really did harbor a variety of stringed instruments. Fourteen of them, all told—including many pianos, grands and uprights, in various stages of restoration. It also contained a full pipe-organ that was fed air through a garden hose, a home-built band organ that played at every Island celebration, and a harpsichord designed and built by the Coop's resident. None of the latter three instruments are included in the book; the fictional Piano Man simply hadn't been in residency on the Island long enough to have accomplished all that work during the story's brief time span.

As for the Piano Man himself . . . ah, yes, indeed, the Island has its own. Paul Whitman, the book's Piano Man, in no way duplicates the real-life version, either physically or character-wise. However, the Island's Piano Man is a character unto himself, and he freely allowed me to borrow his Coop and his profession. He also provided all the technical information the author needed to make the profession of piano restoration believable as it unfolds in the course of the tale. Without him, there would have been no hero; without the hero, there would have been no book.

And so, while my deepest, most heartfelt thanks go to my husband, my children and my friends, who have supported and believed in me for years—decades, in some cases—this book is dedicated to:

Roger A. Russell
His Grace, the Piano Man

Part ONE

Chapter One

The dilapidated old ferry approached Steilacoom and turned for the approach into dock. Her diesels were thrown hard into reverse; the engines churned up foam as they slowed her down, then chopped off and she was allowed to glide the rest of the way in. Her blunt nose bounced from piling to piling until she finally lodged home with a thump that shook the wharf. Her mates scrambled to make her fast, then they dropped the ramp to her deck with a clanking of chains and began to unload vehicles. On this chill October morning, there were three cars and five pickup trucks coming to the mainland, and no foot passengers at all.

There were even fewer going to the Island. Good. That was precisely what he wanted, Paul Whitman thought. Some isolation and solitude. He had watched the awkward docking from the public fishing pier, shivering in the damp cold. A tall, lean man in his early forties, dressed in jeans, turtleneck and a woolen sports jacket, he stood bareheaded in the wind blowing off Puget Sound, his jacket not enough protection against the sharp marine chill. When the loading light turned green, he slung a heavy knapsack over his shoulder and picked up a large, battered suitcase.

Passengers and cars loaded from the same ramp.

Drivers would pull even with the mate and hand their commuter tickets over to be punched, exchanging bits and pieces of local news while they waited. Everyone seemed to know everyone else, and there were hails back and forth between cars. Except for surreptitious glances his way, Paul's presence was ignored.

When his turn came, he surrendered his ticket to the ferry mate, receiving directions to the passenger stairwell without asking. He accepted the acknowledgment of his status as stranger and smiled. "How long a ride is it out to the Island?"

"Twenty-five or thirty minutes, depending how bad the barnacles are." The mate gave Paul a friendly smile. "You're the new Piano Man, right?"

Paul bridled at the term. In his world, a Piano Man played honkytonk in some backwater saloon and spelled Bach with a *k*. He let it pass. "I guess so," he answered simply.

"Well, Old Jeb's meeting you on the other side."

"Would he be Mr. Murdock?"

The friendliness shut down like a closed concert hall. "Nope." The mate walked up to another car pulling up and began visiting with the driver. Paul had been dismissed.

The passenger cabin was a wooden square box set amidships behind the pilothouse, at the top of a steep gangway. It was lined with wooden benches that looked as if they'd been stolen from a park. Windows showed a passenger deck outside, but the October wind sweeping over Puget Sound was too cold to entice him from the warmth of the cabin to watch the departure. On the dock below, the iron gates clanged shut, the heavy diesels revved up, the horn blared like a basso profundo and the ferry lurched into the Sound. He appeared to be the only foot passenger on board this run.

As the ferry left the dock, Paul stared through the salt-stained windows at the islands in the distance. They rose out of the gray, cheerless waters of the Sound, swelling hillocks of shadowed bluffs and somber forests. The stark, grim walls of a state prison standing bleak and lonely on a promontory on one of the islands passed by on the starboard side. On another small island, off the port side, a deserted road twisted up the side of a steep bluff from the small dock at its base to the thick forests on top.

In the distance, nearly lost in the mist, was the third island. Several miles long, it rose like a humpback whale from the recesses of the Sound, a wilderness of sky-scraping firs atop rugged bluffs. A black-bellied rain cloud hovered over the major portion of the Island, casting a black shadow over the bleak forests. That island was to be his home for the next year. From this distance, it looked gloomy and unappealing. But at least it should be peaceful. And after the last few months, he'd welcome that. In fact, if he never had to deal with people again, it would be fine with him.

Still, he didn't exactly know what to expect. He'd been hired by a go-between, told what the job entailed, provided with a map and detailed instructions, and had been assured the check would appear in the mail each week. It had seemed like a good solution to his situation, but now, viewing the Island and seeing for himself the extreme remoteness he'd be enduring, he began to wonder. It was one thing to toss two decades of a life overboard, but quite different to face the resulting reality.

The ferry traveled along the eastern edge of the Island for a while, then made a wide turn to approach the landing. The high, rugged bluffs swooped down to water level several hundred feet south of the dock, but the landing area itself was a gentler slope rising up to the spine of the Island. Portions of the forest had been felled up to the brow of the hill to allow space for the handful of houses scattered across the sloped clearings. A two-lane road climbed sharply to disappear among the sky-scraping firs, its thick forests closing off the interior from casual view. From first appearances, the Island seemed a lonely, melancholy place to live.

The boat docked with another bone-jarring thump against the pier. Paul's written instructions had been clear. Catch the ten A.M. ferry and an old red pickup would meet him at the Island's dock. And there it was. As battered as the old man leaning against a fender.

He was a shrunken gnome of a man, with a slight, misshapen body and a face toughened into leathery wrinkles. Motionless, he watched Paul hike up the long pier to the parking area. When he spoke, his voice was gruff, his face expressionless. "You the Piano Man?"

Inside, Paul bridled again, at the tone of voice as much as at the term, but he merely nodded and stuck out a hand. "Paul Whitman."

The hand was ignored. "They call me Old Jeb." The old man slung Paul's suitcase and knapsack into the truck bed and swung himself behind the wheel with the agility of a man half his age. Following more slowly, Paul climbed into the cab and settled as comfortably as he could among the broken springs.

They jolted up a steep grade, over a badly patched road that twisted and turned through heavy forests of fir and alder for a mile or so, before hitting a narrow, relatively straight, relatively smooth stretch cut through the woods, running south along the spine of the Island.

The place was more populated than Paul would have guessed. Within minutes of the ferry dock, there was a church and a Community Clubhouse. Further along the spine was the Island General Store. Each was set into its own clearing with a small parking area in front.

Beyond the Island store, around a slight bend in the road, a lane marked with a simple wooden sign, CEMETERY, led up a hill into the forest. He glanced up the lane curving out of sight into the woods and made a mental note of its location. Years ago, in their good days together, he and Anna had explored many a country graveyard together, intrigued by the stories that could be pieced together from the headstones.

On the inside edge of another curve sat a one-room schoolhouse.

"Is the schoolhouse still used?" Paul asked, breaking the silence.

"Nope."

"The kids go to school on the mainland?"

"Some do." The old man's tone was grumpy.

"Where do the rest go, then?"

"We got us a new schoolhouse on t'other side of the Island. A two-roomer."

"You have that many kids living here?" Paul asked with some surprise.

"'Pears that way."

"How many families live here?"

"Too many."

Paul couldn't help grinning inside at the curmudgeonly answer, but he kept his face expressionless. "How many's too many?"

"Coupla hundred, mebbe."

Paul looked at the solid wall of forest lining the road. "Hard to believe," he murmured.

The old man stayed silent.

After a few more minutes on the rough-patched road, they finally broke free of the trees and dipped down to a large bay, protected by two long spits of land. Here, the Island seemed more open, more benign. Swamp and meadows spread over gentle hills to the west. To the east, the bay lay gray but placid beneath the brooding sky.

The road followed the graceful shoreline. Paul broke the silence again. "What's that called?" He indicated the water.

"Oro Bay."

Paul waited to see if he'd add anything to it, but nothing more was forthcoming.

Halfway along the shoreline, by the far side of a meadow, the old pickup slowed. Hanging at the road's edge was an old wooden sign with THE COOP painted on it in faded letters. Old Jeb made a cautious right turn onto the steep, rutted driveway and gunned the pickup. They jolted up a steep grade that was little more than two ruts filled with rocks and scattered with potholes.

An old, ramshackle one-story building stretched a hundred feet or better across the brow of the hill. It had weathered board siding and a long line of small windows overlooking the spread of meadow below and the bay beyond. A sparse group of gnarled fruit trees formed the remnants of an orchard to one side of the driveway, and an old shanty of a shed stood behind. The meadow grass was well above knee-height, and overgrown shrubs and vines leaned helter-skelter against the Coop in a random, slightly mad pattern. An air of decay and neglect surrounded the whole place. At the top of the hill, the ever-present forest began again.

Old Jeb turned into a parking area behind the Coop.

"Is Mr. Murdock here?"

"Nope."

"Will he be here?"

"Nope."

"What about the other Piano Man? Is he still around?"

"Nope." The old man jolted to a stop, swung out of the cab and dug in his pocket for a key ring.

Paul retrieved his suitcase and knapsack from the truck bed and followed him through overgrown shrubbery to the back door. Old Jeb battled the lock a minute, then pushed open the door and stepped back out of the way.

A strong odor assaulted Paul. A deep, sickening stench that blared like a trumpet blast. Paul sniffed, trying to identify it.

The old man's sharp eyes took in the action. "Rats. I noticed it yesterday. Damp, mildew—and a dead rat or two."

"As long as they're dead ones."

They'd entered the small living end of the Coop. An area the size of a small hunter's cabin had been partitioned off and a sink, stove, and an ancient refrigerator lined the wall to the right of the door. A plain pine table and wooden chairs sat in front of them. Beyond was a platform bed and a large wardrobe closet. An old club chair and ottoman were pulled up next to a small bookcase with an oil lamp sitting on top.

Around the corner of the partition, stretching to the far, dusky end of the building, was the music studio. It was one long room, ninety feet from end to end, Paul estimated. Heavy beams formed the rafters where once upon a time chickens had roosted. The floor planks were broad and thick, solid beneath his feet. The eastern wall was composed of small wood-framed windows, six over six, overlooking the meadow and the bay below. At the northern end of the Coop, a couple of grimy skylights had been inserted into the roof. Beneath the skylights were the pianos. He went over to them.

There were three: an upright at least a century old, a Chickering concert grand and a baby grand. All three had been battered and abused, as if someone had attacked them with a sledge hammer in a black rage that hadn't eased until every edge and surface had been crushed, fractured and fragmented. The keys had taken their share of abuse, too, for they were cracked and splintered and, in a few cases, smashed into sawdust. He bent to look at the undersides. Each piano would have to be repaired and rebuilt from the soundboard up.

Slowly Paul's focus returned to the room and he became aware of the old man standing in the opening to the kitchen, watching him through narrowed eyes. Paul felt he was being summed up and judged. He straightened from his crouch, not liking the feeling the old man gave him, and headed back towards the kitchen area. "Those pianos have been pretty abused. How'd they come to be that way?"

The old man shrugged, then dumped the door key on the table. "I put in some milk and eggs for you. Need anything else, the store's a couple of miles back. Closes at six. You'll have to do your own cleaning up, the Missus won't come in here no more. I also left you enough wood and kindling for a couple of days. You'd best get a fire going. The nights're cold now and dark comes early. You know how to handle that?" He nodded towards an old wood stove set in the center of the kitchen area. "It can get real cranky."

"I'll manage."

The old man shrugged. "Mr. Murdock says to see to your needs. I'll be by in the morning to check on you." He hesitated a moment, cold blue eyes fixed on Paul, then shrugged once more and was gone.

The chug-chug of the pickup died away and the silence was complete. It caught Paul's attention and he listened hard. Nothing. Not a sound anywhere.

Trying to ignore the silence, he returned to the pianos. For all the windows, the light was dim, and he could find no light switches anywhere. He took the oil lamp from the bookcase and set it on a nearby work table, then began testing wood. He gave each piano as thorough a going-over as he could within a short span of time. Lots of gouges, chips and cracked veneers. But there was no dry rot, soft wood or crumbling that he could detect. If the soundboards were all right . . .

He ran a practiced forefinger up the keyboard of the upright. Nothing. Not a note. Only the sound of the key mechanisms. He checked the other two. They were the same. There were no strings in any of them.

Where the hell were the strings?

He was merely annoyed at first. His vision of tuning one of the pianos and putting on a concert for the forest creatures vanished.

Then the implication hit. That meant no music. Panicky, he glanced around him. There wasn't even a radio. There'd be no music at all.

The silence moved in on him again. There wasn't a sound anywhere. There were no traffic noises, no sirens, no horns blaring, no people laughing, yelling or bustling past, no sense of movement or urgency or busyness. There was nothing. The wind was still. The forest was thick with silence. This was what it would be like when he died, he thought. Simply silence. A cold silence. And no music.

Chapter Two

The Coop was filthy, little more than a tenement. Paul wanted to start the detailed examination of the pianos, but once he started, he'd lose himself in his work, and the real world would fall away from him. As he'd kept drilling into his students, do A before B. His first need was to get the place cleaned up and warm so he could inhabit it with at least some modicum of comfort. The rotten odor was suffocating.

He took off his sports jacket and slung it across the bed, then went back to the kitchen and flicked the switch by the back door. It was only a bare bulb over the sink, but having it on made him feel better. As far as he could tell, except for the one in the bathroom, it was the only light in the place. He rolled up his sleeves, readying himself for the job ahead, shivering as the frigid air hit bare skin.

Warmth came first, he decided. Kindling and quarter-logs were in a tin box by the stove. A small pile of newspaper was stacked nearby. He crunched up the entertainment section, enjoying the irony of that, and laid some kindling on top. The damper was touchy, he discovered. Opened too little, the flame died. Opened too wide, there'd be a quick flare, and the flame died anyway. He finally got a small fire going and satisfied himself with that.

The filthy kitchen was next. Cleaning supplies were sparse. A bar of soap, some liquid detergent, a can of scouring powder and a sour-smelling rag. He scoured the sink and small counter, washed the few dishes and pans he found, then scrubbed out the old percolator. A new can of coffee was on a shelf nailed up between two studs, and he put on a pot, guessing at proportions of water to coffee.

He opened the door to the refrigerator. Milk, butter, eggs, cheese, bread. Why bread in there . . . to keep it from the old man's dead rats? At least the refrigerator was clean, and he had some makings for a noon meal. But he'd have to do some shopping before nightfall. A quick flip of the dishrag over the chairs and bookcase got rid of the worst of the dust and a session with the scouring powder brought the bathroom to usability.

Surrounded by the order he'd brought to the place, he stood in the center and surveyed the living area. The wood stove emanated warmth, the oil lamp glowed softly on the bookshelf, the refrigerator hummed a low E and the percolator played a cheerful tune in the key of C.

It would do.

He turned now to the bed. It was a crude platform sitting gracelessly on the floor, shoved against a wall. Why it was in that spot made no sense. A corner would've helped camouflage the ugliness of it. As it was, it stuck out like an orange crate. The mattress was old, but at least it was dry. A stack of clean sheets, a blanket and a heavy tattered quilt had been dumped on top.

He got the bed made, then hefted his suitcase onto

the quilt and unpacked. His custom-made tuxedos and suits had been left behind. He'd brought jeans, thick sweaters, one heavy jacket, woolen socks, a couple of pair of tennis shoes and loafers, and an old pair of sturdy work boots. Life was to be simple and rough-hewn, not the silk shirts and handwoven ties of days gone by. He pulled on one of the sweaters and picked up his jacket to hang in the old wardrobe standing in the bathroom.

Jacket swung over his shoulder, he opened the door, already reaching for a coat hanger. His hand froze halfway there and he stared. A length of piano string hung from the clothes rod, gleaming in the reflected light of the bare bulb over the sink. One end had been wound around the clothes pole. The other was twisted into a hangman's noose.

Well, welcome to the Island, he thought. He broke his freeze and hung up the jacket, then unwound the noose from the rod. A double-ought G string. Strong enough to hang a man if the notion struck. Someone had a macabre sense of humor. It sure couldn't be Old Jeb, though. The old man had no sense of humor at all, macabre or otherwise.

Well, at least now he had one piano string. He could always install the noose and put on a single note concert. He could call it the One-Finger Symphony. He grinned at the thought.

But then a question occurred. If Old Jeb had had to unlock the door when they'd arrived, how had the noose gotten here?

The silence distracted him again. It seemed like every time he stopped moving, all he could hear was the thick silence. He really was alone in this godforsaken place.

▌

He was in the middle of a luncheon omelet when he heard the bass throb of a powerful engine whirring up the driveway. Paul rose from the table and went into the backyard as a sheriff's car pulled into the parking area and a big bull of a man climbed out, officially dressed, complete with creaking leather, a gun in a hip-holster and a big wad of keys hanging from his belt. He was about Paul's age, broad-shouldered, solid-hipped, with thighs as big as a beef cow's and a way of planting his feet and standing that was more like an oak tree than a man. Clear blue eyes settled on Paul as he went outside to greet him. "You the new Piano Man?"

Paul nodded. "Paul Whitman." He stuck his hand out.

The Sheriff's huge paw enfolded it completely. "Frank Hall."

A familiar chug-chug sounded from down the hill and Old Jeb's pickup topped the driveway. He pulled even with the patrol car, swung down and sauntered over. "Afternoon, Frank. Mr. Whitman."

"Afternoon, Jeb," Hall said. "You looking for me, or for him?"

"Just brought the young feller here this morning. Figured I'd drop by for a cup of coffee, see how he's making out." The old man actually sounded relaxed and friendly.

Paul kept the surprise out of his face. "Let's all have some."

Silence engulfed them as they gathered around the

table. Paul set mugs in front of them. The Sheriff manhandled his, looking around. "Never been in here before. An old chicken coop, wasn't it?"

Paul expected Old Jeb to answer, but the old man sat there, mute. "That's my understanding," he said, finally.

Hall gave a single nod, took a large swig of the coffee, then adjusted his chair back from the table so both men were in easy view. He studied them closely. "Understand you've got a small problem," he said to Paul.

Paul thought of the noose, amazed the Sheriff knew about it already. "Well, it's not that serious."

The Sheriff looked puzzled. "What isn't?"

Paul returned his puzzled look. "What are you talking about?"

"The way I hear it is you've got some piano wire missing. What did you think I meant?"

Paul shrugged, lost now. "The strings, I guess."

"Strings?"

Paul nodded. "They're called strings. Piano strings."

"Okay, strings, then. The way I hear it is they're missing."

"From what I can see, you're right."

"Kind of unusual, isn't it, collecting piano strings?"

"Someone likes his fishing." Paul tried a grin.

The Sheriff simply stared at him. "How's that?"

"They make great leader wires."

"What else can they be used for?"

Paul thought of the noose again, but decided against mentioning it. "Picture wire. Hanging anything heavy. If you use a strong enough weight of string, you could even hang bookshelves from the ceiling, for instance. It makes them appear to float in space."

"Is it like chicken wire?"

Paul hesitated. "No, I don't think so. I'm not really familiar . . ." He turned to Old Jeb for help.

The old man sat quietly, saying nothing. He hadn't spoken since he'd entered the place.

"What about the Piano Man before you? Where's he gone to?"

Again, Paul waited for the old man to answer. Again, he just sat there. "Back to where he came from, I suppose," Paul said, finally. "Wherever that is."

"You don't know where?"

"I haven't a clue."

"Then you didn't know him."

"No."

"Any idea why he left?"

"None."

"Would he have any use for piano strings?"

"I suppose it's possible. Not knowing him, I really couldn't say."

The Sheriff probed some more with his eyes, his face bland, his gaze sharp. Finally, he nodded, finished his coffee and rose, heading towards the back door. Paul followed, Old Jeb moving with him.

"Well, then, I guess that's about it for today. Those missing wi—strings turn up, you let me know." Hall opened the door, pausing to give Old Jeb an amused glance. "Well, Jeb, nice visitin' with you." There was a second amused look, then he was gone.

Paul listened for the patrol car to turn on to the road and disappear, then turned to Old Jeb. "What was that all about?"

"Nothin'." The old man shrugged. "Well, I better be goin' m'self. Thankee for the coffee."

"There's plenty more."

"Another time, mebbe."

Paul stared after the old pickup chug-chugging down the rutted drive. Now why on earth would a sheriff, who one would assume was a busy man with a lot of demands on his time, take a half-hour ferry ride just to inquire about some missing piano strings? And who'd told him the strings were missing, anyway? Interesting. He turned back to the Coop.

He threw out the cold omelet and returned to the pianos, touching them gently, as if reassuring them they were no longer alone. He wanted to start work on them right away, to find out what they'd need, then draw up the lists of parts and supplies so he could get started. But that would take several days, and he knew that once he'd begun, he'd get absorbed, the hours would drift past and he wouldn't get the shopping done before nightfall. Then he'd face a supper of eggs and toast. And a breakfast of eggs and toast. And Lord knew how many other meals of eggs and toast. As Anna had often pointed out, he was the Great Procrastinator.

If you do A before B . . . He unloaded books, parts catalogs and sheet music from his knapsack into the bookcase, then pulled his hunter's jacket from the closet. He considered locking the door, as Old Jeb obviously had, but decided against it. Who could get in, a raccoon? More dead rats? For that matter, who'd want to get in, his friendly neighborhood noose-maker? He slung the empty knapsack over one shoulder and set off.

The gloomy clouds had moved on and the afternoon was clear and sunny. As he descended the rutted driveway alongside the meadow, Oro Bay spread out below him, shimmering a cold but brilliant blue beneath the golden autumn sunshine.

An old wooden tub of a scow was maneuvering through a channel from the bay out to the Sound. A brisk chop set its cabin roof bobbing back and forth. It was a stunning sight, white boat on blue water, sunbeams shimmering on the undulating swells.

Even the Coop didn't look half-bad in the soft sunlight pouring down over field and meadow. Rather rustic, he judged. He began to think his year in exile wouldn't be without its pleasures.

Chapter Three

The Island General Store was small, possibly a tenth of the size of supermarkets on the mainland, and the aroma of fresh-brewed coffee hit him as soon as he walked through the door.

Every foot of floor space was jammed with something. There were aisles of canned foods, shelves of oil lanterns and big cooking pots, walls of dairy and meat cases, and a small hardware department, all crammed together in no logical order. A post office cage ran along the front near the cash register.

A deli area had been carved out of the far end of the store, and a half-dozen tables and chairs were spread around in front of a short-order grill and a coffeepot. The store offered a little bit of something for everyone.

The cash register stood next to the front door and a man of about thirty sat on a high stool behind it, working in a ledger book.

Paul approached him. "Good afternoon."

The young man nodded. "Afternoon." He studied Paul. "You the new Piano Man?"

Again, Paul bridled at the term, but merely said, "Yes. Paul Whitman."

"I'm Thaddeus Webster. Welcome to the Island."

"Thank you. Is that today's paper?" Paul indicated a stack of newspapers setting to one side.

"Yep, the local rag from the continent. Comes in on the first boat every day."

"What time would that be?"

"Six A.M. their side, six-thirty ours."

"And what time do you open?"

"Six-thirty-one," Thaddeus grinned.

The man seemed friendly enough and, after having to deal with Old Jeb, Paul was grateful. "Mind if I stop for a coffee? It smells pretty good." He took out a quarter for the paper and laid it on the counter.

Thaddeus picked the coin up and handed it back. "We'll settle up when you leave. And Jenny'll help you with whatever you want in the deli. She cooks a good meal, too, if you're hungry."

"I've already eaten, but thanks anyway."

At the mention of her name, the girl behind the grill paused in her work to look over at them. She was tall, slender and pretty, about the same age as Thaddeus, give or take a year or two, with brown hair pulled back into a simple bun. A small worry frown nibbled at her strong brows as she studied Paul, her dark brown eyes expressive and sad. It made him feel he had to be gentle with her or she'd bolt like a deer. He'd had students like that, sensitive and vulnerable. Too vulnerable, almost, for life.

"You must be Jenny." Paul smiled at her.

"Jenny Webster." Her smile, when it appeared, was gentle and warm. "And you must be the new Piano Man."

He nodded. "Paul Whitman. Thaddeus thought you might unearth a spare cup of coffee for me."

She pointed to a work area at the end of the counter where two pots of coffee sat on a hot plate next to a stack of styrofoam cups. "It's a self-serve. The orange collar's decaf, black's regular. The first cup's thirty-five cents, refills are free."

Thanking her, he poured himself a cup of regular and, turning, caught three old men staring at him. They were hunched over coffee cups, their faces impassive, their gaze unreadable.

Suddenly, he felt uncomfortably aware of everyone's eyes fixed on him. Including Thaddeus's. Instantly, the young man looked away. As one, the old men followed suit.

Paul took his coffee to a vacant place two tables over from the group and sat down in a corner so he faced all five people, all now purposefully ignoring him. Thaddeus was bent back over his ledger, Jenny had started peeling a panful of potatoes, and the old men were intent once again on their coffee cups. The silence around him was deep. He opened his paper and from behind the front page, he studied each of the old men.

One was portly, with a heavy gray beard, which he absently stroked into a disciplined point. The calmness of his gaze, the slow steady movement of his hand down the beard, the easy way he sat, gave him a thoughtful, commanding air. Using an old trick from his university teaching when confronted with large groups of new students each term, Paul gave him a nickname that he could link to a given name when he learned it. Graybeard.

The man to Graybeard's right was a tall skeleton of a figure, his skin stretching like parchment over face and throat. Freckle-faced, broad-mouthed and loose-jointed, he sat slightly stooped over the table, long gangly arms lifting his coffee cup halfway, his head bowing down to meet it. With every swallow of coffee, his Adam's apple bobbed up and down like a conductor's baton. Adam's Apple.

The third man was as bald as a tuba bell. Shiny skin stretched like a pink skullcap from ear to ear. He was as thin as Adam's Apple, but shorter, much shorter. And where Adam's Apple had kind of an easy, relaxed, good-humored air about him, Skullcap wore a dark, gloomy expression as he brooded into his coffee cup.

The one thing the three had in common besides advanced old age was an air of remoteness. Even Adam's Apple, who seemed more relaxed than the others, had a closed, restrained look to his face. It gave them a secretive air, which intensified whenever he caught their eyes on him, as if they knew something about him he didn't know.

His whole reception on the Island puzzled him. The ferry mate, clamming up so suddenly at the mention of Murdock. The grumpy taciturnity of Old Jeb. A sheriff stopping by over some missing piano strings. And now, the cool indifference of the three old men.

Finally, he shrugged it off as his imagination. He was a stranger here, after all. He refilled his coffee cup and settled in to read his paper.

A sharp voice pierced his concentration. "You the Piano Man?"

The woman was in her seventies at least, a short, stocky, corseted matron, with a head of thinning white hair formed into tight fingerwaves. She stood by his table, hands on her hips, a huge black purse dangling from one wrist. She had the most determined pair of blue eyes Paul had ever seen, and they were fixed straight on him. "You the Piano Man?" she asked again.

He straightened up like a kid caught slumping at his schooldesk. "Yes, ma'am."

Her frank blue eyes appraised him thoroughly. "You gonna stick around?" she demanded. "That other one, he didn't last long."

Two tables over, Graybeard growled, "Grace—"

"Just up and left. No goodbyes, no nothing. And I waited all day for him, too." Her chins warbled with indignation. "Damned nuisance, I can tell you." There was the slightest hint of a twinkle in the strong baby blues, as if she were being outrageous and knew she was being outrageous and was thoroughly enjoying it.

"Grace. . . !"

Confused, Paul asked, "Why were you waiting for him?"

"Supposed to tune my piano. Can't play a decent hymn on it."

Graybeard was rising, now. "Damn it, Grace!"

"Hymn?"

"I'm the church pianist. We got two churches here on the Island—Lutheran and Baptist. You're either a churcher or you're not, and if you are, you're either t'one or t'other. 'Course, I'm a Lutheran myself. Well, now, let's see. You're gonna need time to settle in a mite . . . what you got planned for tomorrow morning? That'd give you the rest of today."

"Actually, I'm still a bit swamped . . ." Paul began.

Graybeard had moved by then. He grabbed her arm and forced her to face him. As short as he was, he towered over her. She glared up at him like a whale on a rampage.

"Quit imposing on people!" Graybeard thundered. "This young fella's got work to do for Mr. Murdock. 'Tain't no good takin' a man from a payin' job to do something for free."

Grace held her stance. "My piano's gonna get tuned," she said flatly.

"And I told you the board would see to it. Now quit this stubbornness and leave the fella alone. Your piano'll get done in its own time!"

"You said that right. And its time has come!" With a final glare at the old man, she turned back to Paul. "Swamped, huh? Okay, I'll give you to the end of the week. And just so's you don't disappear on me, too, I'll do the pickin' up. On Friday. In the morning. Ten o'clock sharp. Be waitin' at the road front of your place. I don't mess none with that driveway of yours if I can help it." Her orders delivered, she yanked her arm free of the old man's grip. "Nice visitin' with you, Abner." She sailed away.

Graybeard gave a heavy sigh of exasperation as he watched her go. "I apologize, Mr. Whitman. That woman ain't got a lick of respect for anything. You just ignore what she says. We'll see to her piano just like we promised."

Paul waved the apology away. "She reminds me a little of my grandmother. She was the town terror, pure bull-headed stubbornness once she got going."

Graybeard nodded sad agreement.

On a sudden impulse, now that the ice was broken,

Paul rose and stuck out his hand. "I'm afraid you have the advantage. I'm Paul Whitman."

The old man had no choice. "Abner Ross."

Paul glanced at the two other men, still sitting.

Abner introduced them reluctantly. "Calvin Brown and Nathaniel Webster."

Paul nodded to each. Calvin nodded curtly, his skullcap reflecting the overhead lights, then brooded some more in his coffee cup.

Nathaniel of the Adam's apple gave him a half-smile. "They usually call me Bobbin." He pointed to his throat and grinned.

"It's a pleasure to meet you," Paul said, smiling. Then he addressed Abner. "Don't worry about your friend, I'll be happy to tune her piano for her."

Calvin looked at Bobbin, Bobbin looked at Abner, and Abner stroked his beard, gazing at Paul. "That's mighty kind of you, but we can't be troubling you like that."

"No trouble at all."

There was a moment of awkward silence. From behind her deli case, Jenny watched them, a small frown worrying her brow. Finally Abner murmured, "We'll see."

Suddenly, Paul had had enough. It was obvious that his presence was causing some discomfort. He folded his newspaper and carried his coffee cup to the trash bin. "I have some shopping to do, so I'll be on my way," he said in an even tone. "It was a pleasure to meet you all."

The old men nodded as one, their faces closed off once again.

Keeping his thoughts to himself, he grabbed an old

grocery cart and wheeled it up and down the aisles. The store had most of what he needed—meats, fresh vegetables, staples, cleaning supplies and a fair selection of wines. He chose as much as his knapsack could hold and took the cart to the counter.

Thaddeus subtotaled his purchases, added a quarter for the paper and thirty-five cents for his coffee, totaled it out and tore off the cash register receipt. He pushed it across the counter along with a pen. "Just sign."

"I can pay for it." Paul pulled out his wallet.

"Sorry. Mr. Murdock's orders. He's taking care of everything."

"Really, I insist."

"Mr. Murdock doesn't want it that way."

Who the hell was Murdock anyway?

"Is Mr. Murdock here on the Island?"

The earlier friendliness was gone. Thaddeus's face was as closed off as the others. "He stays in close contact." He picked up the pen and held it out. "Just sign, please."

Paul let it go. When in Rome . . . He took the pen and signed.

The friendly smile was back. "If you don't want to carry all this to your place, I can drop them off at the Coop later today."

But Paul wasn't buying the friendly act. Not right away, at any rate. "Thanks, I can manage."

Outside, relieved to be free of their scrutiny, he shook his head. Weird people, these Islanders.

▌

By the time he'd returned to the Coop and stowed his groceries, there wasn't enough daylight to start a detailed examination of the pianos. He'd have to leave it until first light in the morning. Which left him at loose ends.

He stared around the Coop, which had once again taken on aspects of a tenement. He'd brought a few of his books with him, so he could settle in for the evening and read. But the old chair with its slanted seat and uncertain springs and worn upholstery wasn't particularly his idea of comfort. And the oil lamp held no romance for him. He could only imagine the eyestrain involved in reading beside a flickering flame.

Suddenly he missed the music room he'd had at home. There were polished oak floors, walls of books, shelves of piano scores, a deep leather chair next to a proper reading lamp and his Steinway sitting in an alcove on its own Oriental carpet.

He poured himself some coffee. If he were home, what would he be doing right now, given this free time? His fingers twitched with the answer. He'd be at the grand, lost in his world of music. Then later on, Anna would come home from work and—

Yes, Whitman? And? And what?

That's where the happy domestic scene broke down. Anna sure as hell wasn't happy. Not with him, at least.

A sharp thump against the outside of the Coop punctured his thoughts. He came to with a start. He moved into the kitchen and set his coffee cup on the table, then peered through the grimy window in the back door. He couldn't see anyone, and certainly had heard no car or truck coming up the drive. Yet the door of the old shed stood wide open. He was positive it had been closed when he'd come back from the store. Was someone in there?

The front of the shed was in shadow cast by a lowering sun in the western sky, and it was impossible to see inside from where he stood. His skin crawled at the thought of a prowler. He was isolated here, without a vehicle, without a phone. There was no way to call for help if he needed it. No one lived nearby that he knew about. In fact, no one from his past even knew where he was. He'd cut all ties to the mainland. If he was in for trouble, he'd be on his own. He took a deep breath and yanked the door open.

A quick tour of the grounds and shed revealed only a thick tree branch lying at the base of the Coop's rear wall. About five feet in length, it was gnarled and twisted into a crooked staff, with a bark that was rough and heavily scaled. It looked as though it had come from one of the fruit trees in the orchard. Apple, more than likely. He glanced towards the orchard in the far meadow, then back at the building. Could he have been so deep in thought he hadn't noticed or heard a rogue gust of wind come through?

The land gave no answer. Up on the ridge, the forest posed against the late afternoon sky, the fir spires lit up by the falling sun like church steeples flooded by spotlights. The trees of the orchard stood quiet, their bare limbs frozen in stillness. The meadow basked peacefully under the lowering sun. And when he rounded the Coop the bay spread smooth and mirrorlike below, a darkening blue under the declining daylight. As far as he could tell, there wasn't a breath of breeze anywhere.

He finally shrugged off the strange appearance of the branch. It had probably been there the whole day and he'd simply not noticed it before.

But the incident had served to forestall a heavy brooding session and he was grateful. He was simply going to have to keep his memories under control if he was to stay rational.

Now that he was outside in the fresh fall air, he had a yen to explore his new world further. If he couldn't work in the fading dusk, and reading held no appeal, then an amble around the Island would kill some time. He went back inside to get ready, the thump forgotten.

Chapter Four

He left the Coop just before dusk and headed north. The bay quickly fell behind him and he was back in the wilderness of forest. Thrashings and rustlings came from the trees as he walked past. Deer? The forest was thick with undergrowth and he couldn't see anything.

As twilight deepened to sunset, the forest blackened. The trees were a couple of hundred feet tall, standing as close together as theater seats, but with aisles permanently clogged by thickets and underbrush. Far above his head, the sky was merely a thin line of cobalt blue where the road cut through the tall trees.

He passed the store once again, sparing only a brief thought for the Islanders he'd met there today. A strange people, he thought again. Then he was back into the woods, striding alone once more among the firs. He passed the church he'd seen on the drive in from the ferry dock, then the Community Clubhouse came into view. Then the road began to slant downhill, twisting and turning its way to the ferry dock, deserted and lonely-looking in the sun's dying rays. From there, a road angled north and he followed it.

Here, along the northern shoreline, the Island seemed less forested and more settled. Trees thinned now and then for a series of old cottages, and a group of summer cabins was clustered along one craggy bluff. Farther on, the road curved into a gentle slope of land that was open to the Sound.

The sky ran forever and in its center, far to the north, the Olympic mountain range stood ablaze in an awesome sunset, one peak following another like crested waves upon the sea. The dying rays had sliced the snowcaps into strips of glowing scarlets, crimsons, and mauves. As the sun sank in a fiery sphere, the colors changed and deepened. It was like watching a heavy layer of lush velvet shimmer under colored spots, a scenic sight unlike anything on the East Coast. Entranced, he trailed the setting sun through a thinned strand of trees to the water's edge, losing himself in the sunset's performance.

It took a moment for the throaty hum of a pickup truck to penetrate his consciousness. It was moving at a speed just above idle, as if its driver were searching for something more than just potholes in the road. Paul had been so lost in the intense quiet that the intrusion startled him. With the stand of trees at his back, he was invisible from the road, and some instinct made him step quickly into a shadow and stand absolutely stock-still until the truck had passed by and disappeared down the road.

The last of the sun was gone, and as he made his way back to the road, he debated whether he should return to the Coop or not. He felt a bit chagrined at the edginess that had made him hide like that. It was almost as if those old men in the deli had intimidated him with their strange behavior, giving him the feeling that his mere presence on the Island was an offense, a violation of their privacy. But the roads were public property, after all, and what was he harming by simply following wherever they led? He turned his back on the way he'd come and set off into the unknown.

The road curved and brought him down the western edge of the Island, past more forest until he reached a cluster of homes built around a deep, narrow bay. Full darkness had set in and lights were on in several of the houses. He watched them for a moment, lost in what he called the lamp-in-the-window syndrome. In the city, this feeling had often overcome him, the lights signifying home to him, and everything good that was wrapped up in the word, like warmth, love, safety and contentment. In reality, the people in those houses were probably facing disappointments and broken dreams just as he and Anna had done. But still, wouldn't it be nice if, just once, that wasn't so?

The road degenerated into a narrow lane that climbed once more into the forest. After a mile or so, it ended at a sharp curve back towards the middle of the Island, in front of a large farm. Hundreds of acres of land had been cleared, and the fields sloped for miles down a gentle hillside. A large two-story farmhouse sprawled across the top of the slope, the fields below, the Sound below that, with a supremely majestic Mount Rainier rising up fourteen thousand feet or more in the far distance. Standing across the road and uphill from the farm, he was caught once again by a view unlike anything he'd ever seen. He selected a fallen tree branch uphill from the curve and sat down on it to rest and enjoy the panoramic splendor spread out below.

His legs were grateful for the respite. He'd been walking for well over two hours and the muscles in his calves ached with the strain. He'd lived a taxicab-type life for too many years, and his body wasn't used to this kind of exercise.

He was beginning to question his ability to make it all the way home when he heard the powerful hum of the pickup truck again. It was far back among the trees, coming from behind him, down the road he'd just walked. This time he was too tired to bother moving out of sight. Besides, why should he? He was on public property this time.

The truck looked as if it were headed for the farm. It was almost past him before the driver saw him in the light of the headlamps. Brakes squealed as it came to a sudden stop. The passenger door opened and Skullcap, one of the old men from the deli, climbed down from the cab. Skullcap, Paul thought, seeking his name. Cap equaled Calvin. Calvin. His name was Calvin Brown.

Paul started to smile in greeting, but Calvin's glower stopped him. The old man obviously was no friendlier out of the deli than he had been in it. "We been looking for you. Get in."

Paul rose, his calf muscles on the verge of cramping. "Is something wrong?"

There was no response. The old man simply held the door. Paul climbed in and slid over to the center, Calvin getting in behind him.

Abner Ross was at the wheel, his gray beard illuminated by the lights on the dash. His eyes were unreadable in the shadows. Calvin slammed the door shut and Abner let out the clutch.

"Is there something wrong?" Paul repeated, directing his question this time to Abner.

"It'd be safer for you if you stayed put for a while. You being unfamiliar with the woods and all."

"I stayed on the road. Except for walking a bit of beach."

"It'd just be safer if you stayed to home."

Paul was too puzzled to argue.

They were heading east now, cutting through the night across the southern end of the Island. The road ended back at Oro Bay, just south of the Coop. The truck turned north, past another farm, then slowed at the Coop's driveway for the turn up the hill. They jolted up the rocks and ruts and swung into the parking area behind the Coop. Calvin climbed down from the cab to let Paul out.

Before Paul could follow, Abner placed a hand on Paul's arm, his face not unkind. "You stay to home, you'll be all right." He let him go.

Paul climbed out and Calvin, with a final glower his way, swung back in. The engine was shoved into gear and Paul watched the truck head on down the driveway. "Thanks for the lift, guys," he said to the night air.

The receding taillights winked back at him. At least *they* were friendly.

Chapter Five

He awoke the next morning to an empty woodbox. The Coop was drafty, damp and cold. Rain was threatening, but rain or no rain, he was forced to attack the woodpile at the back of the shed. He chopped and split wood until his arms trembled and his muscles caught fire. Twenty years of city living had not conditioned him for this.

After an hour, he had only enough logs cut and split to feed the stove for half a day . . . maybe. Out of breath, heart hammering in his ears, muscles screeching a protest, he paused to wipe the sweat out of his eyes and caught sight of Old Jeb trudging up the driveway.

The old man quirked an eyebrow at the small stack of split wood. "Heard you choppin'. Better let me do it."

"I need the exercise."

"Mr. Murdock arranged for me to do it. He wouldn't like it if I didn't."

Paul relinquished the axe. "Where's your place that you could hear me?"

"Next clearing south." The old man set the axe to flying. Wedge, swing, thwack. Wedge, swing, thwack. Within minutes, he'd halved and quartered more logs than Paul had managed in an hour.

Wordlessly, Paul watched for a while, then let his

gaze wander over the hillside. The meadow continued to the top of the hill before the forest began. It was all thick clumps of trees, each fir growing into the branches of the next. A thick undergrowth wound around the base of the trunks, creating a solid barrier of shrubs as high as a man's shoulder and as impenetrable as a stone wall.

For a moment, his mind wandered. Anything could be in there watching him. A raccoon, squirrels and rabbits, or a couple of deer. He'd never had anything to do with hunting, considering it a cruel sport, but if that was the kind of terrain hunters had to penetrate in order to follow their quarry, he felt a sudden respect for the perseverance it would require.

He turned back to watching the wiry old man swinging the axe, and his thoughts moved on to the pianos. "How long's the Coop been unheated, do you know, Jeb?"

Old Jeb stacked a split log and reached for another round. "Since the last Piano Man left, I reckon."

"When exactly was that?"

"Don't rightly remember."

"Do you think he's the one who made off with the piano strings?"

"Have no idea."

"They must be somewhere around."

Wedge, swing, thwack. The old man's face was as closed as his mouth.

"There's a trapdoor in the kitchen ceiling. Any chance they'd be in the crawl space up there?"

"Nope. Ain't been nothin' up there for years."

Paul studied him a moment, then gave up. The first drops of rain began to fall and stirrings of hunger prodded him. "I'm going to fix some eggs. Would you like some breakfast?"

Thwack. "No, thankee." Wedge, swing, thwack.

"It's starting to rain. Are you sure you won't take a break and wait for it to pass?"

"Nope. Thankee anyways."

Paul shrugged and went inside. Hard-headed old man.

After breakfast, he began his examination of the pianos. He probed, pried and tested every part, trying to anticipate problems. The basic frames of all three were solid, and the soundboards were in good shape. But that was the best that could be said for them.

The upright, a worn-out Knabe, built in 1884, was an old soldier of a piano, beautifully crafted with enormous, solid carved legs and columns, and an indestructible oak base. Which was good, for in addition to the abuse the piano had suffered, decades of grime and neglect had taken its toll. The rosewood paneling was dry and cracked. Every key mechanism was stiff and creaky, and the keys themselves were yellowed, either broken or loose or missing altogether. Out of eighty-eight hammer felts, there wasn't one still hale and hearty.

When his examination of the piano was complete, he patted the splintery finish. "Never you mind, old boy, we're going to get you back to top condition."

The ten-foot Chickering, who should've been a real concert lady decked out in gleam and glisten for glittering first nights, was now tattered and frayed. Whole sections of mahogany veneer were gone from around the sides. The lid was gouged and chipped in dozens of places along the edges. And the hinges were too corroded with rust to trust leaving the lid propped open.

But her soundboard was okay. The sturdy legs needed only a new finish to restore beauty to their graceful curves. And the lid was still as level as the day it had been installed. A little surgery to repair the working parts, and some new clothes befitting her station in life, and she'd be a real beauty.

As much as he admired the two pianos, the one he adopted in his heart was the baby grand. Beaten, battered, nicked, scratched . . . the little one had taken more abuse than a pianist from a conductor. There wasn't an area of the finish that had escaped a beating. Every square inch would have to be sanded down and refinished. Some of the keys were splintered lengthwise, others were cracked across and still others had been shattered and crushed into sawdust. The frame box for the keyboard was cracked in a dozen places and a new one would have to be rebuilt. Even the pedals had come in for their share of purgatory; they were bent and dented as if hit by a demon wielding a heavy iron pipe. What manner of person had done this? he wondered. What circumstances would've led someone to such an extreme outburst of rage?

And exactly what had the other Piano Man done, besides swipe the strings? A group of workbenches standing in a far corner of the studio offered every tool known to man. Some repairs could begin before any new supplies arrived. Yet there hadn't been a single spot of work done on any of the pianos. So what had the man done to keep himself busy?

He finally shrugged off the questions. He wasn't going to be able to answer his own questions. And from what he'd seen of the Islanders, they wouldn't be much in the mood to help him.

During the next few days, as rain continued to drum down on the roof, he pored over reference manuals and parts catalogues to compile a list of supplies needed. Then he had to figure out the weights and lengths of piano strings he wanted to install and make a separate list of those.

When he was finally through, he enclosed them with a letter to Murdock, summing up all the repairs needed and the mail order supply houses where the items could be ordered, and addressed the envelope to the agent who'd hired him, as he'd been instructed to do. When everything was ready to send he sat back, satisfied with what he'd accomplished so far. There was fully a year's worth of work here. Which was what he wanted. It would give him the time he needed to decipher the mess that had been his life, and to plan a new one—a new mess? he thought, with some humor—to carry him into old age. He rose from the kitchen table and stretched muscles still suffering from his stint at the chopping block.

Standing by the front windows, he watched the rain gust across the gray waters of Oro Bay. In spite of the bad weather and wicked squalls, two boats made regular trips into the bay. One was an old cruiser rigged for fishing; the second was the same tug-shaped scow he'd seen on his first day on the Island.

He assumed the men who ran them depended upon the sea for their livelihood and couldn't allow weather to stop their work. The sight of them fighting waves and currents made him shiver in sympathy, grateful his work was under cover. Although the Coop could be cold and damp if the fire died away, and the dead-rat stench still assaulted the nose, at least he was sheltered from the rain.

That is, he had been up until now. He glanced over at the letter to Murdock. It needed mailing. And he needed more groceries. And something had to be done about laundry. And he needed to go to the mainland. All of which made the rain his problem, too. It was still cascading down like a vertical river and he didn't have anything close to proper gear for this kind of a deluge. Back home, this all would've fallen as snow, and his heavy woolen jacket pulled on over layers of sweaters and shirts would've worked fine.

But this . . . he wouldn't make the end of the driveway before getting soaked through. He prowled the Coop for a solution.

Nothing.

He prowled a second time, trying to be creative. Still nothing.

On each prowl, he eyed the trapdoor in the kitchen ceiling. Old Jeb had said nothing was up there. Still . . .

Finally, he pulled one of the kitchen chairs underneath and climbed up. He was tall enough to easily reach the square of wood acting as the trapdoor and he pushed it up and over to one side.

Instantly, the putrid stench he'd been living with strengthened. He held his breath and shined a flashlight around. A row of cartons had been lined up along one edge of the opening. He swung them down onto the table.

In the heat of the room, the stink of decay strengthened. Jeb's dead rats?

One of the cartons was grease-smeared on the outside and he opened that one first. Some rotten ground beef, a package of fetid steaks, a half-filled jar of rancid mayonnaise and a carton of milk long soured and congealed, plus a few other unrecognizable unmentionables had all been dumped into the box. Someone had cleaned out the refrigerator and had saved everything. Amazing that someone would've gone to such trouble, considering how filthy the rest of the Coop had been upon his arrival.

Keeping his nose as far back from the carton as he could, he carried it with outstretched arms out the back door and ran through the rain to set it behind the woodshed. If he found some weatherproof clothing, he'd bury the box in the woods. If he didn't, some animal would have a hefty meal—and an even heftier case of ptomaine. At least the stench was explained. Maybe now the Coop would air out and be more aromatic.

Back in the kitchen, he turned his attention to the other cartons. They held someone's scruffy old clothes—worn jeans, small-size boots, sweaters and a lined windbreaker. The kind someone would wear for a working country weekend. From their size, he judged that they belonged to a man much smaller than himself. Otherwise the clothes revealed nothing about their owner. The pockets were empty, the style anonymous, the brands common.

He searched through the garments again. Still

nothing. Puzzled, he stared down at them. Who had they belonged to? And why had they been stored in the attic of a decrepit old chicken coop, next to a carton of rotting food? Could they belong to the mysterious Mr. Murdock?

He repacked the cartons, holding out only the windbreaker. Old, worn, a common-colored brown, it was cut large enough that it might fit him. He managed to pull it on over his sweater. Its owner was obviously several inches shorter than he—the sleeves were too short and the shoulders were tight and restrictive. But it was more protection than he now had against the rain. He kept it out and replaced the cartons in the attic.

The big question, though, concerned Old Jeb. Had the old man really not known the cartons were up there? Or had he lied? And if he'd lied, why?

Chapter Six

The store smelled of wet wool, tobacco and hot coffee. Thaddeus was on his knees, stocking a bottom shelf when Paul entered. He glanced up and smiled. "Well, good morning! I was beginning to wonder if we'd ever see you again." He got off his knees and brushed himself off. "Got some mail for you."

Paul followed him to the small post office cage at the end of the front counter. A murmur of low conversation came from the deli beyond. The same trio of old men were sitting there and Paul nodded a good morning. Abner Ross nodded back, Bobbin smiled with his nod, and Calvin just glowered.

The mail consisted of a single envelope from Murdock's agent. It had to have been from him. No one in the outside world knew where he was. He tucked the envelope in his jeans pocket and handed over his own letter for mailing.

Thaddeus put it in a stack of outgoing mail and came out from behind the cage. "Been saving the morning papers for you. Figured you'd appreciate the news even if it was stale."

"Thank you, Thaddeus," Paul said, somewhat surprised by the thoughtfulness. "I'll take them with me. What I need to know is the time of the next ferry. I have to go to the mainland for some things for the pianos."

The conversation in the deli stopped. Thaddeus exchanged glances with Abner Ross. "Well, uh, actually, there isn't a ferry today."

"No ferry today?"

"Uh, no, uh . . . the ferry's in dry dock. Won't be running for a while."

"What do you do about supplies, then? And the mail? How does that get in and out?" He laid a hand on the stack of newspapers. "And what about these, how'd they get here?"

"We, uh, they're barged over." Thaddeus wouldn't meet his gaze.

"Then I'll ride the barge."

"They don't take foot passengers."

"Just vehicles? All right, then, where could I rent a car? Or a motorbike? Or a bicycle, for that matter, I don't care."

The younger man was obviously in distress. "We don't have any rentals on the Island."

"Then how would I get to the mainland?"

"I guess you don't. Not for a while."

Paul was silent a moment, absorbing the implication of that. "How long is 'a while'?"

"Better part of the winter, I'd guess." His voice turned sharp. "I don't know, I'm not a boater. I don't know about such things."

"Who would know?"

"I don't know that either. The ferry workers, I guess."

Paul studied him. He was aware of the scrutiny he was receiving from the three old men in the deli. Jenny had stopped her work and was watching and listening, too. He kept his gaze on the young store owner while he tried to sort the situation through. Apprehension was spreading through him. Good God, was he being made a prisoner on the Island?

The silence stretched on. There seemed only one attitude to adopt. Don't fight it. Not yet. Not until he knew more about what was going on.

He forced his body into a more relaxed, conversational stance. "Well, then," he said to Thaddeus in an easier tone of voice, "since I can't get to the mainland to bring in what I need, can I order some things through you?"

Relief lit up the bony face and Thaddeus flashed his broad smile. "You bet! Anything at all! You make up a list and I'll see to it it's filled right promptly."

"Then I guess I'll while away an hour or two right here and do that. Clever way of selling coffee." Paul grinned.

Thaddeus gave a surface chuckle.

Paul poured himself some coffee and carried it to the same corner table he'd used the first day.

The three old men stared at their coffee cups. In spite of their differences in postures and mannerisms, they sat like relatives gathered outside a sickroom, awaiting the word of death.

Paul played with that idea. Maybe there was some trouble on the Island unrelated to him. Anna had often said that if he were to enter a room with twelve conversations going, he'd think all twelve centered on him. Maybe that's what he'd been doing here, assuming the strangeness was directed at himself, when in reality there were other, more important concerns capturing everyone's attention.

And maybe it was merely coincidence that the

ferry had gone into dry dock at this particular time. Maybe it really was overhauled every winter, and he'd just happened to arrive on the Island at season's end. Hadn't the first mate mentioned something about barnacles? Surely they wouldn't pull a ferry out of service just to keep some innocuous Piano Man from going to the mainland. Unless Piano Men were that hard to come by that once they got one, they made sure he stayed to finish the work. Like a fish on a line, he thought, amused at the thought. Once hooked, land him and keep him.

Maybe.

He pondered it a while, idly watching customers drift in and out of the store. Hardly the brie and champagne crowd, they were a smattering of all ages from young parents to old great-grandparents, warmly dressed but without regard to fashion, buying staples. No money exchanged hands that Paul could see. Instead, Thaddeus toted up their bread, milk and eggs in a ledger, then pushed it across the counter for them to initial.

Watching it, this simple act of faith and trust had an unexpected impact on Paul. How many years had it been since his own life had functioned that simply? An image of Anna came to mind. Anna, a strong, striking, sleek animal of a woman in her glittering designer dresses, hitting the cocktail party circuit with him under her wing. First to promote his concert career. Then his faculty career. And all the while, her own career in law. Networking, she called it. He tried to imagine the Islanders "networking" and his lips curved with amusement. His America had been very different from this America.

He pushed Anna from his thoughts and began detailing the supplies he needed. Most everything could be purchased at any hardware store—wood stripper, stains, cloths, sandpaper, brushes, cleaning compounds—they would be easy to buy. And Thaddeus's hardware aisle might be able to provide him with enough of those to start some of the refinishing work right away.

The problem he ran into was ordering wood sight unseen. He'd need some rosewood and mahogany veneer, but he really needed to choose the shading and grains himself in order to get the best match possible. He'd also need special woods to fashion new keys that would match those he could rescue of the old, and he didn't know exactly what he wanted. And he needed some kind of hard wood to build a new frame box for the baby grand's keyboard. What should he order for that? Oak?

He really should go himself, to browse among the various kinds of woods and veneers available in order to make the best selection. But how was he going to do that if he couldn't get off the Island? What would it take to get to the mainland? He knew of at least two boats circling the Island. Could one of those haul a passenger over? A paying passenger? Or possibly there were others, too. Smaller runabouts that he could borrow, without having to put anyone to the trouble of piloting him across.

He looked over at the three old men. They sat, impassive as usual, intent on their coffee. More than likely, they would know someone who could help. But their attitude certainly discouraged any approach.

Jenny, then? He glanced her way and caught her studying him with those large, serious brown eyes. Instantly, she glanced down at her work and he discarded his partially formed thought of asking her help. As Thaddeus's wife, she wouldn't be eager to help a stranger if her husband wasn't.

Again he realized how alone he was on this island. There was not one person you could call friendly, and only one—the church hymnist—who could be termed talkative.

But it was more than that. There was something strange about this whole setup, and he tried to decipher what it was that was bothering him. It seemed to be so much more than just reticence around a stranger. Reticence he could understand, the natural reluctance to discuss personal—or even Island—happenings within earshot of someone unknown.

But this—this *remoteness* they displayed—was far more than simple reticence. They acted like people under a terrible strain. Particularly Thaddeus, with his mercurial changes of mood. And Jenny, with her continual serious examination of Paul, as if judging how he'd perform under stress. And the three old men, with their closed-off faces and not so much as a good morning or a comment about the weather. Just that warning to stay at home. Old Jeb, too. He was as talkative as a piano without strings.

And come to think about it, even the casual shoppers seemed furtive, glancing his way then averting their eyes if he caught them, making whispered comments to Thaddeus all the while. The behavior of everyone was definitely odd. Odd and secretive. And—yes, Whitman, say it—ominous. It gave him a chill thinking about it. It definitely gave him a chill. The image of the noose came into his mind, gleaming obscenely in the dusky depths of the old wooden wardrobe.

The pleasure of taking a few minutes to relax over coffee and paper was gone, vanquished by his thoughts. Wanting only to return now to the peace and solitude of the Coop—to the *safety* of the Coop, Whitman, be honest about it—he hurriedly finished his coffee and moved into the main store, simply nodding his goodbyes to the deli folk. A small frown worried its way across Jenny's forehead as she watched him leave.

Thaddeus's hardware aisle provided some of what he needed. He selected several different grains of sandpaper and a can of stripper, had Thaddeus add them to the bill, and slipped them into the knapsack. Then he brought up his concerns about the proper selection of the various woods.

As the shopkeeper listened to Paul's problems, his face took on a troubled look again. When Paul had finished his explanation, he shook his head. "I don't know what to say."

Paul kept his voice low so Abner and his cronies wouldn't hear. "Maybe we could call Mr. Murdock and talk to him about it."

"That wouldn't be possible."

"Why not? He hired me to do a job, he'd want to know if there were any problems."

"No, it just can't be. We'll have to work something else out."

"Who is this Murdock anyway."

"You're the one working for him."

"I was hired by a go-between. A representative of his."

"Then I guess you know all he wants you to know."

"His first name? That's a big secret?"

Thaddeus lost patience. "I've learned over the years that Mr. Murdock tells you exactly what he wants you to know, no more, no less."

Nothing would be accomplished by upsetting him further. "Just thought I'd ask." He began loading his purchases into his knapsack. "By the way, I'm going to have to do something about my laundry. Is there anyone on the Island who takes in washing?"

Thaddeus considered it. "I'll ask around. We'll get you fixed up somehow." He grinned, friendly again. "Shoot, if there's enough money in it, I'd do it for you."

"Oh, I can see that now. A washtub and scrub board behind the counter here, my wet skivvies strung all across the deli, and you with a magnificent case of dishpan hands, waiting on your customers between rinses. Yep, I can just see that."

In spite of his humorous words, Paul felt frustrated. Thaddeus appeared to be an open, sunny person, with an easy grin that showed up at the slightest hint of humor, a person incapable of hiding what was going on inside himself. Yet apparently he was in a situation where he was required to do just that, and his feelings were about as well hidden as the Campbell Soup display next to the checkout counter. Something was very wrong on the Island.

Paul was scheduled to tune the church piano in the morning. Maybe he could get Grace talking and learn what was going on. Maybe she could help him make some sense of things. Maybe she could help him with a boat. Maybe she could help him, period. Somehow he felt he needed it.

By the time he left the store, the rain had softened to a gentle drizzle. At the Coop, he stowed his groceries, then took advantage of the lull to fill the woodbox again. He was carrying in the last armful of logs when he heard the chug-chug of Old Jeb's pickup grinding its way uphill. One of these days that thing was just going to shut down—too old and cranky even to try anymore, Paul thought. But the old truck made it to the top of the driveway—a miracle considering the mudwash it had to climb.

Arms full, he greeted Old Jeb from the doorway. "Come on in," he called out. "This is my last load here."

Old Jeb followed him as far as the doorway and stopped. "Forgot to mention earlier the missus would be doing your wash."

Paul stopped in mid-step and stared.

"She sent me down to pick it up." Still standing in the doorway, his gnomelike body was backlit by the sun, his face indistinct in shadow. "Said to be sure and send the sheets and towels, too."

Paul dumped the load of logs. Murdock again. Not only was the man powerful, he was speedy. "It's not ready. It's not together."

"I'll wait." The old man shifted balance to lean against the doorjamb.

Paul shrugged. "Help yourself to coffee."

"Mebbe next time."

Paul started gathering clothes together, his mind racing. Communication had been swift and sure, which meant Murdock had to be available by phone. Could he be here on the Island? In spite of his exploring trip, the Island was basically unknown to him.

He yanked the sheets off the mattress, used one as a tarp and tied the laundry into a bundle. "I'll need a clean set of sheets."

"I've got 'em with me."

"Then I'll carry this out to the truck for you and bring them in."

"No need." One-handed, Old Jeb slung the bundle on his back as if it were a feather pillow. Gray, stooped and shrunken as he was, he was a bull in a dwarf's body. He trudged out, then back again, a grocery sack of folded sheets in his hand. "I'll drop the clean things by in the morning."

Paul shook his head. "Tomorrow's Friday. I'll be at the church, tuning the piano."

"Didn't anyone mention it?" The old man's face was impassive. "The church board's decided to trade the piano in on an organ. The tune-up's cancelled."

Paul stood transfixed as the chug-chug of the truck faded out of hearing. So much for his visit with Grace.

Chapter Seven

The next morning, he began work on the Knabe upright. Its innards were basically okay. The key action was crisp and the soundboard solid.

Outside, though, the Old Soldier was a battle-scarred, weary old warrior, badly needing plastic surgery and dental work. The finish was wrinkled, splintered and scarred. Some of the keys were cracked. Others were missing completely. New ones would have to be carved, then overlaid with ivory. The cracked ones would just need filling and new caps.

It was the refinishing that concerned him most. The columns would be all right. They were intricately carved from solid rosewood and would take a sanding just fine. As would the legs. But the rest of the upright, the side panels, the front and the top, was simply a veneer over an oak base, and the tolerance of the veneer would be razor thin. He went over every square inch of it, sensitive fingertips smoothing and probing, judging the amount of veneer left. At the end of the examination, he concluded that, with care, the rosewood could be salvaged. He got out rags and stripper.

Tackling the veneer came first. If it wouldn't hold, it was best to find that out right away. He started in a low rear corner, working one small circle through a century of grime, varnishes and stains. He concentrated on every movement of his forefinger, rubbing just so hard and no harder, for fear of damaging the fragile veneer. A work lamp with a good strong bulb would've helped enormously, but slowly, under the light of the skylight overhead, bare wood began to emerge.

After a couple of hours, he set the rag down and examined what he'd accomplished. A small circle, no larger than a fist, shone bare. It looked clean and felt smooth to his hand when he tested it. But its size, compared to the whole of the piano, was equivalent to a single note in a conductor's score. It was going to be one long, tedious job.

He poured himself some coffee, carried the cup over to the windows and stared out at Oro Bay shimmering a deep blue under the October sun. The old tug was back, prowling the Bay again. The boat circled just inside the shoreline, moving at a speed slightly above idle. It finished its circuit, found the channel and moved back into the Sound, where it turned south and disappeared. The bay shimmered on, empty and innocent-looking once again.

He lowered his gaze and stared moodily into the coffee mug. Yesterday, the cruiser had been out, entering the bay every couple of hours. Today it was the tug. These weren't typical fishing hours; this was more like a regular patrol. What was going on?

It strengthened his feeling that he needed to learn all he could about the Island, its layout, its terrain, its people. Daytime was best for that, but unfortunately, with no electricity in the studio, his work was limited to daylight hours. Already, it didn't get workably light until close to eight. What a difference a well-lit work area would make.

A thought floating just below the surface of consciousness nagged him. Something he should've noticed. He hadn't paid much attention to the studio itself, just a quick scan before concentrating on the pianos. But that quick scan had left him with an impression of . . . what?

He refilled his mug and wandered around the studio. There were only the pianos, a supply chest filled mostly with rags, the work tables and a tool bench. He stared at them, wondering what he was seeking.

Tool bench. Of course, the drill. He fumbled for it in the oversized tool box and brought it out. Dangling from one end was an electric cord.

He hunted now. Walls and flooring, on hands and knees. He found one double outlet on the floor under the upright, a second under the supply chest, and a third under the tool bench.

And let there be light, he thought, cheered. He carried the drill to one of the floor outlets and plugged it in. Nothing. He tried another outlet. Still nothing. None of the outlets was live.

He sat back on his heels, puzzling it out. It made no sense. Dead outlets? A job started and never finished? And why had they been hidden? He realized then that what he'd taken for random placement of the pianos and the workbenches had been cleverly arranged to hide the outlets. But why?

He went outside and checked the eaves. At the kitchen end of the building, insulated wire ran in from the road, ending in the fuse box in the bathroom. Two circuits, two fuses. One for the hot-water heater, bathroom light and shaving plug; the other for the refrigerator, bare bulb over the sink and the one appliance plug.

His gaze moved along the eaves to the studio corner. A large eye-screw, as weathered as the siding, protruded at the top of the wall. It was a twin to the one holding the insulated wire at the other end. Thick shrubbery had taken over that end of the building, but there was a small gap between the root balls. He crawled through and found himself staring at a terminus.

He visually measured its distance from the end of the building, then scrambled back out of the shrubbery. Inside, he measured an equivalent space and examined the plain barn siding that covered the walls. One board seemed loose. He pried it off. The fuse box sat well back between a pair of studs, fixed up for three circuits.

He sat back, puzzled even further. Why would you board over a fuse box? It sat at the far end of the long gap left by the board. Twin nail holes punctured the studs on either side of the box. Originally, a board had stopped at the other side of the fuse box, leaving it exposed and accessible. That board had been replaced with the longer one he'd just removed. The fact that the studio was wired for electricity had been cleverly concealed . . . Why? And what had happened to the insulated wire that ran in from the road?

"Yoo-hoo! Mr. Whitman! Mr. Whitman, hey there! Mr. Whitman?"

The hail had come from his driveway. He went

outside and stood at the top of the slope, watched for a moment, then grinned.

The church hymnist made quite a sight. Face flushed, white hair tugged every which way by the cold wind, huffing and puffing, she fought her way up the slope. At the top, she stopped, panting, her corset heaving with each breath. "That . . . driveway's . . . a real . . . killer . . . Oooh!"

"It's a waterslide for ducks. Come on in, Mrs. . . . ?"

"Duncan . . . Grace . . . Duncan," she said between puffs of breath. "Call me . . . Grace. Everyone . . . does. But not . . . whew! . . . Gracie." A last shuddering intake of air and her breathing approached normal again. "Oh, my, that was a climb."

"Okay, Grace, and I'm Paul." He held the back door for her. "I've got some coffee hot."

"No tea?"

"That, too."

"Good. I'll have a cup." She looked around curiously. "So this is what it's like. Kind of dark in here, isn't it?"

"One gets used to it."

"Might help if you washed a few of those windows."

He filled the kettle and set it on the stove. "Might."

"Could use some decent furniture, too."

"It could."

"A rocking chair'd be nice."

"It would."

"Don't say much, do you?"

He grinned. "The quiet type, that's me."

She gave him a shrewd glance. "We'll see."

He set out the tea cup. "You'll have to put up with Lipton's. The fancy life's behind me."

"So I gathered. Makes a body wonder why." She wandered into the studio. "Not much to look at, are they?"

"Ah, but they will be." He joined her among the pianos. "Let me introduce you to my friends. This is the Lady, the grand dame of them all. A sleek beauty when she's got her makeup on. And this, he's the Little One. He'll never have the stature of the Lady, but he'd be right at home in any small kingdom. And this is the Old Soldier. He's been in more battles than you have."

"I doubt that," she snorted. Her bright eyes scanned the three pianos, taking note of their wounds. "How on earth do you ever begin a project like this? To me, it'd be overwhelming."

He explained in detail what had to be done and in what order it had to occur. She listened intently, standing by him, peering where he peered, bending her whalebones to see what he saw.

At the end, she studied him. "You seem to know what you're doing."

"My father had a piano store. He did all his own repairing and restoring. That's how I paid my way through school . . . Let's have that tea now."

Sitting at the table, her tea before her, she focused shrewd eyes on him. "So what are you doing holed up on our little piece of paradise?"

"Recuperation." His own answer caught him by surprise. After a moment's consideration, he nodded.

"Yes, that about sums it up. Recuperation." He looked at her with interest. "Why are you here?"

"I was born and bred here. Oh, I left briefly after Bill Duncan and I got married. He had a yen to move up in life, so we moved to Seattle and he worked for a wholesaler of farm equipment. Once the charm of all those stores and restaurants wore off, though, I took a look around and figured out we'd moved down, not up. So back we came. We bought us a parcel of land and settled in. Built a one-room house, figuring we'd add on once we had our family started. Wasn't to be, though. So I raised food and flowers instead of kids."

He refilled her tea cup. "How did you two live? How did you support yourselves?"

"Bill worked a while making bricks. Good clay on parts of the Island. When that slowed a bit, he helped out at the sawmill. Finally, he hired out on the big farm and worked there till he died. He's buried up at the old cemetery."

"How long's he been gone?"

"Ten years. I still miss him, though. We were good friends. I go up most every afternoon to chat a while. Except when the weather's so bad even the ducks stay home."

"And you never missed the city when you came back?"

"No, sir," she said firmly. "I've seen more of real life on this bit of land than any ten of those city folk. They hide things from themselves. They bury them under their fancy clothes and fancy cars and fancy titles and close the doors of their fancy houses against them. Then they're almighty shocked when natural calamities occur and they end up going to fancy doctors to make themselves right again." The tight curls bounced with the firm shake of her head. "No, sir, I don't miss it at all. You stay your year, you'll see what I mean."

"Of course I'll stay the year, why wouldn't I? I've signed a contract."

"Fiddle, that don't mean nothing. Didn't stop the other Piano Man one whit."

Paul poured himself more coffee. "What exactly did happen to him?" he asked casually. "What was his name anyway?"

"Harrison. Jim Harrison. From what I hear, the loneliness got to him. He couldn't take the isolation here."

"What do you think?"

She finished the last sip of tea, her eyes speculative on his. "I'm not sure what I think. There's whispers that something happened, that that's why he left. Can't imagine what it would be, though. 'Course, there's always whispers, the things-that-go-bump-in-the-night kind of talk."

"What kind of a man was he?"

She pursed her lips and thought a minute. "Kind of a strange duck. Spoke in grunts. Unfriendly. Unpleasant, really. Had a hard, bitter look to his face and a chip on his shoulder. He was a little man, small-boned, about—oh, in his thirties someplace. Much too young to be that bitter. Didn't seem to care about anyone. Leastways, that's how he came across. And for sure, he didn't want to tune my piano. Running off like that was a pretty drastic way of avoiding the work, to my way of thinking."

"Wouldn't someone have seen him on the ferry if

he'd just left? You used the word 'disappeared' the other day."

"The summer folk mostly store their rowboats right at their places here for the winter. What I hear is one of them's missing. Whatever got his wind up, he felt he couldn't wait for the first ferry in the morning."

"The ferry wasn't in dry dock then?"

The change in her demeanor was instant, from easy openness to closed-off wariness. "Oh, no," she said, attempting a casual tone of voice to brush the whole subject away. "Not then. Now. It goes into dry dock just about this time every year." She glanced at her watch. "It's about time for me to get on with things." She gathered her purse close to her side, as if hugging it for comfort, and stood up.

He rose to join her. "Old Jeb told me the church is getting you an organ."

She relaxed again, her eyes twinkling with sudden humor. "Yes, isn't it strange how miracles simply can occur?" she said with a straight face. She moved to the door and paused. "Some people on this island seem to think I'm fresh out of the bassinet. Then I got set to wondering why they were so intent on keeping me away from you. You seem rather harmless. No bodies under the bed, no young girls tucked away in a closet somewhere, are there?"

He chuckled. "Not that I know about. How long will it be before the organ arrives?"

"Only God and the board know that."

"I can still tune the piano for you if it's going to take a while."

She hesitated a few seconds. "The strings are gone," she said, finally.

Startled, he stared at her. "What did you say?"

"Someone broke into the church last night and the piano strings are gone. That's another reason I stopped by today. To see if you could re-string it for me. But you don't have any, either."

His mind raced, trying to make sense of it.

"Then there were a couple of other things on my mind, while I was at it. One is, you might need a friend. If you ever do, for what it's worth, this old body's it. You just light out for my place any time. First house on the Sound, north of the ferry dock."

The offer touched him unexpectedly. He couldn't recall the last time someone had offered to be just a friend. There were no friends in the university or concert worlds. Only sycophants and competitors. "Thank you, I'll remember that."

"You come visiting any time. Except early afternoons when I go up to visit Bill."

"At the cemetery."

"Yes."

"Unless the weather's so bad even the ducks stay home."

They grinned at each other.

"I like you, Paul Whitman. Too bad I'm such an old and dumpy soul. Thirty years younger and I'd show that ex-wife of yours a thing or two."

"How'd you know I have an ex-wife?"

"You've got that married-but-not-any-longer look about you. You'll have to tell me about her one of these times. But not now. Now, I've got to be on my way."

At the door, he stopped her. "You said there was another reason for coming?"

She grew serious and looked at him, long and hard. "We don't really know what happened to Jim Harrison, do we."

■

It was mid-afternoon when the Sheriff's car pulled up the driveway. The sound of the engine drew Paul outside. The chug-chug of Old Jeb's pickup sounded from the road as the Sheriff pulled his monstrous body free of the car. Paul had forgotten how big the man was.

Before he could speak, Old Jeb's pickup topped the driveway and pulled even with the patrol car. He swung down and sauntered over. "Afternoon, Frank, Mr. Whitman."

"Afternoon, Jeb," Hall said. The blue eyes crinkled with amusement. "Been running into you quite a spell lately."

"Have to keep an eye on the young feller here."

"I can see that." The Sheriff turned a bland face to Paul. "Lucky Mr. Whitman, eh?" He leaned his huge body back against a car fender. "The church got broken into last night." He paused and waited.

Old Jeb stayed silent. Finally, Paul spoke. "So I heard."

The Sheriff gave Paul a quick glance. "How'd you hear?"

"It's a small island. Talk gets around."

The Sheriff waited for more. When the silence stretched out, he went on. "As far as I can tell, the only thing taken was some piano wires."

"Strings," Paul corrected.

“Strings.” The Sheriff waited again.

Paul was the one who spoke up. Old Jeb obviously was determined to stay silent. “I heard that, too.”

“From the same place, I expect.”

Paul flushed a little. “Talk does get around.”

“You found any sign of yours yet?”

“Not so far.”

The Sheriff gave a small nod, then his eyes roamed the length of the Coop. “Mind if I look around?”

“Not at all. The coffeepot’s on, too.” Paul led him inside, Old Jeb traipsing after them.

Mug in hand, the big man moseyed through the studio, lifting the lids of each of the pianos, peering into the string cages, taking his time examining everything. He poked through the tool box before he turned back to Paul. “Looks like a major overhaul’s due here.”

“That’s exactly what it is,” Paul said, moving to his side.

With a broad sweep of his hand, the Sheriff indicated all three pianos. “How do you start something like this?”

For the second time that day, Paul explained exactly what had to be done and in what order he planned to do it. Leaning against a nearby wall, Old Jeb sipped his coffee and listened.

The Sheriff heard Paul out without interruption or questions, then studied the Old Soldier where the finish was stripped bare. “Looks like a long job.”

“A careful one. This portion’s veneer. I don’t have any idea of its condition, so I have to work extremely cautiously. An inch-by-inch kind of thing. It wouldn’t do to ruin it.”

"I can see that. That other guy, he damage anything?"

"The first Piano Man? No, he hadn't done anything at all." The question had been asked so smoothly, the answer was out before Paul caught the implications of it.

But the Sheriff merely nodded and started moving back towards the kitchen area. Still silent, Old Jeb moved with them. The big man set his mug on the kitchen counter and paused at the back door. "So what do you think he did while he was here?" he asked Paul. "The other Piano Man, that is. As I recollect, he was here a good couple of weeks, maybe longer."

Paul looked first to Old Jeb for a clue as to the answer, but the old man's face was shut down and unreadable. Finally, he shrugged. "Nothing much, it seems," he said, honestly. "In fact, to be downright truthful, I don't think he ever touched those pianos."

The Sheriff didn't seem surprised. He merely nodded and pulled the door open. "Anything turns up, you be sure to let me know. I'll be around again sometime soon." He paused with the door open. "Afternoon, Jeb," he said, eyes crinkling once again with amusement. "Nice visitin' with you again."

The sound of the patrol car faded in the distance. Paul turned to the old man to find his eyes fixed on him. Old Jeb's forehead was creased in thought as he studied the younger man, as if there were a need to rethink things.

"I'll make some fresh coffee," Paul offered. "That stuff was strong enough to stand up without a cup."

The old man shook his head. "Not on my account. Gotta run."

"All right, then, thanks for stopping in. Sorry the Sheriff spoiled our visit," he added blandly. As if the Sheriff's appearance wasn't the reason for the visit.

"Another time, mebbe. Noticed Grace Duncan's car parked below this morning. She's a real busybody, that one. Got a nose as long as a shotgun barrel. Wouldn't do to get too thick with her. She spreads most of the talk around here." He nodded once and was gone.

Paul watched the old pickup negotiate the mudslide until it was down the drive, then cleared away the coffee cups, at a loss as to what to do next. Unseen and unknown things were swirling like mist about him. To protect himself, he had to find out more. But darned if he knew how to proceed.

His fingers itched for a keyboard. At times like these, restless and unsure of the next move, he'd go to his piano where the music could lift him up and carry him off and he'd drift weightless in that magic dimension of timelessness until his body could take no more, whereupon he'd blink to awareness and discover sometimes that most of a night had passed. Worn-out then, calmed, he'd stumble to bed and sleep deeply before facing a new day.

He rose abruptly from the table. No use in sitting around, brooding. He fixed a couple of hefty meat sandwiches, filled his thermos with the leftover coffee, and packed his knapsack.

The hell with Abner and Calvin and Old Jeb and their old-maid fussiness. Knowledge was protection. He pulled on a heavy sweater, stowed the flashlight in the pack and adjusted the knapsack on his back. The next step was to finish exploring the Island.

Chapter Eight

He set out south. The gray that had clogged Puget Sound skies for days on end had cleared and, on his left, Oro Bay shimmered a deep blue beneath the open sky. Across the water on the seaward side, two spits of land offered sheltered anchorage from storms sweeping over Puget Sound. One spit was forested and wild, the other—the southern arm—was low-banked with cleared lawns and planted shade trees.

On the bay side of the spit, a long dock with slips to the right and left formed a rudimentary marina, now empty for the winter. A couple of smaller, private docks stretched into the bay from broad, spreading lawns that were turning a winter brown. A lone seagull squatted atop an old piling, dozing in the sun. The whole spit wore the boarded-up, closed-down air of a summer compound past its season.

The walk along the bay was pleasant, the road fairly level, the sun warm on his back and shoulders. The tide was out and there was the sharp, pleasant tang of mudflats at low tide. He could taste salt in the air. As he walked, years of sluggish blood started to move and muscles began to loosen. He could already feel a difference in his body in just the few days he'd been on the Island.

Old Jeb's place was closer to the Coop than he'd realized. A double row of firs running from the brow of the hill down to the road separated the two parcels of land. An old, two-story farm house sat well up the meadow, with a full basement, a steeply pitched roof and a recent coat of white paint. There were half a dozen outbuildings behind the house, then a broad apple orchard swept up to the rim of the hill where the forest took over once again. A chicken-wire fence surrounded a huge garden, planted to the side where it could get full sun. Most of the vegetables had been harvested, but fully-grown pumpkins shone a healthy orange, the vines running from stem to stem like an umbilical cord. A peaceful, pastoral scene.

Once Old Jeb's clearing was past, the forest closed in down to the road again. At the bottom of the bay, the road curved around to follow the water, then split into a Y on the far eastern side. Agate Beach Road turned back north, up the spit. Lyle Point Road headed south. How far, he couldn't judge. He knew the northern route would dead-end at the channel into the bay, so he took that route first.

Not much could be seen from the road. Firs left standing at the roadside guarded the waterfront from casual view. An occasional driveway meandered off through the woods, a house gable could be seen now and then poking up among the tree branches, and clearings here and there allowed a glimpse of a sprawling summer home surrounded by lawns sloping to the water's edge. The road dead-ended at a driveway posted with KEEP OUT signs.

On his way back to the fork in the road, he watched for any signs of occupancy. There were none that he could see without turning in every drive and exploring each place separately. It looked like this part of the world had shut down and resigned from life. He regained the Y in the road and turned south.

Lyle Point Road curved and climbed steeply to, he assumed, Lyle Point, another heavily wooded bluff. As the road climbed, a series of summer cabins were perched like eagles along the bluff's edge overlooking Puget Sound. In the distance across the open water, Mount Rainier shimmered in the sun. He paused several times to admire its majestic beauty.

Next to him, the forest kept pace until it moved ahead of him and closed off his way. He considered pushing through the tangle of undergrowth to reach the point itself, but the density of the tangled thickets that wound around and in between trees created a barrier as solid as a cement wall. He turned back from it and searched the clifftop for a way around.

Beside the last cabin, several flights of rickety stairs scaled down the hundred feet of cliffside to a deserted beach below. There were only two ways left for him to go. Back, or down. The blue water of the Sound was empty of boats, the mainland was miles away, and this area of the Island was another that appeared to be used only in the summer. He chose down.

The stairs bolted to the cliffside were shaky, but he managed to negotiate them safely and headed south again, following the beach below the forest barrier on the blufftop. The beach was lonely and barren, composed of pebbles, not sand. At intervals, whole sections of bluff, from base to clifftop, formed headlands jutting far out into the Sound, creating a series of small coves. The tide was out and he was able to make his way around them without getting wet.

The saltwater stretched like a mirror to the distant mainland, reflecting the deep blue of the sky.. The view and the solitude were hypnotic. For the first time in months, he felt totally at peace. He drifted on, not thinking of anything, until a spill of trees from a ravine into the Sound finally blocked his path. The only way around was to swim. Regretfully, he turned and retraced his steps.

Back on the beach at the foot of the stairs, he selected a huge driftwood log, and reclined in the crook of one of its gnarls. He eased into the soft rhythm of the afternoon, listening to the gentle lap of water twenty feet out, and the occasional gull's cry that pierced the peaceful air. Overhead, an eagle soared, checking on this intrusion of its solitude, and he watched it, following the swoops and spirals with a lazy gaze. At the moment, his problems seemed nonexistent. He closed his eyes and gave himself up to the sun.

▌

He wasn't sure of the precise instant he heard the boat. The beat of the diesel seemed the beat of his heart at first, but as it grew louder, awareness came over him. Instinct told him his presence would not be a welcome sight if he was discovered. He scrambled over the driftwood log that had been his pillow and dropped full-length behind it, his cheek pressed flat into the pebbles.

An arch of the log allowed a tunnel view of the water. The boat was the old cruiser he'd seen on many occasions touring Oro Bay. From the distance of the Coop's windows, the boat had seemed a trim, well-kept white craft, but this close, he could see it was badly in need of a paint job and some rust remover. A twenty-five-footer, it had a forward cabin and barren cockpit rigged for fishing, but while it traveled at trolling speed, the three men aboard had no lines out.

Instead, two of the men stood at the cockpit railing, using binoculars to scour every inch of clifftop and beach. The third man, piloting the boat, divided his attention between land and sea. He'd check the boat's heading, rake the cliffs with a long gaze, then turn back to the sea again.

The men with binoculars were young, in their twenties maybe, dressed in jeans and windbreakers. There was no joking, no comradeship, no idle talk. In an almost professional manner, they quartered a section of cliff with their binoculars, examining every square inch within that quadrant before quartering the next section. The cockpit railing came up to their thighs, and with legs spread for balance, their stance appeared menacing.

Paul pressed his body harder against the pebbles. He had no idea how much of him could be seen from the water through the log's arch. When the boat reached his section of beach, he turned the back of his head towards the log and hoped that his brown hair color would blend in with wood, shadows and stones. Barely breathing, he lay motionless.

He stayed prone until the last beat of the diesel had faded, then cautiously raised his head and peered over the log. The waters of the Sound were empty once again.

He stared at the blankness. Were they searching for him?

But that didn't make sense. Up until now, he'd always been at the Coop when they were out on patrol.

No, they were searching for something else. Or someone?

Keeping a distrustful eye on the Sound, he bent down to pick up his knapsack.

A noise behind him made him jerk upright. He peered about the beach, trying to identify it in his mind. A kind of crashing sound.

Cautiously, he turned and examined the face of the cliff that loomed above him. His gaze raked every inch of clifftop, but he didn't see anything. Finally he shrugged. A small animal chasing prey, he decided. Or a piece of deadwood falling. Or something along those lines.

The tide had turned and was coming in now. The sun was lowering fast beyond the treetops and the air took on the chill of an early winter night. Time to go.

At the foot of the stairs, he paused to scan the cliffs overhead once more. It was like looking up the side of a skyscraper that had a scrubby shrub or an occasional boulder poking out here and there. There was no sound whatsoever from above. Whatever the noise had been, it obviously had been a solitary sound.

The bottom half of the stairway was easy. It was simply hard-packed gravel and clay banked into steps by heavy timbers. Steep, but safe. The upper half of the stairs, though, were little more than old wooden ladders zigzagging up the cliff, bolted to rusty iron stanchions protruding from the cliffside. It looked a hell of a lot more rickety and dilapidated from below than it had from the top. But there was no other way up.

He climbed the clay-and-gravel steps, then paused to test the first ladder. The contraption wobbled, but it would hold.

He was part way up the first one when a glint of metal in the shrubbery jutting from the cliff caught his eyes. Holding fast to the rickety ladder, he stretched as far as he could, managing to touch the object with his fingertips. Its perch was precarious. Beneath his fingers, he felt cold metal, then it was gone. Shiny end over shiny end, it tumbled to the beach below, crashing into a thicket hugging the base of the cliff. It sank from sight in its branches.

The object had tumbled too fast and too hard for him to identify what it was. His impression was of a tool of some sort. By the speed of its descent he judged it to be long and heavy. If it had been alive, it would have been killed by the fall. Shuddering, he stared down.

He was better than a hundred feet above the beach now, clinging to one very rickety ladder with a sheer drop down to hard pebbles below. Christ, what would he do if . . . ?

He jerked himself free from his imagination. He was scaring himself needlessly. He'd come down these steps easily enough. He could just damned well go back up them the same way. He climbed methodically, one foot after the other, not looking up, not looking down.

He didn't even slow to test the top ladder bolted to the cliffside. His heart was hammering from both fear and exertion, and if he paused, he'd never move again. He'd spend the rest of his life frozen to this one damned spot. He just kept climbing.

He heard the creak before he felt the sway.

The ladder yawed like a tree being felled. The top of it had separated from the cliff. Caught halfway up, he could race neither up nor down. He had the dreadful sense of empty air beneath him. As the stairs began to tilt sideways in a slow arc, his hand scratched the face of the cliff, seeking a hold somewhere, anywhere.

There was an instant's pause in sound and action. The bottom bolts had held. But for how long?

A boulder jutted out of the bluff a couple of feet to the side. It was knee-height, just wide enough to take his bulk. He held fast to the ladder, breathing shallowly, appalled at the amount of open space between the rock ledge and himself. He stayed frozen for a long moment, not daring to move.

Then wood creaked and the swaying began again. He had no choice. He drew in one deep breath and leaped.

Fear had given his thrust too much power. His body arced through empty space. He was going to overshoot the rock, with nothing beyond to stop him but the beach a hundred feet below.

Instantly, he dropped a leg. His knee smashed into the boulder, tripping his body. His chest slammed down hard and his flight ended. He grabbed rock by the armful and hung on.

The thrust of his jump had propelled the stairway to one side. The rotting wood cracked like the cannon in the *1812 Overture*. The bottom bolts gave way; the stairway came free. It plummeted to the beach far below and broke up into splintered sections.

The last echo of the fall died away and silence spread around him like the gathering night. He crouched on his rock perch, shaking. Pain lanced his knee, but he didn't dare shift position to ease it. He pushed his body hard against the cliffside and fought to regain control.

When his mind finally became convinced the rock was not going to give way, his shaking eased some and he began to breathe again.

Cautiously, he lifted his head and assessed his position. He was about twenty feet below the top. The grade was vertical. Too steep to crawl up. There were two or three shrubs he could use to hold on to—if they held—and if he could find toeholds.

Do A before B. First, figure out how bad the knee was. It had taken the brunt of his crash landing, and streaks of fire were now spreading over the kneecap and running up and down his leg. His fingers explored the surface of the cap. It was swelling up, but it seemed whole. He couldn't detect a break.

Gingerly, he bent the knee. That worked, though it hurt like blazes. Pressing even harder against the cliffside, he pushed himself upright on his good leg, keeping his gaze averted from the open space below. He tested the knee with some weight. The fire spread, but it supported him. Okay, no break. Just pain.

While he was standing, he held his breath and looked cautiously up. Fourteen feet, give or take a couple, from the top of his reach to the top of the cliff. It'd be like scaling a two-story house without a ladder. Still there were some shrubs. And the odd rock or two jutting out.

He raised his arms. A shrub drooped inches above his fingertips. He stood on his good leg and scrabbled with the other foot along the cliff, seeking a toehold. Fresh fires started in his knee. He forced it to bend some more and he finally found a small opening in the cliff. He felt the crack with the toe of his shoe. It seemed tight enough to hold his foot in place.

He jammed his toe into the crack and shifted weight. He used the shrub overhead to help pull himself up, but kept his good leg dangling over the rock perch. He could always fall back if he had to.

But the shrub held and the toehold stayed firm. He was a couple of feet closer to the top. He exhaled. Next step. He reached for a new shrub, found a toehold, held his breath again, shifted weight, then exhaled. Then again. And again. Reach for a new shrub, find a higher toehold, hold breath, shift weight, then exhale. Cautiously, shrub by shrub, he inched up the cliff.

Then he ran out of shrubs.

Six feet to go. The cliff's edge was at head height, a barren stretch of open ground. Not a tree, not a thicket trailed the edge. Of all the times for the forest not to be there. He swore out loud.

The dusk had deepened into full darkness. A black streak in the cliffside about hip level promised the possibility of a crack. He explored it with his fingertips. It would serve as a boosting step, but wasn't large enough to hold his foot for more than a second's push. But it was on his good leg's side. His thrust wouldn't be dampened by pain.

He positioned his toe. This would have to be fast. One smooth motion, and up and over. Before he could think about it, he drew in his breath and surged.

His fingers grabbed wild grass. The clumps were thick enough to hold. He pulled his body up and got the elbow over the edge. Then the other arm. Then the chest—

He banged the injured knee and yelped, but he kept his weight moving upward and forward on it.

He rolled onto the grass and kept rolling, over and over and over, away from the edge until he lay on his back a safe distance away. He stared up at the darkening sky. Stars were turning on like the light bulbs of a marquee. He lay there and watched them until his heart stopped pounding and his trembling eased.

▌

A group of old pickups were gathered along the road in front of his place and a band of men watched him from the top of his driveway as he limped up the ruts. Abner Ross and Old Jeb looked as if they were heading up the mob. They were the only two there he knew.

The back door of the Coop stood wide open and light poured out from the bare kitchen bulb inside.

"What's up?" he asked. He looked from one old man to the other.

They hung back a minute, studying him, then finally, Abner cleared his throat. "Old Jeb didn't see your lights on. He was worried maybe something happened to you."

There must have been twenty of them, all ages, watching him with weary eyes and closed-off faces. "What were you doing in there?" He nodded towards the Coop.

"Just looking for you," Abner said smoothly. He ran his gaze up and down the length of Paul's body. "Looks like you're limping a bit."

Paul refused to satisfy the old man's curiosity. "Tripped over a log in the forest. Hurt my knee some."

For all his scrabbling on the cliffside, the earth had been dry, protected from the rains by the overhang at the top. He'd merely brushed the dust and dirt off his jeans before he'd started for home, and they were almost as clean as when he set out.

That fact didn't escape Abner. Nor the others. Eyebrows raised in skepticism. After the deluge of storms the past week, the forest floor would be saturated with mold and rotting leaves mixed into mud pies that would cake a person's shoes and pants. Especially if he'd fallen.

But no one called him on it.

"We tried to warn you about the woods the other night." Abner's voice was neutral. "They're not safe for a city feller like yourself. You're to stay put from now on."

The previous time it had been a request. Now it was a command.

"And you'd better see to that knee, Mr. Whitman. T'wouldn't do to sicken up. Old Jeb's good with farm stock, he can fix it up for you. He'll come by in the morning. Now, if you're sure you're all right, we'll be on about our business."

"I'm fine," Paul responded briskly.

He stood at the top of the drive, watching them go. At the bottom of the hill, they held a brief consultation, then separated to various trucks. Headlights snapped on, motors turned and caught, and one by one the trucks pulled away, leaving him alone in the black country darkness.

Chapter Nine

Old Jeb showed up at first light, a grocery sack in his arms. "Came to tend that knee."

Paul's body ached with the pain of overextended muscles from his climb up the cliff, but they were mere codas to the concerto of fire that gathered in his knee. Unable to put much weight on that leg, he used the back of a wooden chair as a walker. Without protest, he plopped into a chair and extended his leg on to a second one.

Old Jeb worked in silence. His coarse, work-roughened fingers were as gentle and lithe as a doctor's. The kneecap was the size of a cantaloupe, and he probed the swelling.

Paul bore the pain with clenched jaw as the old man bent and twisted his knee this way and that. The examination seemed to last several lifetimes, but finally Old Jeb straightened up. "Don't think you cracked the kneecap. Might've bruised the bone. For sure, you got some damaged ligaments in there. Gonna be sore for a spell."

"What do I do now?"

"I'll do some doctorin'. That'll help. You stay off it a bit, that'll be the biggest help. I'll tell you when you can put some weight on it."

He dug into the sack he'd brought and extracted a dusky bottle of liquid. "Liniment." He slathered it on, a thick, syrupy liquid with a sharp, foul odor. Then he wrapped the knee with an Ace bandage.

Turning to the sack again, the old man pulled out strips of cloth that looked like cut-up sheets. He started winding the leg up near the hip and continued on down to just above the ankle. When he'd finished, Paul's leg was as stiff as a chair leg.

He mumbled a thanks and watched the old man leave. Weary and in pain, he sat where he was, reluctant even to attempt to move his leg. What do I do now? He glared at the bandages and swore.

Eventually the pain drove him to action. The aspirin was in the bathroom. Using the chair again for support, he hopped his way to the bathroom sink and took two pills, thought about it and took two more.

Hunger was another problem. He settled for a cold meat sandwich for breakfast rather than trying to cope with a frying pan and eggs. The kitchen was cold—the whole Coop was cold. He managed to get the fire stoked up and a pot of coffee percolating. Both helped against the chill.

His head buzzed from the aspirin and caffeine. He walked the chair into the studio, collapsed into the depths of the wing chair, swung the leg up on a piano bench and stared at the pianos. The silence spread around him, thick and lonely.

He was reading one of his piano reference books when he heard the sound of a vehicle coming up the driveway. There was no chug-chug, so he knew it wasn't Old Jeb's. He thought about going to the door, but one flex of the leg muscle convinced him to stay put, and he yelled out, "It's open! Come on in!"

One of the old men he'd met in the deli, the lanky,

freckle-faced man called Bobbin, stuck his head around the kitchen partition. "Hear tell you got banged up a bit."

Paul nodded glumly. "A bit."

"Your order came in down to the store, and when we got to talking about it, we thought maybe you could use it." He came around the corner, his arm muscles bulging from the weight of a carton. "I'll unload it here, so's you can see what's in it, then I'll stow the stuff if you tell me where."

The carton was filled with the hardware items on the list Paul had given Thaddeus. Cans of stains and varnishes, more sandpaper, assorted cloths and brushes and cleaning compounds, spackles—everything was there.

Paul eyed the Old Soldier. "I bet I could rig up a support for my knee and keep working on the upright over there."

Bobbin considered it, then walked closer to the pianos. He estimated the heights of the benches, then nodded. "You right-handed or left?"

"Right."

Bobbin pulled the upright's bench out, positioned himself within easy reach of the piano, and raised the leg twin to Paul's injured one. He judged where the ankle and foot would be and moved the baby grand's bench into place. He tried it once, and nodded again. "It'll work. Hang on, I'll be back in a minute." He headed for the back door.

He lugged in another box, a pair of crutches clamped under one arm. "You go try it now." He set down the carton and held the crutches out for Paul.

The wing chair was low and deep, and Paul struggled to push himself out and up. He planted the crutches firmly under his arms and tested the handholds.

"I guessed at those. You're a bit taller than I am, so I set the handles up one notch."

"They feel fine." On his first step, he overreached and almost fell forward. A chuckle behind him made him grin. "Graceful, aren't I."

"Like a cow dancing upright."

He was more cautious with his next step and made it over to the benches. He positioned himself as Bobbin had done, miming the motions of spreading stripper over the upright's finish, then nodded. "It'll work. You bet."

Pleased with himself, Bobbin bent down to the second carton. "Food, a deck of cards for solitaire, a couple of steamy paperbacks and some good wine."

"Bless you, Bobbin."

"Anything I can get you before I leave? Crutches are okay, but they make it tough carrying stuff."

"A refill of coffee would be appreciated."

Bobbin nodded and disappeared with Paul's cup. He returned with just the one.

"There's plenty," Paul offered. "Have some."

"I can't stay. Thank you, anyway." The old man rose. "Think you've got everything you need for now?"

"I think so. I can't thank you enough, Bobbin. You've saved my sanity by helping me. Now I can keep myself busy."

"No problem. You think of anything, you let me know. Jenny'll be by at suppertime with some hot food for you, so you just send word with her if there's something you need. She's already fixed a sandwich and sent a container of soup for lunch. It's in the groceries. I'll stash them out of the way for you before I leave."

When Bobbin was through, he left with a final hail. Paul listened as the sounds of the truck faded into the distance. This time when the silence returned, it didn't seem so dense, so lonely.

▮

He was spread across two piano benches, concentrating on stripping one small section of paneling on the Old Soldier, when a knock sounded on the back door. Before he could move, the door squealed open and a shrill, female "Yoo-hoo!" rang out.

"In here!" he called back.

Grace Duncan bobbed around the corner, her big, heavy black purse swinging from her arm. She stopped short halfway across the room. "Goodness, you are a sight. And what a smell!" That pronouncement made, she marched up to the piano bench and studied his leg. "Old Jeb's work, I can see. That man must have a monopoly on old sheets. A clear case of overkill."

Paul looked up at her quizzically. "You mean I don't need all this bandaging?"

She frowned. "Well, I wouldn't go so far as to say that. It won't hurt, certainly. Just seems to me you could accomplish what you're after with half the number of sheets he's used. Must be a hotel's worth wrapped around you. But never you mind. Old Jeb knows what he's about. He's cured plenty of lame critters in his time, and every last one of them walked straight as a telephone pole right up until they were carried to their rest, feet first." Her face looked like a happy dumpling as she talked.

Paul grinned. "Thanks. That cheers me up no end."

She sank onto the third piano bench. "So now tell me, just how did it happen? And don't give me any of that tripping over a log story you fed to Abner. He didn't buy it, and neither will I."

Sudden caution rose in Paul. Did she report back to Abner? He wasn't quite ready to tell his story yet. Not until he'd had a chance to go back after the fallen object.

"The log was merely face-saving for me," he said lightly. "I really did crack my knee on one hell of a rock, but I was in the open when I landed, and darned if I could see anything to trip over. Just a thick clump of air, I guess."

"Your full weight must've landed on that rock to cause the damage that's said to be there."

"Oh, it did," he said with utter sincerity. "It did."

She scrutinized him, her blue eyes sharp and shrewd. "Somehow I believe that last sentence. And that's about all I believe."

Paul hesitated, then decided to chance it. "Grace, why are there so many pickup trucks out at night?"

It was like a television set suddenly going off. Her face went blank and her volubility shut down. "Oh, I guess they have things to tend to," she said, finally. She tried for a light, airy tone of dismissal and failed miserably. Like Thaddeus, she was an open, honest person forced into dissembling, Paul surmised. "Like what things to tend to?"

"Poachers, maybe. There's still another few days of hunting season left."

He steepled his fingers and studied her. Under such close scrutiny, she ran dry of chatter and merely sat, fingering the catch on her purse. Finally, he said, "Hunters, huh? Is that why I've been warned to stay at home?"

"Warned!" She looked truly startled. "Who's been giving you warnings?"

"Abner and his crew."

"What kind of warnings?"

"To stay out of the woods. To stay put in the Coop here. Particularly at night."

She'd begun to recover from her surprise and was back to fingering her clasp. "Oh, those."

"Yes, those." He was relentless in his gaze.

She looked down to watch what her fingers were doing. "Yes, I'd guess hunters. Because of hunters."

He let another moment of silence tick by, then said, "Let me ask you, why was I brought here?"

"To restore pianos, of course."

"But why here? On a remote island like this? How were they brought here, who brought them?"

"It's not my story to tell."

"Then there is a story."

Her mouth snapped shut as she stared at him, then she said slowly, "I didn't say there was a story."

"Yes, you did. You just said it."

For an instant, her chin rose to a stubborn, rebellious angle, then it slowly fell as she released a deep sigh. "Well, maybe I did, at that. But it's nothing that concerns you."

"I disagree. I seem to be smack in the middle of it."

"What makes you say that?"

He gave a slow, humorless smile. "I don't think Thaddeus is very good at play-acting."

She snorted, relaxing now. "Thaddeus is one of life's innocents. Always has been, always will be. He can tell you who drinks too much wine, who's coloring her hair, and who's eating himself into an early grave. But as for what's going on around him, really going on, he sees none of it. If he had his way, everyone would be everyone else's best friend. His sister's far sharper than he is, in that way."

"I don't think I've met her yet."

"Certainly you have. Jenny. Jenny Webster. The young lady in the deli."

He leaned forward in surprise. "She's his sister? For some reason, I thought they were married."

She burst out laughing. "I forget how utterly confusing relationships can get on this Island, what they must be like to a newcomer. No, she's Thaddeus's sister, and they're son and daughter to Nathaniel Webster, otherwise known as Bobbin. Thaddeus has a small place of his own, but Jenny lives with her dad. Bobbin's one of the world's nicest men. Very compassionate. He'd do anything for anyone. Abner, too, for that matter. Though he's more reserved."

"And what about the third one—Calvin."

She considered that. "Well, there again, you've got someone who'd pitch in to help if needed. But he's a bit sour, kind of feels that life's gypped him somehow. His wife died soon after they got married and he took it as a personal affront. Bad things should happen to others. Well, as I've told him before—oh, we've talked this out time and again—as I told him, life hands out blows all around, and some of them feel like you're being slapped in the face with a huge hunk of raw liver, but none of us dodge 'em. Not for long we don't. And it's better to wise up to it than run around all moody and broody the rest of your life just 'cause you got yours. You're going to, sooner or later."

In spite of age lines, her eyes were pert and bright and youthful. There was a down-to-earth shrewdness to her that was likable. He suspected she'd had her share of troubles to handle; now there wasn't much that life or people could do that would surprise her.

"So." He grinned. "You're a widow and Calvin's a widower . . ."

"And Bobbin's a widower and Abner's a bachelor and so's Tom Ross and Zeke and a whole bunch of others, and there's not a one of them I'd bother taking home for more than a good home-cooked meal now and then." She was bristling. "So's you can let that bee out of your bonnet right now."

Paul's grin broadened. "I have been properly rebuked and accept it with good grace. So to speak."

She snorted. "I doubt that. And don't think it's escaped my notice that you've successfully avoided answering my questions. There's one thing about busybodies like me, their nosiness usually wins out in the end."

At that, he burst into laughter. "That's probably true."

"Absolutely." She gathered up the huge purse.

"This has been great fun, but now to the serious purpose of my visit here." She opened her purse and withdrew a pharmacy bottle half filled with tablets. "I figure Old Jeb didn't do much about easing your pain, so here's some aspirin with codeine. But take them only if you're not allergic to codeine." She handed it over to him.

The label had her name on it and was dated from the previous winter. "How do you happen to have these?"

"Oh, I've a touch of arthritis that acts up now and again. Nothing serious, but the damn fool doctor insists I have these to help me sleep at night. He doesn't seem to realize that one of these years, I'm going to be sleeping my way through eternity. Who needs to practice up for that?"

She burrowed in the bag again. "And just to make the world a little sweeter . . ." She pulled out a small bottle of dark liquid and turned the label his way. It was handwritten. "Blackberry cordial. Last year's batch. I've brought you two. Be generous with yourself, there's still a basement full of the stuff before we ever get around to tapping this year's supply."

"Grace, you're a wonder."

"I am at times, I must admit." She rose and pulled on her coat. "No, don't get up. I'll see myself out."

"Grace . . ."

She paused.

"Who owns a boat on the island?"

"What kind of boat? There are several. A couple of rowboats, a fishing skiff or two—"

"This would be a cruiser. About twenty-five feet,

small forward cabin, rigged up for fishing. And old. Needs a paint job badly."

"Sounds like Zeke's. He's got some old thing he uses for salmon fishing."

"And another one, looks like a tug?"

"That'd be Tom Ross's. He bought it a couple of years ago from Calvin. Why're you asking?"

He kept his answer casual. "I see one or the other one coming in and out of Oro Bay every day."

Startled, she glanced from him to the windows, then moved over to peer out. She stayed bent a moment, then slowly straightened and turned to stare at him again. "Yes, you would, wouldn't you." She gathered her purse close to her side. "I've got to go," she said abruptly, and she sailed out of there like a cruise ship late for a date with destiny.

Chapter Ten

He'd taken a codeine pill as soon as Grace left and by suppertime he was comfortable enough to answer the knock at the back door in person. He switched on the outside light.

Jenny stood outside, holding a long baking dish in both hands, the night black around her. She'd released her hair from the prison of its bun and it framed her face, falling softly forward over her cheeks. The overhead light picked up red glints among the chestnut strands and played with them as she moved. Her smile was warm and friendly. "I've brought some supper for you."

"Bobbin mentioned you were planning on doing that, and I've decanted some wine and gotten the table set."

She stopped just inside the door, peering past him at the table set for two. "Oh, but I can't stay!"

"Why not?"

"I'm expected home."

"Would your dad be upset if you were just a little late?"

A quick flash of amusement lit up her eyes. "Not upset, just hungry."

"I see. And he's never before cooked for himself. And the Island's so large and filled with so many strangers you're taking supper to tonight, he'd have no idea where you are."

She smiled without responding, and he let it go, content to watch her.

Her motions were all economy. With her heavy, long coat still buttoned up, she placed the dish in the oven, set the temperature, then disappeared outside. She returned with a grocery sack, which disgorged French bread and the makings for a salad. She folded the paper bag and stowed it between a cabinet and the refrigerator, slid off her coat, laid it over the back of a kitchen chair and set to work.

He poured out wine for both of them, then, unable to hobble on crutches and carry things yet, he held it out to her. Wordlessly, she came over to accept it. Their eyes locked and held a moment.

"Thank you," she said softly, before she turned back to her work.

She was dressed simply in a brown woolen skirt and a white blouse buttoned to the neck, which seemed to be her standard uniform for the deli. Her body was as slim as a conductor's baton, her motions quick, graceful and efficient. She had strong hands with long, slender fingers that flew at her work. Radishes, onions, tomatoes, red and green peppers fell quickly under her knife and within minutes were scooped into a colorful array atop a bowl of lettuce.

"With Roquefort dressing, I hope," he commented into the silence.

"I had to guess that's what you'd like."

"Am I as transparent as all that?"

"Not transparent. Cultured."

"Good Lord!" he said, truly startled. "That sounds terribly snobbish."

"Are you? Snobbish, I mean."

"I'd like to think not."

She was silent a moment, picking up the bread and studying it as if considering the best approach with the knife. "What *do* you think of us, Mr. Whitman?"

"I'm not sure I can answer that yet."

"Surely you've formed some impressions." The knife began slicing across the length of the loaf.

"I've only been here a few days. That wouldn't be fair."

The look she gave him was pure skepticism.

"Okay, your brother, Thaddeus, seems like an open-hearted person. Kind, thoughtful, considerate. And trusting. Perhaps too much so?"

She thought about it and nodded.

"Your dad seems rather nice. And thoughtful. He brought out a truckload of supplies for me today. He didn't need to do that just for me. But he did, anyway."

"But that's how we do things around here," she said softly. "We help one another when it's needed."

"Even strangers?"

Her chin was firm, her voice definite. "Even strangers, Mr. Whitman." She appeared ready for a dispute of some kind, but then her expression softened and the smile came back. For the first time, he noticed a slight dimple in one cheek. He found it fascinating. "But do go on," she said. "This is interesting."

"Sort of a bird's eye view of things?"

She nodded.

"Okay, then. Next, Grace Duncan. She's a delight. She is what she is and you take what's there or not at all. A very shrewd lady. She's not going to miss much of what's going on around her. And strong-willed, too. The band's going to march to her beat if she has any say about it."

Jenny gave a soft laugh. "That's about the best description of Grace I've heard. She really is a dear, but she's got some people on this island deathly afraid of her."

"I can understand that. If you were a timid sort, she'd run right over you."

"Actually, that's not true. She's really quite gentle with the timid. Unfortunately, that makes them even more afraid of her." She finished slicing the bread and started spreading some garlic butter. "Go on, please."

"Then there's Old Jeb. He scares the hell out of me. He's very abrupt. And crabby."

"He's got things on his mind."

"What things?"

"Oh, just things." She finished with the butter, wrapped the French bread in foil, and set the package in the oven next to the baking dish. Then she picked up her wine and carried it to the table.

She stared into the glass a moment, then looked up at him. The small worry frown was back, and her eyes were dead serious. "Do you really need this job, Mr. Whitman?"

"Yes, I really need this job. And please call me Paul. Why do you ask?"

"Just curious." She studied her wine some more. Now she seemed melancholy and remote.

"And you? Do you really need the job at the deli?"

She looked surprised at the question. "It helps my brother out for now."

"And later? What about your future?"

"This is my future, Mr. Whitman." With an abrupt motion, she rose and checked on dinner. "Leave that in for another ten minutes or so. Fifteen wouldn't hurt." She picked up her coat from the chair.

"I've upset you," he said softly.

"I said to begin with I couldn't stay." She slid her coat on and buttoned up. It was a fine woolen coat, camel-colored, and somehow seemed more than what an Islander would wear. It made him think of offices and professional work.

The chug-chug of Old Jeb's truck clattering up the driveway penetrated the Coop.

She opened the door for the old man, then stood in the open doorway, on her way out. "His dinner's in the oven. It needs another ten, fifteen minutes. He won't be able to serve it himself. Not on crutches."

"I'll see to it. You go on now."

She nodded. "Good night, Mr. Whitman. Thank you for the glass of wine."

Biting back a protest, he watched her go. He was left with just the company of the stern old man pulling the foul-smelling liniment bottle out of his overcoat pocket.

▮

The next morning, the sound of pickaxes, thumps and muffled grunts drew his attention. Sprawled across two piano benches, intent on his work, Paul hadn't heard anyone approach the Coop. He grabbed his crutches and swung over to the windows.

The Pickup Brigade was out in full force. They were digging holes across the entire meadow in front of the Coop, some swinging picks while others shoveled the loosened dirt. Down on the road, a couple of trucks were loaded with fir trees, roots balled in burlap. A backhoe waited, its huge maw hanging in the air.

He swung his crutches forward in furious strides, grabbed a jacket and raced outside as fast as the crutches could go. "What the hell are you doing?"

Abner Ross stood to one side, supervising the work. "It's just a little landscaping job, Mr. Whitman. It's the best time of year for a bit of tree planting."

"You're going to plant those"—he pointed a crutch towards the firs on the truck—"in front of my *windows*? It's insane! You'll ruin the view and cut off my light. It's dark enough in there as it is!"

Abner was as calm as stone. "Well, let's take a look inside." He moved around the building, leaving Paul to follow him.

Fuming, Paul watched as the old man probed the studio, examining first the windows, then the light slanting across the floor, then the roof. He paced this way and that, studying rafters and roof boards. Finally, he nodded. "Another couple of skylights will do it. Put one in there," he pointed south of the existing one, "and another on the kitchen side. That should do the job. We'll get those in right away for you."

"I don't want skylights. I want my view."

"Sorry." The old man walked out.

Paul fumed some more, but by noon, the trees were in place.

They were young cedars, about six feet tall, with broad spreading branches. The men had planted them far enough apart to allow plenty of room for growth and further spreading, then had planted a second row below them, set so they destroyed any view left between the trees above them. The implication wasn't lost on Paul. He had a clear memory of Grace Duncan, startled, peering out his windows, murmuring that yes, indeed, he could see Oro Bay.

Abner came to the door. "The men'll be taking a lunch break now, then they'll start in on the skylights. Can I fix you something to eat?"

"No thank you." Paul's voice was ice cold.

The old man shrugged, unfazed by the repressed rage directed at him. "We'll be back about one, then."

When the Pickup Brigade returned, they came back with two large panes of glass and some lumber. Throughout the afternoon, men scrambled up and down ladders inside and out. Once the holes were cut for the skylights, fresh light poured in, illuminating the dusky reaches of the studio.

Paul had to admit it was a much better working situation. Already he could see faint streaks on the Old Soldier where he'd thought he'd stripped the finish down to bare wood, but where a faint residue of old stain had been left in the deeper grains.

And the men were friendly enough, joking among themselves, tossing him assurances that his work would be easier now with more light. "Maybe that's not a favor we're doing him," one man shouted from his perch on a rafter, and there was good-natured laughter in response.

Still, Paul was upset. When the work was about finished, he said to Abner, "I presume Mr. Murdock knows of this renovation. This is his property, after all."

"He's left me in charge, Mr. Whitman. But you can be sure, he'll be informed."

"Then he is reachable."

Abner didn't answer him.

When the two heavy squares of glass were in place and the final caulking done, the young man named Tom Ross came over to Paul. He was tall and blond, with a strong sturdy physique. "Now we need it not to rain tonight. If you have any influence up there"—grinning, he thumbed upward—"tell Him to hold off a day or so."

Paul bit back a sharp retort and forced a light tone. "In other words, tonight would not be the night to perform a rain dance in the forest at midnight."

Tom chuckled. "You got it." He began to gather up his tools.

If Paul had it straight in memory, Tom Ross was the one Grace had said owned the old tug. The one called Zeke owned the power cruiser. Was he one of the workers, too? Paul looked around, but there was no way to distinguish one member of the Pickup Brigade from another. He might not even be there. He could be out on patrol again, circling the Island, looking for God knew what. And neither Bobbin nor Calvin were there, either. Were they with him?

Old Jeb arrived with his nightly package of fresh

bandages. He waylaid Abner and took him off to the far corner, out of earshot. They bent over in quiet conversation. Try as he could, Paul couldn't hear what was being said. Old Jeb did some talking, then Abner looked Paul's way and spoke. Old Jeb peered at the Piano Man and nodded. It left Paul feeling like a kid outside the principal's office while his fate was being decided. He found himself getting angry all over again.

The last of the clean-up was finished and the men began to leave. Old Jeb set the sack of bandages down. "I'll be back with your supper."

"Where's Jenny?"

"She won't be coming." He trailed out after the others.

Left alone in the silence of the Coop, Paul swung to the window and stared out. The trees screened not only the bay from his view, but the road as well. He could hear the parting shouts of the men, the slam of truck doors, the startup of engines, but he could see nothing. Except green firs. It gave him a claustrophobic feeling.

Dejected, he swung over to the easy chair, sank into its depths, lifted his injured leg onto the kitchen-chair footstool and brooded upon the injustice of it all.

Chapter Eleven

The skylights helped more than he cared to admit. There still was no electricity in the studio, so his work was still limited to daylight hours, but details previously hidden by the dusky light stood out clearly and the bare spot on the Old Soldier spread rapidly, clean down to the smallest groove.

His knee was improving, too. Old Jeb came by twice a day to doctor it, and under the effects of the foul-smelling liniment, the swelling was quickly down.

When it was gone completely, Paul asked him, "How soon can I put some weight on the leg?"

Old Jeb looked at him with a scowl. "Still a lot of damage in there. Be a week or two. Maybe longer."

"But it's feeling a lot better."

"Ligaments take a heap of healin'. And you did a right fine job on yours. You just mind your patience a mite, keep the leg as still as you can, and you'll be walkin' fine. You go and get fancy on it too soon, well . . ." Old Jeb shrugged, refusing the responsibility for a dire future.

Paul didn't say anything more, but the next time Grace stopped by, he asked her, "You say Old Jeb's fixed up injured animals before?"

She'd taken to bringing his lunch at noon. Today, she'd brought a tuna salad and was spreading it on thick slabs of homemade bread. A jar of home-canned pickles was at her elbow. "Dozens," she answered as she worked. "Why? That rotten-cabbage smell getting to you?"

"It's not exactly eau de carnation. How long does it usually take before they start walking again?"

"Depends on the injury. Just a sprain, it'd be a week or two, be my guess. A real fine job like you've done, could be a few weeks or more. Three months, maybe."

"Three months! Lord, Grace, I'll go out of my mind if it takes that long!"

"Want to borrow some yarn and knitting needles?" She piled the sandwiches on a plate and carried them to the table, poured two cups of coffee, then sat down at her place. She took a hearty bite from one of the sandwiches. Through chews, she said, "You weren't planning to go anywhere, were you?"

"I guess I'm not."

"My, my, a bit grumpy today, aren't we."

"It's called cabin fever. It would be nice to take a stroll, or to walk up to the deli for a cup of coffee."

"Well, I hate to sound like an old grandma, but I'd put up with a bit of inconvenience for a few weeks rather than risk having to put up with it the rest of your life."

"That's what Old Jeb said," he grumped. "You're both a pain, you know that?"

The conversation moved on to a dozen other innocuous subjects, as it always did with Grace. He'd have to bide his time, waiting for the injury to heal further. After all, one didn't just gallop through a

Beethoven symphony. But he still felt at odds with the world.

Bobbin popped in with donuts or cinnamon rolls every day so that Paul wouldn't have to struggle with cooking breakfasts for himself. One morning, though, after Bobbin had left, he looked at the donuts and felt hungry for eggs. He set the donuts to one side, leaned his crutches against the wall and hopped about the kitchen like a one-legged kangaroo, gathering the makings for an omelet. His arms laden with milk and eggs, he began a hop while still off-balance from leaning into the refrigerator and nearly toppled over. With his arms full, he couldn't windmill to keep his balance, so his weight landed hard on his injured leg.

Stiff with sudden fear at the damage he might have done to it, he waited for the shriek of pain to hit.

Nothing.

He waited some more.

Nothing. Not even a twinge.

Gingerly, he touched the sole of his foot to the floor and waited again. Still nothing. He tested it with a small amount of his weight. His leg felt a bit stiff, but there wasn't a sore spot anywhere. He took a tentative step. His knee seemed to work fine.

He walked up and down the kitchen. The bandage, wrapped tightly from hip to ankle, made walking cumbersome, but there wasn't the slightest twinge of pain from the kneecap or the muscles surrounding it. "Son of a bitch," he whispered.

He stopped in the center of the kitchen, his mind racing. He didn't know a lot about the human body. Very little when you came right down to it, but he suspected that if there was no pain, there was no raw injury left to mend. Surely Old Jeb, with a lifetime of healing behind him, knew that.

He stared at the milk and eggs still cradled in his arms, then at the frying pan already out on the stove. A glance at the clock told him Old Jeb would be arriving momentarily.

Still being gentle with the bandaged leg, he quickly replaced the food in the refrigerator, the pan in the cupboard, then grabbed a plate, a couple of donuts and some coffee. He was eating them at the table, crutches by his side, when Old Jeb arrived.

As the old man unwrapped the leg, Paul watched closely. There seemed to be no special trick to the bandage. Start at the top and wind around tightly all the way down. He was silent as the liniment was slobbered on. In another moment, he was bound back up and Old Jeb was preparing to leave.

"Thanks," Paul said, as he did each morning.

"Be back at six," the old man responded, as he did each morning.

"I won't run away," Paul promised. It was their standard routine, and never once had it brought a smile to the old man's face.

Paul kept the bandage on all day, but he tossed aside the crutches except when Grace was there and walked around as much as possible. The bandage kept the leg stiff, so he couldn't bend the knee much, but the small amount he did caused no problems. By suppertime, his leg muscles were aching from use, but otherwise he was fine.

Again, he said nothing to Old Jeb, letting the wiry old man do his work. As a precaution, he used crutches during the evening, when the lights inside the kitchen would show his every movement to anyone watching from the black night outside.

At one point, he scoffed at his own caution. Who on earth would hang around just to keep an eye on him? But he kept up the fiction of the sore leg just the same.

The bathroom had no window, so it provided the one place of privacy. There he packed his knapsack with a complete change of clothes, a couple of heavy towels, some warm socks, an extra pair of shoes, a thermos of coffee and some food. Then he stripped off his clothes, arranging them in careful order across the foot of the bed so he could dress in the dark later on, and turned off all the lights.

In the dark, he unknotted the bandage and unwound it. The rotten-cabbage smell of the liniment, fresh from having just been put on, combined with the old rotten-meat odor that had never really left the Coop, made him want to gag.

Once free of the bandage, he made his way through the dark into the bathroom to wash the liniment smell from his knee. Holding on to the edge of the sink, he did several deep knee-bends. There wasn't a squawk of pain. Just a light stiffness normal for any leg immobilized for a few days. Reassured, he retreated to bed and waited.

The radiant dial of his watch showed two A.M. when he stirred. According to the tables in the newspaper, low tide that morning was at four. An hour's walk, an hour's search either side of mean low tide and an hour home. He'd be back by six. Old Jeb never came until after he'd finished tending his stock, somewhere after seven. He'd have plenty of time.

Enough moonlight lit the countryside to make his flashlight unnecessary. They hadn't had rain since the day of his injury. With dry earth available, he stuck to the side of the road, gliding like a shadow through the night. He saw no one and heard nothing out of the ordinary. Not even a dog barked.

▮

He found the old sprawling summer home on Agate Beach Road without any trouble and made his way easily through the trees that circled the lawn down to the water. He stepped silently on the beach and paused. It was empty both ways, the water lapping quietly at the edge.

He headed south. The cliff started to climb and threw the beach in shadows. Choosing not to use the flash unless he had to, he picked his way along, cautious foot after cautious foot.

As the cliff steepened, the beach narrowed. He rounded a curve and came to an abrupt halt. A headland, forty feet high or better, blocked his path and extended out into the water. A sheer cliff, it offered no way up. He had no choice except to go around it. But he didn't know the depth of the water here, nor the currents. He swore.

He risked using the flash for a quick scan. A few good-sized boulders hugged the base of the cliff, and some driftwood had come to rest nearby. The headland itself jutted out into the water better than a hundred yards, even at low tide. High tide, and the beach would be buried. From his quick survey, he spotted small nooks and crannies at the base of the headland that would provide handholds for wading around it. He'd have to trust to luck as far as the depth went. He sat next to a large boulder and removed his shoes and socks.

He'd just shoved them and his flashlight into the knapsack when the steady ping of a diesel engine drifted over the water. The sound grew stronger. The boat was coming from the north, behind him. He scrambled behind the boulder and crouched down, his head clearing the top enough for him to see.

Captured by moonlight, the boat showed its outline clearly against the dark, quiet sea. It was the power cruiser belonging to Zeke. Spotlights fore and aft swept over beach and cliff. The search was methodical. A dart of light ahead a few feet, then a minute examination backward over the area skipped. Another dart forward and another examination.

The rhythm was almost musical and he picked it up easily, keeping one portion of his attention on the lights' progress even as he tried to probe past their source to the boat itself. But the spots destroyed his night vision and he could see nothing except the rays of brilliant white.

He sensed rather than saw the sudden jump the lights made to the headland. He ducked down a half-second before it lit up the rock shielding him. At the last moment, he remembered the knapsack, still in sight. He could only hope it appeared to be another boulder. He held his breath and stayed frozen.

There was no change in the beat of the engine that would signify they'd spotted anything out of the ordinary. The boat continued its sedate path forward at a steady trolling speed, the two lights dissecting the headland from clifftop to waterline. Finally, the night blackness cloaked him once more.

Common sense told him to retrace his steps and get back to his bed as fast as he could. There was something going on that didn't bode healthy for anyone interfering. He'd be better off simply to do his work until the job was done and he could leave the island. These people meant nothing to him, but his own safety did. A lot.

Instead, he waited until the last engine beat died away, then rose, rolled up his pants legs, shouldered his knapsack and waded out into the water. A small rock buried in the sea bottom caught him unaware and his foot slid off at an awkward angle, a flash of pain shooting through his ankle. Lord, if he came up with another injury now . . . He tested it, but it had been a momentary twist, not a sprain.

As he edged further out, clinging to every jagged handhold the cliff provided, the water lapped higher and higher up his shin. He was grateful for the low tide. Judging from the high water marks on the headland, at peak tides he'd be in over his head and swimming.

The water was cold and his feet and ankles were numb by the time he'd rounded the headland and could wade up to the beach. He debated continuing on barefoot, but his feet needed the warmth of heavy socks. He grudgingly took the minute or so to dry off his feet.

The trip was taking longer than he thought. It was after four already. If the boat followed the pattern it had set on Oro Bay, he had another two hours or so before it would return. He gave himself until five-thirty to complete his errand and be safely off the beach. He picked up his pace.

He had to hurdle two more headlands. He didn't even pause, just plunged into the water, shoes and all. The trips were much quicker than wading barefoot around them.

The third cove was the one he sought. He found the driftwood log where he'd relaxed and dozed, then followed the beach down to where the broken sections of ladder should be.

There was nothing there. He found the clay-and-gravel steps, and the gouge in the outward curve of the bank where the ladder had hit bottom, but there was no sign of rails or steps or even a straight piece of weathered wood. The beach had been swept clean of scraps.

He flashed the light up the cliff, thinking he might've had the wrong location, and froze.

There it was, at the head of the stairs, bolted into place, just like it should be. The breaks had been repaired and whoever had done it had found weathered wood that was a close match to the rest of it. If Paul hadn't spent a lifetime working with wood, it would have fooled even him. With the upper ladder in place, it looked as if the accident had never happened.

Did they know? Did Abner and the Pickup Brigade know this was how he'd hurt himself?

Questions would have to wait until later. He needed to be through and gone.

He turned his flash to the base of the cliff. The shrub should be just to the right of the stairs. It turned out to be a blackberry bush, with vines that wound around themselves into a thicket that cut like a whip.

He ignored the worst of them as he conducted his search. It took only minutes for his light to glint off something metallic.

The tool had caught in a tangle at the rear of the thicket. He worked it free, then stared at it. A combination wrench. As shiny as the day it was bought. And he'd bet his favorite concerto that it fit the ladder bolts at the top of the cliff. Someone had followed him that day and loosened the stairway while he was down on the beach. Someone had done what they could to cause him to die.

▌

It was well after six-thirty by the time he got back to the Coop. Hurriedly, he stripped, then started in on the bandaging. He put the foul-smelling gauze pad over his kneecap, then began winding the sheet-strips, starting at his hip, as the old man had. He had to leave enough slack to be able to bend down to his ankle and get the bandage tied, so it ended up a bit looser than usual, but when he was through, he studied it with a critical eye. To him, it would pass.

Clothed, he switched on the kitchen lights, swung around the room on crutches and got the coffee going. By the time Old Jeb came, he was sitting at the kitchen table, a plate of donuts in front of him, the stove alive and crackling, the percolator chirping in its key of C.

The old man looked drawn and tired, his eyes bloodshot. Had he been on the boat? But tired or not, his eyes were still sharp and they scanned Paul's face and did a summing up of their own. "Looks like you didn't sleep much."

"I didn't. It was one of those nights, one nightmare after another." And wasn't that the truth, Paul thought. "You don't look that rested yourself."

The old man grunted, unwrapping the bandages. "Up with a sick cow."

Paul said nothing more. He merely watched as the old man's fingers did a quick rebandaging job. They'd both lied through their teeth. But he was the only one aware of it, and that gave him some sense of comfort.

He sunk himself into work for the next few days, keeping up the fiction of the injured leg. When he felt enough time had passed, he fussed and fretted through a couple of more bandaging sessions, then called a halt.

"No," he said firmly, as the old man reached for the liniment to tend the unwrapped leg. "No more. My leg seems fine." He got up and walked around. "You see? Not even a limp."

The old man sighed. "I'm tellin' you, it's too soon. You start traipsing around the Coop here, you'll see what I mean."

Paul sat in the wooden chair across the table from him and looked him square in the eye. "I fully intend to be careful. Believe me."

Chapter Twelve

Cold gray skies clamped down over Puget Sound. Occasional sun broke up the monotony, but November started out as one long stretch of bitter, raw grayness.

And the grayer the day, the shorter his working time. With effort and concentrated vision, he could stretch his working time to four o'clock straight up. Once, he tried to push it further, using the flickering oil lamp to supplement fading daylight, but the next day he could see the streaks that had been left on the Old Soldier and he'd had to redo an entire section.

He was pouring morning coffee beneath the bare bulb in the kitchen when he stopped dead, staring up at it. A socket with an outlet, two fifty-foot extension cords and a good work lamp. That would do it.

But would the fuses hold?

He counted the number of outlets wired to the kitchen circuit. The bare bulb, the counter outlet for his coffeepot and one other that held the toaster plug. He could unplug the toaster, move the coffeepot to the bathroom and keep the kitchen light off. That'd work. Why hadn't he thought of it sooner? Why, he could even read by the work lamp at night! Whitman, you're brilliant! A bit slow, maybe. But brilliant. Cheered, he showered and dressed, and headed out for the store in the predawn darkness. A good breakfast wouldn't be amiss, either.

■

Thaddeus broke into a broad grin when Paul came through the doorway. "Look who's out and about! Good to see you, Paul."

"Thanks, Thaddeus. And thanks, too, for all the groceries you sent out."

"No problem, just glad you're healthy again."

Jenny was rolling out pie dough, flour flying in powdery clouds as her strong hands kneaded the dough. She, too, gave him a warm smile of welcome. "Morning, Paul. How's your knee?"

The use of his given name didn't escape him. He felt absurdly pleased. "About like new. Dr. Jeb worked his miracles. Of course I'm going to start mooing any day now."

She laughed. "We'll worry when you start giving milk. Can I get you some breakfast this morning?"

"Two over easy, some bacon, crisp, and a stack of pancakes a foot high should do it."

Nodding, she wiped her hands free of flour.

Paul poured his coffee and took his usual corner table. As early as it was, the three old men were already in place two tables over. "Morning, Abner, Calvin, Bobbin."

Abner sat with head bowed, shoulders slumped, forearms laid flat on the table, hands folded around his coffee mug. He looked dejected and exhausted, and he wasn't stroking his beard as he usually did. He gave Paul a brief nod.

Calvin rode his chair like a horse saddle, his short stumpy body hunched over the mug like a cowboy hunched over the saddle horn, his eyes fixed on the black liquid. His face was remote and moody, and he gave Paul a single glance before he returned to his own thoughts. He looked exhausted beyond caring.

Bobbin looked as weary as the others, the tiredness etched in deep lines running like wrinkled bark down the trunk of his face. But he managed a faint replica of his usual smile for Paul before it faded away.

Paul tried to concentrate on the news of the day as he ate, but he found himself stealing glances at the three men, trying to probe behind the heavy brooding. What did they know? What was driving them to such exhaustion? Had one of them been the one to sabotage the ladder? Or all of them?

He pondered it during breakfast, more worried than he cared to admit. He could tell himself all he wanted that the ladder incident had been nothing more than a prank. A little more serious than most, but still in the bad joke category. But there was enough doubt in his soul to make him feel afraid.

When his breakfast was finished, he folded up his paper. "Good day, gentlemen, it's off to work for me." Some mischievous instinct made him add, "And what're your plans for the day?"

Bobbin stared at him. Calvin flicked a disgusted glance his way. It was Abner who answered for them. "Just the usual."

Paul smiled. All three men looked as if they could fall into bed and stay there a month before they even began to catch up with lost rest. "Well, don't overdo it. You look exhausted."

Paul handed over his food receipt to Thaddeus to be added to his account. "There are some things I need to order from the mainland. Do you have some paper? I didn't make the list at home."

Thaddeus nodded and dug around beneath the counter.

Paul made a list of materials needed for installing a work lamp, then at the last moment, doubled everything. He could plug the extra lamp into the bathroom socket. And a second lamp would eliminate any shadows thrown by the first.

He went over the list with Thaddeus to make sure their interpretations of the items matched. "How soon do you think I can get them?"

"Tomorrow, first boat."

"Good enough. I'll be in to pick them up. Tell Jenny to save me an egg or two." He was struck by a sudden thought. "Never mind, I'll tell her myself." He swung around and returned to the deli counter.

When Jenny saw him approaching the counter, the dark eyebrows raised in question. The three old men came alert enough to watch intently.

"I forgot to thank you for all the dinners you sent over."

A puzzled look replaced the half-smile. "But I didn't. Just that once."

He frowned. "But Old Jeb said . . ." No, Old Jeb hadn't said. He'd intimated the food was from Jenny. The sharp old duck.

"As I understand it, Old Jeb's Missus was feeding you."

Paul gave her a foolish grin. "I guess I jumped to a few conclusions there. In that case, I take back all the thank you's but one."

Her eyes flickered to the three old men, watching

and listening. "You're welcome," she said, a bit coolly. "But I didn't do anything more than I'd do for anyone else taken sick." Not giving him a chance to respond, she turned back to the grill.

His lips pursed in a silent whistle. Was she merely putting him in his place? Or was she afraid of those three old men, and what they might think?

▌

He was deep at work when he heard Old Jeb's pickup chug-chug up the drive. Murdock must've heard about the work lamps, Paul guessed, as he picked up the rag and wiped his hands free of stripper. There was some satisfaction in not being surprised by Old Jeb's appearance. Maybe he was beginning to catch on to some of the Island ways. He went to unlock the back door and let him in.

The surprise was Abner. He entered with Old Jeb, and before saying anything, glanced first at the lock, then Paul. His glance probed a bit, but he didn't refer to it. "Hear you don't have electricity in the piano room. You should have."

"Come with me." Paul led them into the studio and showed them the outlet visible beneath the piano. "There's another under the workbench, and a third under the supply chest. But let me show you where the problem is."

He led them outside and around past the newly planted cedars to the far corner of the building. He pointed first to the shrubbery. "The terminus is in there, at the base of the wall. The fuse box is on the inside. But this is what we're missing." He pointed up to the empty eye-screw under the eaves. "The cable coming in from the road's gone."

The two old men stared up, then moved from behind the trees to study the telephone poles along the road. Abner stroked his beard as he pondered it. "No sign of the wire anywhere?" he asked Paul.

"No. I've searched and searched. It's gone."

Old Jeb scowled. "I should've noticed. I should've spotted it was gone right away."

"Don't feel bad," Abner said calmly. "We planted these damn trees right under where it's supposed to be and didn't notice it gone, either. Pretty hard to see what ain't there to be seen." He turned to Paul. "I gather the work lamps're missing, too. Jeb says there should be two of them."

"Nope. Nothing."

"All right, we'll ship some cable in on the first boat in the morning, along with the work lamps. Tom can rig it for you, he knows that kind of stuff. He should have you lit by noon." A brief glint of humor twinkled in his eyes. "No wonder you put up such a squawk about those trees cutting down your light."

It was no time to argue that shutting off the view of the bay was worse. Paul just shook his head and walked them back to the truck.

Abner paused at the cab door. "If we get you fixed up with live floor plugs, you still need those extension cords?"

"A couple. To give the lamps some mobility. But I won't need the socket plugs."

Abner nodded and climbed into the old truck.

Paul watched Old Jeb turn around and head down the sloppy driveway before he allowed himself a rueful grin. Even his shopping lists were being scrutinized and memorized by Abner and Company. It was a good thing he wasn't trying to smuggle important information off the Island. Whatever he ended up doing with the rest of his life, applying for undercover work wouldn't be one of them.

With the prospect of proper lighting in his near future, he decided to take the day for himself. He hadn't had a proper day off since he'd come here. To date, his treks around the Island had been at dusk or after. He might learn more if he did some exploring in daylight. Besides, it was safer to do his poking around then.

He packed the makings of a good hearty lunch in his knapsack and shoved in an extra sweater and the discarded windbreaker in case of rain. There were predictions of a storm moving in, but for now the day was dry, if gray.

He carefully locked the door behind him.

Chapter Thirteen

The air was a raw cold and he huddled deep into his jacket for warmth. The dark-bellied clouds overhead gave the day a strange, translucent light. As he came abreast of the schoolhouse, the sun found an opening in the heavy clouds and some rays burst through, turning the few remaining leaves on the cottonwoods into golden discs and floodlighting the tops of the firs. He paused, caught by the wonder of it and watched the sun at play.

There was something about this land, something hypnotic yet subtle that grabbed hold of him deep in his soul and stirred up some powerful emotion he wasn't ready to examine and name yet. It was the same feeling that music gave him. It hit him below the mind, subverting the intellect, connecting directly with the soul and the emotions that resided there. If he wasn't careful, he'd fall in love with this place, and he wasn't ready yet to make that kind of commitment to anywhere. But there was no denying the pull, and it seemed to strengthen every time he emerged from the womb of his work.

The clouds cloaked the sun once more, the spell was broken and he moved on.

He paused at the lane to the cemetery and on impulse turned in. The road to the graveyard wasn't much more than a steep, rutted lane carved from the forest. The forest was held at bay by an enormous circular clearing at the top of a gentle knoll. A dirt lane, the width of a hearse, followed the perimeter just inside the tree line. At the top of the knoll, an open-sided pavilion offered mourners protection from the weather, and a couple of spreading oaks and a magnificent black walnut of ancient age stood protecting some of the graves. Bare now, the trees were placed to provide broad sprawls of shade during hot summers. Yet, in spite of the pleasant openness of the knoll, the cemetery appeared secretive and remote, hidden as it was in the forest. Like the Islanders, he thought.

A magnificent marble obelisk stood as guardian over the dead at the top of the graves. It was taller than Paul, of a highly polished black marble. A pair of angels, blowing trumpets and trailing ivy vines, were etched into the glistening surface. The name ROSS had been carved in flowery Olde English letters. Abner's family?

On either side of the obelisk, rows of flat granite headstones stretched into the distance. The earliest Ross grave was dated 1869, a Bessie Ross. The most recent was an Obadiah Ross, dated early in September, just two months before. The birthdate indicated he'd been a man of seventy-six when he died. Related to Abner? A brother, perhaps? Was that why the three old men in the deli seemed continuously sad and weary? They were still grieving?

To Obadiah's right was Priscilla Ross. His wife evidently. She'd been born a couple of years after her husband and had died young, at twenty-nine. To her right, born the day she died, was a headstone for

Thomas Ross, but without a death date. Obadiah's son and Abner's nephew, he deduced. And one of the Pickup Brigade.

Abner's headstone was already in place. His birthdate was ten years after Obadiah's, which made him sixty-six. Not that old, really.

He wandered some more, seeking out the stories. There were a number of children's graves. A half dozen of those were within weeks of each other in 1918. If he remembered right, there'd been a bad flu epidemic throughout the country that year. Some children had individual graves. But another tombstone simply gave the family name with the single word BABIES following it. They could've been twins, quints or singles born years apart; there was no way of telling.

In the Duncan family plot, he found the graves of Grace's dead boys, Joseph and Edward. Their father lay one space over from them. The intervening grave was reserved for Grace. As in other family plots, her headstone was already in place. But not only was the year of death missing, so was the year of birth. Paul grinned. He liked to see a little vanity in women.

Fascinated, Paul moved through neighboring plots. Nearby, he found the Webster family plot. Their family were old Islanders, going back a hundred years or more. He managed to trace most of them through the generations. If he was calculating right, Bobbin, Thaddeus and Jenny were the last Websters left.

He found the tombstone for Bobbin's wife. Sarah. Maiden name, Brown. Calvin's sister, perhaps? She'd died thirty-one years ago. Just about the time Jenny would have been born. So Bobbin had been left a young widower with two children to raise.

Paul sat back on his heels. How would he have felt if Anna had gotten pregnant, then died in childbirth? God, he'd loved her so. It would have destroyed him to lose her during those first years together. Even now, with the love and warmth eroded by the years and the marriage gone, it was tough holding himself together. Imagine losing each other at the height of their passion. Yet here was this man, who'd done what he had to do while carrying a load of pain around in his gut. You couldn't help but admire these Islanders for their ability to endure life. They had one hell of a lot of grit and gumption, as his grandmother would've put it. A hell of a lot more than he had. A hell of a lot more.

He rose from his squat, suddenly anxious to be done. These were the graves of people he knew. Not some quaint anonymous graveyard like the ones he and Anna used to explore as a lark on their weekends in the country, untouched by the stories written there.

But there were still two more family plots to find. The first was Calvin's. The Brown family plot was off to one side, and fairly small. Calvin's grandfather must've brought the family to the Island on his own. His was the only grave of his generation there. Then two sons, one of whom died a bachelor. The second son had been Calvin's father.

Evidently there were only two offspring from that marriage. Sarah, buried in the Webster family plot. And Calvin, whose headstone awaited him. According to his birth year, he was sixty-six, the same age as

Abner. They must've grown up together. Next to Calvin's plot lay his wife, Florence, who'd died twenty years ago. There were no headstones for any children and, from what he'd gathered, he didn't think Calvin had any.

The family name he wanted to find more than any other still eluded him. Murdock. He began an organized, determined hunt, walking up first one row, then another, covering one section completely before starting on the next.

As he progressed, he marveled at the care the plots—the whole cemetery—received. The grass, brown now for the winter, had been thick and closely manicured before the killing frost had come. Many of the graves had permanent holders for flowers and plants at their heads. Almost all the graves were level. Very few had been left neglected and sunken from the dirt settling over time. And there wasn't a fallen leaf anywhere. Someone had put in long hours with a rake.

He finished searching the main section and moved to the far side where most of the graves were unrelated to each other. Here the headstones were neither polished nor finely engraved. Some were marked only by a simple wooden cross, so weathered that many names had faded into oblivion. Was this the Island version of a Potter's Field?

He couldn't figure out later why he hadn't spotted it immediately. The only reason he could think of was that the brown sod and the brown dirt were close enough in shading that the newness of the freshly dug grave had been camouflaged when viewed from a distance. The hump, of course, should've told him right away. But he'd been concentrating on headstones, not on the graves themselves.

The new grave was by itself in a forlorn corner of the Potter's Field. It had no formal headstone, just a simple wooden cross with the name and date of death carved on it. Walter Gibbons had died just a few days ago. No date of birth had been given. Presumably, it hadn't been known. Thus it would follow that he hadn't been an Islander.

Paul counted back. Six days. While he'd been confined to the Coop, nursing his injured knee, a man had died, had been mourned and had been buried. Three people a day had visited him while he'd been laid up, and not one of those three had said a single word about the death.

It made him shudder to think of the stealth going on around him. The stealth of the Islanders and the stealth of death. Somehow it was wrong that death should be allowed to happen so quietly. It shouldn't be allowed to sneak up on one. It shouldn't just be a moment when a person ceases to exist. No, death should come through on thundering hooves with trumpets blaring like a Master at the Hounds, giving fair warning, so the whole countryside would know it was in the area.

As for the stealth of the Islanders . . . Wasn't it a bit strange that no one had thought a man's death important enough to mention? Not Old Jeb—well, he wouldn't. He was too taciturn for gossip. But what about Bobbin? He of the open face and ready grin? And Grace! She'd been quick enough to fill him in on the most recent case of flu, who was getting what for Christmas from whom, and how the plans for the big

Island Christmas Fair were progressing. But a death? Not a word.

His mind tumbling with thoughts and suspicions, he searched the final two rows of the cemetery, knowing he wouldn't find the marker he was seeking among the poor of the Potter's Field section. And he didn't. Nowhere in the cemetery was there any grave marked Murdock.

Which gave rise to a host of questions. Was Murdock an Islander at all? If he wasn't, then why were the Islanders so protective of him? And if he was, was he a relative newcomer who'd managed to win their loyalty in some fashion? And why had they given him their loyalty at all?

Or was it loyalty? Could it be something else, some kind of hold he held over them that forced them to do his bidding? A case of a rich man buying the poor, like the black-hearted villain in some old-time melodrama, waving the mortgage over the poor heroine's head while she pleaded for mercy?

And was Jenny that heroine? Was that why she always had that river of sadness flowing underneath the calm exterior?

He stood at the bottom of the slope near the head of the lane and gave the cemetery a final sweep of his gaze. Something was nagging at him, something he'd missed—no, not missed. Just not noted in a meaningful way.

He gnawed at the half-formed thought a minute, then gave it up. It would come to him, and he could come back then if he had to. In the meantime, he ran his eyes over each row one last time, seeking a headstone overlooked or a section skipped. There were none. He'd checked each and every one. No Murdock was buried in any marked grave here.

He turned and headed down the lane. He'd learned more than he'd expected to, but less than he'd hoped. But he'd come away with an unexpected nugget. Who was Walter Gibbons and how had he died?

He ran over possible sources of information in his mind. There was only one real candidate. Grace Duncan. And she'd invited him to visit her anytime. If he could work the conversation around . . .

The afternoon ahead sketched itself out in his mind. First, he'd find a quiet place to eat his lunch and mull over the morning's findings. Some woodland glen where he'd be secluded from curious passersby. Then he'd do a thorough trek of the Island, examining it closely in daylight. And when he was tired from that, and ready for the warmth of a fire, he'd drop in and visit with Grace for a while. At the very least, it might gain him a glass of blackberry cordial. And perhaps—just perhaps—it might gain him more.

Chapter Fourteen

Grace Duncan's property began at the ferry dock and ran north from there along Larson Road. She had a considerable amount of land; a wood rail fence edged the property for half a mile or better before he reached the driveway. Except for the clearing where the house sat, the land was heavily wooded with madrona, alder and fir. Thickets twisted among the trees, curling in on themselves like some incestuous family.

The house itself had a narrow, two-story farmhouse front with a single wing spreading from one side. It was saved from homeliness by gables and dormers and shutters and dormant flower boxes. The siding was a weathered gray shingle, the trim a Federal Blue. It looked like a piece of the New England coastline transplanted to the Pacific Northwest.

A long gravel driveway curved around the front. As Paul climbed the broad steps to the porch, the outside light snapped on and the door opened.

"I thought I heard feet crunching on the gravel!" Grace exclaimed. "Come in, come in!"

Paul entered a large foyer. "I decided to accept your invitation to stop by sometime."

"Perfect timing. I've a man-sized stew on and no man to eat it. Let me have your jacket." She hung it on a peg and led the way into the living room.

The room took up the whole of the side wing, dominated by a massive fireplace on the far end. Windows lined both front and rear walls, with a pair of French doors in the center of the rear wall that opened to a brick terrace and the water beyond.

His attention was immediately caught by the view. Across the water, the lights of the prison on MacNeil Island shone out of the dark like a city dressed up for a concert, disguising its grim purpose. He stood by the French doors, mesmerized by the lights glinting off the calm waters. "Beautiful," he sighed at last.

Grace stood silent behind him. He hadn't seen the piano yet. When he finally turned, she watched his eyes find it, a half-smile on her face.

It was a small Chickering grand, and he moved to it as if in a trance. With care approaching reverence, he rubbed his fingertips along the black mahogany lid. Its highly polished finish gleamed in the soft glow of the lamps and firelight. "This is what the Lady will look like when I'm through with her," he said to Grace.

He leaned over the keyboard, his face naked with need and hunger. He reached with a fingertip toward a single key, a slight tremble in his hand. Abruptly, he halted. His finger hovered over the keyboard for a long second before he yanked it back, as if from a hot stove. Slowly, a step at a time, he backed away.

The last twenty years roared through his memory like a freight train. Without warning, a full-scale brooding gripped him and he moved to the French doors, peering out at the water, swamped by the pain.

Dimly, from a great distance, he heard the rustle of

Grace's clothes as she moved out of the room. There was an instant's silence, then she was at his side, a warm coat on, carrying his jacket. "Put this on. I want to show you my pride and joy." She hustled him out to the terrace.

The rear of the house was L-shaped, with the two-story wing projecting deep into the rear of the property. Behind the wing, near what he assumed would be the back kitchen door, was a large greenhouse.

The door wasn't locked. Grace pulled it open and reached for the light switch. "Now you're expected to ooh and ahh properly. It's called singing for your supper." She flicked the switch on.

Masses of poinsettias spread over a dozen rows of potting benches, segregated by color. Reds filled one whole side of the greenhouse, whites the middle, pinks the far side. Heavy timbers formed the skeleton of the greenhouse and hundreds more poinsettias hung everywhere from hooks heavy enough to hold a side of beef each.

"Good Lord." He stopped dead in the doorway. The enormity of the sight swept his black mood away.

"They're for the Christmas Fair. The extras go to nursing homes and hospitals on the mainland."

"There's enough here to supply the whole nation."

"Six hundred and seventy-three, to be precise. I lost a few. Didn't report them in time when they were little."

He began to grin. "They'll be sorely missed."

"Now, now, let's have a little respect, if you don't mind."

She showed him around with obvious pride. A

clear, rigid plastic had been used in place of glass, pulled taut over the timbered skeleton. The air was warm and humid, but not uncomfortably so. She showed him the electrical heating strips powered by a portable generator, the venting fans in the gables, the tables behind the mass of poinsettias with grow-lamps hung above and flats of seedlings underneath, the thirty-gallon cans of soil, fertilizer and peat moss, and the center table at the rear, the warmest spot, where several orchids grew.

"These are my children," she said, supporting a slender lavender flower with a careful palm. "I think of them as teenagers. Cantankerous, rebellious, willful, hard to get along with, and beautiful." She laughed at herself. "Silly old woman that I am, I give them more attention than people sometimes. But it's my escape. When the world gets too strong and over-ripe, I come in here and lose myself for hours."

"Does the world get to you often?"

"More than I'd like to admit. Let's go have some wine."

Back in the living room, she sat in a wing chair by the fire, warming her feet in their black, no-nonsense Red Cross shoes. In the soft glow of the firelight, she was ageless. Her face was plump and unlined, her eyes a still-bright sapphire blue. Her hair was china white, flowing in fingerwaves back from the porcelain face. Her corseted body maintained a royal posture.

He studied her. "This is a beautiful place. Especially the greenhouse. So why did I have this image of a one-room cabin?"

"This was it." She pointed towards a rear corner between fireplace and terrace. "My kitchen was there, the table was where I'm sitting now. We had rockers along those front windows and the bed was where the hall door is. The rest of the house grew from this."

"It's charming."

"It's what Bill and I spent our life creating. Bit by bit. It came slowly." The sapphire-blue eyes fixed on him. "Are you missing it much, the life you left?"

He thought a minute. "Some. But not as much as I expected I would." He hesitated, but her face encouraged trust. "There's so much to work out. . . . What's the old saying, 'misspent youth'? I've misspent twenty years, and that's like receiving a healthy inheritance at twenty-one and waking up one morning to find it's all gone. That's hard to deal with. Whenever I look ahead, there's nothing there to see. There's no building of anything, bit by bit, as you've done here. I thought I had, but I was wrong. The foundations were false and the building came tumbling down."

"If they truly were false," she said softly.

"Oh, they were, Grace, they were." He sighed deeply. "In looking back, I can see now it started when I was a kid, repairing pianos with my dad, and thinking the whole while that I'd do better than he had, that I'd be more than just another Piano Man. And I built a life on that thinking, never examining the basic premise—was I good enough to be more? Instead, I let my thinking become a habit and built a life based on it. It didn't work. It couldn't work. But I didn't dare admit that, so one habit piled on top of another. That's what the last twenty years have been, I'm afraid—just a collection of habits. Anna used to accuse me of running away, of using the keyboard to escape reality. I'm beginning to see she might've been right."

"That's rather a harsh judgment she made, isn't it?"

"She didn't get much from the marriage. A failed concert pianist doesn't make any money. That was a strain for her. It grew worse when she passed the bar. She started earning some pretty hefty wages and began to meet other men doing the same. Not that she wasn't loyal. Don't misunderstand me, she was as loyal as any wife would be. Still, the comparison was there. And then to not get tenure at the university . . . The teaching job was my final proving ground as a husband, and when I didn't win the appointment, it was simply too much for her to swallow. So here I am. With the clothes on my back and a year of work ahead, and nothing much beyond that."

"Things'll come clear for you eventually, Paul. The Island makes a good stopping-off place. Some might call it running away, I call it good sense . . . stopping every now and then to figure out what's what." She tilted her head in an examination of him. "Seems to me you're looking better fit these days. I heard about your walk this afternoon. Otso Point, Amsterdam Bay, Higgins Cove, Carlson Cove—that was quite a hike."

He smiled. "I see the Pickup Brigade's been at work again." He set his glass on the coffee table and rose. He moved to the fireplace and stared into the flames a moment, then turned to study her, leaning an elbow on the mantel. "Grace, why are they keeping such a close watch on me? What are they trying to keep me from finding out? What is everyone concealing?"

For a long moment, she stared into the distance at some private vision, her face troubled. Then she merely dropped her gaze and shook her head. When she looked at him once again, the plump face was as smooth as usual. "Oh, they're just making sure you don't come to any harm. The woods can be dangerous, you being a stranger and all. Why don't you refill our glasses while I stir the stew and plop the dumplings on."

He gave a polite smile and nodded. He wondered what her reaction would be if he told her someone had tried to kill him. She'd probably just "plop" more dumplings on.

▮

They ate at an old oak table in the high-ceilinged dining room. He was ravenous and the food was delicious—a rich brown gravy loaded with thick chunks of beef, potatoes and vegetables, well-seasoned and tasty.

His attention was on the food until the hard edge of hunger had eased, then his curiosity reasserted itself. "I was up at the cemetery this afternoon and some of the gravestones told quite a story. I saw the grave for Bobbin's wife. Did she die giving birth to Jenny?"

Grace nodded. "She hemorrhaged, and none of the Island ladies could get it stopped. That was before we had MAST, our medical helicopter service to the mainland. Today, she'd have been saved. Then, it was a different story."

"I was thinking when I saw the headstone how I'd have felt if that had happened to Anna. I'm not sure I could have coped. Certainly, not as well as Bobbin has."

"Don't let appearances deceive you, Paul. For a long time after Sarah died, we worried about Bobbin. He kept blaming himself. He kept saying, over and over, if only she hadn't gotten pregnant, if only he hadn't gotten her pregnant. He seemed to take on the sole responsibility for her pregnancy, as if she'd had no part in it at all. They say the Lord never gives us more than we can handle. I don't buy that for a minute."

"I guess a shock like that would be enough to make a man lose some of his marbles. Temporarily, at least."

Grace's eyes began to twinkle. "Oh, most everyone on earth's missing a playing card or two. It's just more noticeable here than other places."

"So Bobbin lost his wife and Calvin lost his," he mused. "What about Abner?"

"Abner never married. He preferred being everyone's favorite uncle."

"Was Obadiah Ross related to him?"

"His brother."

"He died just recently."

"About two months ago," she said reluctantly.

"Any relation to Tom Ross?"

"His father."

Paul studied her. "Why do I have this feeling I'm pulling teeth?"

Grace looked down at her plate, then back up at

him. "It's still pretty fresh, you know. We try and care about one another here."

Quickly, Paul apologized. "I'm sorry, I didn't mean to be insensitive. I gather, then, it was sudden?"

Grace nodded, her reluctance increasing. "He fell off a cliff."

His insides froze. "Where?"

"On the southern end of the Island. Lyle Point. You probably haven't seen it yet."

His thoughts whirled. The scene of his own near escape. Had Obadiah's death really been an accident? That's how his own would have been viewed, he knew. "And who was Walter Gibbons?"

For a moment, he thought she wouldn't answer. Her face closed down as it had earlier in the living room, and frown lines furrowed across her forehead. He sipped his wine, letting her wrestle with the decision, knowing she was too independent to be influenced by anything he could say.

At last she sighed. "I guess there's no harm . . . Walt was a drifter. A transient. What we'd call a hobo in the old days. He'd wander the whole country from coast to coast, riding the rails. Or whatever else he could find. He first showed up on the Island—Goodness, it must be sixty years ago now. Better than fifty, anyhow. He'd do odd jobs for a meal and a night in the barn. Fell trees, chop wood, clear fields, mend fences, that sort of thing. He'd stay, oh, maybe three or four months, usually spring or summer, then he'd move on, and it'd be a year or two, sometimes four or five before he'd come back again. We never knew where he was born, where he'd just come from or where he was headed. He'd just show up and pick up an ax and start chopping wood again. Harmless old fellow, really. He thought his own thoughts, seldom spoke and minded his own business."

Paul couldn't help but grin. "The kind of stranger the Islanders prefer."

"Well, he didn't go around asking a lot of nosy questions like some I could name."

"Now you see what a working piano would do for me. If any of them were playable up at the Coop, I'd spend all my spare time at the keyboard and wouldn't have the energy left to ask about anything."

"How soon do those piano strings arrive?"

He laughed out loud. "Weeks, yet. Back to Walter . . . Obviously, this last visit was his final one. What exactly happened?"

"To put it baldly, this last trip he arrived dead. Tom Ross found his body washed up on the beach. He'd drowned."

"He doesn't sound like the kind to either own a boat or go for a swim. How do they figure it happened?"

"He had some kind of an old, leaky scow hidden away. He always rowed over in it. He never used the ferry. I don't think he had the money for passage. As to whether the rowboat was his, or just—borrowed?—I don't know. But they think he took one too many trips in it and it fell apart halfway over."

"Did they find the boat?"

"Not a stick of it. It'll wash up on some shore somewhere during some storm, just another pile of rotten timber."

"Then who paid for his funeral?"

"I wouldn't exactly call it a funeral," she said slowly. "Calvin built a plain box, and there's a section of the graveyard reserved for those who don't have anything much, and they simply buried him there."

"Someone carved a marker for his grave. On a wooden cross."

"That'd be Calvin again. He's by way of being the Island woodworker. I think it's the one thing that's saved his sanity through the years, his woodworking. He's a beautiful craftsman. He's built everything from my potting benches to my kitchen cabinets. But that's just his bread-and-butter work. What he really loves is wood-carving. He does the finest carvings I've ever seen. Very intricate. A scene within a scene. It's a sight to see. Someday, when he knows you better, he might invite you to his place."

"I love wood, you know," Paul said, slowly. "The shape, the texture, the patterns. All kinds of wood, too. Everything from simple driftwood sculpted by the sea to the richest mahogany money can buy. And I've often thought I'd enjoy doing some carving. Do you suppose Calvin would be willing to take on a student? Especially a beginner?"

"He might. He's tried it a time or two over the years, but they never stuck with it. He's so good at it that I think it discourages people and they end up quitting."

"I don't think I would. I think I'd take it as a challenge and do everything I could to become that good."

Her gaze on him was shrewd. "I'm sure you

would. I think that's probably both your strength and your weakness."

"You mean my inability to ignore a challenge? Such as, trying to find out what's going on around here?"

"You do seem reluctant to let things be."

"Would it be such a terrible thing if I did find out what the problem is? I just might be able to help, you know."

"Some of us have talked about it. Maybe in time . . . Can I get you some coffee? And what about a piece of apple pie? With ice cream?"

He grinned. "Yes, to all three."

He cleared while she served and poured. He took particular notice of the cabinets Calvin had built. They were of a richly grained fruitwood—apple, he suspected—and finished as smoothly as a piano key. The wood gleamed like polished ivory, as if it had several coats of hard lacquer on its surface, but on closer examination, he decided it had been merely waxed to a fare-thee-well. As Grace had said, the craftsmanship was superb . . . right down to the hidden hinges and the hand-carved drawer pulls.

"Beautiful," he murmured.

Nodding agreement, she finished scraping the last of the dinner scraps into an old plastic butter container. "Now you start earning your keep. Take this on out to the compost pile and dump it in. It's around back of the greenhouse."

He grabbed his jacket from the peg in the front hall and went to the back kitchen door. "Can I get through this way?"

"Yes, but watch out, the backside of the greenhouse isn't lit. You'd better take a flash." She rummaged in a bottom kitchen drawer and handed him an old, battered flashlight.

The night air was bitter, raw, cold. It enveloped him instantly. Grayish-black clouds covered the moon and stars, so absolutely nothing around him could be seen. Other than the gentle lapping of water against the breakwater, black stillness encircled him. The lights of the prison on the island across the Sound gave him a feeling of people nearby, but it was an illusion. He was alone in the night.

The realization made him shiver. It seemed to him there'd been a lot of violent deaths on the Island. Maybe it was as Grace had pointed out, that in a confined area like this, you were brought face to face with death as a normal part of life. Whereas in town, it was an anonymous shadow riding the city streets, hidden among such a vast number of people that it rarely touched anyone you knew.

But still—a fall off a cliff? An unexplained drowning? Within a two-month period? Was that why the Sheriff took the trouble to come all the way out to the Island simply to check on some missing piano strings? And just what exactly had happened to the first Piano Man? For that matter, just what exactly was happening to the second Piano Man—namely himself!

Suddenly shivering again, he found the compost pile, quickly dumped the contents of the bowl into it, and hurried back to the warmth, lights and safety of the kitchen.

Chapter Fifteen

The next morning, the Pickup Brigade showed up shortly after daybreak and Paul went outside to meet them. They were led by Tom Ross and Zeke, a short, stocky man with dark, swarthy skin and flashing brown eyes. He looked like a heavyweight boxer who'd been on the wrong end of a knockout punch, but he had a huge grin that turned his battered face into a friendly mug.

"Hear tell you need some wiring done," he said to Paul. "Can you show me where the terminal box is?"

Paul led the group around the house and pointed to the back corner. "Behind the shrubbery there, down low."

The men all trooped over and probed and peered and consulted. After a few minutes, a couple of them broke away and strode down the slope to the telephone poles. They examined two, craning their heads back to inspect the crossbars, then studied the third and nodded. One of them headed across the meadow to his truck. A few minutes later he emerged in spikes with belts of equipment dangling from shoulders and waist.

Old Jeb's pickup came chugging up the drive, and the lineman picked up a thick coil of cable from the old man's truckbed and headed down the hill once more.

Abner climbed out of Old Jeb's cab and both men made their way to Paul's side and stood next to him, watching the activity in silence.

The men still by the corner of the Coop had cut the shrubs back enough to clear access and were studying the terminal box. Zeke made a comment to Tom Ross, and he nodded and came over to Paul. "Fuse box?"

"Inside. I'll show you."

Abner and Old Jeb followed them in.

Paul pried the siding up, exposing the fuse box. Tom removed the fuses and stuck them in his pocket, then disappeared outside again.

Old Jeb studied the gap left by the board, then the board itself. "That don't belong there. The one that goes there is a good two feet shorter. You can see the holes for it t'other side of the box."

"Any idea where it might be?" Paul asked him.

Abner frowned. "It's not here anywhere?"

"Not that I've found."

Old Jeb shook his head. "Don't know then. Looks about an eight-footer that's gone." He glanced in the direction of the pianos.

Paul saw where his thinking was going. "It wouldn't have anything to do with those. There's no need to use any scrap lumber on the pianos, ever."

Abner exchanged glances with Old Jeb, but they said nothing more.

Paul stared at the two old men standing thoughtful in the dusky daylight. "Don't you think it's about time you let me in on what's going on here?"

There was another exchange of glances. "Nothing but some petty thievery," Abner said smoothly.

"Bound to happen now and again when a place ain't been lived in a while."

Paul merely shrugged, but inside an anger flared, and he went outside to get away from them.

The lineman had run a bypass at the junction for the power flow moving down the road and was connecting the new cable to the pole. Helpers draped cable across the lower meadow and through the newly planted trees. Reaching the Coop, they handed it up to a buddy on a ladder, who threaded it through the eye-screw in the eaves and dropped the end back down to them.

At a signal from the lineman, the men pulled the cable taut and held it, while another bared the wires and connected the ends to the terminals in the box.

Tom Ross double-checked all connections and waved for the bypass to be removed. Everyone stood motionless, watching. Nothing sparked, arced or crackled. He nodded in satisfaction and came over to Paul. "Let's put the fuses back in and see what we get."

Old Jeb and Abner, talking in low voices over by the pianos, stopped when the younger two men entered. Paul didn't spare them a glance. He was still angry with them. And their attitude.

Tom screwed the fuses in, waited a minute and, when nothing happened, grinned up at Paul. "They're either live or dead," he said cheerfully. "Let's test them out. How about that old toaster over there, does it work okay?"

"Yes." Paul disconnected it from the kitchen circuit and carried it to the floor plug next to the Old Soldier.

"Better let me," Tom said. He pushed the plug in, listened for a long second, then pushed the plunger down on the toaster. After a minute, the coils glowed red. "There we are. We've got ignition." He grinned at Paul. "Don't thank us, feller, we've just lengthened your workday."

In spite of himself, Paul had to laugh. "Then consider yourself unthanked. But I'm going to appreciate electricity in here. It'll be nice to be able to read at night. And maybe get a radio and have some music again."

The other man nodded and clapped his shoulder. "You betcha. Next thing you'll want is a phone to accept all the social invitations flying around these parts." His laugh boomed from the rafters and even the two old men cracked small smiles at his youth and humor.

Still chuckling at his own jokes, Tom made a quick trip out to his truck, returning with an armload of work lamps and extension cords. He unloaded those, went out again and returned with the tall ladder and some heavy hooks and metal chains. "Okay, let's get you fixed up."

Working together now, he and Paul studied the rafters and the position of the pianos, discussing where the work lamps would be the most effective. Old Jeb and Abner joined in, and eventually consensus was reached. The four of them adjusted the position of the Lady and the Old Soldier some, then Tom scrambled up the ladder and installed the heavy hooks at various places along the rafters, each hook dangling a length of chain.

They had brought four work lamps for him. "We

felt you were a bit modest in your request," Abner explained.

The unexpected thoughtfulness threw Paul's anger off-stride. Damned Islanders. Just when you think you've got them all figured out and neatly pegged, they turn around and do something like this.

Smiling his appreciation, Paul took two of the lamps and hung them on each side of the Old Soldier at a good working height for him, then he arranged the height of the remaining two so that they eliminated the last of any shadows.

Tom hitched each of the four lamps up to their own extension cord and plugged the cords in. "Now, let there be light."

Paul switched them on, one by one. The brightness chased the daylight dusk back to the far reaches of the Coop, and the lights bathed the Old Soldier from all sides like floodlights on a statue. He felt like cheering. "Thanks. I can't tell you what a help this'll be."

"Glad to oblige. One last thing. I want to check the wiring under the floor. Make sure a bunch of happy mice aren't gnawing away on the wires under there. Where's your trapdoor?"

"Jeb?" Paul turned to the old man. "I've looked and looked and haven't found one. Do you know where it is? Outside, maybe?"

Old Jeb studied the place a minute, then pointed towards the bed platform pushed against the wall at the other end of the Coop. "Should be under there."

Under the bed, of course, Paul thought. If the pianos, supply chest and workbench had been moved to cover the floor plugs, then surely the trapdoor would be covered, too. The previous Piano Man had certainly been a strange old duck.

He and Tom pushed the heavy wooden platform into the center of the room. A two-foot square of flooring nailed together like a raft formed the cover. Paul bent over the recessed ring and tugged. It came up hard, creaking all the way.

Tom moved to his side to help. Old Jeb and Abner looked on.

As soon as they had the cover clear of the rim, they got their fingers under it and lifted it clear.

Pale daylight from the room wormed its way into the cavern of the crawl space. Tom and Paul both stared down, frozen.

The half-man, half-skeleton stared back. The bloodied brass of a piano string wrapped tightly around the neck glistened in the pale light.

Tom exhaled first. "Holy shit," he breathed.

Paul let out a shaky breath. "Yeah," he whispered. "Oh, yeah."

He swerved his gaze to break eye contact with the corpse and caught sight of the two old men standing across the opening from him. One tall and portly, the other little and scrawny, at the moment they were carbon copies of each other as they, too, stared down into the hole. Their heads were bowed, their shoulders were slumped in weary defeat. They looked a hundred years old.

As they broke their gaze from the dead man and looked at each other, their expressions showed not so much shock as confirmed suspicions. Paul could've sworn they hadn't known the dead man was there. But he also could've sworn they'd known that the man was dead somewhere. The location was the surprise. Not the death.

With instinctive timing, he and Tom moved simultaneously to replace the trapdoor in the opening. They were gentle with it, so as not to disturb the corpse below. With that thought, Paul knew he was on the verge of coming apart, and held on with grim control. "Okay," he said to Abner, "let's talk."

The sound of his voice broke the tableau. "You tell the men outside to go on home now," Abner said to Old Jeb. "Then go on down to my place and make the necessary phone calls to the Sheriff. Tom, you go on out to my truck and poke around under the driver's seat. Should be a bottle of brandy tucked back in there. Our young friend here looks like he needs a shot. So do you." He thought a second. "So do I, when it comes to that."

Chapter Sixteen

After Old Jeb had gone, Paul parceled out the brandy in jelly glasses, then led the way to the studio and indicated two piano benches for Tom and Abner. He stood behind the third, facing them. Outside, pickups roared to life, then faded down the driveway. Old Jeb's chug went last. Then the silence returned.

Paul's stomach kept breaking into waves of nausea in spite of the brandy. He fought against showing it and stared hard at the two men in front of him, much as he'd done countless times to recalcitrant students. Macabre 101 was now in session. He addressed himself to Abner. "Start at the beginning," he said quietly, "and don't leave anything out."

Abner's eyes were filled with the deepest despair and there was no resistance left in him. "It was the Murdock kid. Not the dead one over there. That's a fella by the name of Jim Harrison, the first Piano Man. It was the Murdock kid who did it. Leastways, I'd guess that's who did it."

Tom nodded agreement. "The kid's a psycho. Crazy as a loon."

"A few years back, maybe six or seven now," Abner said, "Jason—that's the kid's name—got himself into a heap of trouble over in Minneapolis. That's where his home is. I don't know what happened, exactly, but a jazz pianist got himself killed and Jason was charged with the crime. But they determined he wasn't responsible for his own actions, so instead of prison, he got shipped off to an insane asylum."

"A mental institution," Tom interjected.

"He spent some time there," Abner continued. "A couple of years, maybe three, all told. Then Ben Murdock—he's his dad—got him out of there and shipped him here for us to look after. Ben keeps a place here on the island and that's where he put the boy. We been watching him ever since."

"My God, why? Who is this Ben Murdock anyway?"

"He's a local boy who made good. Real good."

Paul exploded. "What in the hell has that got to do with anything? We're talking a major crime here. No one makes it that good!"

Abner stayed calm, adjusted his position on the bench and settled in more comfortably. "Let me back up a bit. Ben's dad came here as a farm hand, his wife dead, Ben just a tadpole, not able to crawl yet. He grew up one of our own. Didn't suffer none from lack of mothering. He was a nice kid, Ben was, smart as a whip, and good-hearted. Hard times fell on the Island. Weren't no work less'n you owned your own land and could farm it or log it. Even then, it was a hardscrabble living. Ben, smart as he was, could see that, and when he was grown he left the Island, looking for work. When he left, he swore that when he made good, he'd be back to help the rest of us. He made good. Founded a construction firm, moved from building houses to building skyscrapers—his company does work all over the world now. And while he got bigger and richer, life here got worse. The Island wasn't big enough to compete with the big logging sections or the big farmers. Ben came back and bought us all out of foreclosure. He closed out the banks completely. He got us all restocked with heavy milkers and some good layers, got us some timber contracts, set Thaddeus up in the store, and bought the ferry and got the contract with the county away from the pocket-robbers who were grinding us down even further."

"In effect," Paul said, "he bought himself an island."

"No, sir!" Abner's voice was sharp. "No, sir, he didn't. We all have our deeds free and clear. Only string he put on us was, we're free to leave the land to family, but if we go to sell, he gets first refusal."

Paul thought it over. "That sounds fair. So, what about Jason?"

"Well, now, in the beginning, Jason seemed an okay little fella. Cute as could be. Tow-headed, blue eyes, big grin. And big. He was a big kid. Took after his mother's side. She was a Swede, and tall herself."

"Was she an Islander?"

"No. Ben met and married her in Minneapolis, where his company's headquartered. Shortly after the wedding, though, he brought her out to meet us all. He'd picked himself up a parcel of land on the southwestern corner of the Island, just south of Amsterdam Bay, and built himself a place on the hilltop. His missus and the boy'd be out every summer, with Ben stopping in whenever he could get away. Her name was Ilsa, and that's about all any of us can tell you about her. She didn't really cotton to the Island—or to the Islanders. She even brought in her own household help. Though occasionally she'd use Old Jeb's Missus when she had to. And Ben, of course, kept Old Jeb hired on year-round. But Ilsa, she kept to herself, playing her piano, and the only time we Islanders would ever see her would be passing back and forth on her way to the ferry.

"Jason, now, he was a different story. When he grew big enough, he ran all over the Island. He loved it here. Got to know every hill and holler we got here. Got along just fine, he did. Leastways in the beginning. The trouble started the summer he was seven or eight. It began right enough, the summer seemed normal—except that Ilsa used Old Jeb's Missus that year, instead of bringing her own help in. Later on, Jeb's Missus said that all Ilsa did was play the piano all day long. She was quite a pianist, I gather, and would play all different kinds of tunes. But that summer, it was all slow, heavy, moody kind of music. It about drove Old Jeb's Missus batty. Then one night, Ilsa just ran off, and that's when Jason went off his belfry.

"At first, it was feared she'd gotten hurt in the woods. But when a search of the Island turned nothing up, and we discovered Ben's old boat was gone, then we knew she'd run off. Nobody was much surprised. She didn't seem to like Ben—or Jason, for that matter—much more than she liked the Island or us. She was a beautiful woman, and rumor had it she'd found a man more to her liking in Minneapolis and had run off with him. But Jason adored her, and when he wasn't off running about the Island, he'd be right beside her, on the piano bench, listening to her play. He took her leavin' real hard. Real hard.

"And that's when the trouble started. Jason struck out at everything he loved. He had a little Scottie, and the dog was found drowned in the creek running through Ben's land. He also took an iron pipe to the first piano. That's the upright over there you been working on, Paul. Jason had been learning to play on that. Then he took the same iron pipe to the small black one over there that his mother used to play on. And I'm not talking just once or twice. Every time he got out from under whoever was keeping an eye on him, he'd take something to the pianos, screaming and yelling the whole time he did it. The kid just plain went nuts. Ben finally took him back to Minneapolis and that was the last any of us seen of him until Ben shipped him back a couple of years ago."

Questions, dozens of them, tumbled through Paul's mind. "I can understand a little boy taking his pain out on some pianos, but drowning his dog? Are you sure that's what he did? He drowned his little dog?"

"It appears so. The poor little thing was found dead the next day. No proof that Jason done it. And he cried and carried on like he'd lost his last friend. But it was crocodile tears, some folks say."

"Jesus, knowing all this, why'd you let him come back at all then?"

"After what Ben did for us, how could we not?"

There was no answer to that. Paul shuddered. "Jason's been here now—how long, this time?"

"A couple of years."

"Where?"

"Up to Ben's place. The younger men—" he nodded toward Tom—"they took different shifts watching him 'round the clock, glad of the work, to be honest."

"And has there been any other trouble up until now?"

Tom and Abner exchanged glances. "Could be," the old man said cautiously.

"We're not sure," Tom added. He'd been silent through the recital, nodding agreement at different points, but refraining from any comment. His face was suffused with misery now. "There's been a couple of accidents lately. You're probably not aware of it, but my pa, Obadiah Ross—that's Uncle Abner's brother, too—he fell off a cliff a couple of months ago. And we've just had a drowning. An old tramp who'd show up every few years. The Sheriff's written them up as accidents. No proof they weren't. But my pa was a woodsman. He knew this Island like the palm of his hand. It just don't make sense that Pa would get that careless that he'd take a tumble like that."

Paul thought back to his own near-escape on the beach, but didn't say anything.

"He fell off of Lyle Point," Abner put in, his voice neutral, his eyes shrewd. "That's the place the ladder fell when you were climbing it, the day you hurt your knee."

Paul flushed slightly. They knew about his escapades, then. The jungle telegraph at work? "I guess what I don't understand is, if you know my every move, why don't you know Jason's, too?"

"You're a stranger. He's not. And up till now,

every time Jason'd get away from us, he'd be gone a day or two, but he'd always come back—"

"Get away from you! I thought you said he was guarded night and day."

"Well, basically, he was. Only now and then, he'd slip around a corner and be off. Only he always came back. Up till now."

"How long's he been missing this time?"

"Since summer."

"Summer!" Paul started pacing, his mind whirling a hundred revolutions a second. "My God, how could a man stay hidden for all this time? I mean, the Island's not that large. It can't be any larger than what, twenty square miles, max?"

"Eighteen." The old man sighed. "You have to understand, there aren't more than a couple dozen of us able to look at any one time. While we search one part of the Island, he's got the whole rest of it to hide out in. And he can move through these woods as silent as a deer."

"He's got to have food."

"Plenty of game. And gardens. And root cellars."

"Fire to cook it over?"

The old man shrugged. "No trace of one so far. But some of those stands of trees are a couple of hundred feet tall. A man'd have to fly, to see any smoke coming up."

"Summer. He's ducked you since summer." Paul was still appalled. "And you haven't called in the Sheriff to help look or anything?"

"We were never sure. You see, it was like the Scottie . . . there's really no proof, is there? We were just never sure."

"Well, now you have your proof." Paul jerked his head towards the trapdoor and the dead body below. "And when did he disappear?"

"Around Labor Day."

"Right after Jason 'slipped away,' as you call it."

Abner gave a reluctant nod.

"My God, this is incredible. A murderer on the loose, and for two months he's been running circles around you."

Abner's voice was sharp. "How many 'coons you seen since you been here?"

"Two. Maybe three."

"The Island has thousands. How many deer you seen?"

Paul held up a hand in peace. "All right, I get your point. Besides, the Sheriff'll bring out his men and comb every inch of this place now. They'll find Jason in a hurry."

Both faces turned expressionless. Tom's eyes probed the rafters. Abner stroked his beard. "Well, now," he said, finally, "we weren't figuring on the Sheriff being in on this part of the story."

Paul stared at him. "What!" The old man didn't have to repeat it. He'd heard the statement clearly enough. "I don't believe you," he said flatly. "You can't hide a murder like this. Besides, you've already sent Old Jeb to call the Sheriff."

"We don't intend to hide it," Abner said. "We're just not planning to volunteer all we know. After all, there's no proof so far in any of what we've said. It's all conjecture."

Tom nodded agreement. "Speculation," he added. "All we've been talking is speculation. We don't know what happened in Minneapolis. Just some story we've heard. We don't know that my Pa didn't fall, that Walter Gibbons didn't simply fall overboard and drown. We don't know any different, do we?"

"We sure as hell know that Mr. Harrison over there didn't wind the piano string around his own neck," Paul said grimly.

Abner didn't miss a beat. "But we don't know for sure who did it, either, do we? That's why none of us—none of us, Mr. Whitman—will be pointing a finger in any direction. Isn't that right, Mr. Whitman? None of us will be pointing any fingers."

Paul ignored the threat. "You're simply going to let him go on killing others. If it was a pianist in Minneapolis, and a pianist on the Island, as long as he sticks to pianists—"

His voice faded, his throat suddenly dry. He swallowed. "I'm the bait, aren't I." He stared at the two of them. "You thought that if one Piano Man disappeared, you'd bring in another, and keep an eye on him, and sooner or later . . ."

The men's silence was answer enough.

Horrified, Paul sank onto the piano bench. "No."

"We need you to help catch him," Abner said. It was said smoothly, without the slightest touch of regret. A simple statement of need.

"No."

"Once he's caught, Ben's putting him in a private institution for the rest of his life. He won't be a threat to anyone anymore."

"No."

"There's simply no point to a trial. They'd just

end up doing that same thing, committing him for life."

"No."

"We'll watch over you. You won't come to any harm."

"Not a chance, no."

"In fact, Tom has a couple of guard dogs—"

"I don't like dogs."

"That'll work out," Tom said. "The ones I got don't like people."

Chapter Seventeen

The Sheriff flew in by helicopter with a single aide. The crime lab crew and cars would follow by barge.

Frank Hall was as implacable as ever. He stared down at the body calmly, took a slow tour of the Coop, then set up an inquisition chamber in the studio, with himself at the grand piano, his aide taking notes at the baby grand and the four Island men—Abner, Old Jeb, Tom and Paul—seated on wooden kitchen chairs arrayed in front of him.

Abner did the talking and he kept the story simple. They'd installed some work lamps in the studio area for the Piano Man, had lifted the trapdoor to go below to check the wiring and had found the body. Old Jeb had gone to call the Sheriff. Other than that, all he knew was that the dead man hadn't been seen since Labor Day.

The Sheriff studied each of the four men. Three stared back at him impassively. Paul attempted to do the same. He didn't know what else to do.

With lazy motions, Hall pulled a toothpick from his breast pocket and began to chew it. "What do you know about Harrison, Jeb?" His voice was folksy. His eyes weren't.

"Not much. Quiet fella. Kept to himself."

"What was his background?"

The old man shrugged.

"How'd he come to get this job?"
Another shrug.
"Well, how'd you learn he was coming?"
"Ben called me."
"And?"
"Ben arranged for me to take care of things."
"Which was?"
"Bringing in food. Chopping wood. Cleaning up a bit in here afore the Piano Man arrived. Just helping out."
"Harrison have contact with anyone else on the Island?"
"Kept to himself mostly."
"Abner? Harrison talk to anyone you know?"
"As Jeb says, he kept to himself."
"What about Thaddeus? He must've needed groceries now and again."
Abner thought about it. "Far as I recollect, he'd come in, make his own selections, have Thaddeus add 'em up and leave. He never stopped for coffee, like Mr. Whitman here. Never said anything to anyone. Can't recollect even hearing his voice."
"He take advantage of the area—fishing, clamming, hiking?"
"Not that anyone noticed."
"Just put his nose to the grindstone and ground away, eh?"
Silence.
"You come visit him for coffee, too?" Frank asked Old Jeb.
The old man and Paul both saw what was coming and exchanged looks. There was no ducking it, though. "Nope," the old man said.

Frank's shrewd eyes moved lazily to Paul. "You're an honored man then, aren't you, Mr. Whitman, to be accepted by the Islanders like you are."

Paul kept still.

The studio was chilling down. The stove needed attention. But Paul couldn't get his wooden muscles liquid enough to move. As if reading his thoughts, Old Jeb muttered something about adding a log and moved to the woodbox.

The silence stretched on, so deep and thick Paul could've cut a slab for a piano lid.

The Sheriff kept his eyes on Paul until Old Jeb was through and had resumed his seat. "You been here how long now?"

"A month. Maybe five weeks."

"That one of those missing piano strings wrapped around his neck?"

"Possibly." Paul nodded. "Probably."

"Anything else missing you've noticed?"

"A few things."

"What things."

"Odds and ends mostly. A board, some work lamps, things like that."

Hall's eyes roamed the floor and lit on the plug nearest him. "New?"

Discolored and battered, obviously it wasn't.

Tom Ross fielded that one. "No."

"Why'd you need to get below then?"

"Just to make sure the wiring was okay. That it wasn't frayed, rats weren't gnawing on it."

"Wiring already in place, was it?"

Tom nodded.

"Fuse box okay? Wiring connected there okay?"

Another nod.

"What about the connections outside?"

"The terminal? That was okay, too."

"So then you were just missing the cable running up from the road."

No one spoke.

"So now we got heavy cable wire gone missing, like the piano wire. What else is gone that you haven't happened to mention?"

Silence.

Hall was unperturbed by it. He just kept studying them, chewing the toothpick thoughtfully. He'd withdraw it long enough to ask a question, then chew on it some more while the answer was given. Or no answer was given. He held it free of his mouth again. "How come there's a gap in the wall alongside the fuse box?"

Again, Tom answered. "Hadn't gotten around to putting the board back on before we lifted the trapdoor."

Hall eyeballed the length of scrap lumber laying on the floor. "Looks a mite too long. Fuse box needs to be where you can get at it easy, don't it?"

"Usually. But we have to use what's on hand here on the Island, and you get some pretty strange buildings that way. Folks often don't do the usual thing."

"Apparently. Different kind of wood, too, isn't it?"

Tom shrugged. "I just know electrical."

"Jeb?"

The old man shrugged, too.

"Okay, so we're missing a board. Eight feet of one-by-twelve, looks like." He dismissed that subject and his eyes roamed the rafters. "All this electricity around and no lights until now. Amazing. How'd you manage to see to get any work done, Mr. Whitman?"

Paul cleared his throat. "The skylights helped."

"Kind of curtailed your working hours, didn't it?"

"That's why we strung up new wiring today."

"Ah, so the cable *was* missing." Hall waited a beat, then focused on Abner and Old Jeb again. "How long you reckon it's been missing?"

"Hard to say," Old Jeb said.

"How long these pianos been here now?"

"Years."

"How many years?"

The old man shrugged. "Can't rightly say."

"Where'd Ben get them?"

The old man shrugged.

"Why does he keep them here?"

"Guess 'cause he had the building settin' empty here."

"Freight bill must've been a killer. These valuable pianos?" he asked Paul.

"Very."

"Worth any investment?"

"Well, worth the cost of the freight, yes."

"And your pay to fix them up."

Paul nodded.

Hall returned to Old Jeb. "Anyone work on the pianos before Harrison came?"

"Nope."

"When'd he come?"

"August sometime. Early part."

"And disappeared Labor Day?"

Silence again. Hall chewed and waited. Finally Old Jeb nodded.

Like a coon dog sniffing air, the Sheriff tried a different direction. "That bed always been in that spot against the wall?"

Old Jeb hesitated. "Nope," he said finally. "It was against the wall, yes. But further down."

"So the trapdoor was clear."

The old man nodded.

"When'd you first notice the bed had been moved?"

"When I came in to ready things up for Mr. Whitman here."

"But you looked the place over when the first Piano Man disappeared, didn't you?"

"A time or two."

"Wasn't moved then, was it?"

A pause. "Nope."

"You, Abner? You, Tom? Either of you move it?"

Two negative shakes of the head.

"Know who did?"

More negative shakes.

Hall went back to Old Jeb. "Was the Coop kept locked after Harrison disappeared?"

"More or less."

"More or less," the Sheriff echoed. "You mean sometimes it was and sometimes it wasn't?"

Another nod.

"How many keys are there to the door?"

"A couple."

"You had one, Harrison must've had one, Mr.

Whitman must have one—any others out? Ben have one?"

"Could be."

"But he's still in Minneapolis, right?"

Old Jeb nodded.

"He know about the trapdoor?"

The old man shrugged.

"Your pa do the original wiring here, Tom?"

Tom nodded.

"He just died lately, didn't he? Here on the Island."

Another nod.

"Fell off a cliff. Right after Labor Day, if I remember rightly."

Tom stayed silent.

The Sheriff settled back with the toothpick again. "Well, now, let's think this through a bit," he said slowly, his eyes resting on each of them in turn. "Seems to me the Island folk hereabouts might know a little about this place. When it was built, who owns it, when it was converted from a chicken coop to living quarters. Some of the Islanders might even know the layout. The kitchen at that end, the studio at this one." He paused, letting a stretch of silence in, watching all four with ease. "But where the trapdoor is? That's pretty intimate knowledge for just a mere noddin' acquaintance with the place. It'd take someone special to know that, don't you think? Maybe someone who'd lived here. Or someone who'd built it. Or someone who'd worked on it." He paused again. "Or . . . maybe even a kid who'd played in it."

Four pairs of eyes stared back at him.

"I guess the next question is, who'd want to hurt a Piano Man? Seems a harmless enough breed to me."

They were saved from any response by the arrival of more deputies and the lab crew.

▌

Now that he had adequate help, the Sheriff changed his methods. While the technicians toted in equipment and settled on the logistics of their work, Hall took on each of the Islanders alone, leaving the other three grouped under the keen gaze of a trooper stationed well within earshot.

Abner was first. Hall simply took him outside for a walk. Tom and Old Jeb sat slumped on kitchen chairs, sightless eyes aimed at the floor. Paul slumped with them.

The Sheriff seemed to take forever, but when Abner returned, Paul sneaked a glance at his watch. It had been less than fifteen minutes.

Old Jeb was next. Expressionless, he followed the Sheriff out.

Abner gave a short shake of the head towards Tom. The younger man nodded to indicate understanding of the message.

This time, the trip outside seemed short. Too short. Paul glanced at his watch again. Only five minutes. Why? Were there fewer questions to ask Old Jeb than he'd had to ask Abner?

Paul had expected to go last and was startled when the Sheriff beckoned him next.

It was cold out. Godawful cold. The wind was picking up and it instantly sliced through his jacket and cut through to his bones.

The Sheriff seemed unaffected by the raw air. He

led the way to where the official cars were grouped, well away from the Coop, and leaned against one fender, removing a fresh toothpick from his shirt pocket. Then he chewed and watched Paul for a long moment.

Paul chose a fender opposite him. Suddenly he wished he smoked a pipe. Or anything else to keep his hands busy. He shoved them into his jacket pockets, crossed his feet in an effort to appear in control, and returned the Sheriff's gaze.

"Okay if I call you Paul?"

Paul nodded.

"And I'm Frank. That's less intimidating than Sheriff, don't you think?"

The broad face was bland and friendly, and Paul didn't trust it a minute. He merely nodded.

"Must've been quite a shock."

"Dreadful."

"You want some brandy?"

"I'll be all right."

"I've ordered the men to search underneath that crawl space. Just to make sure there are no little surprises left down there."

"Thanks."

"We'll have to seal the place for a while. Most of the day, maybe part of the evening. But we should be clear of it in time for you to bed down there tonight."

The thought of sleeping there sickened Paul.

Frank Hall read his mind. "Or, we could take you back to the mainland with us tonight."

It was an unexpected lifeline. God, what a lifeline! Paul straightened, his mind racing at the thought. He'd become so habituated to the idea of being stuck on the Island, he'd never thought of this as his way off. And the advantages listed themselves like a computer readout. Freedom. Disassociation from the problems here. And safety. His own. Don't forget the safety factor, he told himself.

Quit, Anna had urged at the end of his concert career, when finally he'd been so outclassed during the preliminaries of an international competition that he'd felt like a kindergartener just learning his treble clef. "Your problem, Paul," Anna had said, "is you just don't know when it's time to quit. So I'm telling you, quit. You're way out of your depth. Your time has passed."

He was way out of his depth now. The sensible thing would be to follow Anna's advice. Quit. Go back to the mainland with the Sheriff and carry on with the rest of his life.

Of course, this was the very same lady who, when Paul found he couldn't abide faculty life and its continual petty feuds and the back-stabbing battles for position, had turned on him and said, "You're always ready to quit, Paul. You're always ready to give up whenever things get the least bit difficult! Really, Paul, when are you going to settle down and stick with something?"

It was an odd time to realize it, with a dead body lying inside and his own life on the line, but he suddenly realized it was the reversal of attitude that had extinguished the last of his love for her. That she could be so irrational and unreasonable and lacking in self-awareness, while so quick to see and point out the flaws in him . . .

Without knowing he was going to do so, he

slumped back against the fender and said to the Sheriff, "Thanks, but I'll take my chances."

Hall sighed. "The Islanders really have taken you in, haven't they? What is it, some kind of vampirism? They bite you in the neck and you become one of them?"

Paul mustered a grin. "Seems that way, doesn't it?"

The Sheriff gave a mutter of disgust. "That fairy tale they told in there—that the way it happened?"

"That's the way it happened."

"So it's the truth, then."

"It's the truth."

"The whole truth?"

"They told you the truth, just the way it happened."

"I'm sure they did." Hall sighed. "And the amount of truth they told would fit in a teacup. What worries me is the potful they've left out." He tossed the toothpick on the ground and straightened. "Might as well go back in and go through the routine with Tom. Just for the sake of the report. 'Were all the witnesses questioned?' Hell, yes."

The Sheriff traded Paul for Tom. When they'd gone outside, Abner said to Paul, "We're taking you to my place for a while, then you'll bunk in at Tom's the next few nights."

There was an undertone of urgency in Abner's voice. His eyes indicated the keen-eared trooper nearby, then pleaded with Paul not to question the arrangements at the moment. Having already thrown in his lot with the Islanders, he merely nodded. He had no other choice. For now.

Chapter Eighteen

The minute he walked into Abner's cottage in the woods and saw the stranger standing between Calvin and Bobbin, Paul knew who it had to be.

His image of Ben Murdock had evolved from the time of the first store receipt he'd been forced to sign, and it wasn't flattering. He'd pictured a Nast-style backroom politician, cigar jutting out of a fleshy mouth above jellied jowls, diamond pinkie ring cutting into a fat finger, orders whipped out to underlings in the guttural imperatives of a medieval lord. In short, a repulsive man filled with his own sense of self-importance.

The reality was as far from that image as a violin was from a tuba.

Murdock was a man in his fifties, medium-built and trim of weight, with a pleasant open face, a thick head of boyishly undisciplined black hair and warm brown eyes that viewed his surroundings with sharp curiosity and interest. He greeted the other Island men first, his manner easy, then he extended a hand to Paul. "It seems, Mr. Whitman, that I've placed you in far greater danger than I'd anticipated. I cannot apologize enough for that."

The man's deep brown eyes were hypnotic, and in spite of hardened feelings against him, Paul raised a hand to be shaken. The grasp was firm without being harsh.

Ben indicated a comfortable chair near the wood stove for Paul, then turned to the other men. "Jeb, I know you and the others haven't eaten since breakfast, and this promises to be a long afternoon. Why don't you fellas go on down to the deli, then regroup back here in about an hour, hour and a half. And I haven't eaten either. When you're through, would you mind having Jenny fix up something for Mr. Whitman and myself? Would a hamburger suffice, Mr. Whitman?"

It seemed a rather inappropriate time for the social graces, but rather than be irritated by it, Paul watched it happen with an amused detachment. The man was a first-class operator, all right. "A hamburger would be fine."

After the men had left, Ben poured coffee for the two of them, then sat on the couch opposite Paul, placing his cup on the big slab of wood that served as a coffee table. The pleasantries over, his face turned serious and his eyes reflected worry. "Calvin and Bobbin have outlined what happened today, but I'd like to find out some of the details. I'd appreciate it if you'd tell me exactly what went on."

Paul told it straight. The need for the work lamps, the missing cable, the lifting of the trapdoor to check the wiring below, the discovery of Harrison and the Sheriff's inquisition.

When he was through, he leaned back in the chair, studying Murdock. The man was a listener. He'd fixed his eyes on Paul and had let him talk uninterrupted, his thoughts hidden behind a well-practiced poker face. Paul could well believe Murdock played successful hand after hand in the high-stakes game of international development.

"Has Abner told you about me, about the situation with my son?"

"Yes."

"Then I imagine you have a couple of hundred questions you'd like to ask."

"Yes, I do. But first, I'd like to hear your story. I'd like to know more about your son."

"Fair enough. You know that he's brain-damaged, don't you?"

"No, Abner didn't mention that."

"He's quite retarded, Mr. Whitman, though he can talk a little and do a little math. Count apples up to ten, that sort of thing. Physically, he's big. Big and strong. He's six-three, blond hair, and weighs better than a couple of hundred pounds. Or he did. I imagine he's lost some of that now. But he looks like a big, gangly Swede. He took after the men on his mother's side." As he paused to consider his next words, his eyes filled with pain. "When I said he can talk, I mean simple words and simple sentences. He can tell you if he's hungry, or wants a drink of water—but if it's something out of the ordinary, he simply doesn't have the language skills or the smarts to get it across. This, as you can imagine, can be frustrating for everyone. You have to keep commands simple, and it's nearly impossible to explain intangible concepts to him. His reasoning process is very limited, and very primitive. But he has certain instincts. Animal instincts. And one of them is for the woods.

"I'm not sure how he does it, but he knows his way around the Island here like an animal. When he was little, many times he'd lead me deep into the woods until I'd be completely turned around, lost. But he knew every stick, bush and gully, and always knew where he was, where he was headed and how to get back. That's one of the reasons I liked him being here as much as possible. No matter where you go here, eventually you end up at a shoreline, so there wasn't any worry in turning him loose and giving him some freedom. Particularly since he was afraid of water. Very afraid. And that kept him from trying any kind of stunts on that beach. It was—I felt—a safe, self-contained environment for him. And much better for him than the city, where he was confined like a dog to the yard. His mother didn't agree."

Ben paused to sip his coffee, his face troubled. "The key to understanding Jason today is in understanding his mother then." Abruptly he set his mug down, rose and moved to the window to look out. The silence was deep, the crackling of the fire the only sound. After a moment, he turned, his face controlled.

"The summer when Jason was seven was a bad one all the way around. Ilsa—his mother—was a gifted pianist. How gifted was never really proven, but I'd say she had all the talent needed for a successful concert career. You'd know more about that, though, then I would. But whatever her gifts, it was a major problem between us. She accused me of taking her away from a great career and trying to bury her on the Island. That simply wasn't true. I did everything to encourage her to pursue a concert career, including providing her with all the household help and all the care for Jason she'd need. She was completely free to devote herself to a career no matter where in the world it led her. And I'd made sure the money to support her attempt was there for as long as she needed it. It was years after she ran away that I realized that rather than my keeping her from a great concert career, I'd provided her with a good excuse for not having to try. But, as I say, it was years before I realized this. When she left, I was devastated. Just devastated. And Jason was even more so.

"Jason had been raised by a series of nurses and nannies from birth. When it became apparent that he wasn't normal, Ilsa would have nothing to do with him. But I don't think Jason understood rejection. He adored her. Absolutely adored her. In many ways, he was his mother's son. They both, physically, were beautiful people. And Jason had a particularly sunny nature, always smiling and laughing and good-humored. Every chance he got, he'd try to get his mother's attention. He'd pick flowers for her, he'd bring her pine cones and wild berries—anything to try to make her love him. But she was cold, aloof, unyielding when it came to him. He was damaged goods and she'd have none of it.

"Then it turned out Jason had a gift for music. In particular, the piano. When he was only three, he'd hear a tune on the radio once, then go over and pick it out on the piano. By five, he was playing songs with chords. By seven, he was playing Chopin. When it turned out he had this gift, Ilsa finally did take some interest in him. Enough to see that he got some proper training, at least. And that, of course, just made Jason love her even more. He'd finally won her attention. From four until he was seven, Jason's world was complete. He had the Island and his woods. And he had his music and—at last—his mother.

"He also had one other love. Animals. We had a series of pets—dogs and cats and hamsters and pet rats and guinea pigs—a real menagerie. There was never any incident with them. Jason was the gentlest of people in dealing with them, and all the animals trusted him. His favorite, though, was a little Scottish terrier, Campbell, called 'Cam' for short. Cam traveled with Jason back and forth from Minneapolis to the Island. The two of them were inseparable. When Jason played the piano—and he would for hours on end—Cam would lie right next to the pedals, never budging an inch. And when Jason ran off into the woods, or went to play with some of the Island kids, Cam'd be right at his side. They slept together every night. They were inseparable, just inseparable.

"Well, that summer, as I said, was a bad one. Ilsa never liked coming to the Island. She always claimed to be a city girl, and she wanted her restaurants and theaters and shopping and taxicabs, and that summer she was even more reluctant to come here than usual. But it was so good for Jason to be here that I insisted. I shouldn't have. It was the first of a series of mistakes I made that summer. A series of bad mistakes. So Ilsa came, and she spent her time at the piano, playing hour after hour. And when she wasn't at the piano, she'd lock herself in her room, not speaking to anyone. We'd had a maid quit that year, so instead of bringing our own help to the Island, we arranged for Old Jeb's missus to come in and run things for us. Old Jeb already worked for me year-round, taking care of the place. He didn't much cotton to Ilsa—and she couldn't stand either of them—so there was quite a bit of enmity there. Still, even allowing for local color, the reports I was getting were disturbing. The piano playing, the brooding in her room. And she was ignoring Jason a greater amount of time than usual.

"I was scheduled to come out late in August for a couple of weeks as I usually did, but when the reports of Ilsa's behavior kept coming, I decided to come out a few weeks early. Every night, she'd play the piano late into the midnight hours. A sad, heavy, brooding music. And every night, she'd stop in mid-chord, make a thundering crash of discordant notes, as if she'd brought her fists down hard on the keys, and slam the lid down. Then she'd go out afterward, not coming in until nearly dawn, when she'd exhausted her anger, or rage, or whatever she was feeling. When I questioned her about it, she claimed that nothing was wrong. Nothing besides having me as a husband and Jason as a son, that is.

"Then one night, she didn't come back. We searched the Island, but somehow I knew that she'd finally left me. I had an old runabout of a boat that I used for fishing and getting back and forth to the mainland when I needed to. We found it later, tied up to the public wharf in Tacoma. She was long gone by then, with too great a head start to get any trace of her at all.

"Jason kept asking for his mother, and finally I

had to tell him she was gone and wouldn't be coming back. He took it hard. Damned hard. He ran screaming out of the house and raced off into the woods. He went so fast when he ran out that his little Scottie, Cam, got left on the wrong side of the door. Cam was going crazy, trying to get out to go after him, so I opened the door and he tore off into the woods after Jason. That was my second mistake." He shook his head. "I wish I could redo that whole summer. I'd do so many things differently.

"I wanted to follow Jason, but Old Jeb advised me to leave him be for a while, to let him stomp out some of the emotion and wear himself out. Another mistake, I'm afraid. Jason did come back, though, about suppertime, as Old Jeb had predicted he would. Usually, after a day in the woods, he'd come in and play the piano until it was time to eat. But that day, I found him sitting on the couch, just glaring at the piano. He wouldn't talk, and when I tried to comfort him a little, he ran off to his room. It was at that point that Abner came in carrying the little Scottie in his arms. The dog was dead. He'd been hit hard on the head with a rock and his muzzle held underwater until he'd drowned. Abner found him floating in 'Coon's Creek, which runs through the back section of my place.

"I was sick inside. Jason had to be dealt with, of course, and I went into his room and asked where Campbell was. 'Gone,' is all he'd say. 'All gone.' Then he cried and cried and cried. I should've made him confront the body of the dog, I suppose, to drive home the terrible thing he'd done, but he'd buried his head in his pillow and was crying his heart out, his fists hammering the mattress. So I simply rubbed his back until he'd calmed enough to fall asleep. Old Jeb buried the dog in the woods that night.

"When we got up the next morning, the boy was already up and out of the house. Again, Old Jeb advised me to let him be. Some bread had been taken from the kitchen, so I knew he had food. And there were other things that had to be done. We were still searching the Island for Ilsa, making sure she wasn't lying hurt somewhere. Off and on throughout the day, I could hear Jason in the distance, calling out for the dog. It about tore my heart out to hear it. Old Jeb felt he was too young to understand exactly how final death is. But Jason never came close to us and we never caught sight of him. Early in the afternoon, his voice faded away and we heard nothing more from him the rest of the day.

"When we got back to the house at suppertime, Old Jeb's Missus was there and she had a queer look on her face. She beckoned me to follow her. In the living room, an old iron pipe had been tossed on the floor and the baby grand that was Ilsa's piano was a battered ruin. Then she led me to the game room and showed me the upright we'd shipped out for Jason's use. It, too, had been attacked with the pipe. Then she led me down the hall, and there was Jason, sprawled across the bed. He was sound asleep, but it was obvious he'd been crying. His face was filthy from the woods, and there were streaks of white showing through where the tears had run down.

"I woke him up and showed him the piano and the pipe. 'Did you do this?' I asked him. He looked at the piano with dazed eyes and said, 'No more. All gone. No more.' As much as I coaxed and cajoled, that's all I ever got out of him. 'No more. All gone. No more.' And he never played the piano again."

Abruptly, Ben's voice cracked and he swung back to stare out the window at the woods, his shoulders high with the tension of keeping control.

To give the man some privacy, Paul sat quietly, staring into his coffee mug. His heart was filled with the pain the other man was feeling. This was no chairman-of-the-board act, designed to motivate one recalcitrant employee. This was real, a searing of a man's soul as he'd relived the events he'd related.

When Murdock's breathing sounded normal again, Paul looked up at him. "So his mother and dog disappeared forever from his life on the same day," Paul said softly.

His back still turned to him, Ben nodded. "Yes. He lost them both. And took it out on the pianos."

"Those were the two pianos on the Island, then—the upright and the baby grand?"

"Yes."

"What about the Chickering?"

Ben swung around now, back under control. "Another mistake, I'm afraid. I should've sold it as soon as I got back to Minnesota. Instead, I found a special school for Jason and sent him there. And over time, he seemed to be all right. They cared for him and kept him busy and taught him some simple skills. All the reports were encouraging. A somber boy, they said, but docile. No temper tantrums, no rages. Kept to himself and did what he was told. But he wouldn't have anything to do with any of the animals there. Or with music. Otherwise, he was fine. So I really felt that the issue of the pianos was over. Then one year, when he was twelve or so, I held the company Christmas party in my home instead of a restaurant, and somebody started playing Christmas carols on the Chickering. Jason didn't say or do anything. He simply left the room, as he'd been trained to do at school, and when I checked on him later, he'd gone to bed and was asleep. And he was still asleep when I left for the office the next day. It was about midmorning when the housekeeper called me home.

"The Chickering had been virtually destroyed. Jason had found some plumbing pipe in the garage, left over from one of Ilsa's remodeling projects years before, and he'd used it on the piano. He also had his bag packed to go back to school. I told him I understood why he felt the way he did about pianos, that he didn't have to leave, that I'd send the piano away, not him, and I was sorry I hadn't moved it out before. I couldn't sell it; it was too battered. So I called some of my men over and we shipped it out to the Island that day, to be stored with the others until I could get them restored."

"Was that when you fixed up the Coop?"

"No, that was done earlier. After the summer Ilsa left, I didn't have much stomach for the big place I have here, and I wouldn't allow Jason to come back here at all, so I converted the Coop for me to use when I had to come here on business."

"And the piano strings? Would Jason know enough about pianos to be able to take them off?"

"I don't know. We're not sure what he knows and what he doesn't know. He doesn't talk enough for any of us to find out. But I know he's done things that indicate a far greater understanding of the world than I would've guessed."

"Was his IQ ever tested?"

"Yes, but I don't know the number. They just said he was trainable. That's all they've ever told me. He can count money in small amounts, so he knows some math. That's what I meant by doing things that I would've guessed he couldn't."

The mild questions Paul was asking had helped steady the man. But the rest of the story had to come out now. "What happened in Minneapolis?" he asked quietly. "To the pianist."

There was a long moment's silence as Ben stared again at the past. Then he sighed. "Jason was in his early twenties by then, and had progressed far enough in his schooling to get a job at Goodwill Industries, unloading trucks. He lived in a group home run especially for people like him. He had his own room and could keep it clean himself. And he knew his bus route to and from work.

"But he didn't have any judgment. That was one of his deficiencies. Oh, he knew right from wrong. In fact, once he learned what was right, he became inflexible about it. But about people, he had no judgment at all. If strangers smiled at him, they were his friends. If they laughed, they were happy. He couldn't conceive of anyone ever trying to hurt him. And he didn't know what a taunt was.

"Well, the bus broke down one night while he was on his way home. The route took him through a rough section of town, filled with porno houses, adult book stores and drinking dives, that kind of thing. When the bus gave out, the driver pulled over to the curb and radioed for a replacement. He made the passengers disembark to wait for the new one to get there and strolled off to have coffee, or a beer, or whatever.

"The sidewalk was filled with hoods and pimps and prostitutes—those kind of sidewalks usually are—and a couple of the hoods spotted Jason and his buddies from the home for what they were and decided to have a little fun with them. They got them away from the other passengers—the normal ones who might've stepped in and helped the boys out—and asked them if they'd like to go to a party.

"Of course they said yes. They had lots of ice cream parties at the halfway house, so parties were good things in their minds. The hoods took the boys into this dive, made them hand over all their money and bought them beers. Not ever having had any, it only took two or three to get them higher than a skyscraper. By now, a whole group of derelicts had joined in, and they told the boys to do stuff like clap their hands and climb on the tables and dance around and things like that. Like performing bears. The more the boys did it, the more everyone laughed. When Jason saw that he could make everyone laugh, he did it all the more. This was a party, right? People laughed at parties, right? The more they laughed, the better the party. This was fun, right? Jason—none of the boys—had any way of knowing these bastards were laughing at them.

"There was an old player-piano against one wall. Someone went over and started pumping the player to accompany the dancing. As soon as he heard it, Jason stood stock-still, then, before anyone knew what he was doing, he hopped off the table, grabbed a bar stool with iron legs and bashed the back of the guy's head in. Then he started in on the piano. Of course, Jason was big anyway. Big and brawny. No one was about to tangle with him. Or try to take that stool away from him. He was still hacking away on the piano when the cops got there.

"The cops were pretty disgusted by the whole thing, but even though the boys had been set up by scum, one of the scums was dead. My attorney met with the DA and we worked out a guilty plea for manslaughter, with attenuating circumstances. In return, Jason was sentenced for a period of three years in a mental institution. When his sentence was up, I shipped him here to the Island and hired a couple of the Islanders to stay with him at all times. The rest you know."

"My God," Paul said softly, "what a time that kid's had. And you. You've been to hell and back."

"Several times."

"What about his mother?"

"Ilsa? She made a clean getaway. No one saw her go. No one saw her arrive in town, and Lord knows where she headed after that. Or what name she was using. In spite of what mystery books and television shows lead you to believe, most people are too unobservant to notice or remember strangers. Especially airport clerks, who see thousands of unknowns every day. We know she had a lot of money on her. We know she'd socked away a small fortune during the years she was with me. She wasn't a stupid woman—she'd have had her plans well made. In fact, I suspect that accounts for the moody music all that summer long. Whatever she'd planned in Minneapolis before leaving for the Island, the timing wasn't right until August, and the waiting must've been unbearable."

"What about your marital status then? What did you do legally?"

"I have a corps of highly paid attorneys. They found a friendly judge, we filed the proper legal notices, a divorce was granted and I was awarded full custody of Jason. That's why I did it. I didn't care about me. I'll never marry again. But I didn't want any problems over Jason's custody."

The older man gave a shaky sigh, then his gaze refocused on the present. He slumped into a chair, his eyes filled with pleading. "Will you help me find him, Paul? Will you stay on the Island and help me find him? There'd be a good deal more money in it for you, naturally."

Paul thought a minute, then said slowly, "Jason started off hurting his dog. Whether he knows the difference between hurting him and killing him is moot at this point. He moved on to battering pianos, now piano players. His violence is escalating. Who'll he go after next? Aside from me, that is."

"He has no reason to hurt anyone else."

"He had no reason to hurt his little Scottie, either."

"The doctors think that was a reaction to his mother's desertion. He must've heard her playing late that night, the thundering crash of the keys, and then she was gone. Gone forever. Her leaving and the pianos are somehow all linked together in his mind.

And the impotence and rage he must've felt . . . well, Campbell was a too-handy object for it all."

"Perhaps. A stoning of the animal I could see. Or a beating, perhaps. An explosion of emotion—rage and grief. But knocking the dog out, then drowning him? That's pretty cold-blooded."

"That's one way of looking at it. But suppose he knocked the dog out accidentally—throwing a rock, for instance, just as the dog ran up to him. And suppose he tried to bring the dog around with cold water, and was clumsy about it. Supposing that?"

"Would he know that cold water can bring a person to?"

"I don't know." Ben sighed. "That's the problem with this whole thing. No one knows what's locked up in his mind."

"That's my point exactly," Paul said quietly. "No one knows what he'll do next, or who's safe and who isn't. Except for me. We can pretty well be sure I'm not safe. With two Piano Man notches in his belt, we know he'll keep on after me."

Ben thought a minute, then some of the businessman came back. "Now that we know what's happened to Jim Harrison, I cannot in good conscience bring in a new Piano Man. Do you agree with that?"

Paul nodded reluctantly.

"Second, Jason's got to be found. Do you agree with that?"

Paul nodded again.

"And third—so far, at least, he's chosen to leave the Islanders alone. Which means, they're not a threat to him. He has no reason to come after them and harm them. On the other hand, we know he knows you're here. He's already tried for you on Lyle Point, according to the reports I've received. And now that you know what this is all about, not only can you protect yourself from him, we could set a trap, using you as the bait, and the next time he tries for you, we'll get him. If we haven't flushed him out first."

Paul made one last attempt. "Why not turn the whole thing over to the Sheriff? A little manpower and he'd have him."

"Whatever Jason is, he's my son," Ben said with quiet firmness. "I don't want him shot and killed like some poor wretch of a deer. Besides, Frank Hall doesn't have the manpower for a concentrated search like this. That's one of the joys of working in a public agency in this day and age of budget cuts, not enough men to do a proper job of things."

"From what Abner told me, Jason's been on the loose for over two months now, and no one's caught him yet."

"That's been two months of part-time looking. That's why I'm here today. To organize a manhunt the likes of which you've never seen. There's a couple of hundred able bodies on this Island, and we're going to start using them around the clock. Jason has got to be caught."

"And then what?"

"He'll be locked up for life. I've got a place all ready to receive him. It's a pleasant place, with a lot of kindness and warmth and help. He'll have good people there taking care of him. And he'll be removed forever from society."

"And Jim Harrison? What about his death?"

"It'll remain unsolved. Officially, that is."

"The Sheriff's not a stupid man, by any means."

"No, you're right, he's not. But he simply won't get any answers to his questions."

Suddenly, Paul ran dry. He was tired and emotionally exhausted and leaden-hearted. Nothing was simple about this situation. His sympathies lay with the simple-minded lad who couldn't cope with the cruelties of a world he would never understand. Yet, because of these same cruelties, the simple-minded lad had evolved into a murderer and had to be stopped. The question was, what was the best way to stop him?

He studied Ben. Was he a man of his word? The Islanders seemed to think so. If Paul cooperated and Jason was caught, would Ben fulfill his promise and confine Jason someplace for life? Again, the Islanders thought so. What did he himself think, though?

The man had been painfully honest. His story wasn't an easy one—or a proud one—to tell. It took a basic courage and a certain kind of dignity to lay your life bare in front of a stranger. But was that enough? Was that reason enough to join in with what amounted to a flagrant disregard of the law?

An image of Anna came to mind. She'd buried her sleek, sexual, almost jungle-like animalism beneath the strict, staid, disciplined folds of the gray business suits she'd adopted, until the body motions and personality began to reflect what she wore. As the years had passed, she'd become more and more inflexible in her approach to problems and people. They were to meet her standards, or they were failures. It was one or the other, never a compromise.

And what would she do in this case? She'd walk to the nearest phone and turn the whole situation over to the Sheriff. If a young man's life was needlessly sacrificed in the process, so be it. She would point to the piano player in Minneapolis and the dead man at the Coop and term her actions justified. And she'd be right. That was the thing that stopped him, that had always stopped him in dealing with her. Legalistically, she would be right.

Paul felt caught between conflicting impulses. During his concert career, he'd often been torn between one or another interpretations of a concerto. Each approach had its own merits, and it was never an easy decision. To make it, he'd had to crawl deep inside of himself and listen to the way his soul said it should be played. It hadn't made him popular with conductors. Or famous, either, he thought wryly.

Ben gave Paul some time with his thoughts, then suggested, "When the men get back, we'll tell them we worked things out, shall we? We'll let them know that you'll be helping us."

In his mind, Paul could hear Anna's scream of mental anguish. He gave her a single last thought, then nodded. It was decided. He was in. "What do we do next?"

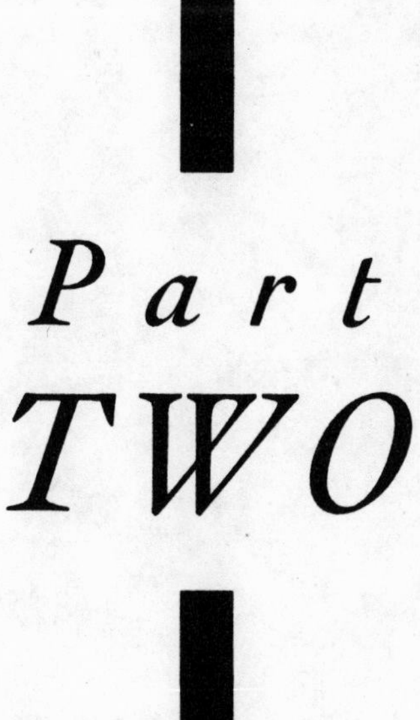

Part TWO

Chapter Nineteen

Tom's place was a log cabin on the western bluff of the Island, with a magnificent view of water and the snowcapped Olympic Mountains. A thick cloudbank was moving across the mountain range by the time he and Paul got there, but a few stray sunbeams escaped the black clouds to play light games on the vast stretches of snowfields below. Fascinated by the tension of light and darkness, and needing some relief from the gloom of the long afternoon, Paul stood lost in the beauty of it.

Tom came to stand next to him. "My grampa bought this land when he first came here. It took him most of his lifetime to pay it off, and he never had a chance to build on it. Pa had his own place up the road a piece, next to Uncle Abner's, so this was left to me."

"You're a fortunate man."

"Yes, I am." Tom led the way to a porch spanning the full rear of the cabin. "Ready for the assault by the guard dogs?"

Paul could hear dogs whining and scratching beyond the door. "Can you control them?"

"Most times," Tom said with a straight face. He turned the knob, shoved the door open and stepped back.

A small black blur rushed out and wound around

Tom's leg. A more dignified golden retriever followed, tail swinging in a wide arc. The retriever received his pat on the head from Tom, then lay on the ground in front of Paul and rolled over on his back for a chest rub, feet spread wide in the air.

The black blur turned out to be a wire-haired dachshund, with a body long enough to play piano on, a tail going faster than a metronome set at *pizzicato,* and a tongue as long as a conductor's baton that slurped out sloppy kisses along any face within reach.

"Guard dogs, huh?" Paul bent down and scratched the retriever's stomach.

Tom grinned. "Meet Elmer and Irma. My protectors."

"That true?" Paul asked the retriever. "You the protector here?"

Elmer sighed, stretched further, his tail, curved up between splayed legs, waving like a flag in a lazy breeze. Irma swiped a wet tongue across Paul's chin. Stooping now and laughing, he scratched her ear while his other hand kept rubbing the mound of thick fur stretched on the ground in front of him.

The cabin was larger inside than it had appeared. It had a great room open to the ridgepole that spanned the entire rear wall, with high windows framing the view. The front half of the cabin, facing the road, was a large bedroom and fair-sized bath. A half-loft overlooked the great room.

Some comfortable chairs and a couch had been grouped around a flat-topped wood stove churning out a steady amount of heat. "You can bunk there for a few days," Tom said, indicating the couch. "It's not too bad to sleep on."

"Thanks, I may do that."

"I'm going to make some coffee for the others for when they get here, but how'd you like a drink for now?"

"A whiskey would be nice."

Paul slumped into one corner of the couch, stretching his feet out towards the stove. Through the window wall, he watched the storm building up over the mountains. A wave of tiredness swept over him, so strong it nauseated him. The drink helped.

Tom sprawled in a chair opposite. As if they'd verbally agreed on it, they avoided talking about the day. Instead, Tom began telling the story of his cabin, how he'd built it himself using trees he'd felled in clearing the homesite. He'd trimmed them, skinned the bark off by hand and cut them to length. When he had enough, he'd held a log-raising party for the whole Island, with the younger men hefting logs, the women supplying the food and the old-timers supervising everyone. "Fueled by lots of wine and beer," Tom added. "The cabin ended up more upright than they did."

As they talked, daylight waned and the view faded like a stage going dark. Finally, Tom set down his empty glass, fed the dogs, then pulled a couple of thick steaks out of the refrigerator and tossed them into a frying pan. Paul pared and sliced potatoes for fries. The dogs curled up together near the wood stove, comfortable and drowsy after their supper. The fire, visible through the screen of the stove, danced and bobbed like a cheerful sun. Glancing around the cabin at the warm, tidy layout, Paul thought, this is enough for any man.

▌

The seven men gathered around Tom's big scarred kitchen table. Ben Murdock had a chair to himself at the head of the table. Old Jeb and Calvin sat on his right, facing the night-black windows. Abner and Bobbin were across from them. Tom and Paul shared the foot. They all had mugs of coffee in front of them and Tom had brought out sheets of paper and pens for taking notes.

Murdock waited until the men were settled into place, then took control of the meeting, his face grim. "Before we pour our energies into organizing a hunt for Jason, is there any chance at all that he's left the Island?"

Abner shook his head. "He can't have swum to the mainland. He wouldn't have lasted thirty minutes in water as cold as that. We've had watchers on every ferry and barge. Nothing. And we've done a daily check of all the boats moored on the Island. None of them's budged so much as a hair."

"Is there a chance he tried to swim for it and didn't make it?"

"We've talked about that a time or two," Abner said. "South Puget Sound's a dead end. A body'd have to thread its way sixty miles north or better among all the islands that'd be in its path before it'd hit the Straits of San Juan de Fuca. Then it's another hundred miles or so west before it'd get to open sea. If a body would turn west at all. Given the right currents, it could drift on up into the Canadian San

Juans. I just don't see it making that kind of a trek without washing up on some shore somewhere. Not to mention all the shipping traffic coming in and out of the Sound. That's a lot of heavy boating for a bobbing body to escape notice."

"Then he's on the Island."

"He's on the Island," Abner agreed.

Murdock looked over at Tom. "You're only a few years older than Jason, and he used to tag after you a lot. If you were him, and you were going to duck the old Wise Men here, how would you do it?"

"Well, first off, food," Tom said slowly. "I'd stay away from meat, chickens, eggs—anything that needs cooking. You don't have to have a fire that way. Besides, the root cellars are so full this time of year, nobody'd miss a few potatoes or carrots. I'd wait until market day and the family's gone to town and help myself."

Murdock's eyes lit up. "And different folks go to town different days . . . By God, I think you've got something there. What about shelter?"

"I'd set up different places. Some in the woods, some in the cellars of the summer folk. I'd find an empty cabin or two. A boathouse, maybe. Deserted barns. I wouldn't have just one place. Then you've still got the forests. The thing you've got to remember is that Jason's pretty top-notch in the woods. He loved them as a kid and was always disappearing into them. They were friends to him. And as a kid, he'd be able to get to places the grown folk couldn't."

"You think he'd remember them after all these years?"

"We don't know for sure, do we?"

Tom had said it gently, but it still brought a shadow that dimmed Murdock's eyes for a second. "No, I guess we don't," he murmured.

Something flickered beneath the moody, remote attitude Calvin always wore. More a tilt of the head than a change in facial expression, it indicated—what? Paul thought. Empathy? It was hard to tell. The man wore a habitual glower that put people off.

Abner had been sitting back, deep in his own thoughts. Now he straightened. "First, we need to eliminate as many areas as possible. Cut off his food and as much of his shelter as we can. The summer houses should be first. We'll search them from top to bottom, then board them up."

Bobbin nodded agreement. "There are those barns tumbling down out to the old farm. There'd be a good amount of boards available from them."

Murdock pulled a small notebook out of his jacket pocket and wrote in it. "What you haven't got, we'll ship in."

"Added to that," Abner continued, "we'll padlock all root cellars, basements, sheds, any barns, any buildings that would provide him with food or shelter. That goes for the Coop, too. We should get a double-keyed deadbolt on the door so no one can go in or out without a key."

Old Jeb shook his head. "It'd be a lot safer if we keyed the door on the outside only, with a turning bolt inside. Lots of flammables in there, and that wood's old and dried. Anything catches, the place'd go up like a bonfire on the Fourth of July."

"No," Paul said firmly. "I want a double-keyed deadbolt. If Jason does get in somehow, I don't want it easy for him to get out again. And I'll keep the key handy, in case of fire."

Old Jeb looked at Murdock, received a nod, and shrugged. "You'll have it by sunset tomorrow."

"Okay," Abner said, "assuming he's been eating from the various root cellars, now we've got our lad confined to the forest with no food or shelter. He's going to get pretty hungry and do one of a couple of things. Either he'll catch some game—deer, 'coon, whatever—which means a fire. Or he'll break into a year-round place. Either way, we'll get a fix on his whereabouts. Assuming he does neither—maybe he has food already stashed somewhere—at least we'll know he's confined to the forest. Of course, that's about as much help as a newborn chopping wood."

They began, now, to discuss methods of actually cornering Jason in the woods. Paul sat silent, the city slicker among the knowledgeable woodsmen. But as the discussion twisted and turned with every new idea proposed, he began to see the magnitude of the problem.

The Island was roughly eighteen square miles, three-quarters of it forests thick with fir, madrona, alder, nettles, huckleberry thickets and salal bushes. The odd wild blackberry shrub just added to the jungle. Then there were ravines too wild, too steep and too deep to search thoroughly and marshy areas where a man would bog down the second step he'd take. Jason could hide one thicket away from the searchers and still escape detection.

At one point, Murdock sighed. "What you're leading up to is clearing away all the undergrowth. An inch-by-inch search."

Abner nodded. "Don't see a way around it."

"Wouldn't a 'dozer do as well?"

"Too many big trees. Besides, all a 'dozer'd do is cut a path through the woods. We got some of those now. It's off the path that's the concern."

"Where do you peg our chances of actually finding him?"

"It's hard to say, Ben." Abner stroked his beard, considering it. "There's the noise of the chainsaws. While we're doing all the clearing, the noise'll give Jason an exact fix on where we all are while we won't have the slightest idea where he is. On the other hand, once we've cleared the woods and they're all open to us, then we've got a real chance to corner him. It's better than hiking up and down a few deer paths like we have been doing while he hides behind the nearest bush, thumbing his nose at us."

Ben thought it over. "This is all going to take time."

"I know you're anxious, Ben, but we haven't any way of laying our hands on the lad today." Abner shook his head in sorrow. "I wish it were otherwise, God knows, but it's not."

The dogs, asleep all evening through the droning of the discussion, both came awake as one. They cocked their ears, listened a minute, then raced to the back door, whimpering.

The door burst inward and a dark, swarthy face peered in at them. "Sheriff's coming."

"Thanks, Zeke."

Zeke's appearance startled Paul. He'd had no idea a frontier scout had been posted outside the log cabin. Everyone else took it in stride; only Paul seemed surprised.

As if a bell had rung to end class, Tom smoothly gathered up the notes they'd made, shoved them in a kitchen drawer and scooped up the coffeepot. Zeke disappeared back outside, taking the dogs with him.

Tom posed with the coffeepot, waiting. The men kept silent.

Within seconds, the sound of a motor taking the incline up the driveway reached them. Tires crunched on gravel in the parking area and the soft murmur of a powerful engine died away.

Tom held his pose until the knock sounded, then he opened the door and managed to put the right amount of surprise in his voice. "Frank! Come on in." Tom held up the coffeepot. "I was just refilling cups. Come join us."

Ben Murdock had slipped his own notebook back into his pocket, and he rose and moved toward Hall. "Frank," he said, extending his hand. "Good to see you."

Tom set the coffeepot on a hotpad in the center of the table and quickly moved another chair into place next to Ben's at the head of the table. "Have a seat, Frank."

The Sheriff's broad face wore an amused expression. "Well, now, a regular gathering of the locals. Evening, Mr. Whitman, doing a comparison study of coffee beans, are we?"

"Actually," Ben said smoothly, retaking his seat, "we were comparing notes to see if we could come up with an answer or two."

The Sheriff accepted a mug of coffee from Tom and settled himself comfortably at the table. "And?"

Ben shook his head. "I'm afraid we're being outwitted."

"When'd you get here, Ben?"

"Just this evening."

"Why?"

"It was my employee found murdered on my property. I felt a certain responsibility."

"And Mr. Whitman here? You feel a certain responsibility for him, too, Ben?"

"Of course. That was my second reason for coming. To make sure he was all right."

The Sheriff beamed at Paul over a sip of the coffee. "Mr. Whitman, I find a continual amazement in the amount of care and concern you're receiving from the Islanders."

Paul grinned slightly. "It is amazing, isn't it, Sheriff."

Hall leaned back on two chair legs and studied each of the men. After his eyes had made a leisurely tour around the circle, he focused on Ben once more. "And the third reason?" he asked softly.

Ben frowned. "The third reason?"

"Well, Ben, you see, it's this way. I read all them weekly news magazines. *Time, Newsweek,* stuff like that. Lots of mentions of you and your company. Building cities in Saudi Arabia. Showing the Japanese how to build a tract house. Importing construction techniques from Norway for use up in the Yukon—"

"Sweden."

"From Sweden. Not to mention all those skyscrapers going up all over the place with your name on them. Toronto's next, isn't it?"

"Saint Louis. Then Toronto."

"Must be a couple of million bucks' worth of contracts in all that."

Ben grinned. "Billions. A couple of billion. But do go on, Frank, don't let me interrupt."

"So you hire a guy to come to a remote, godforsaken island to fix a couple of pianos you've got stashed away here—God knows why—and he goes and gets himself nicely murdered, and you come running on out first thing. Makes me wonder a bit."

Ben kept his eyes steady on the Sheriff. "It makes you wonder what, Frank?"

The Sheriff took another swallow of coffee. "Well, now, for instance . . . Say a welder gets pushed off an I-beam high in the sky while working on one of your skyscrapers. You gonna rush off to that site on the first plane? Or a carpenter gets mugged in Saint Louis, and his brains get splattered all over the alley wall, you gonna hightail it there? Or maybe a half-built wall collapses on a worker in Japan, pushed over by a buddy lusting in his heart after the dead man's wife. You gonna head there first thing, too?" The Sheriff shook his head, his eyes still amused. "Seems to me you'd send flowers, a bonus to the widows and go on about the jillion and one other things you have to handle each and every day." He stopped, waiting for a response.

Ben remained calm, shaking his head in mock dismay. "You're more suspicious than my security guards in the Mideast, Frank. The differences between the welder on the skyscraper, a carpenter in

Saint Louis, a worker in Tokyo and a Piano Man on the Island here are twofold, Frank. First, I'm a home-grown boy. That gives me an emotional interest in what goes on here, not just a business one. And second, the other jobs are for the company. This one isn't. It's for me."

"So it's personal."

"Yep, it's personal."

"And this is just a good old-fashioned, old-time reunion of some good old friends and fishing buddies. Excepting Mr. Whitman, of course."

Both men stared at each, the Sheriff with his amused, mocking expression, and the corporate CEO with an easy grin on his face, used to playing cat-and-mouse.

The silence deepened as it went on. Abner stroked his beard thoughtfully. Calvin studied his coffee mug. Bobbin looked worried. Old Jeb sat motionless, waiting for the chips to finish flying and land somewhere. Tom was thoughtful, like his uncle, his gray eyes level and steady on the Sheriff. And Paul watched them all.

The Sheriff chuckled finally, breaking the standoff. He gulped the last of his coffee and rose. He shook his head, chuckling at Ben once more, then turned to Paul. "You still alive tonight, Mr. Whitman?"

Startled, Paul pinched his wrist. "I seem to be." He took his own pulse. "I bet I'm good till morning, at least." He grinned, then thought of what he'd said and the grin slowly faded.

"Glad to hear it. I take it you won't be needing that hitch back to the mainland then."

"Nope." He felt the instant suspicions of the others, a current that washed through the room like a shock wave. "The Sheriff kindly offered to airlift me off the Island if I wanted him to," he said easily to the others. "I told him thanks, but no thanks, I'd take my chances."

The Sheriff gave one last look around. "Well, I'll let you get on with your reminiscing." He walked to the door, his powerful tread shaking the floorboards, and paused with his hand on the doorknob. "Oh, by the way, if you happen to—just happen to, mind you—come up with an answer or two, you might give me a call."

The men sat expressionless. Finally, Abner nodded.

Hall's gaze found Paul. "And Mr. Whitman, if you happen to find yourself dead in the morning, why, you give me a call, too."

With a final mocking smile, he was gone.

Chapter Twenty

Over the course of the next few days, the hunt for Jason moved into high gear. Summer cottages were searched, then boarded up; sheds, root cellars and basement doors were padlocked; boats were sent out to patrol the miles of Island shoreline. The wild forested areas of the Island were sectioned like a road map and two-men crews were formed to search each segment.

The forest teams began at the northern tip of the Island, clearing their way southward. They were ruthless with their chainsaws. Thickets were shorn back to bare earth, scrub trees were felled to stumps, and earthen caves were pickaxed into heaps of loose dirt. As small sections of forest were cleared of any hiding places, the debris was wheelbarrowed out to the road's edge where other teams came along in pickups and carried it off to the Island's landfill.

Daytimes, Paul worked on the Old Soldier; nights from six to midnight, he helped clear forests. He'd been paired up with Bobbin and they were assigned a thickly forested arm of land forming one of the Island's northern spits. At one time, a logging trail had been bulldozed through the forest for fire access, and they began working along the overgrown path. With chainsaws and a wheelbarrow, they cleared the trail, then moved into the woods to hack away at the next layer of tangles.

It was grueling, back-breaking, arm-wrenching work. First there was the undergrowth to clear away—blackberry vines and huckleberry thickets and broad thick clumps of salal bushes, all with long, winding branches that grew every which way. How anyone could pass through such a tangle was beyond Paul's comprehension.

Then there were the trees—the firs, madronas and alders. At best, they allowed narrow crooked alleyways between them. At the worst, they befouled each other, young ones growing up beneath the lower branches of century oldsters, united in a symbiotic closeness that created a solid barrier even a clump of air couldn't get through, never mind the solid body of a man. When they ran into walls of those, they'd leave the trees standing and go off at a right angle until a space could be found to press forward again. Paul quickly learned that there was no such thing as a straight path in the woods.

By the end of his first shift, his muscles were knotted into torturous cramps that merged and spread during the night into a single pain encompassing the whole of his body. Simply climbing out of bed in the morning was an exercise in agony.

Over breakfast at the deli, learning that Bobbin was heading out with Abner and Calvin for a second shift on another section of woods, he stared at the three old-timers in awe. "Do you have any aspirin back there?" he called over to Jenny. "I need a couple." Then he grinned at the three old men. "I'm not as young as you fellows."

That night, Paul watched Bobbin bend his arthritic back to pick up the chainsaw for his turn. If Paul had no arthritis, yet he still was one giant sore from head to toe, how much pain must Bobbin be feeling?

He waited through the old man's turn with the chainsaw, then his own. When Bobbin came back to trade again, Paul shook his head. "I'll stick with this, if you don't mind. I'm determined to master it."

In the dim perimeter of the miner's lamp, Bobbin's eyes were shadowed, but even so, Paul caught the faint flicker of relief that flashed across the bony face. He'd guessed right. Wheelbarrowing was easier on the old man. Without anything more being said, Paul finished out the night on the chainsaw.

The soreness of the night before had been only a foreshadowing of that night's pain. Even his toes were curled tight into cramped knots from all the squatting he'd had to do. He felt as if his legs were made of bricks as he trudged his way to breakfast. Without asking, Jenny served up aspirin with his food, grinning as she did so.

Daytimes, he was busy with the Old Soldier. All the parts for the pianos had come in, except the strings. The stripping was the most time-consuming part of the restoration, and with that about done, he was hopeful that the pace of the repairs would pick up a bit. If so, by Thanksgiving he should be ready to stain the stripped wood.

Despite the constant activity, a part of his mind was always aware of the dangerous position he'd placed himself in. During the day, he was alone in the Coop, vulnerable to attack. The nights were even worse. As his workday ended and dusk set in, his nerves stretched taut like overtuned piano strings. He twitched at the slightest sound, and he found himself staring at the trap door, as if it were an open grave with his name on it. Somehow, through sheer discipline and willpower, he managed to keep his fear under enough control so that it didn't interfere with his work, but he never felt completely at ease. In retrospect, his first weeks on the Island, when he'd read by lamplight in the quiet of the night, seemed serene and peaceful and he yearned for their return.

He'd been staying at Tom's, the one place on the Island where he felt safe. But he couldn't continue staying there; it was too much of an imposition, no matter how much Tom denied it. Besides, his couch was too short for Paul's lanky frame. Yet before he could return to the Coop to sleep, he had to resolve the problem of the platform bed.

Whenever he was in the Coop, his eyes couldn't seem to stay away from the bed. Even when he was deep in his work, his gaze would stray in that direction at regular intervals. The specter of Harrison's face decomposing in the crawlspace below was so vivid, it might just as well be lying out in plain sight, rotting away on the pillow while Paul watched. And whenever he pictured himself sleeping above Harrison's temporary grave, his stomach roiled with nausea like a storm-tossed sea. Yet if he moved the bed, he'd expose the trapdoor, and he wasn't sure that would be better. At the moment, at least, the platform bed prevented some hideous creature from emerging from the bowels of the earth and claiming his soul as he slept. His options, it seemed, were to sleep over the damn thing or have it in plain view. Either way, he'd be haunted.

In the end, Paul moved the bed across the Coop and down a bit from where it was, positioned where he could lay on his side, watching the trapdoor if he needed to.

Once he'd made the move, it took another day before he could work up enough courage to try it for one night. His worrying turned out to be a waste of time. By midnight, after finishing a grueling six hours clearing underbrush, he was so exhausted his imagination sank into as deep a sleep as his body did, and he knew nothing until morning. He moved back into the Coop permanently the next day.

His mood wasn't helped by the Sheriff, who'd taken to popping in on Paul at odd times, any time after the first ferry in the morning to just before the last ferry at night. There was no pattern, no routine to the visits; they occurred with random frequency. Although the Sheriff took Paul back over the story of finding Harrison's body a couple of times, his purpose didn't seem to be gleaning new information as much as it was simply sniffing out the atmosphere. Paul tried to probe below the surface to get a sense of what the man was thinking, what direction his suspicions were taking, but it was impossible. The man returned the stare with a blandness that defied interpretation. And it seemed to Paul that with each visit, the Sheriff's expression grew more bland, his eyes more suspicious.

The Sheriff's nosing about the Island was particularly exasperating to the hunters, forcing them to suspend their search whenever he was around. Fortunately, Paul didn't start his shift in the woods until the last ferry was leaving the dock, so there was little concern that the man would catch him with a chainsaw in hand. Still, the man's constant visits were unnerving.

One of his visits occurred just after Paul had finished removing the hammers from the Old Soldier. The Sheriff came into the kitchen, shook the cold from his body and picked up the old plastic butter container holding the salvageable hammers. "These look like sliced mushrooms on toothpicks. What are they?"

Paul explained what they were, showed him where they went, told him what they were supposed to do and picked up one to point out where the new felt would go.

The Sheriff followed it all with close interest. When Paul was through explaining, he studied the old piano a moment, then said, "You really know what you're doing, don't you."

"I should. My dad did it before me, and this is how I put myself through the conservatory, tuning and repairing pianos. Want some coffee?"

"A cup would be nice. Storm's brewing and it's colder than Iceland out there."

Paul filled two mugs and they each took a piano bench. The sky outside was leaden with ominous clouds. "If there's a storm coming, what are you doing out here on the Island?"

"Just moseying around," Frank said blandly. "Crime's not some kind of a pantywaist sissy afraid of a little bad weather."

"Yes, but what if the storm breaks while you're still on the Island? Aren't you afraid of getting stuck here?"

"Never known the ferry to be shut down by a little storm coming through."

He studied the big man sitting at ease on the Grand Lady's bench, one elbow resting on the closed lid case. "Any leads on Harrison's killer?"

"We make a little progress now and then."

All at once, Paul was curious. "How do you go about something like this?"

"What? Investigating a murder, you mean?"

Paul nodded. "Where do you start?"

Hall shrugged. "Just nose around, pick up a bit here, a bit there, trace a few movements, pretty soon a picture forms and bingo, you've got it. Nothin' to it. Takes patience, is all."

"You strike me as the kind of man who has an endless supply of that."

"You might say so." The Sheriff took another giant swallow.

"So what picture have you formed?"

"Well, now, that'd be giving me far more credit than I deserve. Can't form the picture until all the bits and pieces are to hand."

Paul shook his head. "That's equivocation if I've ever heard it."

The Sheriff was amused. "Equivocation." He pronounced each syllable distinctly. "I like that. Equivocating. Yes, sir, I sure do like that. Puts me to thinking it's a good word for what the Islanders are doing, don't it you?"

Paul put down his coffee mug, irritated with himself. The man was dangerous. He knew that and yet the blandness the Sheriff assumed had led him into playing word games, and that was too perilous at this point. He'd give the whole thing away if he wasn't careful.

He mastered his irritation and said calmly, "I wouldn't know. Well, I should be getting back to work now."

"Me, too." The Sheriff set his cup down and rose, his thick legs flexing muscles visible through the cloth of his uniform. He stood flat-footed, legs spread at ease. A massive man. "Speaking of work, I noticed some new trails being cut into the woods."

Paul kept his voice casual. "Clearing timber, I guess."

The Sheriff pursed his lips and nodded. "That's what I heard. I caught up with Abner and his cronies the other day, getting ready to log a section."

The Sheriff waited, but no response was required. Paul stayed silent.

"Strange time of year to be logging, though."

"I wouldn't know."

"No, you being new and all, I guess you wouldn't. Speaking of being new, it must feel right good, being taken in by the Islanders like you have."

Paul sensed danger. "It's made working here more pleasant," he said cautiously.

"Yep, a regular protection outfit you got going for yourself. Why, they're as closed-mouthed about you as they'd be one of their own. Kind of makes a fella wonder why." The Sheriff smiled slightly, ice-blue eyes shrewd on Paul's. "Well, thankee for the coffee." A wave and he was gone.

An icy wind began about suppertime and made the work in the woods that night miserable. The cold was bitter and talking was impossible over the noise of wind and chainsaw. Paul had to wait until he and Bobbin were hunkered down on break behind a broad stand of trees that gave them some protection from the fierceness before he could report his conversation with the Sheriff.

Bobbin heard him out. "He's sniffing the air for a scent. I wouldn't worry about it. You handled him well. And we knew he was bound to see the cuts. They's why we've actually been doing some logging during the day."

"He's a dangerous opponent."

"Yep, he's that, all right. At times we need a smart Sheriff, and at times we need a dumb one. It's a pity you can't get both in the same fella."

Paul nodded. "Amen." A sense of futility and frustration swept over Paul. "Are we really doing Jason a favor by all of this?" A sweep of his hand indicated the trail. "Doing it without official help, I mean?"

Bobbin thought about it a while. "Could be argued either way, I'd guess. Jason's gonna be one scared maverick, whoever corners him. Maybe the Sheriff could find him quicker, I don't know. But his men'd all carry guns, and comin' out of a corner like Jason's bound to do, he's not gonna stand much of a chance of living through it."

"Is starving him to death any kinder? We've locked up every potential food source we could find."

"Well, now, I've got some thoughts on that, too," Bobbin said, slowly. "Either he's alive, or he's not. If he's alive after all this time, means he's found a food source somewhere. And if he's not, then we'll find that out, too."

Paul sighed. "I don't know, Bobbin. If he hid beneath a thicket and stayed quiet, we could hack away two trees over from him and never find him."

"That's why the name of the game's cut-and-look, cut-and-look." Bobbin dumped out the dregs of his coffee. "All we can do is the best we can. If he's to be found, he'll be found. God bless him either way."

Chapter Twenty-one

Overnight the wind strengthened to gale force. Paul fought its force to go to breakfast, his head bent low against the icy edge of it, each footstep hard won.

Only four of them made it to the deli—the three old men and Paul. As they ate, the wind clawed at the window, seeking entrance, and the store lights began to flicker. Thaddeus stayed close to the cash register, oil lamps at the ready. Jenny twitched at each wind-lash.

The howling grew so fierce that Abner finally set his fork down. "If this don't let up, it won't be safe to work today."

Bobbin considered it. "We got a real beauty on the way, no question about it. I hate to lose a day, but I vote we call it off till it's come and gone."

Calvin nodded, his glower deepening into a full-blooded scowl. "S'pose we'll have to," he grumped.

Bobbin turned to Paul. "If I don't come by your place at six tonight to pick you up, then I'll be by tomorrow night, same time. Assuming the storm's passed by then."

"Good enough." Paul ate quickly. "I can use the time at the Coop." The idea of some real rest that night erased some of the tiredness. He could work straight through the day without interruption, into the evening if he chose to, then top it off with a good night's sleep.

Bobbin slowed him with a hand. "Have you some lamp oil at your place? In this kind of wind, the Island's sure to lose its electricity."

"Sure do. And a couple of lamps. That's what I read by at night. Or I used to. Now I use one of the work lamps."

Bobbin looked thoughtfully at him for a minute, then nodded. "Be careful."

"You, too." He smiled and was gone.

Going home was a breeze—pun intended, he thought. With the wind at his back pushing him into a half-run, he reached his doorway just as the first rain lashed him.

As Bobbin had predicted, the storm was a beaut. The heavens threw it all at the earth. Thunder, lightning, sleet, rain and hail. The wind tore at the Coop, seeking entrance. The rain slashed against the windows. Branches snapped and fell with cracks as loud as thunder. Trees crashed to earth, one near the studio end, jarring the building as it slammed past it to the ground.

Paul kept the fire going hot, as much for cheerfulness as to fight the icy fingers of wind that found their way in through the siding. He kept an oil lamp lit in case the power went out and set out the second, ready to go if needed. He put together a stew and set that on the back of the wood stove to simmer, then worked steadily at the kitchen table all day, replacing felt on the hammers.

He missed having music playing in the background

as he worked. Missed it dreadfully. The smell of the stew and the cheery red warmth of the fire made the Coop feel comfortable and cozy, and music would have made the feeling complete.

He stretched a time or two, going to the pianos where he imagined them uneasy, voiceless, unable to protest. He admired the Old Soldier. "You're going to be outstanding," he told him. He eyed the baby grand. "And you're next. We'll save the Lady for last." He stroked the battered ebony lid of the Chickering as though to ease the hurts of its wounds. "You'll be the star," he told her.

Then he shook his head, laughing at himself. "If anyone I knew," he said in a normal tone to all three, "saw me standing here, talking to you, they'd commit me." Chuckling, he returned to his work.

The storm accelerated. Hail beat on the skylights and thunder rolled overhead like cacophonous bass drums. Lightning split the air. The cold north wind, already gale strength, howled out of the woods to slam against the Coop. Fir branches swayed broadly under its force, like a conductor's baton gone berserk. Unbidden, an image of Jason came to mind. Paul pictured a giant blond man hunched up somewhere against the cold fury of the elements. Poor lost soul, he thought.

Then, as if resting between movements of a symphony, the storm paused. In the sudden quiet, Paul could hear the gentler rain pattering on the roof, the steady ticking of his alarm clock, the crackling of the fire in the stove, the soft chatter of the lid on the stewpot dancing lightly over the steam. The worst seemed to be over.

The pause ended. The wind returned with new violence, thunder rolled and the concerto resumed. A monstrous crack sounded from down by the road and the Coop went dark.

By the flickering light of the first oil lamp, he lit the second. He set one lamp on the kitchen counter and left the second on the table. Shadows flickered on the walls of the kitchen. The studio was in darkness. He wasn't comfortable with that.

He split the lamps, placing one near the Lady. That was worse. The Coop was filled with strange shapes and shadows. He wished he'd picked up more lamps at the store. Or at least some candles.

He finally settled on both lamps in the studio, counting on the glow of the stove to lighten the darkness at the kitchen end. Using his flashlight as a kitchen light, he ladled up some stew, set the pot on a trivet on the counter to cool, and sliced some French bread to go with his meal. There was enough wine for a single glass. He carried his food and glass to the baby grand and, using a carton lid as a placemat, sat down to dinner.

But his mood had turned. He couldn't regain his earlier sense of contentment. Each crack of lightning made him jump. Then he'd sit motionless, waiting for the roll of thunder to come and be gone. He continually looked behind him over towards the corner, where the trapdoor lay in wait. Finally, he moved his plate around to the other end of the piano so he faced it head on.

He ate because he needed to eat, tasting nothing, his eyes fixed on the square of wood guarding the entrance to the underworld. The pauses between thunder and lightning lengthened, and their sounds moved off into the distance. The wind quieted some, and there was now just a steady downpouring of rain on the skylights.

As the storm abated, his mood eased a little. Not much. He still felt on edge. He finished his food, downed the wine and carried his dishes to the sink, rinsed and stacked them, then wandered through the dim lamplight to the pianos, his fingers flexing with the need to pour pent-up emotions out onto the keys. It was moods like this that drove him to play.

It was one of Anna's favorite accusations. You turn to the piano, Paul, she'd say time and again, never to me. He sighed with the knowledge that she was right. Would it be different with any other woman?

His thoughts turned to Jenny. Was she all right in this storm? Surely Thaddeus would've closed up the store. No one would be out in this. They'd have to be crazy to. Since she lived with her dad, and Bobbin was the kind of man who'd build a sturdy home to shelter his family, he wasn't really worried about her.

Grace Duncan popped into his mind and he moved suddenly, peering out the windows. Grace would have been alone in the storm. She was probably all right. At her age, she'd weathered a lot of them.

Still, she did play piano. And Jason had a definite fixation on pianists. And what better time than a black stormy night to strike? It wouldn't hurt to check on her. It was too perfect a night for murder.

Chapter Twenty-two

The cold hit him as soon as he opened the door and he shivered violently as he locked the deadbolt. The storm had more strength left in it than he'd realized. By the time he'd reached the road, the wind had driven enough rain inside his collar to run down his shoulders and back and soak through his shirt. His flashlight showed only the footstep immediately ahead.

Well, the hell with it. He was already wet. And cold. There wasn't much else the storm could do to him, and he continued up the road.

The store was dark, but Thaddeus's van was parked out front and the mellow glow of oil lamps lit the windows. Neither sleet nor rain, Paul thought as he passed by.

It was during the long stretch of deserted road beyond the store that he began to doubt his own wisdom. With well over a mile to go before the next clearing, the forest loomed up on either side of him, a solid black. No one in the world knew where he was at this moment. Just like no one in the world knew where Jason was. And if Abner's suspicions were true, and Paul's every movement was being watched by the crazed young man, then he certainly was providing him with the perfect opportunity.

The rustlings of leftover wind through the tree

branches didn't help, either. He picked up his pace, condemning himself for his own stupidity. He should be heading straight back to the Coop and the safety of his deadbolt.

He argued with himself all the way to the ferry dock. His need to check on Grace was all out of proportion to reality. She'd lived on the Island all her life, for God's sake. And Jason probably didn't know she played piano. He wouldn't consider her a pianist, as the man in Minneapolis had been. Or Harrison. Or himself. As for the storm, as he'd realized earlier, she'd weathered her share. What need was there for him to walk three miles or better on a bitter stormy night, through a forest hiding who knew what, just to hear her say she was fine, anyway? But by the time he did reach the ferry dock, he was so close to her house that the short distance left didn't matter anymore.

Slanting rain cut his visibility to the footstep in front of him, and he heard the pickup before he saw it. In fact, he heard it only seconds before it raced past. The headlights, coming toward him, loomed out of the rain, passed him and were gone, all in a second. It was so quick, he never had a clear look at it, didn't know what color it was, nor what make or model. He knew it wasn't Old Jeb's simply because of the engine noise. This one didn't chug, it purred.

And with all his heart, he wished he knew, for in that brief second he paused, the pickup had sent the entire contents of a deep puddle over both his legs. His shoes squished with each step. He was frozen to the bones, wet and miserable. All he could think about now was getting dry and warm.

To his surprise, Grace's house had lights. He hesitated a moment in front of her drive, unprepared for what he might find. His imagination was wired high tonight.

But she opened the door as if he were an expected visitor for Sunday tea. "My goodness, Paul, come in, come in! What a night to be out!"

"I'll second that. I'm surprised you've got lights."

"And heat," she exclaimed, helping him off with his jacket. "Oh, my, you're soaked through. You'll catch your death that way. I'll just get a blanket while you get that sweater and shirt off and I'll pop them into the dryer. Your socks, too. Set your shoes by the fire, and we'll have you warm in no time. A bit of a hot toddy wouldn't hurt, either, I'd bet."

She bustled about, making him comfortable, wrapping him in the blanket, and producing an excellent Tom-and-Jerry.

He took a grateful sip and stretched his bare toes out toward the fire. "Do you hire yourself out?"

She laughed. "If I did," she said, her eyes twinkling, "it'd be to someone twenty years younger than you. Hear tell you've been told the story of Jason. What do you think of our unhappy lad?"

Paul thought a minute. "If it weren't for the killings, I'd feel kind of sorry for him." Paul studied her. "Did you know his mother at all?"

"Lordy, yes. She used to summer here every year, and when she couldn't stand it at home anymore, she'd come sit at my kitchen table."

"What was she like?"

"She had three passionate interests in life—music, men and herself. She hated Jason for being what he was, hated this Island for being what it was, and hated Ben for forcing both of them on her. They lived in Minneapolis most of the year and summered here. Ben liked to have Jason here as much as possible—it was the only place where the boy really had any freedom. But Ilsa chalked us all up as a bunch of illiterate hicks and holed up in the big house and brooded over her piano all day long. I don't know what life held for her after she ran off like she did, but I guess through her eyes, anything had to be better than this."

"You said something about men . . ."

"Lordy, Paul, that woman'd bed down with anyone just to get back at Ben. Oh, not here on the Island. Men hereabouts had too much respect and liking for Ben to lay a hand on his wife. But I guess in Minneapolis it was a whole 'nother story. I guess she'd pick up anything in pants with a zipper down the front.

"Anyways, she used to sit at the kitchen table and tell me about it. Even if half of it was made up, which I suspect it was, that still left more men in her life than trees on the Island. I'll tell you, Paul, I've met many people in my lifetime—good, bad and in-between. But that woman was a piece all to herself. She didn't care about right nor wrong . . . she had no conscience at all. She'd take whatever she wanted from anyone and the devil take the hindmost."

"It's a wonder Ben stood for it."

"I'm not sure he knew. And Jason adored her, so even if Ben did suspect some hanky-panky, he'd have more'n likely looked the other way. Besides, she was pretty, she was gifted and she was charming. When she had a mind to be. And when that woman played the piano, she really played."

"So when she left, Jason took his hurt out on the pianos," Paul said. "How did Ben handle her leaving?"

"Ben's pretty much of an honest person. Ilsa gave him so many problems that, even though he never said so, it was probably a relief to be shed of her when she finally did take off." She pushed herself to her feet. "Let me have your mug. I'll fix us a refill and check on your clothes. I put the heat on low so as not to shrink your sweater."

While she was gone, he stretched out farther in the blanket, toasting his toes by the fire. There was something comforting about this room, he thought. Something comforting about Grace, too. Something old-shoe about her. She was practical, down-to-earth, with a lot of plain, old-fashioned common sense. In that way, she was much like Bobbin.

Her return interrupted his thoughts. "You look pretty serious there." She handed him a fresh Tom-and-Jerry.

"I guess so." He shifted in his chair. "I guess I'm still trying to figure out what makes Jason tick. Bobbin said he was simple-minded. That was the word he used, 'simple-minded.' I keep trying to translate that into a mental picture. Did you know Jason as a little boy, too?"

"Yep, we all did. He was a real favorite on the Island. He was a lovable child, with silky blond hair, big blue eyes, and a huge smile that lit up his whole face like a lamp going on. And he was affectionate. He hugged everyone. Including some of the old sourpusses on the Island. And we've got a few of those, too, I'm sorry to say. But Jason treated everyone like a friend. To him, everyone was a friend. He was very trusting."

"Too much so?"

"Very much too much so. That was part of his simple-mindedness. He simply didn't have any judgment. He could be taught right from wrong, but if it was a new situation and he hadn't been taught, he didn't know what to do, what was expected of him."

"It sounds like he was at the mercy of the world."

"He was. And I don't know whether losing his mother like he did helped or hindered that. Eventually, he'd have caught on that while he adored his mother, she had no use for him. Sooner or later, he'd have learned that. So would it have been better if she'd stayed, and he'd learned the most important person in his life had no use for him? I can't rightly say. I know that once she left, Ben protected him as much as possible. And whether that was a favor or not, no one could tell you either. I doubt that Ilsa would've taken the time—or had the interest—to do much for him."

"Poor kid."

"Exactly. That's how we all felt."

"And now?"

Her shrewd eyes fixed on his. "How much have they told you about these last few months?"

"I know about Harrison, obviously. And we talked about Obadiah and Walt Gibbons and their accidents. If they were accidents."

"Then you know about as much as we do."

"I understand why Jason would go after Harrison.

He was a Piano Man. What I don't understand, Grace, is why the other two. If Gibbons was a drifter, it wasn't likely he had any connections to pianos. And Obadiah—was he a pianist?"

"Nope. Never so much as sang a note in his whole life, as far as I know. We don't know why Jason went after them. If they really weren't accidents. But it's got us all worried. It's like there are no rules anymore. We thought we had Jason pegged, and it turned out we don't." She sighed heavily. "All I pray for is that he's found quickly, and this trouble all comes to an end."

He set down his empty mug. "Well, I don't want to rush my visit with you, but if the dryer's done, I'll be on my way. I just dropped in to make sure you were all right."

She nodded. "And it's getting on toward my bedtime." She gave a wry grin. "If someone had told me when I was twenty-one and wild as an Indian that I'd ever voluntarily go to bed this early, I'd have sent them to the loony farm. But that's what old age does for you."

While she went to get his clothes, he wrapped the blanket around him like a cape and wandered to the piano. The lid was up and the keyboard waited, a black and white shining that drew him like a hypnotist.

He was tempted. He reached out a hand, fingers already flexed and positioned for a B-minor, then drew it back. No, he decided, he wasn't ready to try it, yet. It was just possible that Anna was right; he'd never thought beyond the keyboard. For now, he had work, shelter and food. But it was not yet time to play. Not yet.

He turned to find Grace watching him from the doorway, his clothes over her arm. She smiled as if she could read his thoughts, then bustled over to give him his things. She picked up mugs and carried them out to the kitchen while he dressed.

He was tying his shoes when she came back in. "How about coming for Thanksgiving dinner, Paul? I've a whole gang coming in. Abner and Tom, Calvin, Bobbin and Thaddeus and Jenny . . . why don't you come, too?"

"I'd really like that, Grace. Thank you." He rose. "Would it be appropriate to bring a bottle of wine?"

"Just one?" She grinned at him. "I'd sort of counted on you for a couple of bottles. Or three. Or four."

"Would a case be enough?"

She considered it. "Possibly."

"Consider it done."

He was halfway down the front walk when she called after him. "Paul, I almost forgot! Thaddeus called just before you got here. You're to stop at the store on your way home. He's got a carton for you."

"How'd he know I'd be here?"

She laughed, waved good night and shut the door. Like last time, the downstairs lights were turned off and the upstairs turned on before he reached the end of the drive.

The rain had eased up and was definitely on the wane. Which was encouraging. Somehow the forest didn't seem so black and dense. And visibility was good enough now that if he had to, he could protect himself from another drenching by a passing vehicle.

What was even more encouraging was that the store had lights. "Do you think my lights might be back on, too?" he asked Thaddeus.

"Might be. Hard saying. I don't know if you're on my power line or not." Thaddeus lifted a carton onto the counter. "Dad left this for you. Said to keep the stuff as long as you can use it."

"What's in it?"

Thaddeus shrugged. "Darned if I know. He gets all kinds of curious thoughts sometimes. Well, I'm just about ready to shut her down. If you want, I'll give you a lift up to your place."

Paul judged the weight of the carton, then nodded. "I'd appreciate that."

Thaddeus locked up, then guided the van slowly down the road, weaving in and out among fir branches broken off by the wind and tossed every which way. "Must feel good to have a night off," he said to Paul, "even if it took a lollapalooza of a storm to do it."

"My weary muscles appreciated it, yes."

"I feel sort of bad I can't help with the search. How's it coming anyway?"

"I guess we're making some progress, Thaddeus, I don't know. It's hard for me to tell." He fell silent a minute. "My heart kind of goes out to Jason, out there somewhere, alone and scared, especially on a night like this. You must've known him as a kid. What was he like?"

"Kind of a neat little guy. He was—oh, a good six

or seven years younger than me. He wasn't much on reading and writing, and only talked in very simple sentences. Couldn't form most words. Or remember them. I don't know which. Still and all, he had some sharpness to him. His eyes took things in, know what I mean? He'd tag around after us, watch us play baseball, and after a while, he could catch a ball himself and swing a bat. Couldn't connect real often, but still he knew they went together. His eyes just took it in."

"What about now, Thaddeus? Would he know enough to hide himself in the woods and keep himself going as he has?"

"You bet." Thaddeus slowed to make the turn up the steep driveway to the Coop, then brought the van to a complete stop. From the bottom, the driveway appeared to be pure mud.

"I can walk from here," Paul suggested.

"No problem, I got four-wheel drive on this little critter." Thaddeus grinned as he shifted the drive lever. "She's as ugly as sin, but a beauty of a workhorse." Crawling and jouncing, they made the top. He brought the van around in a sweeping U-turn, aimed back down the hill. "Sure enough, your electric's back. Your place is lit up like a shopping mall."

"I must've forgotten to turn the switches off when the lights went out. Thanks, Thaddeus, I appreciate the ride. And the visit."

"Me, too. You play cribbage, by any chance?"

"No, I never had time for cards. I was always practicing the piano."

"Good. I'll teach you when this is over. It'll be nice to have a patsy for a change. Abner's always drubbing the hell out of me. Back to your question about Jason, yeah, these woods were home to him. He could climb a tree like a 'coon, pass through brush as silent as a deer, keep as motionless as a log. He knew all the berries to eat and the ones to leave alone. Somehow God made up for the lack of a mind with an overabundance of animal instincts. Yeah, he's out there somewhere, if that's what you were meaning. And he'll lead you a merry chase before you catch him."

Paul nodded thoughtfully. "Thanks, Thaddeus. And I'll look forward to that card game."

Thaddeus grinned. "No, you won't. Not after the first one. But we'll just keep you at it till you do."

Paul set the heavy carton down to unlock the deadbolt, carried it just inside and stopped to lock the door again. He extinguished the oil lamp he'd left burning on the counter, reconstituted the fire and put on a pot of coffee. Then he opened the carton.

Inside, carefully bundled in newspaper, was a small brass reading lamp. A cream-colored shade was stuffed with butcher paper to keep it from getting crushed. Another package held the light bulb, a couple of spares and some extension cords.

He assembled it, placed it on the bookcase by the old club chair, plugged it in and turned it on. A mellow aura of golden light encircled the chair. He grinned with pleasure and turned off the harsh work lamps. Dear Bobbin.

There were still some flat rectangular packages at the bottom of the carton. He took the largest out, unwrapped it and stared. Then he hurriedly unwrapped the other two. It was a small cassette player with speakers. The last package revealed an assortment of tapes, most of them classical. The gift damned near made him cry.

He put the player on the closed lid of the Lady, connected the various wires and chose a Beethoven symphony. He made a few adjustments—treble, bass, volume—then sat in his chair and let the music swell around and through him, his heart swelling with it. He gave up all thought and lost himself in the music.

Steady rain pattered on the roof. The freshly fed fire crackled as it warmed the room. The smell of coffee drifted through. The lamp by his chair threw out a golden halo of soft light and music filled the Coop to the rafters. He showered to Tchaikovsky, then drank a final cup of coffee laced with brandy to Chopin. The tape player had an automatic stop, so when he was ready to climb into bed, he put in a Brahms tape and turned the volume low. Contentment filled his soul. For the first time, the Coop felt like home, and he felt safe and secure.

Kicking off his slippers, he peeled down the bedcovers, then froze.

A small pile of white bones lay heaped in the center of his bed.

Chapter Twenty-three

In a near rage, Paul yanked on shoes over bare feet and jacket over pajamas and, unmindful of the cold rain, marched through the woods to Old Jeb's place. He banged on the door until lights went on upstairs and kept banging until the old man opened up and peered out.

Paul snapped out orders like a stage manager. "Get Abner over to my place, right now. You, too. And bring some long boards and a couple of dozen house nails with you."

Without further explanation, he tromped off.

They were quick to get there. Abner brought Tom with him. Calvin rode in with Bobbin, and Old Jeb followed right behind, his truck bed loaded with boards and bags of nails.

Without a word, Paul pointed to the pile of bones on his bed, then took the heavy lumber from Old Jeb and dumped it over by the trapdoor. He set the first board in place and hammered in a fury.

The men talked quietly a moment near the bed, then Tom and Abner disappeared outside with their flashlights. Old Jeb went to the back door to inspect the deadbolt, and Calvin and Bobbin stood to one side of the trapdoor, watching Paul hammer.

Paul finished the first board and reached for the second.

Calvin bent down and slowed his arm. "You pound the nails straight in, a good shove from underneath will push that board right up again. Come from the end, and slant them inwards. Nothing will pull them out then."

Paul was startled out of some of his anger. "Thanks." He toed a nail in and banged away. By the time he finished the last board, Abner and Tom were back inside. Paul brushed dust off his hands.

Old Jeb broke the silence. "Deadbolt ain't been touched. You sure you locked it when you went to Grace Duncan's tonight?"

Paul exploded. "Does everyone on this goddamned island know every damned thing I do? Christ, you must spend the whole damned night on the goddamned phone!"

"Not exactly," Abner said blandly. "Jeb calls two, they each call two, those two call two more and pretty soon the Island's covered."

"A Noah's ark. Wonderful. And where the hell were the two men supposedly guarding the Coop?"

"Following you to Grace's."

Paul shook his head in disgust. "I can't keep up with any of you. And yes, I locked that deadbolt when I left tonight. I know, because Thaddeus drove me home with a carton from Bobbin—which I'm sure you all know about, too—and I had to set the damned thing down on the steps to unlock the deadbolt so I could enter this wonderful safe haven of mine."

Abner nodded soberly. "We found where he got in. Part of the lattice work that covers the crawl space was muddied up. We shook it a little and it pulled right off. Soon's the rain lets up, we'll cement in all around the foundation and you won't have that problem anymore. In the meantime, this"—he pointed to the boards nailed over the trapdoor—"will keep you safe."

The force of the anger was gone and Paul felt tired and empty. "Yeah, until he finds another way in."

Abner thought about it. "Tom, you check every foot of flooring. Look for loose boards, missing nails, anything that would give access."

Calvin looked up to the roof line. "What about the skylights?"

"We'll wire them shut, too," Abner said. "Should've done it to begin with."

Old Jeb was over by the bed, studying the bones. He moved a piece or two and studied them some more. He made a couple of adjustments and nodded. "Look at this."

They all moved over and stared down. A partial skeleton had emerged.

"My guess is a 'coon," Old Jeb said. "Been dead a long time. There's no flesh at all. Missing some parts, too. But it's a 'coon all right."

Frowning, Paul began shaking his head. "No, I don't think so," he murmured, lost in his thoughts.

Abner swung to look at him. "You don't think it's a 'coon?"

The question brought Paul to awareness. "Oh, yes. Yes, I do. I meant something else. In fact, I'd bet it was a 'coon. Or something like it. I'm almost sure of it."

"Found some loose boards," Tom called out. "This floor's a sieve. Jeb, you got more nails?"

"Bags full." He pointed to the kitchen table, then gathered up the bones, dumped them in the carton used for the lamp and radio and carried it out.

Tom grabbed a handful of nails, took a hammer from the workbench and started pounding floor-boards. Calvin picked up the one Paul had used and toed in some fresh nails in the first board Paul had laid. Old Jeb came back in, empty-handed, and he and Abner talked together in low voices. Paul stood by the window, staring into the darkness.

Bobbin came up to him. "You got something on your mind," he said softly.

Paul leaned an elbow on the sill and studied the old man. Who to trust? Bobbin, as skinny as he was, had the right build for the suspicions that were beginning to creep into Paul's mind. Yet, the arthritis had him fairly well crippled, and it would take a certain litheness to do what he was thinking. Then there was the man's openness, a sincerity hard to deny . . .

He decided to take a chance. "There are a couple of things bothering me," he began in a low voice. "From all I hear, Jason's a big, brawny giant of a Swede."

"He is." Bobbin kept his voice low, too.

"There's not a great deal of depth to that crawl space. A couple of cinder blocks high at the most."

"That occurred to me."

"It would take someone with a pretty skinny body to maneuver their way through that crawl space to the trapdoor."

"That occurred to me, too." A quiet humor lit his eyes. "A pretty skinny body, like mine."

Paul met his gaze. "Yes."

The humor deepened. "No, I didn't do it. But go ahead and ask if you've a need to."

Paul held his gaze a moment longer, then gave a small smile. "No, I don't need to. But you do understand what it could mean?"

"You're thinking it wasn't Jason at all."

"That's precisely what I'm thinking. Listen, Bobbin, Jason wasn't all that bright. Don't you think something like this is a bit subtle for someone like him to think up?"

It was Bobbin's turn to study him now. Finally, he nodded. "Paul, I've gone along with this hunt because Jason has to be found. But there's been some question in my mind all along. It almost seems like he's getting help from someone—" He broke off as his gaze moved past Paul.

Paul swung around. Tom Ross was approaching and was within hearing distance.

"We'll talk more about this tonight," Bobbin murmured. "I might have a thought or two that'll help."

Tom took the last few footsteps to reach them. "Well, Paul, you're all fixed up now. You've practically got a new floor going here. No more surprises in bed . . . unless you invite them in." He grinned.

Paul adopted a light tone. "If I invite them in and still get surprised, shall I call on you for help?"

"Anytime. What's a pal for if he can't help a good buddy out in a situation like that. We're about set to leave, but we'll be back, crack of dawn, to fix that skylight. Once that's done, and we get the foundation cemented in, even an ant will be hard put to gain entryway."

After they were gone, Paul locked himself in and poured a generous helping of brandy. He let the effect of the first swallow spread throughout his body, then he put on a Schubert concerto and settled into his chair. It was going to be a long night.

Chapter Twenty-four

The rain stopped during the night. The wind veered north again and the cold moved in like a new ice age. The thermometer fell to near zero. Dawn raised it only slightly.

As a thin winter sun edged over Oro Bay, Tom showed up with the Pickup Brigade and several ladders. They swarmed over the roof, inside and out, and within a short time had the skylights wired over and sealed shut.

Paul thanked them and saw them out, then ran both hands over his face, digging grit out of his eyes. His body felt heavy and ponderous with tiredness. He should dress, go for breakfast, then start work. But he was so damned tired. And the cold outside had an ice edge that penetrated the cracks and corners of the Coop.

The hell with it. He stoked the fire and crawled into bed. He gave the bones that had been lying there a single brief thought, pulled the heavy covers over his own bones and sank instantly into a deep sleep.

Sturdy pounding at the door startled him into wakefulness. He dragged himself out of bed, slung a robe on and stumbled to the back door. A sideways glance at the clock as he passed by showed it was almost eleven. He fumbled with the key and finally got the door unlocked. "Jenny!"

She was bundled up in her heavy coat, a woolen scarf and mittens. Steam clouds drifted from her mouth at each breath and she was shivering. A small grocery sack was in her hand.

"Come in, for heaven's sake, it's freezing out there." He opened the door wider.

She came into the kitchen and paused uncertainly. She looked half-embarrassed. "How does the old saying go? If Mohammed won't come to the mountain . . ." She gave a small wry laugh and held out her bag. "I brought you breakfast. And your morning paper."

"Thanks, I appreciate that. You take your coat off and warm up by the stove while I get some coffee going." He filled the percolator, put some grounds in and plugged it in. "How'd you get away from the deli?"

"Grace offered to babysit the coffeepot."

Dear Grace, he thought with amusement. "How thoughtful of her," he said with a straight face.

Jenny stripped off her outer things and held her hands out to the stove for warmth. "We heard what happened last night." She shivered some more. "I don't think I could've stayed here after that."

"I wasn't sure I could," he said honestly. "I confess, I stayed up all night on guard duty."

She fell silent. Her brown hair was parted in the center and pulled back into a knot at the back. She surveyed him with her steady brown eyes. So like her father's, he thought. "You look terrible," she said. "You go clean up and I'll start the bacon."

"Thanks, it won't take me long."

Showered, shaved and dressed, he emerged from

the bathroom to the smell of the bacon. Instant hunger pains hit hard. "I hope you're cooking enough for both of us." At her nod, he set the table for two, then sat watching her work.

Head bent over the frying pan, her face was in shadow, the clean lines of her profile backlit by the kitchen window. Her chin was firm and her lips curved up slightly at the corners. She moved with graceful motions, her wrists delicate but her forearms strong and rippling with muscle as she hefted the heavy cast-iron skillet with a practiced hand. The curves of her slender body were clearly outlined in spite of the thick heavy sweater she wore. Paul had a sudden urge to undo the knot of hair at the nape of her neck and let the thick mane cascade free.

"I can't remember the last time someone fixed breakfast for me," he said.

Jenny smiled. "I can. It was yesterday morning, and the morning before that and the morning before that . . ." She spread cooked bacon on a paper towel and cracked eggs into the hot fat.

"You never seem to take a day off," he commented.

"There's not much point in it this time of year. Besides, I can use the money and Thaddeus can use the help." She flipped the eggs over. "Come spring, when the garden needs attention, I might take some time off then." She served the eggs and brought the plates to the table. Bacon and toast quickly followed.

They ate in silence, her appetite a match for his own. He noticed her hands, slender, with long fingers. Pretty hands, he thought. A pianist's hands. "Do you play piano?" he asked.

"We never had money for lessons when I was young."

"What about Grace? Couldn't she have taught you?"

"I suppose so, if I'd asked her, but there was just plain too much work to do and we all had to pitch in and help in order to eat. It was a matter of survival. What was your childhood like?"

"I was fortunate. My growing up was built around music. My dad repaired pianos, so there was always an excuse to play one."

"Did you start pretty young?"

"I guess. By three, I could play little tunes, by five I knew some of the simpler classics, by eight I was performing at local schools in the area. My parents saw to it I had the best training they could provide."

She hesitated, not wanting to pry, but at the same time, wanting to know. The brown eyes were large and round with unspoken sympathy. "I know you were a concert pianist. Ben told us that when he hired you. Don't you play at all anymore?"

"Just for myself. Not as my profession."

"Why not? Why did you stop?"

The million-dollar question, he thought. Why had he? Unspoken pressure from Anna to conform? A desire for the respectability and prestige that accompanied the title, University Professor? A need to be part of the straight life?

"I didn't mean to pry," Jenny said hesitantly, into his silence.

Her comment brought him sharply to the present. "No, no, it's not that, Jenny. It's simply that you've asked the same question I've asked myself a hundred times in the last five years. There's a living to be made by playing the piano. If you can accept your level of talent. Maybe that's where the problem was. I wasn't willing to accept being less than the best. I aimed for the top, and I wasn't that good. I just plain wasn't that good."

Now that he was started, the words seemed to flow. "There are several levels of talent at the top. The topmost, of course, are the truly gifted, the world-class pianists, the ones that play the famous concert halls of the world and fill them to standing room only. They're the ones with name recognition, with the tours and the albums and the devoted followings. Next level down, I suppose, would be those who are members of a major symphony orchestra. But unlike the violin or woodwind sections, where there's a good numerical probability of a spot opening up, a symphony generally only engages one pianist. Thus the openings are few and far between. To be honest, though, I'm not sure I would've gotten a spot with a major symphony anyway. To help you place me on the talent scale, I was slightly above a saloon player."

"Is that why you went into teaching?"

"No. There was Anna's career to think of. Attorneys don't just hop around the country with a wandering minstrel, joining any law firm on the nearest street corner. They join one, and stay on to build up their practice and eventually, if they're lucky, receive a junior partnership. I joined the university faculty solely to save my marriage. I enjoyed teaching the young, but I hated every other aspect of university life. And they knew that, the powers-that-be. It was fairly obvious. I was difficult to control. I absolutely refused to play politics, refused to take part in the petty feuds that went on—in short, I refused to play their game. When a tenured slot opened up, there were two of us eligible for it, and the other guy got it. And frankly, he deserved it. To put it crudely, he kissed so much ass, his nose will never lose its tan."

She burst out laughing. "I like that. You can be sure that quote'll make the rounds of the Island. Grace'll love it."

He grinned. "Grace strikes me as having quite a naughty streak."

"She's as raunchy as they come. When she was younger, she had red hair, and they called her 'Raunchy Red.'"

"Oh, really!" He sat back with amusement. "Now that's a blackmailable fact if I've ever heard one. Now, what about you? You've heard my life story. It's your turn."

The sadness never far below the surface emerged again. Her gaze dropped to her plate. "There's nothing much to tell. I haven't been all over the place the way you have."

"You've lived off the Island, I know."

She gave him a swift look of astonishment. "How do you know that? Did Grace say something?"

"Grace hasn't said a word. No one has. Your coat gives you away. It's a bit high-quality for the kind of clothes the Islanders wear."

"I'll be darned." She sat back and stared at him. "I never would've thought of that . . ."

"I'm sure you wouldn't have." He delighted in her amazement. There was something innocent about her, an almost childlike quality, that precluded cynicism of any kind. Not like Anna. No, no, he thought, not at all like Anna. Jenny was a warm person, with a somewhat serious outlook on life. Sincere, he decided, that would be the word for Jenny, sincere. While Anna—well, Anna was a tawny-haired animal, ambitious and aggressive, explicitly sexual in her motions, wild in bed, headstrong in life. Things would be done her way or not at all. The magnetism she exuded was apparent from the very first glance, whereas Jenny's appeal was a quieter, calmer, deeper kind of attractiveness that grew upon you. The difference between the two women was extreme, much like the difference between the music of Chopin and Wagner, he thought.

Jenny's eyes were fixed on him, huge, warm and sympathetic, and suddenly he hungered for her. He wanted to feel that warmth, to nurture it into closeness and intimacy, to lose himself in it and cleanse away the disorder of the past twenty years.

She broke eye contact just then, dropping her gaze to her plate, fighting against some internal feelings of her own. Finally she spoke. Her voice was husky, but the words were light. "All right, Mr. Detective, what else does the coat tell you?"

He was grateful for the return to the pragmatic world and focused his concentration on her question. "Let's see. My guess is that it cost more than a waitress makes in a month, so I suspect either a rich boyfriend or a high-paying job."

She'd recovered from the intensity of their silent exchange and could laugh again. "Or a pinched budget."

"I see. But then, that wouldn't fit in with what I sense of your character. Reverent, brave, thrifty—"

"You forgot clean."

"And clean. Definitely clean. And perfumed. My guess is you held a professional position on the mainland."

She nodded. "I have a degree in aeronautical engineering. I worked for Boeing." She gave a small laugh. "Doesn't everyone who has a degree in aeronautical engineering work for Boeing?"

"My God, I am impressed." He stared at her, taking in this new dimension of her. "How'd you manage that? The schooling, I mean. You said things were tough here on the Island."

"Ben Murdock. He's set up full scholarships for any Islander's child who wants to go to college. That and a couple of waitress jobs saw me through."

"And after all that work, you gave up engineering to come back here?"

She chose her next words with care. "I guess I found out what Grace found out when she was off the Island. I hadn't move up, I'd moved down. I felt a need to return to values I understood. And to people I've known since birth. There aren't as many unpleasant surprises that way."

"I have a suspicion that there are always unpleasant surprises along the way. It sounds like you've been badly hurt."

"No more so than anyone else." She hesitated, searching his eyes for understanding. "I guess I just took it harder, that's all."

"What happened?"

"He was a liaison engineer from Lockheed in

Southern California, assigned up here." She flushed, somewhat uncomfortable with the telling. "He gave me quite a rush. Really kind of swept me off my feet, I guess. Anyway, I fell in love. I thought we were serious. Unofficially engaged, I guess. Anyway, we went house-hunting, found the perfect place for us, which he bought in his name, and after he'd signed papers on it, he thanked me for all my help, and said he'd be away for the next week, moving his wife and family up." She swallowed hard, fighting to keep her voice level. "I was shocked, of course, and he was shocked that I was shocked. He didn't seem to realize that his being married changed everything. I told him I wouldn't see him again, that I was through, but he didn't believe me, and wouldn't accept it. He said he had no intention of giving me up. He saw nothing wrong with living with his wife and seeing me on the side."

She faltered to a stop, unshed tears glistening in her eyes. It was a moment before she regained her composure, then she tossed her head, her chin held at a proud angle. "That was on a Friday night," she said, her voice even again. "I came home here for the weekend and thought about it, and went back in on Monday and resigned. I forfeited two weeks' pay in lieu of notice, so I was gone before he returned. They play by different rules out there, and I decided I didn't want any part of it."

Paul reached out a hand and covered hers. "I'm sorry, Jenny," he said gently. "I'm sorry there are people like that in the world. But not all of them are, you know."

"I suppose."

"How long ago was this?"

"It's been a year now."

"They say it gets easier."

"They say it does. I don't think I quite believe that yet."

"I'm sure you don't. But you will."

She'd recovered some of her composure and was able to give a half-smile. "Now you sound like Grace."

He grinned. "That's about the highest compliment you could give me." He paused, wondering how she'd take the idea that had just popped into mind. "You know," he said tentatively, "I could teach you to play piano. Can you read music at all?"

"The treble clef. I took choir in high school."

"So you sing?"

The warmth and humor were back. "Dad says I sound like a frog having a hard day."

"Then we'll definitely skip the operatic studies. But I could teach you the bass clef for the piano. It's not hard. The bottom line's G and it goes up and down from there."

"What would I do for a piano? Yours are all missing their strings, I hear."

Her words shredded the fragile cocoon he'd wrapped around the two of them. He came back to reality with a crash. Back to the Coop, site of a noose in his closet, bones in his bed, and a body beneath the trapdoor.

Without thinking, he released her hand. "Grace would probably let you practice on hers," he said absently. What difference did it make if Jenny learned to play the piano or not? Or whether she'd been badly hurt by some first-class jerk or not? All he was, was the Piano Man, here to restore three instruments and then be gone. What the hell had he been thinking of? His first priority was to figure out what he was going to do the rest of his life. And in order to do that, he had to survive. That sure as hell took precedence over some dalliance that would never lead to anything anyway.

His mind focused on the problem at hand once again. "You knew Jason when he was young. What was he like?"

She considered the question seriously, looking a bit puzzled by the sudden shift of topic. "I'm not sure how to answer that. I'm not sure what you're looking for in an answer."

"I'm not sure either. From what I hear, he was pretty simple-minded. He operated more on an instinctive animal level rather than like a reasoning human being."

"Yes, that's true. Though he was affectionate and lovable. You didn't think of him as an animal. Just a little guy who didn't quite have all his marbles."

"Well, suppose someone on the Island's helping him. Feeding him, housing him—"

Her back went suddenly rigid. "What are you saying?"

"Well, you can't deny he's been lucky. These are experienced woodsmen hunting out there. If he has a hiding place, they'd have found it."

Her eyes grew huge. "That's a terrible thing to say," she whispered. "That would mean someone's condoning murder, and that simply cannot be!"

"All right, what do you think? What other explanation could there be for Jason's success in escaping us?" he asked mildly.

"Several that I can think of. I don't mean to hurt your feelings, but it's obvious you know nothing about these woods. I could be dressed in bright red, hiding in a thicket one bush away from you, and you'd never see me. Second, these 'experienced woodsmen,' as you called them, are babes in the woods compared to Jason. I mean that literally. He could lead you around your own backyard in ways you could only guess at. And third, to think of us Islanders being capable of condoning such a thing as murder—well, again, I don't want to hurt your feelings, but that shows just how little you understand us. We would honestly be incapable of such an action."

He thought a moment. "All right, supposing I accept your arguments. Then where do you think Jason is hiding?"

"I'm not sure I could even make a guess," she said slowly. "I guess if you have someone operating on animal instincts, you'd have to look at where animals hole up."

"A den, you mean? Like a fox?"

"Why not?" She glanced at her watch. "I've got to get back." She rose and plucked her coat off the chair. "I just know that you—all of you—have a long job ahead of you, ferreting him out. It isn't going to be easy, and it isn't going to be quick. I'm sure Jason's set himself up to keep himself fed, warm and dry, and that's going to increase your difficulties." Her voice gentled. "But the good news is, you've got time on your side. He doesn't."

She paused in buttoning her coat to smile down at him and the enchantment caught him once more. "It's the nice thing about the Island, there's always a tomorrow here." Then her tone lightened and her eyes softened, lit with the quiet humor he found so intriguing. "Any messages for Grace?" she asked.

He smiled. "How would she feel about working at the deli again? A full shift, every day?"

Blushing, she gave a small laugh. "I'll tell her you asked for some more blackberry cordial." With a final grin, she was gone.

He cleared away the dishes, then spent the afternoon working on the Old Soldier. As his skilled fingers trimmed, fitted and sanded replacement keys, his thoughts roamed over the whole of the Island—the people, the woods, the puzzle of Jason's hiding place. And Jenny. Especially Jenny.

Chapter Twenty-five

Bobbin was due to pick him up at six. At five, he stopped work for the day, cleaned up his mess, made a fresh pot of coffee for the thermos and fixed some thick meat sandwiches for supper.

The night outside was clear, the sky dazzling with hard brilliant stars. The thermometer read three above zero and he dressed as warmly as possible—two pairs of heavy socks, a long-sleeved undershirt, a cotton shirt, a flannel shirt on top of that, and a wool vest under his fisherman's sweater. He'd pull his heavy jacket on when Bobbin came. He set out a ski cap and his heavy work gloves.

It was only five-thirty when he heard an engine coming up the drive. It lacked the throaty roar of Bobbin's pickup. He glanced out the kitchen window and his heart sank. It was the Sheriff.

Quickly, he pushed the thermos, ski cap and gloves out of sight, grabbed the morning paper and a full cup of coffee and was sitting, reading, when the Sheriff knocked.

"Door's open," he called out.

The Sheriff entered, shivering from the sudden warmth. "Colder'n an iceberg out there. They say it's gonna get down below zero tonight. That'll set a few records around these parts." He sniffed deeply. "That coffee smells kind of good."

Resigned, Paul poured some out. "Aren't you doing rounds a little late today?"

"Oh, just nosing around. Last ferry's at six-thirty, so I still got time to chat a spell." The Sheriff helped himself to a chair and eyed Paul's clothes. "You look like you're headin' to the North Pole."

"I'm working up my courage for a walk. I try to go every night, but the weather's not cooperating lately."

"Takes a lot of gumption, a night like this." The Sheriff rose and wandered to the Old Soldier. "The new strings come in yet?"

"Any day now." Paul picked up a piece of dogwood and held it out. "Feel that."

The Sheriff ran a finger up and down its sides. "Slick as a car hood."

"That's rough yet." He turned on a work lamp. "It's cut from dogwood. If you hold it up to the light, you can see the pink of the wood."

The Sheriff held it close, turning it this way and that. "Sure enough. That's a good-looking stick. What're you using it for?"

"For the sharps." Paul took it from him and slid it into a blank place on the keyboard. The long end stuck out over the ivory keys. "I'll trim it off, sand it down and seal it, then slip it into place."

"Thought those were supposed to be black keys."

"They can be. I'd use ebony then. But the dogwood's just as good. And it'll look beautiful on the upright with its rosewood paneling."

The Sheriff peered down at the keyboard. "You gotta do each one of those like that?"

"Yep."

The Sheriff shook his head in amazement. "The patience it must take."

"You have to enjoy the process. If you try to hurry to get it done, you'll end up frustrated."

"Sort of like a murder investigation."

"Well, yes, I guess." Paul turned off the work lamp and ushered the Sheriff back to the kitchen, sneaking a glance at the clock as he went past. Almost six. He prayed Bobbin would be late just this once. Not much chance, though. The man was as prompt as Sunday morning church bells.

The Sheriff escaped Paul's escort to the kitchen and veered off towards the trapdoor. "Nailed her down, I see."

"Keeps the rats out."

"You wired closed the skylight, too, I noticed. With that new deadbolt in place, it's as safe as a jailhouse in here."

"It seemed the prudent thing to do."

"Yep, I'd say so." The Sheriff finished off the last of his coffee standing, then smacked his lips and set the cup down. "Anything special prompt all these prudencies?"

Paul grinned. "Just my cowardly soul."

"And a devotion to continued life, eh?" The Sheriff grinned back and clapped him on the shoulder. "Well, guess I better mosey on down to the ferry dock. Wouldn't do to get stuck on the Island all night. Thanks for the coffee. It chased the chill from my bones clear to the other side of summer."

Relieved, Paul nodded.

The Sheriff paused at the door. "And you're sure

everything's okay? That there's nothing that needs to be talked about?"

"I'm sure."

"Good." The Sheriff's big hands swallowed up the doorknob. "By the way, those bones Old Jeb gave me . . ." His face was bland. "Any idea where they might've come from?"

Paul scraped up an innocent tone of voice. "Bones? What bones?"

"Just some old bones Jeb found someplace in his wanderings. He asked me to find out what kind of bones they are, so I've sent them on to the state lab for analysis. We should hear back in a few days." The Sheriff gave a single nod. "Well, as long as you're all right, good night now. Enjoy your walk," he added gently.

Paul was openly sweating as he closed the door behind the Sheriff. Cat and mouse, cat and mouse. And the Sheriff was just too good as the cat.

He poured the last of the Sheriff's coffee into the sink, then sat at the table with his own cup, listening. The sound of the Sheriff's car died away in the right direction for the ferry dock. Then there was only silence. A cold, brittle silence. He glanced at the clock. After six. God had answered his prayers. For the first time since Paul had known him, Bobbin was late.

He drank his coffee and waited. Ten past six. Quarter past. Twenty past. At six-thirty, he decided he'd misunderstood and he was supposed to meet Bobbin at the woods. He retrieved his things from under the sink, pulled on his ski cap and gloves and picked up the thermos and the flashlight. He made sure the door was locked behind him.

The cold was harsh, ice-edged and bitter. It penetrated his jeans immediately and wormed its way through the layers of chest clothing seconds later. By the time he hit the bottom of the driveway, the pain of ice-fire filled his lungs with every breath.

The dark night spread out around him. In spite of the clear sky, there was no moon yet, and the firs towered into the sky like a tangle of black monoliths. An occasional branch cracked in the frozen air. Otherwise, it was all silence.

There was enough starlight to see by, but when he turned onto the trail, the woods closed it out and he had to use his flashlight.

There was no sign of Bobbin's truck, and for a moment he wondered if the hunt had been called off again. The cold was ferocious and certainly reason enough. But wouldn't someone have let him know?

The wheelbarrow was there, about a quarter-mile in. No chainsaws, though. He stopped and called out Bobbin's name, then listened.

Silence.

He shouted again.

A tree limb cracked. Then more silence.

He was undecided. The dangers of the night seemed overwhelming. His instincts screamed to get the hell out of there.

A tree limb creaked again. From the same direction, way down the trail.

It was just the cold. The cold froze moisture in the limbs, the limbs swelled and expanded, the bark cracked open. It was just the cold.

The crack came again. Same direction.

He sighed. What the hell, it was only a few minutes' walk to the end of the trail they'd cut. Might as well check it out. Brave talk, for he had to stifle his fear and give his feet orders to move.

He took it a step at a time, pausing to swish the flashlight over the brush on either side. He stayed light on the balls of his feet, fully expecting something to jump out at him, prepared to defend himself if it did. Heart hammering wildly, he reached the solid wall of trees where they'd been forced to make a right-angle turn, and paused.

The creaking sounded again, clearer now. He used the flashlight to peer down the new path ahead.

Something shiny about waist high reflected back, then was gone.

He hesitated, his light still trained in that direction.

It winked again.

He took a step forward.

Another wink. Another step. He could barely make out something dark beyond the wink.

Another step closer and an outline began to form. Another step. It looked like a shoe dangling from a shrub.

Why would a shoe be caught in the underbrush that way?

He swung the light up to see what held the shoe trapped so high. It took him a moment to realize he was looking at a leg. A human leg. Someone's leg.

He stared at it blankly a long moment while the meaning penetrated to his brain, then slowly raised the flashlight up. Up over the hips, up over the stomach, up over the stilled chest until it reached the face.

Bobbin hung from a tree limb, a length of insulated electrical cable twisted into a noose around his neck.

Under the dead weight of the body, the tree limb cracked again.

Chapter Twenty-six

Choppers and barges shuttled back and forth between the mainland and the Island, bringing the Sheriff, his men and their equipment. Portable floodlights bounced off the forest walls and illuminated the road, the trail and the body. A work area at the road was cordoned off. Beyond it, the Islanders gathered, standing in somber groups, more and more arriving as the word spread of Bobbin's death.

The Sheriff, his car not there yet, borrowed Tom's pickup and led Paul to it, turning the motor on to heat the stone-cold cab.

Paul shook everywhere. He crossed his arms hard across his chest and pressed his knees tight together in an attempt to stop it. His muscles hurt from the tension he exerted over them. And he felt tight, brittle. If someone said "Boo," he'd fly apart.

Hall studied him a moment, grunted and climbed out. A minute later, he reappeared with a thermos and a flask. He mixed some of the contents of both together and handed it to Paul. "Coffee and brandy. Drink up."

Paul's hand shook so badly he spilled some on his jacket before he could get it to his lips. He took a gulp, kept the cup pressed against his mouth to prevent further spillage, then gulped some more. The warmth hit his stomach like a shotgun explosion. The fiery liquid butted up against stomach muscles tightened into a ball and a battle of nausea swept over him. Then the brandy did its work. Its fire ran through his veins, easing muscles and stilling the tremors. He up-ended the cup and emptied it.

The Sheriff rolled down his window and beckoned to a deputy. He spoke in an undertone, pointing to Abner and a few of the other Islanders. Then he rolled up the window and put the truck in gear. "Your place is closest. We'll head on there."

"No," Paul said sharply. "I need to go to Jenny."

"Grace Duncan's taking Jenny home with her. And Zeke's gone to be with Thaddeus."

"Then they know."

"Yes, they know."

Paul leaned back against the seat and closed his eyes against it all.

Once at the Coop, the Sheriff took over the kitchen, putting on some coffee and tossing a log into the wood stove. Then he led Paul into the studio, sat him on a piano bench and moved to the Old Soldier, where he leaned an elbow on its top, studying him. "All right, before the others get here, tell me one more time."

"Bobbin was supposed to pick me up at six," Paul said in a dead voice. "When he didn't get here, I finally walked down to see if I had understood wrong and was supposed to meet him. I followed the trail in, and found him. That's it, that's all I know."

"What made you go down that trail? The Island's full of them. Why that one?"

"That's where we were supposed to meet."

"But why there?"

The impact of the question slowly permeated the fog around him. He straightened then, paying more attention to what he was saying. "What do you mean, why there?"

"I mean just what I said, why there? Why were you supposed to meet him there?"

"I—I—" Paul's brain was still too thick with fog to think. He finally gave it up and shrugged.

The Sheriff studied him. "All right, let's try the wheelbarrow. Why was there a wheelbarrow in there?"

"Uh—they were doing some clearing. I guess it was to take the brush out."

"Why were they clearing it?"

"I don't know, I'm not sure."

"Was that what drew you down the trail, the wheelbarrow?"

Paul sensed a trap, but wasn't alert enough yet to know what it could be. He hesitated, hoping the Sheriff would tire of waiting and move on to something else. But the Sheriff outwaited him, and finally he sighed. "I guess."

"What was it about the wheelbarrow that attracted your attention?"

"Well, nothing. It wasn't the wheelbarrow by itself. It was Bobbin I was looking for."

"And the fact that the wheelbarrow was probably used to cart his body there had nothing to do with why you picked that particular trail to walk down."

"Well, no. I didn't give it much—" Paul straightened. "What do you mean, it was used to cart his body there?"

"My guess is, he was killed first, and strung up

second. There's a layer of piano wire under the noose."

"Oh my God." Paul stared at the Sheriff for a long moment before his gaze drifted off into the distance. Strangling Bobbin first, then stringing him up, made it seem like killing the same man twice. Murder twice over, he thought. It was ghastly.

The arrival of Abner and some of the others stopped the questioning. Paul was extremely grateful for that. He sank back against the Chickering behind him, letting his shoulders slump in grief and fatigue.

Abner, Calvin, Tom and Old Jeb came in together. The Sheriff stood, large and flat-footed, in the center of the studio, hands on hips and studied each of them. Without speaking, he indicated the other two benches and motioned for them to sit down.

The Sheriff waited until they were all settled, then stared a long moment at each of them. The familiar blandness that cloaked his thoughts and feelings was gone. His arms were crossed, his jaw clenched tight, his blue eyes an angry cold in their cage of wrinkles. "All right, I want to know what's going on. Why are there trails being cleared, and why was Mr. Piano Man here supposed to meet Bobbin there?"

Absolute silence greeted his question. Frank let it build, boring in on first one man, then another. The men avoided looking at each other, finding various places around the studio for their eyes to rest. Even Abner, normally given to stroking his beard when he was thinking, sat with the stillness of a statue.

Frank let the tension mount before finally speaking. "All right, then, let me start with some easy ones. When's the last time any of you saw Bobbin?"

The men exchanged glances.

Tom spoke first. "Last night. Here."

The others nodded.

"He wasn't at breakfast with you this morning, then."

Abner shook his head. "Breakfast was—disorganized this morning. Some who normally are there, weren't. Just one of those days, I guess, where everyone scattered in separate directions."

"To do what?" the Sheriff snorted. "Clear trails?"

Another silence was building, and the Sheriff just let it, probing each man with angry eyes in turn. Paul had the feeling the Sheriff was barely keeping himself under control, as if there was a volcano ready to erupt from the depths of the massive mountain of a man.

Finally the big man sighed. "You've been ducking me, misleading me, avoiding me, thinking you could handle whatever's going on all by yourselves, thinking I'm too stupid to notice you've been playing with me. Now, by God, one of your own's been hit. This isn't some stranger like the first Piano Man, where you're not really involved. Or a drifter like Walter Gibbons, who comes from God knows where, then disappears back there again at regular intervals. No, by God, this time it's one of your own who's been murdered. So now the question is, are you gonna give me credit for having a smattering of smarts and let me in on what's going on? Or are you gonna stall around and let some more killings take place before you decide to speak up."

Tom Ross fixed worried eyes on the Sheriff. Old

Jeb pursed his lips. Calvin's glower deepened. After a moment, all three looked over at Abner.

The old man sat alone on a piano bench set off to one side. His head was hunched over his barrel body, his gaze aimed toward the floor. As the silence stretched on, he rubbed his eyes with a thumb and forefinger. Finally, he nodded. "I guess we've taken it about as far as we can." He straightened up and looked at Hall. "It's Jason Murdock. He's the one you want. And he's out there, hiding in the woods somewhere."

"You'd better tell me about it."

Abner did, his voice filled with despair. He went back twenty years, beginning with the disappearance of Ilsa and its effect on Jason, and brought it up to present day. The only thing he omitted was his suspicion that Jason had killed his brother, Obadiah. Since neither pianos nor piano wire was involved in his death, it couldn't be totally discounted as an unfortunate accident.

The telling took the better part of an hour. As Abner spoke, the Sheriff showed no surprise. He even nodded a few times, as if beliefs of his own had been validated. But he asked no questions, letting the old man tell the story in his own way without interruption.

When Abner was through, silence overtook them again.

The Sheriff finally broke the stillness. "That the way you know it?" he asked Paul.

Paul thought back. Abner had pretty well covered all of it. Aside from Obadiah's death, the only other thing omitted was Paul's conversation with Bobbin the previous night. And he wasn't about to bring that up with the rest of the men—particularly Tom—sitting in the room with him.

The Sheriff waited, his eyes shrewd on his.

Paul nodded.

"How'd you learn the story?"

"Abner. Abner and Ben Murdock. They told me."

The Sheriff snorted with disgust. "So you all decided you could keep it in the family and handle it yourselves. Turned out to be a sorry decision, didn't it." He surveyed them once again as a group, still visibly angry. "Well, no more solos, understand? We'll get a hunt going and we'll get him found. But I'm taking over from here, I'm in charge. Got it?"

Abner nodded agreement. "There's one thing, though, Frank. Ben's afraid some harm will come to Jason in the catching of him."

"It's possible. Not likely, but possible. We'll do what we can to protect him. You gonna call Ben and tell him about Bobbin? Or you want me to?"

"I'll do it. It'd be best if he hears it from me."

"Okay, I'll get my men organized and the search underway. Tom, my car should be on the Island by now. I'll take your pickup down to get it, then send yours back with a deputy."

At Tom's nod, the Sheriff strode out. His footfalls were heavy and formidable as he crossed the planked floor, and again Paul was struck by the pure massive size of the man. Now that he was taking charge, however, there was comfort in his hugeness.

Silence engulfed the men as Tom's pickup roared to life outside, then faded into the distance. Abner moved first, his body slow and ponderous. "Best get that call made."

"I'll go with you." Calvin's voice was thick, obscured by sorrow. His normal dark spirit had blackened and he seemed sunk beneath the weight of his grief.

At the door, Abner turned to Paul. "You still game to clear trails?"

"I thought the Sheriff was taking over."

"He'll need the help."

"After what the Sheriff said, you're still going to keep going?"

"The way I see it," Abner said slowly, his eyes taking Paul's measure, "nothing much has changed. Jason's still out there somewhere, and he still has to be found. It doesn't really matter much whether it's the Sheriff and his men who do the finding, or Calvin and Old Jeb and the rest of us. It's the finding that's important. So the question is, are you still game?"

Paul was nodding before the old man was through speaking. "You bet I am."

"Good," Calvin growled, "good. You can team up with me, then."

Old Jeb had been silent throughout, deep in thought. Now he looked around in a vague way, not really seeing the rest of them. "I think I'll check on my Missus up to the house . . ."

Abner nodded. "What Frank said about not doing any solos . . . seems to me it'd be wise for any of us not to be alone. Jenny can stay on at Grace's and Zeke can stay with Thaddeus. And Paul, you better go back to bunking in at Tom's place."

"No," Paul said, shaking his head. "I've got my

work here. Besides, the Sheriff stopped by earlier and saw the wired skylights and the nailed-down trapdoor. He says it's as safe as a jailhouse in here. I'll be just fine."

Abner looked skeptical. "You sure?"

Paul nodded. The last thing Paul wanted was to be alone with Tom Ross. The image of the man approaching them last night as he and Bobbin talked about Jason was burned like an acid etching into Paul's memory. "I'm sure."

Chapter Twenty-seven

The little church in the clearing was full for Bobbin's funeral. Islanders jammed the pews and lined the back and side walls, and when it looked as if not one more person could be squeezed in, everyone moved closer still and made room.

The casket, closed, was set to one side of the pulpit, a single spray of deep red roses laid on top. Candles flickered in the dimness as soft organ music drifted down from the choir loft. Grace played a reputable Bach, Paul thought.

He stood in a rear corner of the church, well out of the way. Jenny sat in the first pew between her brother and Tom Ross. Thaddeus hunched forward, eyes aimed at the floor. Abner and Calvin sat next to him.

Just before the service started, the Sheriff arrived and stood beside him. Paul had not seen him since Bobbin had been found and he glanced at him curiously. "Found anything yet, any sign of Jason at all?"

The Sheriff sighed. "Nothing. Not a trace so far. It's slow going. I keep dreaming that he'll simply walk out of the woods and give himself up. I think it's called a pipe dream."

Grace pushed the volume of the organ high and the first notes of the opening hymn swelled.

The service was simple and brief. The minister, a

tall, lanky man, concentrated on the ascent of the spirit. Abner gave the testimonial. Thaddeus stayed hunched over, staring at the floor. Jenny held her head up, eyes fixed on the speakers, face composed. But from the angle of sight from where he stood, Paul could see an occasional tear slide down her cheek, and his heart ached for her.

After the final prayer, the Sheriff beckoned to him. "Need a ride to the cemetery?"

Paul hesitated. He'd planned to wait for Jenny. But when she and Thaddeus emerged, they were surrounded by friends. "Yes, thanks."

After the close, overheated air of the little church, the cold air was sharp and mind-clearing. The Sheriff's car was the first one at the cemetery, and he pulled off the circular drive at the top of the slope, well above the graveyard proper. By then, the cold had eaten its way into their bones and he let the engine idle to gain some warmth from the heater.

Bobbin was to be buried in the Webster family plot, next to his wife. The gravesite had been prepared and a heavy green cloth stretched over the planks covering the hole.

Paul fought back a sudden surge of despair. How could a fine man like Bobbin just be snuffed out that way? Grace was right. Life—and death—were bare bones on the Island.

The hearse glided up the road, leading a long line of mourners, and drove around the circle to the far side of the graveyard. The Islanders parked their cars and trucks off the shoulder of the driveway behind the Sheriff until it was full. The rest parked below and walked up.

Although inside the tiny church the crowd had threatened to burst its wall joints, in the cemetery there was more room to spread out and their numbers seemed sparse. It struck Paul how really isolated the Island was. Used to the massive crowds of the city, the university and various concert halls, the group here seemed a mere handful of people. Yet, he was sure everyone was present.

He ran his gaze over families standing together in somber groups, recognizing more than he'd have expected. Between the Pickup Brigade, the searchers gathering to eat in the deli and the shoppers wandering through the store, he'd seen most of them a time or two. A couple of dozen of the men were tall and lean, like the minister, and after he noted them, he wondered why he'd bothered noticing them at all.

The casket was set in place next to the green cloth. Abner and Grace guided Jenny to the graveside. Thaddeus followed, Tom and Zeke by his side. At the sight of the coffin ready for burial, Jenny's composure broke and she leaned suddenly against Abner, burying her head deep into his shoulder.

Paul couldn't bear to watch any more. He let his eyes roam the cemetery, forcing himself to notice mundane details in an attempt to keep himself under control. He counted headstones. Thirteen in one row, fourteen in another, six in a third down at the bottom of the slope. One headstone was crooked, probably from frost upheaval, and a second had been laid off-center. He counted level graves, most of them, then counted the humped—two. Only one grave was sunken.

When he'd noticed every single thing there was to

notice, his emotions had calmed to a slow simmer and he went back to scanning the crowd. Old Jeb stood to the rear, next to a tiny old woman, shrunken by age into a question mark, who must have been his Missus. Next to them, Ben Murdock stood quietly. His eyes looked sunken and weary, his face fallen into wrinkles of despair. He'd flown in to the Island as soon as he'd learned of Bobbin's death and word was that he was staying this time until Jason was captured.

Paul was too far uphill to hear the minister's words, but the crowd as one bowed their heads in prayer. After a moment, Thaddeus went over to the floral spray brought from the church and drew out two red roses. He gave one to Jenny, then offered his arm. They moved slowly up to the coffin. The two of them stood silent, staring down at the casket for a long moment, then each leaned forward to gently lay the rose on top of the plain varnished wood. The minister spoke a few final words and the services were over.

As the crowd began to mill around, the Sheriff sighed. "Damned shame. He was a good man."

Paul merely nodded.

"You going up to Grace's for some food?"

"I suppose."

"You okay?"

"Yeah, I'm okay."

❚

The gathering at Grace's was subdued. The men talked in quiet voices, marking time until politeness and duty had been served. They ate some food, drank their one drink, then looked at their watches and each other, anxious to be back at the search again.

The women stuck near Jenny, seeing to her needs. Paul managed to make his way to her once to express his sympathy. There was little to say except, "I'm sorry, Jenny, so very sorry."

"Thank you." Her face was pale and drawn, her voice faint. As quickly as the words were spoken, the next person in line pushed forward and her attention was forced onward.

Tom came to get him. "You planning on doing more piano work today?"

Paul glanced over at Jenny, where she stood with quiet dignity, then shook his head grimly. "No, let's get this bastard found."

Chainsaws sprang to life and their whine echoed night and day up and down the roads of the Island like a swarm of mosquitoes gone berserk. The Sheriff, short of men, had deputized the Islanders. Working over a map through the night of Bobbin's murder, Ben and Abner helping, the Sheriff had sectioned the Island and assigned pairs of searchers to clear out each parcel of wilderness. Once cleared, regular deputies would be sent in to search and secure it, then guards would be positioned to keep watch.

Grim-faced men bent willingly to the work, their saws screeching for vengeance. Each branch sliced from a trunk was one less screen to cloak the fugitive. Each thicket sliced at its roots was one less hiding place. Each fallen tree and dead log sawn into sections and carted off was one less hollow offering shelter.

After a couple of days, Paul returned to working on the Old Soldier with men posted in the woods around the Coop to keep watch, but at night he put in a full shift working with Calvin. By now, he'd learned his way around the woods and was able to translate different degrees of blackness into rocks, gullies, tree roots and rotting leaves and other small treasures the forest produced to trip the unwary. He bent his back to the work with the same passionate vengeance as the rest of the Islanders.

Whenever he had to follow a path carved deep into the forest, he'd tense with dread, wondering what awaited him this time.

By Thanksgiving, a good quarter of the Island had been cleared.

Still, Jason eluded them.

Chapter Twenty-eight

Thanksgiving Day dawned bright, clear and cold. A new storm front was building up off the coast of Washington, but it hadn't moved inland across the Olympic Peninsula yet and the high pressure system hovering above Puget Sound promised to hold for the day.

Dinner at Grace's was scheduled for four o'clock. Paul set the alarm clock at the Coop for early afternoon, so he wouldn't lose track of time while working. When it rang, he was just about through applying the first coat of varnish to the Old Soldier. He finished the last brush stroke, then backed off to examine the piano.

The keys were all in place now, the ivory a pearly-white against the pale rose tint of the dogwood sharps. The leg columns, sanded free of pits and gouges, rose with broad curves to support the keyboard case. Lighter curves climbed either side of the music rack, buffed to the smoothness of marble. And now, the varnish, glistening wetly, brought out the subtle grains and patterns of the wood. He'd known there was a handsome fellow underneath all the scarring and abuse, but the actual beauty of the instrument was breathtaking. He suddenly felt proud. Proud and deeply satisfied.

He kept his euphoria in check as he began to clean

his brushes with turpentine. One more week of light sanding between coats of varnish, then the piano would be ready for stringing and tuning. It might even be ready to play by Christmas, he thought, as he covered the varnish can and put it on the far side of the workbench. If only the damned strings would get here.

Tom was scheduled to pick him up at three for the ride to dinner at Grace's, but he was ready to leave an hour earlier than they'd planned. On impulse, he decided to walk. After working all morning among the odors of varnish and turpentine, he needed to breathe some fresh air. He left a note taped to the back door for Tom, turned the deadbolt and tested its security, then set off.

The air was cold, but not unbearably so. His stride was leisurely and he stopped now and then when something of interest caught his eye. Being cooped up with pianos during the day and attacking the woods at night had so narrowed his life that he'd forgotten how peaceful the forest could be when not viewed as the enemy. It was hard to feel any sense of danger with bright sunshine pouring down over the meadows. Darkness was Jason's ally, not daylight.

He was abreast now of the store. A CLOSED sign was hung on the front door, but Thaddeus's van was parked in front. Paul knocked on the plate-glass window.

Thaddeus was doing bookwork at the counter. When he looked up and saw who it was, he shuffled over and turned the key in the lock. His face had aged with sorrow and his eyes were ringed with black circles of grief. He managed only a slight smile of greeting. "I'm closed, Paul, I shut her down at noon for the holiday. But if you need something . . ."

"I saw your sign, Thaddeus. No, I don't need anything. I just wondered if Jenny'd like to walk down to Grace's with me."

"She's already there. I took her down to help with dinner as soon as we closed up."

"What about you? You about ready to go?"

Thaddeus glanced at his watch. "It's only a little after two. We're not eating till four and I need to finish up this bookwork. Unless you need a ride?"

"Nope, I'm fine. I'll see you there, then."

He headed north on the Eckenstam-Johnson Road. Pickup trucks began to pass him as the Islanders paused in their manhunt and headed home for holiday dinners. Paul recognized all the members of the Pickup Brigade now and exchanged waves with them as they went by. Abner and Calvin went past with Ben and Old Jeb just behind. All four had been invited to Grace's for dinner, but only Abner and Calvin had accepted. Ben wasn't in a mood to see anyone, so Old Jeb's Missus would be fixing a dinner for the three of them up at his place.

Ambling along, taking his time, Paul could hear the distant whines of chainsaws in the woods. The Sheriff's men would be working straight through their shifts as usual. The Islanders wouldn't have stopped either, if Ben hadn't insisted. He felt his son had caused enough grief on the Island without taking men from their families on a holiday. But the Sheriff had no such sensibilities. There'd be no holiday for his men.

Paul thought of a scared Jason, huddled somewhere in the cold. He'd be listening as the search grew closer, and Paul wondered if he was at all befuddled by the commotion going on. If he was as simple-minded as they said, he might not link his actions and the resulting search as a single episode of cause and effect. It was possible he was treating it like a lark, an advanced version of Hide-and-Seek. In any event, regardless of his thinking, there wouldn't be a holiday dinner for him either.

Paul strolled along the ribbon of road carved like a canyon through the walls of firs, the bold winter sun warming him through the woolen sports jacket he was wearing. As he followed the turn in the road leading east, he topped the last rise and, at the foot of the hill below him, an empty ferry dock stretched out into the glistening waters of the Sound. A sea gull made a lazy circle above the dock and drifted to a stop on one of the pilings.

A tremendous feeling of freedom swept over him as he stared at the calm and placid beauty of water and sky. In spite of the problems on the Island and the loss of Bobbin, life was pretty damned good. There were no demands on him beyond his daily work and the search at night. No longer was he pulled this way, then that, torn into bits and pieces that were handed over to the control and whims of others. Time had taken on a different meaning, stretching ahead of him in an unbroken flow instead of being chopped up into the abrupt segments of life in the city. Life was more of a whole here and he liked the feeling that gave him.

Then there was the Old Soldier. God, he was proud of it! Proud of the way it had turned out. He strolled down the hill and turned north on Larson Road. There was such a deep satisfaction in turning the ugly duckling of an upright into the beautiful swan it had become. Occasionally, in his concert years, one or another of his performances would be so inspired as to approach the lofty heights of art. It was a sensation like no other. The head spun with dizzy excitement, the heart pounded deep in the gut, and the eyes would close in pure gratitude to the gods. But no matter how he strained to hold on to the feeling and make it last, it was short-lived, fading soon after the last echoes of the music had died away.

But the Old Soldier! My God, the beauty of him! A solid, lasting testament to the rightness of things. Not the ephemeral feeling of a great performance, but a feeling that could be renewed merely with a glance. The Ephemera, he mused, newborn in the morning, adult in the afternoon, dead at nightfall. That was the life of the concert hall. Whereas what he was doing now seemed deep-rooted and permanent. He might die this evening, and his music would die with him. But the Old Soldier would live on. He now had a legacy to leave the world. It was this, he realized, that his father must have felt in his own work.

He'd have liked to have shown the Old Soldier to his father. Or to Bobbin. Both old men would've appreciated the time, care and work that had gone into re-creating its beauty, and that would've deepened the pleasure that much more. Suddenly, he missed Bobbin like crazy. If he could have found any of those missing piano strings to make the Old Soldier playable, he'd have dedicated a concert to his memory.

He stopped dead in mid-step. Strings! Why hadn't they uncovered Jason's cache of piano strings?

He did some mental arithmetic. Three strings per note, times eighty-eight notes, times three pianos—four, counting the church's—that was over a thousand piano strings missing. That was one hell of a lot of wire to store anywhere. Why hadn't any of it been found? He resumed walking, his mind intent on the puzzle.

He was ready to turn into Grace's driveway when Tom's pickup drove up and stopped. He glanced at his watch. Three-fifteen. Normally, it was only an hour's walk from the Coop to Grace's place. This time it had taken better than an hour and a half. He'd really dawdled. Paul had deposited the promised case of wine in Tom's pickup the day before, and he unloaded it to present to Grace.

Inside the house, the two men were welcomed effusively by Grace and given a quiet greeting by Jenny. Like her brother's, her face was pale and her eyes were sunken into the center of dark circles of fatigue. She looked as though she hadn't slept much since her father's death. She took their coats and hung them up while Grace set Tom to fixing drinks, then retreated to the kitchen. Shaking her head in sad dismay, Grace hurried after her.

Tom surveyed the bar that had been set up to one side and lifted a bottle of liquor. "Wouldn't you know. Wild Turkey."

"God save us all," Paul sighed. "Well, dump mine over a couple of ice cubes and drown it with ginger ale." He carried his glass over to the hearth and absently stared at the fire, his mind grappling with the mystery of the missing strings.

Thaddeus arrived next. He mumbled a hello, accepted a drink, then moved to the couch, sinking into a stupor of grief. Paul was tempted to go to him, but Tom caught his eye and shook his head. Instead, they stayed by the hearth, discussing aspects of the manhunt in quiet tones.

Abner and Calvin didn't get there until almost four. They came separately but within minutes of each other. Paul waited until the welcomes were over and they had drinks in their hands, then beckoned them to the hearth to join Tom and himself. Thaddeus remained slumped on the couch, not noticing them.

In a tone low enough that Thaddeus wouldn't hear, Paul brought up his question of the piano strings and their whereabouts.

Abner frowned, his face puzzled. "I sort of assumed they were just a handful or so. Like twine. How large a bulk are you talking about?"

"In aggregate, maybe a trunkful. Split up, a couple of small cartons, maybe three. It's not a huge amount, not a warehouseful, but they have to be somewhere."

"What about the woods?"

"You mean randomly scattered under a bush somewhere? Or buried in a hole in the ground?" Paul shook his head. "I shouldn't think so. Jason would want them near and accessible. And dry, too, I should think. No, they almost demand a shelter of some kind."

Tom gave a heavy sigh. "Every damned place we

boarded up had cartons stashed away. In basements, in attics, in lofts, in closets. They could be anywhere. You mean we'd have to open up every one of those damned places and go through them from top to bottom again?"

A new thought struck Paul. "Maybe that's why electrical cord was used on Bobbin. Maybe there wasn't enough piano string under it to support the weight of a body. Maybe we've cut Jason off from most of his source, and that's why he used the cord."

"Well, that's both good news and bad news," Abner said wearily.

"Would he have gotten rid of them?" Tom asked. "Just tossed them out after using them on Harrison?"

"What about the ones missing from the church piano? That happened after I got here, long after Harrison was dead."

"Maybe that's why he took them," Tom said. "He killed Harrison, got rid of the strings, then decided he needed some after all, and helped himself to the church's."

"Then why use electrical cable on Bobbin?" Paul thought a minute. "In fact, why swipe the cable at all?"

Abner turned to Calvin. "What do you think?"

The old man glowered. "I think we've got a major problem here. I think they're in a carton or two in somebody's summer house, that's what I think."

Abner pondered it. "Then the question is, do we search every carton in every house, or do we let it go, figuring we've cut him off from his source of supply?"

Tom sighed. "I hate to think of all the unboarding and reboarding we'd have to do."

Jenny and Grace appeared at the door with platters of hors d'oeuvre.

"Let's think on this through dinner," Abner said in an undertone. "We'll talk some more on it later on."

When Grace herded them to table, Paul surveyed the feast. A beautifully roasted turkey took center stage, surrounded by bowls of sage dressing, mashed potatoes, peas-and-onions, cranberry sauce, two different kinds of squashes, relishes and a huge basket of homemade yeast rolls. The aromas brought back pieces of his childhood, his mother and the other women laughing and chattering in the kitchen, his dad sprawled on the sofa, in easy conversation with the men. He smiled at Jenny across the table. A traditional Thanksgiving, he thought. Normal Rockwell personified.

Chauvinistic, Anna snorted in his mind.

Irritated at the sudden thought, he bowed his head for grace.

Abner's blessing was brief. "Thank you, Lord, for the bounty on this table, and we promise, no complaints. Amen." Then he concentrated on carving the turkey and the food was passed and served.

Conversation was awkward at first. Bobbin's ghost sat with them, and Jenny and Thaddeus were obviously struggling with internal battles of grief. Grace, usually such a face-up-to-the facts person, became flustered for a moment. To cover up the awkwardness, she chattered on about mundane things—the squash wasn't as good that year, didn't they think?—until finally Abner set down his fork and glared at her.

"No sense in pretending, Grace, we're all missing Bobbin." He indicated the lavish spread. "Bobbin would've loved all this. You know how his appetite was." He turned to Paul. "He was the only man I knew who could down three platefuls of food and lose two pounds in the process. Why, I remember one time . . ." And he was off and running with a story of Bobbin's legendary eating capacity.

One reminiscence led to the next. There was gentle laughter at the memory of an eight-year-old Bobbin swiping and hiding a whole Thanksgiving pumpkin pie. He'd successfully averted suspicion from himself, only to discover later that night that his dog had had a Thanksgiving treat of his own. He'd blown his secret by running to his mother in tears. At the end of the tale, Jenny laughed softly with the rest, then she blinked back a sudden surge of tears.

Grace, now back in control, would have none of it. She took charge of the conversation and changed the topic immediately. "Moving from Thanksgiving past to Christmas future," she said, "the Island Christmas Fair is a week from this coming Saturday and we need to get the tables and booths and display boards set up at the clubhouse. Tom, I've been thinking you and some of those cohorts of yours could see to the planking and sawhorses for the tables. Calvin, you and Abner can truck some of the craft things down for the various ladies. Jenny's taking charge of the bake sale. And, Paul, since you won't have anything special to do, you just plan on helping me tote poinsettias early that morning. Thaddeus, of course, will have to tend the store, but he could lend Paul his van, couldn't you, Thaddeus."

Paul shook his head. "Nope, Thaddeus, I just wouldn't feel right borrowing your van."

For the first time, a touch of his old good humor flashed in his eyes as Thaddeus saw the distressed look covering Paul's face. "Don't give it a second thought, Paul. I lend my van to some poor beleaguered soul every year for those poinsettias. It's only right and proper I make some contribution, after all."

Tom turned to Paul. "I think that's a long-winded way of saying, You've been had, Dad."

Abner nodded gravely. "I do believe you're on the hook, Paul. If it's any consolation, we've all been there. And if you'll take a tip from this old hand, while you're at the Fair, you'll scout the territory and choose your own poison for next year."

"Don't bother, Paul," Grace said. "I shanghai whoever pleases me. This year, you do, and if that's so next year, you do then, too."

"I'm not sure why," Paul said, "but somehow I don't feel quite as honored as I probably should."

"You're just not appreciative of opportunity, you mean," Grace snapped back.

Jenny giggled, her eyes filled with a sudden merriment as they found Paul's. For that brief second of time, they connected through her grief across the space of the table, and he was shocked to find that his heart had leaped like a schoolboy's.

The teasing went on, and Paul listened idly to the easy ebb and flow of the talk for a few minutes before his listening sharpened. His sense of hearing, conditioned by years of music, had been honed into a conduit that could damn near hear a tuning A before the fork was struck, and he picked up the noise of a heavy hummingbird coming toward the Island.

Of the group at the table, he'd heard it first. But as the thrumming grew louder, they all looked upward, as if they could see through the shingles into the sky.

"That's a chopper," Grace murmured.

"It's coming for someone," Jenny whispered. "Oh, God, maybe they've found Jason."

"Maybe it's just the Sheriff," Paul said lightly, "on his way to cadge a drumstick or two."

"Did I tell you I invited him to dinner?" Grace said calmly. "He's been divorced for years, you know. But he declined. I even told him who'd be here, and he still turned me down." Her attempt at lightness was lost beneath the tension of hard listening.

The chopper flew towards them. It came in low, skimming treetops, a thundering machine shaking earth and house, making the blood pound in sympathy with the pulsations. Then it was over and past, curving beyond them to the southwest. The vibrations faded, the noise died off and silence engulfed the house again.

They waited, trying at first to keep a conversation going, then one by one falling silent until the only sound in the house was the mournful dirge of the chainsaws coming from the woods.

Within minutes, they heard a truck pull up out in front. Abner went to open the door and when he returned, Old Jeb and Ben were behind him.

The three men stood behind Abner's empty chair

at the foot of the table, their faces grim. Their eyes sought out Paul's.

When Ben spoke, his tone was gentle, his face full of sympathy. "It's the Coop, Paul." He immediately held up a hand as instant panic climbed within Paul. "Now, it could've been a lot worse. There was some damage done, but not as much as could've been. The Sheriff's there now."

"What? What was done?"

Ben was reluctant. He looked at Old Jeb for reassurance, then back to Paul, and said the word he dreaded hearing most. "Fire."

Chapter Twenty-nine

Paul had envisioned the Coop as a total loss, with walls burned down to the studs and charred rafters open to the sky. But the building itself was basically intact. The back door swung loose on broken hinges where Old Jeb, in a miracle of strength, had broken through. One of the Sheriff's men was examining the lock as Paul arrived.

The Sheriff met Paul in the kitchen, his face reflecting the same sympathy that Ben's had. "It could've been worse, Paul." He led the way into the studio.

The air was thick with smoke, and the smells of turpentine, varnish and charred wood wrapped themselves into one sharp, acrid odor that assaulted him. His nostrils stung, his lungs hurt when he breathed, his eyes burned and his stomach knotted tight into a nauseated fist.

As he moved forward, the further reaches of the studio began to emerge from the smoky haze like some surrealist painting. At first glance, it appeared all smoke and no damage. The rafters were untouched, the roof was in one piece. With the skylights wired shut, the harsh, pungent burning odors had no way to escape, and they hung over everything.

Relieved that the studio was untouched, he turned

his attention to the pianos. They seemed to be all right. The Old Soldier stood angled in towards the middle, where he'd left it that afternoon. The baby grand stood farther off to one side and looked all in one piece. The Lady had the back rear corner to herself and sat placidly amidst the haze.

Then he saw a blackened, mountainous heap on the floor next to the Old Soldier's end panel. He stared at it for a full moment before he realized it was his bedding, tumbled into one massive bundle. He took a closer look at the Old Soldier in the thick haze and his heart sank.

The flames had feasted on the wet varnish, eating their way up one side, across the music rack and up the curved columns to the top. In some places, the veneer was gone, exposing blackened wood. In others, where the flames had skipped parts of the finish for their own insane reasons, the veneer was blistered and coming away in peels. Blackened keys marched across the piano like a mouthful of rotting teeth.

He stayed put until he'd absorbed the worst of it and had himself firmly under control. With as much detachment as he could manage, he toured the other pianos, assessing them for damage. They'd been untouched.

He examined the floorboards next to the Old Soldier where the bedding was piled. The fire had carved a pit in the wood, but the sheer thickness of the planking had prevented it from going through. The planks were probably strong enough to support the weight of the upright, he decided, so there was no immediate danger of the upright falling through. Still, they'd have to be replaced. He wasn't ready yet to deal with the details of the damage to the Old Soldier.

Tom had been hovering nearby, tactfully giving Paul his privacy, but ready to be of help if he could. He moved to his side now. "You gonna be okay?"

Paul nodded.

"You better plan on bunking at my place for a few days. I'll give you a ride up there when you're ready. Now, I'm gonna check things out." He indicated the scorched floorboards.

Paul nodded again, then turned to locate Frank Hall, who was talking quietly with Abner and Ben. Calvin and Old Jeb stood with them. The discussion halted as Paul approached. He zeroed in on the Sheriff. "If I can interrupt a moment, I'd like to hear what happened."

"We won't know for sure until the arson folks get through. But it's pretty straightforward from what I can see. Wood was piled next to the upright over there, some live coals from the stove were scattered over the wood, and the turpentine and varnish cans were piled on top. A simple operation with a built-in delay."

"What about the bedding? Where does that come in?"

"Old Jeb used it to beat out the flames and smother the coals."

Paul spoke as if Old Jeb wasn't in the area. "How'd he come to find the fire?"

Hall turned to the old man. "Jeb?"

"We was up to Ben's, fixing dinner, and the Missus forgot to bring her turkey platter. We came on down to get it, and on the way back, I thought I saw some smoke drifting around this end of the Coop. Thought I'd best check it out."

"My God," Paul breathed, "a forgotten turkey platter."

The old man nodded. "I can tell you I was mighty put out at having to run all the way home for a plate just to hold some turkey. Ben must've had a couple of dozen big platters that would've done. Leastways, in my book. But nope. Nothing would do but it had to be 'The Platter.'" His face screwed up in wrinkled astonishment. "Guess I won't complain again."

"How'd you get in?"

"Busted through the door. You could see smoke edging out of those skylights up there, so I didn't waste no time. I went straight for the woodpile outside and grabbed the heaviest log I could heft and just battered my way through. Don't even remember how many times I hit it, but it didn't take a whole bunch." He glared at Paul. "'Course, if'n you'd've listened to me, you'd have had a turn knob on the inside of that deadbolt, just like I suggested. Then I could've just broken the glass and reached in and turned it. Would've saved some wear and tear."

"A turkey platter," Paul repeated once more, still awed. Sudden affection for the crabby old man welled up, for caring enough to both use super-human strength in getting through that door to save the Coop and for lecturing him on the lock afterward. He turned to the Sheriff. "How did he"—he indicated the charred bedding—"whoever . . . get in?"

"The arsonist? Far as we can tell, he walked through the door as if he owned the place. You happen to walk off and leave it unlocked today?"

"No. I know I locked it. I tested it before I left. Besides, if I had left it open, how would he have locked it up without the key?"

"Good point. How many keys are out?" The Sheriff looked around the circle. "Any of you got one?"

Ben nodded. "I do. And Jeb has one, too."

The Sheriff took Ben first. "You still got yours?"

"I'll have to check. It's in the desk at the big house."

"Do that. And Jeb? Where's yours?"

"Should be on a hook by the back door."

"You sure it's there?"

"Should be."

"By your back door, huh? You and the Missus been spending most of your time up to Ben's. You keeping that door locked while you're gone?"

The old man looked defiant first, then sheepish. "Never been a need."

Nobody put it into words, but the implications were clear. If Jason had a key to the Coop, he'd have a warm, cozy place to hide in every time Paul was out.

Hall shook his head in exasperation. "You check that key out, Jeb. Maybe it's still there. If it is, see if it's been moved or anything. Maybe put back in the wrong order or something."

"I'll go now."

"You go with him, Ben. Look for your own key, too." He pointed to Calvin and Abner. "And you two, each of you go with one of them and stick with him. I don't want none of you wandering around alone."

When the men had left, the Sheriff studied Paul,

measuring his control. When he was satisfied, he said, "That piano was pretty far along, last time I saw it."

Paul nodded bleakly. "I just finished putting the first coat of varnish on it today."

"What time did you get through?"

"About one. A couple of minutes afterwards."

"Then what?"

"I cleaned my brushes and capped the can of varnish and put everything against that far wall. I did not leave the stuff out by the piano, believe me."

"And then?"

"I showered and changed for dinner at Grace's. Tom was supposed to pick me up at three, but I was ready early, so I decided to walk. I left a note for him taped to the door, locked the place up and left."

"And what time was that?"

"Shortly before two. Maybe a quarter to. The General Store was closed when I got there, but Thaddeus was doing some bookwork. I stopped and asked him if he was ready to go on down to Grace's. But he glanced at his watch, said it was only a little after two, and he had time to finish up before dinner. The store's about a twenty-minute walk from here."

"What time was dinner set for?"

"Four."

"And Tom was supposed to pick you up at three?"

"Yes. We were to come for drinks anytime after three."

The Sheriff looked around. "Tom? See you a minute?"

Tom and Zeke had been pacing out the area around the blackened floorboards, carefully avoiding a coveralled man scraping charred wood into a glassine envelope. At the Sheriff's hail, Tom pointed an area out to Zeke, spoke a few words, then joined them.

"You come here today to pick up Paul?"

"Yep. We were supposed to ride down to Grace's together for dinner. But he'd left a note that he was walking."

"You see anything, hear anything, smell anything when you were here?"

Tom frowned. "No, and that's bothering me. I feel like I should've noticed something. But I didn't. The whole place seemed just like it always did."

"You didn't hear any brush crackling anywhere, like someone standing there watching you?"

Tom thought back, then shook his head. "Nope. Nothing."

"What time do you figure you got here?"

"Three, on the dot."

"You hang around at all?"

"Nope, I read the note and left."

"That would be about right, Frank," Paul put in. "Tom overtook me at Grace's driveway about three-fifteen. It's about a fifteen-minute drive."

The Sheriff thought a minute. "Let me ask you, Tom. If the fire was just smoldering, if it hadn't broken out into flames yet when you got here, would you have noticed it?"

"You bet. We're alert to fire around here. My God, Frank, look at this Island. It's all trees. You get a dry spell and one careless match, and this whole place's history. You bet I'm alert to fire."

"And you'd be able to detect the difference between the smell of a wood stove banked down for the day, and a pile of smoldering wood?"

"Well, now . . ." He thought about it, then nodded. "Yeah, I would. Somehow I would. We burn mostly alder and fir in the stoves. That has a different smell from building lumber. And my nose is pretty keen. Yeah, I'd be able to tell."

"And there was nothing at all about this place that set off any suspicion in you."

"Nope, nothing. There was no fire brewing when I came by." His tone was definite. "Have you searched the woods around here yet for some sign of Jason?"

"My men are out there now, circling the area."

Paul stirred, suddenly uneasy, but he couldn't decipher the cause of the feeling. He stayed silent.

The Sheriff caught the slight motion and raised a quizzical eyebrow.

Paul merely shook his head, shrugged, then asked, "Have you pinned down a time yet?"

"Old Jeb discovered the fire about five. My experts figure it was set somewhere an hour or two ahead of that. They'll be pinning down the time as they learn more, but for now, we're looking at the two-thirty to four o'clock time slot. Old Jeb drove down to his place about three. He passed Tom coming the other way, so the times all fit. And he didn't notice anything that first time by, either. So I figure we can narrow it down to between three and four. Once Jason was in the Coop, it wouldn't take long to set. No more than a couple of minutes."

Paul frowned. "Old Jeb went to his place at three, and came back at five? Two hours to pick up a turkey platter?"

The Sheriff grinned. "It was one of those marital things you had to be there to see. He was plenty put out at having to make the trip down, so he decided to make his Missus wait while he tended his animals, so he wouldn't have to come back this evening. But since he was making her wait, she took the opportunity to catch up on some things that needed doing in the house, and when he was through with his chores, she wasn't done with hers, so he still ended up waiting for her. Between the two of them, it took two hours to pick up the turkey platter."

The men on the key search returned. Ben had been successful. He held out a clear plastic sandwich bag to the Sheriff. "It was in my desk drawer where it was supposed to be. But just in case, I used tweezers to pick it up."

The Sheriff's eyes glinted with humor. "Thank you, Sherlock Holmes." Then he looked Old Jeb's way.

The old man looked plain mad. "'Tain't there, Frank."

The Sheriff's response was kind. "Don't feel bad, Jeb, that kid's running circles around all of us."

Old Jeb's face turned fierce. "He won't get in the place again."

Paul shifted his stance. The uneasy feeling was back. The feeling he was missing something, something that should be spotted. What the hell was it? He thought back, but couldn't identify anything that triggered it.

The Sheriff's eyes were on him again.

To avoid another question, Paul turned to Ben. "I haven't examined the upright thoroughly, so I don't know whether it can be saved or not. It could be it won't be worth salvaging, but I'd like to try. However, I think I ought to bow out of searching at night and move back in here full-time. This place shouldn't be left unguarded."

Ben hesitated. "I suppose. As far as the upright goes, we can just go ahead and scrap it. You've already spent so much time on it . . ."

"That's why I want to see if it can be saved. It looked absolutely stunning this afternoon, and if it's not structurally damaged, if the soundboard's all right, then it can be that way again. I'll know tomorrow."

Ben swept a hand around, indicating the Coop. "This place won't be fit to stay in tonight. The smell alone will keep you out. It's enough to make you sick to your stomach."

The Sheriff nodded agreement. "My men'll be working here most of the night, anyway. You sleep up at Tom's while the worst of the smell airs out. You'll need a new door, and a new lock, and those planks replaced in the floor over there. That'll take some time. But I definitely agree, the search is out for you from now on."

Abner nodded. "Yep, that's the best way. You leave the manhunt to us. Now, we'll go change out of our party duds and get back to it."

The Sheriff turned on him. "No, sir," he said flatly. "No searches tonight. My men are hunting in weird and wonderful places tonight and I don't want them mistaking you for their prey. You get a good night's sleep, all of you, and start in fresh in the morning. Paul, I'll give you a ride up to Tom's.

There's a couple of things about those pianos I need to ask."

"I'll tell Tom."

As Paul passed the charred area, there was no way to avoid looking at the Old Soldier. The sick feeling returned. God, he'd been so beautiful . . .

He concentrated on the task at hand. "Tom, the Sheriff's driving me up to your place, so I won't be needing a ride."

"Okay, then I'll run on down to Calvin's. He thinks he's got enough lumber stored in his shed to replace a hunk of the floor here. I'll check that out, and if he does, we'll get all the materials rounded up tonight. Then we can start right in to work here at first light."

"Thanks, Tom. I can't seem to do without your help these days."

"Just being neighborly." He looked at Paul quizzically, tilting his head in the Sheriff's direction. "Why's he driving you up there?"

Paul shrugged. "He wants to quiz me on pianos, he says."

Paul walked into the winter darkness outside, drawing in deep breaths of the fresh cold air, feeling nearly light-headed from the oxygen rush. The Sheriff was doing the same. A deputy had driven his car over on the last ferry and they climbed in.

Hall started it up and moved forward, then came to a dead stop at the top of the driveway, glaring at the steep grade down. "Two ruts and a hump. Ever hear of a grader?"

"I plan on selling white-water rafting tickets in the spring."

"Mud tobogganing'd be more like it." Hall shifted into low gear, his foot riding the brake. "Here goes nothing."

It was a painful, bone-jolting descent. At times, the front of the car slewed sideways, sending the headlights off into space, and whole sections of driveway were lost to the blackness. Oh, for a street lamp, Paul thought.

He held on tight, unconsciously flexing his muscles to help the car stay on course. "I'm glad Jason's found other things than killing me to keep him amused. With the way you're sliding down this hill, I'm not going to live long enough for him to bother with."

The Sheriff made some comment back, but Paul suddenly wasn't listening. He was focused on what he'd just said. Why had Jason stopped short of killing him? Granted, there was this attack on the Coop, and earlier, the bones in the bed. But neither were deadly. Yet he'd tried hard enough to kill him on the cliff that day. Wouldn't it make sense that if Jason had started out to do him in, he'd keep on until he succeeded? What had distracted him from his program? The need to kill Bobbin? Or was there something more, something else as yet unknown?

They finally rounded the bottom of the driveway and hit smooth pavement. The car purred along now, a cream puff. The Sheriff grinned. "Safe and sound, like a baby in swaddling clothes."

"Next time, remind me I know how to walk."

They rode in silence a while, then the Sheriff gave

a large shake of the head. "Paul, I feel just about as bad about that piano as you do. It's been a mystery to me how you transformed it from what it was to what it became. It was kind of like watching a stevedore turn into a preppie."

Paul gave him a curious look. "You've been fascinated with this restoration from the beginning. You planning on changing your line of work?"

"Sometimes I'd like to. But it wouldn't be to what you're doing. Window-washing, more'n likely. Nope, I guess mysteries just naturally get my juices going. Take yourself, for instance. In some ways, you're a mystery to me. A man never quite knows what you're thinking."

"One of Anna's favorite charges."

The Sheriff ignored his comment. "But I get a sense of you now and then. A fleeting glance, so to speak. For instance, I get the distinct impression that something's worrying you about this whole business with Jason."

"I'm just trying to save my skin."

The Sheriff eyed him blandly in the dim glow of the dash lights. "In addition to that. Something deeper."

Paul stared straight ahead, watching the headlights push back the night. The car turned onto Tom's road.

Finally, Paul came to a decision and straightened up. "Yes, there are a few things bothering me. Maybe it's because I've lived all my adult years in one city or another, and I don't know enough about the woods and nature to understand. Whatever the reason, let me ask you, how is Jason surviving out there?"

"What do you mean?"

He twisted in his seat to face Hall. "Let's assume, right or wrong, that Jason's found a hole in the woods that gives him shelter. And let's assume he's wearing enough warm clothes to keep from coming down with pneumonia. And let's assume he has a stash of food to see him through. Sometime, somewhere, he has to defecate. So far, no one's found a trace of his spoor. Either we're awfully dumb, or he's awfully smart."

"What're you suggesting?"

Paul peered a long moment at the other man through the dash glow. "Could it be he's being protected by someone on the Island? Housed in a basement or a loft or a woodshed somewhere?"

"You're thinking of Old Jeb's unlocked door."

"Sure, or any of a dozen others that are probably left untended simply because of habit. Frank, all we've checked are summer houses and weekend cabins. We've never searched the year-round places. We've never actually searched Abner's place, or Calvin's, or Zeke's—or even Ben Murdock's. Or, to get back to Old Jeb, he seemed to have some pretty strong feelings for the boy . . . would he be helping him out somehow?"

"A couple of weeks ago," Frank said slowly, "I'd have said yep, there'd be a good possibility of that. But since Bobbin's death, I'd say chances are slim. Bobbin was too well thought of and too well respected for any Islander to hide his killer now. No way could any of them justify doing something like that."

"So he's out there somewhere. A man who leaves no trace of himself."

"That's the thinking."

Paul sank back into his seat. That was the thinking. But somewhere the thinking was wrong. He was almost sure of it.

Chapter Thirty

The gathering storm along the Washington coast held off, strengthened, held off, strengthened again and still held off. It was as if the world had taken on the cold, deathly stillness of a crypt. For two nights and three days, the Islanders waited for the storm to break. At the Coop, the Pickup Brigade came and went. New floor planking replaced the charred boards and the harsh odors eased, finally drifting away on their own. Before the storm arrived, Paul was able to move back in.

When the storm hit, it hit hard. Driven by gale-force wind, the rain swept across the Island in knife-sharp sheets. The wind pounded against buildings in a fury, howling past corners and roaring across clearings. Branches cracked and crashed to earth. Trees toppled like wooden soldiers facing a firing squad. Old barns collapsed and shed roofs careened across field and meadow. Sleet and hail attacked everything like a mass of ice picks. The debris smashed up against trees and buildings in window-high trash drifts.

The manhunt was halted, school was cancelled, and the ferry stayed at home on the mainland. Old Jeb fought his way to his animals and bedded down in his barn. Thaddeus closed the store and moved into Grace's place along with Jenny. The Sheriff, trapped on the Island by the suddenness of the onslaught, holed up at Ben's place. The Island shut down completely to weather the onslaught.

Paul stayed alone in the Coop, the second new deadbolt tightly locked against the wild pummeling outside. Its rage suited him. The fury matched his own as he attacked the Old Soldier's injuries with the precision of a field surgeon. He had a supply of wood, veneer and ivory on hand and he worked around the clock, by electricity when he had it and lamplight when he didn't, pausing only for an occasional bite of food or a bit of sleep. When icy fingers of wind found their way in and defeated attempts by the wood stove to warm the place up, he simply put on more sweaters and kept working. He felt like some mad scientist, dashing from one task to another in an insane fury of activity.

The Old Soldier had lost one end panel and most of its veneer to the fire. Some of the ivory was beyond salvage and most of the dogwood sharps had been singed raw. But the intricate carvings of the legs and the music rack were untouched except for blistered varnish, and the flames hadn't had the chance to eat their way inward to the soundboard or the main frame of the instrument.

He sawed and stripped and sanded the wounds, then cut and measured and glued the grafts into place. The patches of new woods and fresh veneer showed up like white patches on a red jacket. He experimented with stains on the varying woods until he could bring the injured parts into harmony with the whole. He mixed and tested until he found exact matches and wiped on coat after coat. While each staining dried, he cleaned and repaired the keys, replacing burnt ivory and carving new dogwood pieces, working undisturbed. Even though the storm had forced the men watching the Coop to leave, he felt protected by the ferocity of the storm. No one could get to him and there was comfort in that. As long as the storm raged, he was safe. And as long as he was safe, he could work.

The storm lasted two full days and on through the second night. As dawn of the third day spread over the Island, the wind gave one final howl then moved on past. The sleet and hail turned first to a calmer rain, then eased up to a drizzle that eventually drifted to a stop. By the time the storm was over, Paul's own fury was exhausted. The piano was ready for varnishing once again and he felt back in control.

Wearily, he pulled on a jacket and went out to walk his land. A weak winter sun was edging up over Oro Bay. The now-placid waters were bathed in a soft reddish-gold light. In the distance, the snow-covered peak of Mount Rainier stood tall and proud, clearly outlined against a lightening sky, its new coat of white a rosy pink beneath the sun's slanted rays.

He stood quiet, watching sun and shadows play among the folds of the mountain, lost in the grandeur of the dawn, not thinking, simply absorbing it, pressing it into memory.

When the kaleidoscopic sunrise had finished its show, he began to circle the Coop, checking for storm damage. He'd lost some shingles and some of the siding boards had come loose. Flying branches had been caught against the stove pipe on the roof, creating a massive tangle of fir, alder and madrona.

Guy wires holding the freshly planted trees upright had bent or snapped and three of the trees had toppled. Several others were leaning precariously, dripping water from sodden limbs.

He rounded the final corner of the Coop and turned his attention to the driveway. The heavy rains had turned the hump into mud. It was one river of sludge now, littered with branches, rocks and missing shingles. In a word, impassable.

The field down by the road looked like a flea market sponsored by Mother Nature. Large fir branches heavier than a man could carry lay strewn like matchsticks. The new cable bringing power to the studio had snapped completely and both ends of wire lay a field apart in their own wind-whipped pattern. The cable to the kitchen was sagging heavily, but it had managed to hold together. At the bottom of the meadow, he turned to face uphill and surveyed the property as a whole. The damage, he supposed, could've been worse.

The slow chug-chug of Old Jeb's pickup sounded south of him. Paul watched as the old man zigzagged the truck through a maze of broken branches littering the road. A final swerve and he eased to a stop next to Paul.

"Mornin'," he grunted. "Started over a time or two to check on you. Couldn't make no headway against the force of the blow. You make out okay?"

"Not too badly. The Coop lost a few shingles and some of the siding's loose. Three of those young trees toppled over and there's a million branches down everywhere. And no light, of course. One of the cables has snapped. Otherwise, the Coop did fine. What about your place?"

"About the same. Lost a few shingles, a couple of trees, lots of branches, and the power. That's about it. Thaddeus should have the store back open by now. You going down to breakfast?"

"Nope. I'm not leaving the Coop unattended anymore. I've just finished repairing the damage from my last sabbatical and I don't intend having to do it again."

Old Jeb nodded. "You do what you gotta do. After we get a bite, we're gonna clear roads so the power trucks can get through. You should have electricity by the end of the day." With a wave, he chugged off.

Paul was prying the lid off the can of varnish when he heard a noise at the door. His first reaction was a sudden, cold fear. He grabbed a poker from the side of the wood stove and stood to one side, out of sight of the window. "Who's there?" he yelled.

"Just me and Zeke!" Tom's voice rang out.

Paul unlocked the door, swung it open a small amount and peered out.

Both men stood there, scraping their boots against a derelict branch, attacking the mudcakes packed around the sides and toes of the worn leather. Tom spoke in a muffled grunt. "Can't get these damned boots clean!"

He opened the door wider.

Tom entered first, Zeke behind. "Ben sent us over to make repairs, but we can't get the truck up here." Tom grinned. "You've got enough mud out on that driveway to raise a passel of happy pigs."

"Oh." Paul eased his grip on the poker. He could think of nothing more to say.

Zeke's near-black eyes were fixed on Paul.

After an awkward silence, Tom's face took on a puzzled cast. "We interrupt you or something?"

"No, no, not at all." Stuck with the poker in his hand, he opened the door to the wood stove and poked at the coals. "Just worn out, is all. I worked throughout the storm."

Tom seemed satisfied. "Old Jeb's down for breakfast with the others. Says you need a baby-sitter for the pianos while you go eat. Zeke and I'll stay here while you go on down. We'll tackle those shingles and loose boards. That driveway's gonna have to wait, though. Can't 'doze her down till she's dried up a bit."

"Thanks, anyway, but I'd rather stay and help."

They split up the work. Paul nailed siding while the other two scrambled over the roof. They finished before he did and began splicing the power cable together, unhitching it from the pole first. As Paul pounded nails, he watched them working.

Zeke was the gopher, trudging down to the road to bring up whatever was needed from the pickup. To Paul, Zeke was a cipher. He mulled over what he knew of the man and came up with little that gave a clue to his character. He acted as Tom's sidekick, but an aide rather than an equal. He had little to say, seemingly content to let others talk while he listened. He laughed when appropriate and scowled when he should, his dark eyes absorbing everything, while giving nothing back. There was no outward indication of his own passions, his own beliefs. He seemed to run in neutral most of the time. An unknown.

Paul pounded the last nail in, climbed back down and headed down the slope. Zeke was down at the road, checking connections at the pole. Tom was wrapping the last of the splicing with heavy insulated tape. He looked up as Paul approached. "We'll string her back up and she'll be as good as new again, Paul. But it'll be most of the day before you have some juice running through."

"Old Jeb indicated that already." Paul squatted down and looked over the joining. "Was there much storm damage on the Island?"

"A few lost sheds. A couple of old barns gone. Lots of trees and branches down. But no. No one had a tree crash through the roof. That's always a fear here."

Tom checked the repair one final time, then began to wind excess cable. "You hear the Sheriff got stranded here by the storm?" A broad grin spread across his face. "Choppers were grounded, ferry was cancelled, nothing smaller'n a battleship could cut through those waves. And no phones. Hear tell he muttered something about the next island he visits'll be Manhattan."

Paul laughed. "Is he still here?"

"Hell, no. First light, he was gone. Didn't even wait for his chopper to fly in and get him. He hornswoggled Calvin into taking him across in his boat."

"I thought Calvin sold that boat to you."

"He did. But I guess selling a boat's like marrying

off a daughter. You never quite break the ties that bind."

Zeke climbed the slope to where they stood. "It's all okay down there. Looks like we strung her up too tight the first time. Wasn't enough slack to bounce with the wind. One good gust and she snapped like a green bean. I'll take up the extra slack at this end, but let's let her droop a little."

Paul watched him as he walked uphill. Like most of the Islanders, Zeke walked with a steady, unhurried stride that managed to eat up yards of ground all the same. "What's Zeke's background, Tom? Has he always lived on the Island?"

"Nope. His pa came here with the electricity. The Island didn't get power until 'sixty-four. His Pa came to string the poles and simply stayed on. Zeke was seven or eight at the time. When his pa sickened up and died a few years back, Zeke stepped into his shoes and carried on. He's a real genius with wire. Knows everything there is to know about the flow of electricity. Well, let's tackle those trees that're down, see if any can be saved. The general cleanup'll have to wait till we get that driveway fixed. Unless you want to 'barrow the debris down to the road."

"I'll wait."

The fallen trees were pronounced questionable, but they replanted them anyway on the off-chance they'd take hold.

As the men were getting ready to leave, Paul asked, "What's going on about the manhunt? Is that going to start up again soon?"

Tom nodded. "Some of the men are already at it.

We split into two groups—cleanup and searchers—and divvied up the work. We'll spell each other off. 'Course the Sheriff's men are all back at it."

"You think Jason's still okay in there?"

"If the storm didn't get him."

Zeke nodded agreement, his eyes inscrutable, then bent down to pick up leftover strands of guy wire. The man simply made Paul uncomfortable. He didn't like being around people you couldn't read. Anna had been that way, too. Her jungle brown eyes were always surveying him, as if watching for the next transgression. And it was most definitely an uncomfortable feeling.

Remembering the sudden fear that had swamped him when Tom and Zeke had arrived and his foolishness with the poker, Paul rummaged in the shed in the back and came up with some old lengths of pipe. They appeared to be pieces of some kind of watering system—for the chickens? he wondered—and he selected several of the shorter lengths and hid them throughout the Coop, out of sight yet handy to him no matter where he stood. Then he returned to work.

With sunlight brightening the studio through the skylights, he gave the repairs to the Old Soldier a minute examination. He'd matched the stains almost perfectly. There was the slightest shading difference between the new veneer and the old, but it looked no different than the shift of tones any piece of furniture took on due to changing angles of light.

He'd just chosen his brush to begin the varnishing when Ben Murdock arrived to check on the storm damage, Old Jeb at his side. Paul set the brush down and showed them around, explaining the damage and pointing out the repairs made. He stopped at the trees in front of the windows. "Tom wasn't sure how badly the roots were damaged, but we took a chance and replanted them anyway."

Ben considered them. "If we get a thaw good enough to loosen up the ground, we'll move them somewhere else. All of them. The storm proves you need the light when the electricity's down, and we don't need to screen you off from anything anymore. I want to get that driveway fixed, too. And it's about time you had something to get about in. I'll talk to Thaddeus about using Bobbin's truck."

"I think Jenny's planning on using it."

"Is she? Then we'll ship one in for you."

"Thanks, Ben, but I'd rather have a phone. Those strings still haven't shown up yet, and I know if I could call the manufacturer a dozen times a day, they'd be on the next truck out."

"I'll have my office follow up on that. In any event, you should have a phone, anyway. It won't do you any good in a storm like this one, but in between, you should have it."

Paul grinned. "Hear tell you had a caged lion of a Sheriff for a house guest the last couple of days."

Humor eased some of the tiredness around Ben's eyes. "That's just about what it was, too. I figure he owes me his next ten years' salary. He plays a lousy game of gin rummy. Too busy grumping around to concentrate. Claims he's putting in for a transfer to the Caribbean. Says hurricanes would be more fun."

"I heard it was Manhattan."

"That, too."

"What about you, Ben? Are you staying on?"

A shadow of sadness filmed his eyes. "Until it's over. It's all I can do." His eyes skimmed across the wide band of forest edging the meadow. "It's the least I can do."

Paul wanted to assure him that Jason was all right, that he was safe in his forest hideaway and had survived the storm just fine. But survived the storm for what? He remained silent, leaving the man to the privacy of his thoughts.

Abner and Calvin arrived at noon. By now, Paul guessed he was being baby-sat by the Islanders just as he was baby-sitting the pianos. It amused him, even though the interruptions were a nuisance.

He set the brush across the varnish can and let them in, wiping his hands on a turpentine-soaked rag.

"Just stopped by to get you for lunch," Abner said. "Calvin's volunteered to set a spell here so's you'd feel comfortable about leaving the pianos."

Paul shook his head. "I'm in the middle of varnishing the piano and can't stop just yet. I'll eat here. Thanks, anyway."

"How's it coming?" Abner asked.

"Come see." He led them into the studio.

The two men circled the Old Soldier, examining everything. Finally Abner straightened. "You're good, you know that? If I hadn't seen it myself the other night, I'd never have suspected how bad the damage was."

Calvin nodded agreement. Without touching anything, he peered at every joint, traced out the patterns of grain with his gaze, searching for the patchwork, then leaned over and examined the keys. "You make those?" He pointed to the dogwood sharps.

Paul remembered that Calvin had the Island reputation as wood-carver. He nodded and waited for the verdict.

Calvin took his time. He worked his way slowly from bass to treble. Every inch of dogwood came under his microscopic scrutiny. "Not bad," he grunted, finally.

Paul thought he detected a tinge of respect in the old man's look. The habitual moodiness returned to cloak it almost instantly, but still he felt pleased. He indicated the wet, half-varnished leg. "Sorry I can't join you."

"Next time," Abner said.

"Are you two on cleanup crew today?" he asked, as he led them to the door.

"Yes," Abner said. "We finally got all the roads open, now we'll start clearing off the shoulders. They're a right mess."

"Hear tell the Sheriff's men are back on the search. You think Jason made it through the storm okay?"

Calvin shrugged.

Abner stroked his beard a minute. "Might've." His eyes had a bleakness to them, though, as if he didn't really think so.

❚

In the early afternoon, Thaddeus showed up. Amusement swamped Paul's irritation this time. Only Grace, Jenny and the Sheriff were left to check in.

Thaddeus entered the Coop, toting a carton of groceries. "Figured you'd be out of bread and milk by now."

"And wine."

Thaddeus set the carton on the kitchen table, rummaged a minute, then held aloft a large jug. "Would I let a good buddy down? And there's brandy, too. I had some shipped over on the first boat that ran."

"Thaddeus, with your sense of enterprise, you'll go far in this world. Want some coffee?"

Thaddeus shook his head. "No time. I've had a real run on the store today, and Jenny's down there handling it alone. That's why I'm so slow in coming up here. Should've brought these up first light, in case you were completely out of eats."

"I guess everyone's anxious to get back to the search for Jason. At least that's the feeling I'm getting."

Grief erased the lightness in the younger man's eyes. "I guess." He hesitated, peering at Paul as if deciding whether to trust him or not. After a minute, he spoke, his voice grim with intensity. "You know, I never thought I'd ever end up hating anyone. But I do." He shook his head, slightly embarrassed by the confession. But his chin was set at a stubborn angle.

"I would say that's normal."

"Maybe. I just never thought I'd be the type to say it. Well, I've got to get back now." Still embarrassed, he left.

Suddenly weary of the misery and trouble everywhere, Paul sank into a chair at the grocery-strewn table and glanced around at the shabbiness of the Coop. Maybe he should take the Sheriff's offer and leave, move on. There was work everywhere for a good Piano Man. Playing saloons or restoring instruments. It was a portable line of work. He could pick his spot and make a living. Somewhere normal, where roads led in and out of town, connected to the rest of the world. Somewhere not hemmed in by water, loneliness and murder.

He let the idea grow. He'd banked all his weekly checks. With Murdock paying all his expenses, there'd been nothing to spend money on, and now he had more than enough for a fresh start. He could climb on a plane headed anywhere. Preferably someplace warm. Or he could buy a car and drive until he found a spot that appealed to him. A mountain town with a good tourist trade and an ample supply of saloons. Colorado, maybe.

That's right, Anna said, run. You ran from the concert stage, you ran from the university and you ran from me. So run some more. That's your style, Paul. You're nothing more than an escape artist, running away from everything. So just keep on running.

He jerked upright in his chair. Oh, stuff it, Anna, he thought, tiredly. Just stuff it. You don't know the first thing about me and you never did. I was just a picture in your mind from some glossy magazine—an elegant man dressed in a tuxedo standing in the spotlight next to a grand, making his bows. I was never flesh and blood to you. So stuff it, Anna. Just stuff it.

He began to put the groceries away. Shabby or not, it was home for now. His home. And Anna could jolly well find one of her own.

Grace came at three, just as he'd finished the varnishing and was ready to clean his brush. She wrinkled her nose at the turpentine smell, then collapsed into a kitchen chair, huffing from the climb up the slope. She patted her hair into place, though not one strand of the blued waves had dared budge from their assigned spot.

"What are you doing out alone?" Paul asked, more sharply than he'd intended.

She blinked in surprise. "I was up to the cemetery. I always check on Bill after a storm. What's making you so peevish, your liver acting up?"

He laughed then. "All right, point made. Would you like some coffee?"

Her eyes twinkled. "I think I've taken on a bit of a chill."

"I see. Well, then, brandy's definitely called for."

"If you insist. But only in my coffee. Wouldn't be seemly to be drinking this time of day, otherwise."

While he prepared their mugs, she got up and wandered to the studio doorway, then stopped, a look of amazement spreading over her face. "Oh, Paul, it's beautiful!"

He came up behind her, holding the two mugs. "It did come out nice, didn't it?"

She moved closer to the piano. "Lord, you've a gift. You ought to show this to Calvin. He'd be mightily impressed."

"He's seen it. He was up this morning. And yes, I do think he liked it." Paul still held the two mugs. "Where are you planning to sit?"

"At the table. The fumes are too strong in here."

With a last look, she returned to the kitchen. "The strings come yet?"

"Nope."

She accepted her mug from him and took a chair. "You know, Paul, sometime in the next century before I die, I'd like to hear you play. What would you say to playing at the Fair? We usually sing carols at the end of the day."

"Instead of toting poinsettias?"

"After. Of course."

"Of course. Who'd play if I refused?"

"I would. But don't give that a thought. My fingers are starting to slow down a mite. They're not bad yet, but still, the timing's a smidgen off, I can feel it."

The thought had appeal. Surely, in public like that, with just carols to play, there wouldn't be any harm. Under their own impulses, his fingers flexed. But could an alcoholic have just one drink? "Let me think about it, Grace."

She nodded and finished her coffee. "I need to start home before dark. Frank Hall'd have a fit if he caught me out."

Paul froze. "What do you mean?"

"Oh, honestly, he's such an old lady at times. Wants to lock me up like some museum treasure in a glass case." She pulled her coat on and wound a scarf around her throat. "I'll be by for you tomorrow about noon. I'll honk from the road. I'm not about to climb this mountain again."

"Now, hold on a minute. One thing at a time. About the Sheriff—"

"Oh, pshaw. See you tomorrow at four." She marched to the door.

"Wait a minute, Grace. What's at four?"

She paused with her hand on the doorknob and her face took on a broad, innocent look. "Why, setting up the Fair. We always do that the day before. And building the poinsettia booth is part of toting them." With a last twinkle, she was gone.

America's lost a great president, he thought. After all, what other requirement was there for that office if not the great art of conning a majority of the masses into doing precisely what you want done?

The Sheriff didn't show. Which surprised him a little. Neither did Jenny. Which didn't. Thaddeus had said they were swamped. But he was now at loose ends. After the furious burst of activity the past few days repairing the upright, work was stalled until the varnish dried. He couldn't begin repairs on the other two pianos. That would stir up dust and grime that would cling to the wet varnish.

He roamed the Coop by lamplight. The power still wasn't on, so he wouldn't even have music tonight. As darkness fell, the night stretched ahead of him, long and lonely.

Now, in a city . . .

A knock sounded. Heart thumping wildly, Paul recalled the placement of each and every pipe length. Then he chided himself for his fear. Murderers don't go knocking. Paul unlocked the deadbolt.

Tom stood on the step. "Brought you a friend." He held out a portable cassette player. "Figured with no electricity, and cooped up here like you are, you'd need this so's at least you could listen to some music. Have fun." With a wave of his hand, he was gone.

Paul closed the door and stared down at the player. "I'll be damned."

The evening turned pleasant. Surrounded by the richness of his favorite symphonies, he fixed himself a good meal, then settled into his easy chair and read by lamplight until bedtime.

His urge to run had slipped away like some stray, trivial whim.

Chapter Thirty-One

The next day, the piano strings finally arrived. At mid-morning, Tom and Zeke dropped them off. They went out to examine the driveway while Paul opened the cartons. He checked the number of strings against the order and relaxed a little. The strings were all there. At least Jason hadn't increased his reserve supply.

Tom poked his head in the back door to turn thumbs down on 'dozing the driveway yet. "It's still too soon, it's not dried out enough. Listen, we've got to help down at the Clubhouse, so we gotta get going. You got everything you need now?"

"I think so. I do need to get a message to Grace, though. She said she'd be picking me up at four so I can set up her poinsettia booth at the Clubhouse, but I don't want to leave the Coop unguarded. Would you explain it to her and tell her thanks, but no thanks?"

"Sure, no problem. There'll be plenty of extra hands down there to build it, anyway. Don't give it another thought."

"Good enough. I appreciate this."

"Of course, if she does corral me into building it for you, you're gonna owe me one. A big one." He grinned and was gone.

Paul began to look for a place to hide the strings.

He was damned if they were going to disappear like the others had. He searched the Coop, but nothing seemed secure. He stood in the middle of the studio and surveyed it. If you want to hide a book . . . he thought. Unfortunately, that principle wouldn't work for the strings, not with the other ones missing.

He stopped in mid-hunt, caught for a brief second, caught on the breath-holding edge of sudden vision. His mind circled it—

And there were those maddening circles again.

It faded. He stood still, hoping to trigger the near-thought again, but it was gone.

He resumed his hunt.

The best he could come up with was to make room for the carton in back of the cleaning supplies beneath the kitchen sink. He resealed the lid, sat back on his heels to study it, then got a couple of neatly folded bed sheets, opened them into a rumpled heap and tossed them over the carton. If someone just glanced in, they'd think he merely had the quirky habit of stuffing used bed sheets under the kitchen sink.

He'd just started applying the second coat of varnish when the Sheriff arrived. His face wore a heavy scowl and, without asking, he helped himself to a mug and filled it with coffee.

"Welcome and good cheer to you, too," Paul said.

The Sheriff gave him an even grumpier look, then wandered over to the Old Soldier where Paul had been working and moodily stared at it without interest. "Grace make her way here yesterday?"

Paul bent down and picked up his brush again. "As a matter of fact she did."

"That damned broad."

"Why, what happened?"

"I put my best man on her—Charlie Pearson. He's supposed to keep watch on her, and she gives him the slip. Pulls a scam no rookie would fall for. She invites him in for tea, gets him settled at the table, says she's going out to that greenhouse of hers a minute to get something, and disappears. He gets hold of me, and I had to pull a dozen men off the job just to search the woods around her place, looking for her. She's gone more'n two hours and comes back just as calm as you please. Without an explanation. Wouldn't say a damned word about where she'd been. Simply says, 'A woman needs some time to herself now and then.' Damned broad."

Paul had to bend low over the varnish can to hide his grin. When he was reasonably sure of keeping a straight face, he looked up at the Sheriff. "I'll give you a tip, but don't tell her I told you, or I won't have a hide left. She usually goes to the cemetery every afternoon to visit her husband. She stopped by here afterward."

Then Paul frowned. He laid the varnish brush across the can and straightened up to stare at the Sheriff on eye-level. "What do you mean, you put your best man on her?"

"Just a precaution." He glowered. "It's important to find the killer, but it's just as important to keep everyone who's alive still alive. But we're having a fine time of it keeping up with these damned Islanders. This whole thing's outta control. Christ, everyone runs off and does what they want, and I can't keep track of any of them. Do they think they're in danger? No, sir, not a one of them! And will they cancel this damned fair of theirs? No, sir, not on your life! The whole goddamned thing's outta control!"

"You really think there's danger in holding the Fair?"

"Damned right I do."

The Sheriff stomped into the kitchen, Paul behind him, and plunked his mug on the countertop with a thud. His glower had been general, but now it focused on Paul. "And I guess I better tell you," he barked, "for what it's worth, I've assigned a man to the Coop here, too. He's off in the woods at the top of the field there, freezing his ass off. His orders are to stay put and watch this place. That means you stay put, too. I haven't got the manpower to spare to put one on the Coop and a second on you as you go traipsing around God knows where. So you stay put, too." The glower deepened. "Understand?"

Paul nodded.

"This damned Island." The Sheriff yanked open the back door. "I'd like to pull the plug and sink it!" He slammed the door behind him.

The Sheriff had planted the seed. With one of his men watching the Coop, there was no reason Paul had to stay to guard it. Except for the Sheriff's warning, of course. Which he could choose to forget if he wanted to.

He fought the growing idea during the next few hours. The Fair had plenty of help. Tom had said so. They didn't need him. And yet, it might be interesting to see how an Island fair was put together. And he had agreed to help with the poinsettia booth.

On the other hand, he'd promised the Sheriff to stay put. Well, not promised, not quite. More like nodded. Still . . .

Still, maybe Jenny would be there. If she wasn't there, then maybe he could stop at the store and see her.

He wished he knew why he was so continually worried about her. He didn't feel that way about any of the other Islanders. Somehow, there was a vulnerability to her the rest of them lacked. They could take care of themselves. He wasn't convinced she could. And yet, she'd managed to get along all her life without him. What did she need with him, a broken-down Piano Man?

Yet, there was that damned promise to the Sheriff.

And yet . . . and yet . . . and yet. Back and forth the battle raged.

Finally, he came to a corner on the Old Soldier, a good stopping place. The hell with it. He was going, that's all there was to it. He cleaned his brush and capped the can and carefully stowed them away.

A bedlam of sounds spilled from the Clubhouse. Abner and Ben were unloading heavy folding tables from the opened end of Abner's pickup. As Paul walked in from the road, Abner grunted from the weight of his end of a table, successfully maneuvered it to the ground, then grinned at him. "Pure madness in there."

"Sounds like it," Paul said. "Need some help?"

"We got more helpers than jobs. Always that way. Thanks, anyway. Just make sure those damned poinsettias make it here okay in the morning. Why that woman can't bring 'em down the night before is a mystery to me. She says they need that last shot of greenhouse care, but they're all going in people's houses anyway, every last one of them, and people here don't live in greenhouses. Stubbornness is all it is. Plain, ordinary, everyday stubbornness."

Ben grinned at Paul. "It's an annual complaint."

"A common one, it seems," Paul said.

"You got someone watching the Coop?" Abner asked.

"Nope, I booby-trapped it."

Not wanting that line of conversation to continue, Paul walked past them and up the porch stairs to the doorway. He stopped dead and stared. Madness understated the case. Pandemonium was more accurate.

The inside of the building was one long rectangular room, with a stage at one end, a kitchen at the other. The building was jammed with a hundred people doing a hundred different things. Voices babbled and yelled from every corner, raised in hails and greeting, raised in barking orders, and raised in argument, all overlaid with a lot of laughter and miscellaneous whooping. Banging hammers punctuated the noise, buzzing saws underlined it. Instinctively, Paul fingered each ear, as if to clear it.

He scanned the room, looking for Jenny. She was standing at one end, dressed in jeans and a red sweatshirt, her hair tied back out of her way, looking young and fresh and pretty. She was watching his reaction to the bedlam with amusement, waiting for his eyes to find hers. When they did, she smiled and his heart went wild.

She pushed through the crowd to his side and

slipped her hand into his. "I was hoping you'd come," she said. She squeezed his fingers tight. "This is more fun than the Fair itself. Almost."

He grinned down at her. "Almost, eh?" Her eyes were magnetic and he was hypnotized. After a moment, he pulled himself out of it. Without releasing her hand, he started looking around, trying to sort out the sights and make some sense of it.

Men on high ladders were stringing red and green streamers and long clusters of balloons from the ceiling. Booths were being built everywhere by Zeke and the Pickup Brigade. Old Jeb was erecting scaffolding, with pipes spanning the supports instead of planks. Down by the stage, Calvin was supervising the setting up of a huge Christmas tree, while Tom tested strings of lights.

Off to one side, the Sheriff viewed it all. Taller and bigger than most, he stood flat-footed and amazed, a giant overseeing a flurry of elves. He directed an exasperated look Paul's way when he saw him enter.

Jenny had to shout into Paul's ear to be heard. "I want you to meet a few people." She pulled him into the crowd.

In one corner of the room, protected from the chaos by a couple of tables set at an angle, an old man sat rigid on a straight-backed chair. A cane stood between his knees and his hands were folded over the top. A pair of milky blue eyes surveyed the activity swirling around him.

As Jenny made the introductions, Paul lost some of her words in the noise, but he caught "Isaiah" and "patriarch of the Island." The old man offered a palsied hand. The bones felt as fragile as a bird's wing and Paul shook it gently.

Jenny shouted again. "Isaiah is the father of seven, grandfather of twenty-three, great grandfather of fifty-seven. And so far he has twenty-one great-great-grandchildren."

Isaiah followed the words and shook his head. "Twenty-two last month." He looked up at Paul. "I'm ninety-eight years old and still got my hearing, my eyesight and my own teeth." He laughed with a heartiness that belied the fragile body. The laugh was contagious and Paul joined in.

The young minister who'd presided at Bobbin's funeral pushed through the crowd and grabbed Paul's elbow. "I understand you play the piano a little," he shouted, his freckled face sincere.

Paul smiled at him. "A little."

"We have a candlelight service at the church on Christmas Eve. Would you play some of the carols for us?"

"I thought Grace was your organist."

"She is. This was her idea. We'd move in a piano for you and she'd play the accompaniment on the organ." He clapped his hands in rhapsody. "Oh, I can hear it now! It'll be the highlight of the service!" Before Paul could refuse, he rushed off.

Paul scowled at Jenny. "That damned Grace."

She kept a straight face, but her tone wasn't quite right when she echoed, "That damned Grace."

He studied her suspiciously, but couldn't decide if it was specific or general humor turning up the corners of her eyes.

They kept walking until they reached the stage end of the room, where some measure of order prevailed. The sharp tang of freshly cut pine surrounded them as Calvin and his crew balanced the stem of the tall tree in a bucket with bricks and stones. A crew of sidewalk superintendents shouted out orders to tip it left, tip it right, tilt it forward, tilt it backward, cut off more bottom branches, don't cut off more bottom branches, top the tree some more, leave the damned tree alone.

Exasperated, Calvin came to stand by Paul and judge for himself. "More to the right!" he bellowed. "More! More! Okay, easy now! Now forward! More. More. Nope, too far! Back a touch. Okay! That's got her!" He tossed a triumphant scowl at Paul and returned to the bucket.

Tom Ross knelt near the tree in front of the stage, untangling a string of lights. "Glad you made it down," he yelled at Paul. "Who's baby-sitting the Coop?"

"No one," he shouted back. "I booby-trapped the place."

"Good for you. About time you were out and about. What're you up to now?"

"I'm showing Paul the local entertainment," Jenny shouted down to him.

Tom grinned. "Tomorrow this'll be calm and orderly."

"That's hard to believe," Paul shouted back. A swell of noise drowned out his words and Tom grinned again and shrugged. He hadn't heard him.

Paul gave up.

Old Jeb was working on scaffolding supports

nearby, his missus handing up lengths of pipe to him. Paul asked Jenny what he was doing.

She put her mouth up close to his ear to be heard. "The ones near the Sheriff are to hang afghans and quilts from. These by the tree are for Grace's poinsettias, the hanging ones."

"I should be there, helping."

"There's time for that." Jenny started explaining the general layout. "The plants and greenery's at the stage end, crafts and handiwork are in the center, and the food'll be down by the kitchen."

At one of Old Jeb's scaffolds, the Sheriff stood arranging a quilt over the top pipe, a heavy glower on his face. A tiny bird of a woman supervised every movement and every fold. At Paul's approach, the big man glared at him. "Nice to see you," he said sarcastically.

"Thanks," Paul grinned. "Nice to see you, too."

Jenny tapped the tiny woman on the shoulder. "This is Isaiah's wife, Nellie," she yelled to Paul. "She's the Island quilter."

The little woman fixed bird-bright eyes on him. "You the Piano Man?" She barely topped his belt buckle and had to lean way back to get any view of his face.

Paul could see pink scalp through the scanty white hair. He nodded.

"You got a grand piano up to your place?" she asked.

He nodded again, puzzled.

"Been thinking of doing one on a quilt. I'll come take a look-see at yours. How's Sunday after church?"

"Sure. Anytime."

"I said Sunday after church, didn't I? Then that's when I'll be there."

He began to grin. "Perfect."

"Be sure and be home. I drink tea." Dismissing him, she turned back to the quilt.

Jenny burst into giggles.

The Sheriff had watched it all with a grin. "She's a tartar," he said. "She's kept Isaiah toeing the line for near on to seventy years now."

"Over seventy," Jenny corrected. "They celebrate their seventy-fifth wedding anniversary on Valentine's Day. The Island's planning a big party for them. She married him when she was fourteen, so she's quite a bit younger than he is."

Paul chuckled. "That makes her only eighty-nine. A mere whippersnapper of a girl." He turned to Jenny. "You going to be that vinegary when you grow up?"

His question amused her. "At least." Her face grew serious as she looked up at the Sheriff. "I guess you don't appreciate all of this much, do you."

"The only advantage I can see is that all the Islanders are in one spot where I can watch them."

Paul glanced around. "I don't see Grace."

"She's at the house," the Sheriff said, "working on her plants. She's got Pearson helping her. I think he's in love."

"How old is he?"

"Oh, about thirty. Married, with three kids."

Nellie homed in on Paul. "You haven't done a thing around here." She pointed to a pile of lumber. "We need some stands for the wreaths. Hop to it."

He looked to Jenny for rescue, but she shook her head. "I'm due in the kitchen for hot chocolate duty."

The Sheriff edged away with a muttered, "Gotta see Abner now."

Paul was left to the mercies of the eighty-nine-year-old fireball who had none. He built and she supervised. They were rather simple easels, but still it took a couple of hours to get them up.

Just when he figured he could escape, she grabbed hold of his sleeve. "Oh, no, you don't. You still got wreaths to hang."

"Yes, ma'am."

It was full dark outside by the time he had the last wreath hung to her standards. Finally, she harrumphed and dismissed him. "Sunday morning, right after church."

He grinned down at her. "And you drink tea. I won't forget."

The squeal of a loudspeaker slashed through the noise, quieting voices for a second. On stage, Zeke and Tom worked over a tape deck and the sound of bells filled the room. Everywhere, people paused in their work.

All eyes turned to Calvin as he climbed up the high stepladder. In his arms, cradled as tenderly as a babe, he carried a large wooden angel dressed in a silvery-white gossamer silk. Her face was round, her mouth curved into a sweet smile below apple cheeks and her halo glowed a soft gold.

Carefully Calvin set her in place on top of the tree. He adjusted the wings, then made a signal to Tom. The multitude of colored tree lights sprang to life, reflecting off the satiny reds, blues and whites of the glass ornaments. At the top, the angel glowed in all her shimmery glory.

There was a collective "ooh" of wonder from the crowd, then the music from the tape deck swelled. A hundred voices or better broke into a lusty, off-tone version of "Jingle Bells." The red and white streamers drifted overhead, balloons jouncing beneath them. The fragrant aroma of hot chocolate and fresh-baked cinnamon rolls permeated the air.

The hot chocolate and rolls were served. Paul was introduced to so many people he couldn't keep faces and names straight. There was a lot of visiting and laughter and talk of family doings for the holidays. When the rolls were gone and the chocolate pot had run dry, the cleanup began.

Nellie headed straight for Paul again. "You haven't done much around here." She pointed to the sink.

Inwardly, he groaned. "I know, hop to it."

He washed and she supervised. He had to wash the last pan twice before she dismissed him. Before she could say anything, he held up his hand. "I know, Sunday morning, after church. And you drink tea. I won't forget."

Jenny finally took pity on him and led him outside.

Whether it was the weather, the season or his mood, even after they left the warmth and noise behind, the Island seemed to sparkle. Above the treetops, stars glittered and glistened, brilliant in the cold. Their footsteps crunched on the frozen ground, the snaps and cracks sounding as loud and cheery as wood popping in a fireplace. He breathed in a hefty lungful of the sharp fir-scented air and a sense of peace spread throughout his soul.

Jenny was still staying at Grace's and a soft lamp glowed from the living room window when they pulled up in front. The rest of the house was dark.

Paul had driven Bobbin's old truck, Jenny sitting quietly at his side. As he stopped in front of the front walk, she stirred. "You know," she said, slowly, "I didn't think of it till just now, but Grace usually gets there in time for the lighting of the tree and the hot chocolate. She never showed up tonight."

"Oh, Jesus." He jumped down and stood still, trying to penetrate the shadows. "Where's the deputy, wouldn't he be outside?"

Jenny reached his side. "On this cold a night? Grace wouldn't hear of it."

He ran up the front walk. Any minute, Grace would throw open the door and laugh at his fears. Surely, she could hear his pounding feet. No sound came from the house.

"Is the door kept locked?" he called back to Jenny.

"Yes, but I've got a key." Behind him, Jenny fumbled in her purse as she ran.

He reached the porch and grabbed the doorknob. The door *wasn't* locked. He pushed it open and took a minute to listen. Nothing. "You look through the house," he ordered, "I'll go straight out to the greenhouse."

He raced through the kitchen and burst through the back door. That wasn't locked either. The whole goddamned place was open to anyone wandering by. Jesus!

He knew, though. Deep inside, in the bowels of his being, where the dark spots of a man's soul lived, he knew. He wrenched open the door to the greenhouse, flung on the lights and froze.

She'd dressed for the tree lighting in a soft red woolen dress the shade of her poinsettias. Her hair was freshly curled and newly rinsed. Her feet were encased in the sturdy, black, no-nonsense Red Cross shoes she favored. They dangled in the aisle between tables of plants, about on a level with the blossoms. The strands of copper piano wire glowed softly in the overhead lights as they wound around a beam then dropped to her neck. She had been dead a long while.

Jenny opened the door of the house.

Instantly, he switched off the light and closed the door. Turning, he used his body to block the entrance.

His stillness brought Jenny to a halt. In the pale moonlight pouring down on them, he could see knowledge cross her features.

"No!" she screamed, her voice a whisper. She tried to push past him. "No!" her whisper screamed again. Maddened, she struggled against him, clawing to get past. *"NO-O-O-O!"*

He wouldn't give in. He grabbed her arms and pinned them to her sides. When she tried to back away to free herself, he locked his hands together behind her back.

Pinned against him, she struggled until her strength gave out. Slowly, like a sail in a dying wind, she collapsed and sank against him. "Oh, *God!*" she wailed into his chest. She clung to him with fingers like claws and softly keened.

Swallowing hard, he held her until her body calmed and the keening died away, then he waited a few extra heartbeats. "Jenny," he said. His voice came out a croak. "Jenny, you'll have to go and get help. Get the Sheriff. I don't want to leave her alone. You'll have to go. Can you do that for me, for her, please? Please, Jenny?"

Her frenzy died into dullness. She nodded. Shoulders slumped, she took the truck key he pressed upon her and shuffled away.

He listened as the truck engine died away in the distance, leaving just the sound of an easy surf lapping at the shore a few yards away. The greenhouse and the woods were silent around him. In the distance, a seagull cried.

He sank to the ground, leaned back against the greenhouse door, drew his knees up against his chest and held them tight.

Then he cried, too.

Thirty-two

The funeral was held on Monday.

Numbed, Paul sat with Jenny and Thaddeus in the little church. Barely two weeks ago, he'd stood in the rear during the services for Bobbin. Then he'd felt grief and rage. Today he was beyond that. He was ice inside. Dangerous, pointed shards of ice. For the first time in his life, he knew he was capable of murder.

They'd determined that Grace had been killed sometime late in the afternoon on Friday, between three and six. The deputy had yet to be found. The deputy. With a wife and three kids waiting for word on the mainland. They—everyone—knew he was dead. If he'd been merely conked on the head, he'd have woken up by now and have made himself known.

That's what Paul wanted. He wanted the deputy to wake up and make himself known. He wanted Grace to wake up and have it all not be true. He wanted to have Friday afternoon back again, so he could do things differently. He wanted Grace back.

Jenny, too. On Friday afternoon, she'd gone straight from the deli to the clubhouse, knowing all her customers would be there and Thaddeus wouldn't be needing her. Since the deputy was on watch, she hadn't worried about Grace, hadn't bothered to check on her. Now she was twisted with guilt and remorse. And Paul couldn't help her. He was too cold inside. If he couldn't have Grace back, he wanted one other thing and one other thing only—he wanted the killer's neck between his bare hands.

The church was jammed. Next to Paul, Abner cried openly. Calvin's forehead was sunk into one hand, his head bowed to his chest. Tom batted the rolled-up program against one palm. Zeke stared at the floor. Old Jeb and his Missus shriveled back into a pew. Paul himself sat rigid in icy isolation, Jenny weeping softly at his side.

The service came to an end. The pallbearers bore. The congregation shuffled out. The cortege began. The line of cars was orderly, subdued.

Thaddeus and Jenny rode with Paul in Bobbin's truck. He parked in turn on the paved road and they walked up the dirt lane to the cemetery. Pick-axes had broken through the permafrost. The grave had been dug. Up the hill, beneath the alder she'd planted to shade Bill's grave, Grace was laid to rest.

Silently, the Islanders returned to their cars. There would be no gathering today, no wake. The men were grim. Like warriors, they'd bury their dead and get on with the hunt. Chainsaws whined around the clock. Men worked until the last muscle cramped, slept a bit, then went back at it.

The Fair had been postponed. Fear governed the Islanders now. Wives cleaned house in groups. Children were kept at home. People spoke in hushed murmurs. They peered behind every tree.

Jenny moved in with Thaddeus and was never out of her brother's sight now. Paul stayed alone at the Coop, Bobbin's old shotgun borrowed from Thaddeus by his side. The Sheriff had made no direct comment about it, but Paul's situation was a worry and they'd had it out about it the night of Grace's murder.

It had been around four-thirty in the morning. At about one, Paul had been driven home from Grace's place by one of the deputies, and he'd already gone through one potful of coffee and was halfway through the second when the Sheriff had shown up.

He'd poured a brandy for the Sheriff and another mug of coffee for himself. He didn't dare touch alcohol. He'd kill someone if he did. Silently, he handed the Sheriff the brandy glass and walked to the window, staring at the dead black pane reflecting the room back to him. The night beyond was impenetrable. Cold and impenetrable. Like death.

The Sheriff eyed him warily, measuring his mood. He swirled the brandy, watching the amber liquid form and reform light patterns like a kaleidoscope. He took a large swallow, then returned to watching Paul.

At last, he sighed and broke the silence. "I'm going to have to take my man off watching the Coop. Having just one man on the job is ludicrous. Pearson's proven that. I'm not having my men work alone anymore, and I can't afford to have two men sitting guard here. Two," he snorted. "More like six, working in eight-hour shifts in pairs around the clock. That's without a day off. Even if we went to twelve-hour shifts, that'd still be four. I just don't have the manpower to spare. Fucking taxpayers."

Paul didn't move. "I understand."

The Sheriff shivered suddenly. "Is it cold in here?"

Wordlessly, Paul set down his mug and moved to the stove. The Coop filled with the clank, thump and stir of the fire being tended. Then silence fell once more. He resumed his stance at the window.

The Sheriff became absorbed in the brandy once again. "The point is," he said slowly, "I want you doubling up with someone else. You choose your housemate. I don't care who it is, but you can't stay here alone."

"No."

"No? That's it? Just a plain no?"

"That's it. No."

Abruptly, the Sheriff set the glass on the top of the bookshelf. "Look, Paul, talk to me. Don't close off this way. I've seen it in my men now and then, and it doesn't do anyone any good. So talk it out, friend, talk to me."

Paul stared at the reflected room.

The Sheriff sighed. "Then I'm gonna send you to the mainland. I'm gonna have Ben Murdock fire you and ship you out. You're history, Piano Man. Just a footnote on the fucking page."

"I won't go."

"Oh, you'll go. This is Murdock's place and I've got a couple of judges who owe me one. I can have an eviction notice drawn up by dawn. Or simpler yet, an arrest warrant as a material witness. One way or another, you're outta here."

Paul turned then. His voice was ice. "Maybe you can throw me off the property, but you can't throw me off the Island. I'm staying. And skip the threats of arrest. You won't do that and we both know it."

The Sheriff's tone turned mild. "Then pick a roomie and move in. Jenny and Thaddeus want you up at their place."

"You're not very bright tonight, Sheriff. Someone's out to get me and anyone I'm involved with, and you want me to move in with Jenny and risk her life? Your brain's turned to dogshit."

"There's Murdock's place."

"Old Jeb and his Missus are there. I'd be a danger to them."

"Well, I could go on mentioning one Islander after another, and you'd find fault with each and every one." He sighed. "We're not getting anywhere this way, we're just going 'round in circles."

At the window, Paul froze. He swung slowly around and stared at the Sheriff. "What did you say?"

"I said we're going around in circles, not getting anywhere with this."

There it was again. Circles. Always it came back to circles. What in the hell was there about it that caught him up short like that every time it was mentioned?

"You've got that look on your face again. What is it?"

"Circles," Paul said slowly. "Circles. Every time I think circles, I stop cold."

"Circles and you? Circles and what's happened the past few weeks? Circles and Jason—?"

"Circles and Jason. Circles and Jason." Paul concentrated hard. "From what everyone's said, Jason's simple-minded."

"True."

"Action/reaction. That would be his way. His mother plays the piano, he adores his mother, his mother abandons him, the piano stays, so he takes his fury out on the pianos. From that day on, pianos mean pain to him. Who does he assault in Minneapolis? A Piano Man. Action/reaction. Who does he kill here first? A Piano Man. Again, action/reaction."

Rising excitement forced him to move. He paced among the pianos. "Then the pattern changes. Obadiah. He doesn't play the piano. Walter Gibbons. He's just a drifter. Bobbin. Why Bobbin? He didn't have a musical bone in his whole body. And Grace. She was an organist, not a pianist. At least, not like Harrison, and the man in Minneapolis, or me. Suddenly the pattern changes, Frank. Instead of action/reaction, it's cold-blooded killing." Paul halted abruptly, his eyes widening.

"Go on," the Sheriff said quietly.

"Look at that bar in Minneapolis, Frank! Jason hates pianos, someone plays the piano, and boom, in front of a saloon full of people, he bashes the guy's head in. Right on the spot. He doesn't go away and plot their demise. No. He simply picks up a bar stool and goes for it, right there! Straightforward. Action/reaction. He's not calculating enough to swipe piano strings or cut down electrical cable to use as nooses sometime in the future. He lives in the here and now. He lives with what's going on this very second. He takes this second and the next second and the next and the next in the order they arrive and handles each one according to what happens then! In an unbroken, straight line of action/reaction.

"But then, suddenly, the pattern changes. He starts running circles around us, devious circles designed to lead us astray. But Jason's not devious." Paul's face glazed over with shock. "Frank, Jason's not devious! He doesn't have that kind of mentality. But that's who we should be looking for . . . someone devious. My God, we're not looking for Jason at all!"

The big man gave a small, grim half-smile. "So you finally figured it out," he said softly. "No, you're right, we're not looking for Jason at all."

They moved into the kitchen where Paul put on a fresh pot of coffee. Sunrise was a couple of hours away yet and the cold winter night pressed blackly against the windows outside, isolating the two of them from the rest of the world. Anyone could be out there watching them and they'd never know. He quickly turned back to the light of the room.

He filled the mugs with fresh coffee and carried them to the table. "I don't think Jason's alive."

"No, I don't think so either."

"Then why the charade of the hunt?"

"His body has to be somewhere."

"In the woods?"

"That would be my guess. If he'd been dumped in the water, he would've washed ashore somewhere by now. And if he'd been put in any of the summer houses, the killer would've done something to keep the men away from that particular one during the boarding-up process."

"So the hunt's to continue."

The Sheriff nodded.

Paul looked down into his coffee mug for a long moment, then raised his eyes to meet the Sheriff's gaze. "It almost certainly has to be an Islander," he said softly.

"Almost certainly."

"Have you any suspicions at all about who?"

"None."

"Or why?"

"Ah, the why and wherefores." The Sheriff shifted again. "I can't fathom a guess as to why Harrison was killed. Apparently, he was the first. The others, though . . . that was simple paranoia, I think. I'm only speculating, mind you, but I think Jason saw our man, whoever it is, kill Harrison. He'd gotten away from Ben's place, which he did on a regular basis, and being as childlike as he was, he probably just walked in on the killing and said, 'Why are you hurting that man?' Or something as equally simple. So Jason had to go."

"And Obadiah?" Paul asked.

"Same thing. He must've seen something, or known something . . . or possibly he put two and two together and said something. He had to go. Enter Walter Gibbons, the drifter, who had a habit of showing up at the oddest times, so exit Mr. Gibbons. As for Bobbin, he probably suspected something, too—"

Paul nodded. "He told me he did."

"What?" The Sheriff straightened. "When did he tell you that?"

"The night before he was killed."

"You better tell me what happened," he said grimly.

Paul thought back to that night. "Actually, I guess I was the one to bring it up. I didn't exactly put it the way I did with you earlier, otherwise I might've caught on sooner. But even back then, I guess I had some doubts about this all being Jason's handiwork. I did question how someone so simple-minded could continually outsmart everyone. And I thought the dumping of the bones in my bed was a bit subtle for someone like that."

"So. The bones were found in the Coop here. By the way, they were 'coon bones. The report reached my desk yesterday."

"That's what old Jeb said they were. And yes, they were found here. I'd gotten ready to go to bed, turned back the sheets and there they were. I'd spent the evening at Grace's, so the Coop was empty for a while. Whoever did it must've done it then."

"How did Bobbin come to be there?"

"When I found the bones, I marched straight over to Old Jeb's place to borrow some boards and nails. You must remember, Frank, we'd only just found Harrison's body a short while before, but we'd never nailed the trapdoor shut. Since I'd locked the deadbolt, I figured Jason had to have come through the crawl space. Only now, of course, I guess it wasn't Jason. Anyway, Old Jeb called the others and they all came out to check the Coop over. While they were doing that, I hammered the boards over the trapdoor and nailed it closed."

"What exactly did you say to Bobbin?"

"I don't remember my exact words, but I was

questioning how Jason could be consistently outsmarting us. There was also his size, too. He'd been described to me as a big, gangling man, brutally strong. He'd have had a hard time maneuvering through the crawl space. It's pretty shallow under there."

"Who all was here?"

"Bobbin. Old Jeb. Abner, Calvin, Tom Ross. That was it. Ben wasn't on the Island that night. He didn't fly in until after Bobbin's death was discovered."

"Not true." The Sheriff smiled slightly. "By then, he was making regular trips to the Island to check on the progress of the hunt."

Paul sat, thunderstruck. "But I knew nothing of those."

"You weren't supposed to. They saw no need for you to know, would be my guess."

The thought troubled Paul. If Ben was coming and going so silently, and with such freedom as the Sheriff indicated, then what else had been going on while he'd worked away in the isolation of the Coop? Had Grace known about Ben's visits, as well as the others? And Jenny? Did she know, too?

Paul ignored the Sheriff's somewhat amused glance. "All right, then, Ben was on the Island. But he didn't come here that night. That I know."

"So you had Tom and Calvin and Abner and Old Jeb and Bobbin here. What exactly did Bobbin say to you?"

"When I mentioned my doubts, he said he'd had some himself and that he'd talk to me about it the next night when we met. We were paired up in the woods at that time. He didn't seem all that surprised."

"Anyone overhear you two talking?"

Paul hesitated. The memory of Tom Ross approaching them was clearly etched. Finally, he shook his head. "I couldn't say for sure."

The Sheriff eyed him. "Well, who was closest to you?" he said in a patient tone.

"No one. We were off by ourselves in a corner of the studio."

Hall finally let that pass. "Okay. Then what?"

"Nothing. I worked the next day—"

"So you wouldn't know where anyone else was that day."

"No."

"And the last time you saw Bobbin alive was the night before, here."

"Yes."

"Did you see anyone else that day before you found Bobbin?"

"Jenny. She came for lunch."

"Did you mention your doubts to her?"

"Yes, I did."

"And how did she react?"

"Well, at that point, it didn't occur to me that Jason might be dead. I just thought someone on the Island was helping him. So that's the idea I brought up with her. But the thought that someone she'd known all her life was condoning murder . . . she simply didn't accept that thought at all."

"Anyone else come by that day?"

"Just you. You stopped by just before I was due to go out and meet Bobbin."

"To get my usual serving of pap." His tone was humorous, but his eyes were dead serious.

Paul hesitated, then nodded. "We probably should've brought you in on all of this earlier."

"Probably," he said, with only a slight tinge of sarcasm. "Well, then, that gives us a motive for Bobbin's death. Someone overheard you talking with Bobbin that night. Either he—or Jenny—might've mentioned it to someone else. Whatever, by then, paranoia was running wild in our killer's brain waves, and that was reason enough to have to eliminate Bobbin."

"Are you saying Jenny may be in danger?"

"Not necessarily. She may not have mentioned your comment to anyone. She might've been too upset to do so."

"But you don't know."

"No."

"What about Grace then?"

"I would guess that by now the killer's reading suspicion into every weird look that comes his way. Grace must've known something, or said something, or done something, or merely looked a certain way . . . whatever, she had to be eliminated."

"What do you do now?"

The Sheriff sighed. "Good old-fashioned police work. In a word, drudgery. Opportunity, means, motive. We start by backtracking movements to eliminate those who couldn't have done any of the killings. Once we've formed our list, then we examine it for the whys and wherefores."

"You're looking, then, for the killer to make a slip."

"Oh, he's made several already. Up until Bobbin's death, he was pretty well home free. There was no firm time of death. Harrison's body was too decomposed to place the day of his death except within broad parameters. Obadiah was pushed off the cliff during the night. Few people have alibis for snooze time. Walter Gibbons? Well, we know about when he was drowned, but as to the time of day, forget it. And Jason's body hasn't been found yet. Even when it is, it won't narrow things down much. If the killer had stopped there, he'd have gotten away scot-free.

"But with Bobbin, we know he was killed sometime during the afternoon. He was last seen at lunch, and you found his body at dinnertime. Still, that's a fairly broad span of time to cover. And with the search going on, the Islanders were scattered all over Kingdom Come. It would've been pretty easy to slip away unnoticed for thirty minutes or so. But it does mean we can eliminate anyone who was off the Island that day, everyone who spent the day with friends, everyone who worked in the woods in constant sight of another, or was out on patrol in one of the boats."

"And with Grace?"

"With Grace, we get a few breaks. We're going to be able to pin the time of her death down to pretty fine parameters. The greenhouse had a constant temperature, and the medical experts will be able to pinpoint almost exactly when she was killed. Plus the Islanders were grouped together all day setting up the Fair. It was a mess down there, sure, but you'd be surprised who you remember seeing and who you don't."

"So that was a major error on the killer's part."

The Sheriff shook his head. "No. The one that's going to narrow down the list is the fire you had here in the Coop Thanksgiving Day. That's the biggie. A holiday like that's the time to be surrounded by family and friends. Anyone's absence—or lateness—would be noticed. Setting that fire was a grave miscalculation on the killer's part."

"Why did he do that, try to burn down the Coop? And why heap a bunch of bones on my bed? Surely, if I hadn't been scared off before, that wouldn't scare me off either."

"That wasn't the purpose. At least, I don't think so. It was just a ploy to make everybody feel that Jason was still alive and active in the woods."

Paul rose to refill their mugs, his mind going over dozens of implications. "But now that you suspect he isn't, wouldn't it be better to warn the Islanders so they can take steps to protect themselves?"

"I've thought of it. At this point, though, I don't want the killer to know I know it's not Jason. I have more freedom of movement that way, and he'll be operating under a false sense of security."

"But if you know it's one of the Islanders, shouldn't you be questioning them?"

"You mean, instead of sitting here, drinking your coffee?" The Sheriff smiled. "Oh, I've managed in amongst my other little duties to spend some time with a few of them. I had to be careful not to give the game away, but I probed a bit here and there, figuring someone might know something they didn't know they knew . . . if you get my meaning."

"Did you learn anything?"

"Well, they all gave a good imitation of a stick of

lumber. You know how communicative the Islanders can be. They stick together like tapioca pudding. So no, so far I haven't learned a lot. If they suspect something, whether they're aware of it or not, they're keeping it to themselves."

"Doesn't that worry you?"

"Sure. So does cancer. And in either situation, I can only do so much." He glanced at his watch, rose and pulled his jacket from the back of the chair. "I'd best be on my way. You haven't had any sleep tonight."

"I probably won't," Paul said absently. A question had occurred to him. "Was your visit here tonight part of your efforts to learn something?"

The Sheriff gave him a hard stare. "I figured you had a few doubts about Jason."

"How did you know that?"

"You've been asking some very bright questions." The Sheriff gave a grim smile. "I just hope no one else has noticed."

Chapter Thirty-Three

Because of his suspicion of Tom Ross, Paul had lost all trust in him, but when it came time to lay the Old Soldier on its back for the stringing, he could think of no alternative but to ask Tom for help, and through him, the Pickup Brigade. Abner, Calvin and Old Jeb were too far up in years to handle the kind of weight the old upright entailed.

Tom brought Zeke and four other brawny souls with him. Paul placed two at the front, and four at the back, their hands ready to catch the weight when the piano was tipped backward.

Tom and Zeke were pushing, not catching. As they each grabbed a corner to begin the tilt, Paul was struck by the size of Tom's hands. Big, thick-knuckled, and heavily muscled, they pushed the piano over as if it were made of Styrofoam.

The thought of those hands tightening piano wire around Grace's throat fired Paul's icy rage up to a white hot fire. He fought it down and they slowly lowered the piano to the floor on its back.

The six gathered around the fallen Soldier, staring with some awe at the abdominal cavity. "How you know what you're doing is a mystery to me," Tom said slowly. The others nodded solemnly. Then he broke the spell with a clap on Paul's shoulder. "Well, fella, we'll leave you to it."

Paul damned near grabbed him then and there. Instead, he kept his eyes fixed on the Old Soldier, as if studying his next move, and merely nodded. "Okay, guys, thanks."

❚

The stringing went slowly. It was tedious, backbreaking work. Each key had one string and two pins. The wire was wound around the first pin two and a half times, then the pin was pounded into its pin-hole on the bottom board. It took seven or eight good sturdy blows of the hammer to seat it properly.

Once seated, the wire was run up to the top of the opening, around the hitch pin and back to the bottom board. Measuring three-fingers' width of extra, Paul clipped the wire, coiled it around the second pin and tapped that one into place next to its partner. He gave each pin equal turns until he could hear the wire pop into the groove on the hitch pin at the top. As he ran wire up and down, he wove braid over and under alternate strands, creating a horizontal band of gold shimmering across the brass.

He worked in a half-stoop half-squat, an awkward, tiring position, and the strength called for in his fingers often made them cramp into painful claws. He could only work on the stringing for short periods of time before having to stretch and walk away from it. He spent a lot of time at the front windows, staring sightlessly at the young trees blocking his view of Oro Bay.

Again and again, his mind replayed every scene of the last two months. He looked at the killings from every angle, digging deep into memory to recall who said and did what. But each time, it came down to that one memory of Tom approaching the corner where he'd been talking with Bobbin. And Bobbin had been killed the next day.

The third afternoon following Grace's funeral, he felt himself drawn to the cemetery. It was a moody, gloomy day out, with a low gray sky threatening rain. Eying the sky, he decided the showers would hold off for a while, pulled on his jacket and locked the Coop. He skipped using the truck, choosing to walk instead.

At the cemetery, he climbed the slope to the alder tree. Grace had been buried three days, but none of the settling of the dirt had taken place yet. He stopped and picked up a wilted rose from among the spray that had been laid across the grave. He held the rose absently, staring at the dirt hump, and pictured Grace lying there, cold and still. He couldn't believe yet she was gone. She'd been so alive and warm, pumped up with energy and enthusiasm and wit. Now, nothing. The heart didn't beat, the lungs didn't breathe, the mind didn't work. Nothing.

An image of Tom's monstrous fingers came to mind. The rose stem snapped in his hand.

He tossed the two parts of the wilted flower on the humped grave, turned away and started.

The Sheriff was leaning against a post of the pavilion, watching him.

Paul made his way over to him. "I didn't hear anyone," he said.

The Sheriff's face remained bland. "Oh, for a big man, I get around silent when I want to. 'Course it's like an elephant walking on tippy-toes, but I manage."

"How'd you know I was here?"

"Well, we may not be watching you full-time, but once in a while, I sneak on by to check things out. Saw you start out and felt a sudden need to take a walk, too." He pulled a small rolled-up pamphlet from his back pocket and handed it to Paul. "Thought you might be interested in this."

Paul unrolled it. The Island telephone directory. Eight pages of names and phone numbers. With most of the names crossed out.

"We've done the eliminating we talked about the other night. The names that are left are the ones who were alone during the time the fire was set." The Sheriff leaned his head back against the post and closed his eyes. "Read them aloud."

"Brown, Calvin."

"Not seen by anyone else from a quarter to three until four-thirty, when he arrived at Grace's." The Sheriff's voice was flat, the facts reeled off in a monotone.

"Fowler, Jeb and Hilda. That Old Jeb and his Missus?"

"Yep. Up at the house for the turkey platter. Jeb outside, Hilda in."

"Gruber, Ezekiel. Ezekiel . . . Zeke?"

"Unseen for two hours."

"Murdock, Benjamin A."

"Alone for two and a half hours, while Old Jeb and his Missus went for the turkey platter."

"Ross, Abner."

"The same as Calvin. They rode in from the woods together in Abner's truck. He dropped Calvin off first, then supposedly went home to change. Showed up at Grace's just ahead of Calvin around four-thirty."

Paul drew in a deep breath at the next name. "Ross, Thomas."

"Left the woods at one. Arrived at Grace's—according to you—at three-fifteen."

"Webster, Thaddeus. Thaddeus?" he asked, startled.

"Alone with the store closed from noon till almost four."

"But I saw him there shortly after two."

"Nothing to prevent him waiting until you disappeared down the road, then climbing in his van for a quick run out to your place."

"I suppose not." Paul closed the booklet slowly. "You probably could eliminate Old Jeb's Missus. I've seen her. She's a little scrawny old woman. She might have the strength to kill them, but she couldn't loft the bodies on high like they were. Not without help."

"That's our thinking."

"Which leaves Calvin, Jeb, Zeke, Ben, Abner, Tom or Thaddeus. It has to be one of them."

The Sheriff nodded. "I'm sorry to say."

"What about Grace's death? Everyone except Thaddeus was at the Clubhouse that day."

"Abner left to get a load of lumber that afternoon. Calvin went home to get the treetop Angel, which he'd forgotten. Tom was short an extension cord for the lights, so he went to scrounge one up. Ben helped a while, then went back up to his place to make a few business calls. Zeke was running a pickup service to bring the crafts in, so he was all over the Island that day. Old Jeb worked on the scaffolding for the quilts, then Nellie sent him out to start picking them up and bringing them in, so he was out and about, too. And Thaddeus was up at the store. He made one cash sale all afternoon. And that was before two."

"Then every single one of them had the opportunity."

"Afraid so."

Paul kept his voice casual. "You got a favorite candidate yet?"

"Not until I know the reason why. I have a feeling the motive points straight to the killer."

"So what do you do next?"

"We set a watch on them, and hope our man panics and makes some more mistakes."

There was nothing more to be said. Paul's gaze wandered over the cemetery, picking out Bobbin's grave. The earth there had settled already. Some grass seed in the spring and the rawness would be gone. It would blend in with all the others and look as if it had always been there.

Eventually, so would the other raw graves. Grace's and Obadiah's, still humped. And over in Potter's Field, Walt Gibbons's, level. Would the caretakers wait for all the graves to settle before they planted the grass?

Impatient with his own morbidness, he started to turn back to the Sheriff. What was this fascination with graves and humps and settling anyway? He'd done that during Bobbin's burial, too. Was it because he personally knew two out of the last four people who'd died?

Piano strings came into his mind. When he'd been

hunting for a place to hide the new strings, a thought had crossed his mind. What was it? Piano strings.

Then it came to him. His thoughts stopped and he looked again at the graves. Obadiah's humped, Bobbin's level. A difference in grave diggers?

"Frank, come have a look a minute."

As Paul explained his thoughts and pointed to the various graves, a monstrous scowl cleaved the Sheriff's brow. He tilted his head this way and that. He walked down and studied the graves from one angle and another. He pushed his toe against the dirt. At last, he muttered, "Nah. Just a difference in soil. You get some clay in some parts of the Island here and even a tropical storm depression wouldn't sink it none. And two feet over you can have soft loam going twenty feet deep with a ten-foot hole in the middle of it. Nope, nothing to that theory."

Paul half-listened, wandering around the raw graves once more, pausing now and then to scoop up clumps of earth. Bobbin's grave, one of the level ones, was the soft sandy loam that would settle, as Frank said. But so was Obadiah's, and his was humped. "Sorry, Frank, think again. They're all loam. You'd better get someone up here to check it out."

The Sheriff's eyes narrowed in calculation. He studied first one grave, then another, stooping low to judge the height of the humps. "Nah," he said again, finally, rising and brushing loose debris from his pants. "Nah, you're all wet this time, Piano Man."

Paul's stubborn streak got going. "If you won't do anything about it, Frank, then I'll get someone who will. I'll call the state troopers if I have to, or the Attorney General's office, or whatever it takes. But something's not right about those graves, and we'd better find out what."

The Sheriff glowered first at Paul, then the graves. Not quite smothering a long-suffering, put-upon sigh of imposition, he led him down the dirt lane to the main road where he'd parked his car. "You sure turn long days into longer ones, Piano Man. Climb in."

He drove up to the cemetery and parked at the bottom of the slope. He used his radio to call for some deputies, then climbed out and circled Obadiah's grave again.

Two cars arrived and four men piled out. The Sheriff conferred with them, then they tramped from one new grave to another, studying them, consulting among themselves. Finally a captain separated himself from the group and surveyed the graves once more. After a long moment of speculation, he looked over at the Sheriff and nodded.

The Sheriff strode to his car and used the radio again. Two more deputy cars pulled in, spilling out more men. Then everyone waited.

When crackling sounds filled the air, the Sheriff leaned into his car, on the radio once again. He hung up and nodded to the men. "That's it, let's go!"

They took shovels from the trunk of one of the deputy's cars and set to work on Obadiah's grave. Ignored, Paul stood near the pavilion, close enough to have a general view.

A few inches down, too close to the surface to be the coffin lid, a shovel hit a solid obstacle. The men scraped away dirt.

The toe of a hiking boot poked through first. Then a jeans-clad leg. At the opposite end of the grave, a head was uncovered. Even through the decomposition and the clumps of dirt, a thatch of blond hair could be seen. Paul drew in a sharp breath. Jason Murdock.

The captain dropped a blanket over the body where it lay and stared at it a minute. Then, with sudden suspicion, he stared up the slope to the fresh hump on Grace's grave. "We'd better check this one out, too, Sheriff," he called out.

The Sheriff gave an even deeper sigh. "You two," he pointed to two of his men, "you go to work on that one. The rest of you get down to the road and block any of the Islanders from coming up here. Except for these." He wrote down a half-dozen names in his notebook and tore the page out. Then he trudged down to his car radio again.

Within minutes, a shout came from Grace's grave. "We got an extra body up here, too!" A few more scrapes of the shovel and the same voice called out, "Jesus, it's Pearson."

The deputy guarding Grace had been found, still guarding Grace.

Abner's truck nosed from the dirt lane onto the drive and stopped behind the deputies' cars. Ben Murdock climbed out, Old Jeb right behind him. A second truck following them released Tom, Zeke and Calvin.

The Sheriff went down to meet them. He talked a couple of minutes, then as Ben made a move to go uphill, he placed a quick, restraining hand on his shoulder. Instead, it was Abner who went up the slope with him to Obadiah's grave.

A deputy raised a corner of the blanket. Above his beard, Abner's face went dead white. He froze for a long heartbeat of time, then nodded.

At the truck, Ben had kept his eyes fixed on Abner. At the nod, he sank slowly to the running board. Then he buried his face in his hands as Calvin awkwardly patted his shoulder and Abner went back down to join them.

Choppers flew in the official personnel. The M. E. clomped past Paul. "This keeps up, I'm getting a weekend place over here." When he recognized Paul, he paused. "How's that young woman doing? The one with you when you found the old lady?"

"Jenny?" Paul said with some surprise. "She's doing all right. Actually, she's doing remarkably all right, given the circumstances."

"A pleasure to treat a live one now and then. Keeps the skills up." He moved on to where the Sheriff waited.

The Island men had formed a loose group of support around Ben. Paul wandered down to join them. There wasn't much talk, just the comfort in not being alone at the moment. For a while, Paul watched the lab crews working, then his eyes wandered over headstones and graves, wondering what other secrets the graveyard contained.

Ben sat now by himself, staring blankly at the far woods. His face was lined and gray, his shoulders slumped in defeat. Paul wandered over and leaned on a fender next to him. He didn't say anything; he simply stood there for him.

After a bit, Ben murmured something Paul couldn't make out. He squatted down to hear better. "Sorry?"

"I'm trying to decide," Ben said in a low voice, "if it's better to have a son alive and guilty, or dead and innocent."

They were beginning to attract the attention of the rest of the Island men. Suddenly frightened on Ben's behalf, not knowing how the killer was going to read the scene, Paul patted his arm as if in sympathy. He kept his voice low. "You watch out for yourself, you hear? You keep a sharp eye out."

"You're beginning to sound like an Islander." But Ben had heard the warning and nodded agreement. "How'd you guess Jason was here anyway?"

"Ever heard the theory that the best place to hide a book is in a library? I wanted to hide the new piano strings from the killer and wished I'd had some old ones around to disguise them."

Ben mustered a wry smile.

Paul gave him a comforting pat on the arm, then rose to join the group of five men watching them . . . one of whom was a madman.

His eyes sought and found Tom Ross.

Chapter Thirty-Four

A broad band of warm air moved up from the south and met frozen land, creating thick ground fog and effectively shutting down the Island. As the fog thickened, Paul spent long tense days alone in the Coop. Isolated even from a view of the fields, the Coop was suddenly too big, too cavernous and echoing, a drafty barn of haunts. The fog was worse at night. It swirled an ashen mist against the windows. With a darkened room behind him, all he could see was a flat-faced blackness. Anyone could be out there, and he'd never know.

Daytime, the stringing went on and on. His body had fallen into the rhythm of it now, and he did it without thought. Which left his mind free to concentrate on Tom Ross.

There was nothing he wanted more than to trap the man. To somehow create a situation that would force him to give himself away. To trap him somewhere alone, where he could cut loose with all the rage built up inside of him.

A simple confrontation wouldn't work. All Tom would have to do was to stand fast and deny everything, and he'd walk. Paul concentrated on coming up with some plan that would force Tom to give himself away, concocting one scheme after another. The trouble was, not one of them was worth a damn. He didn't have the devious type of mind it required. Still, he kept trying to figure out something that would work.

In spite of the fog, the Sheriff stopped by often, partly to check on him and partly to talk. He was there when Paul tapped in the last of the Old Soldier's pins.

Paul made the turns and snapped the copper wire into place, then straightened up, rubbing his back. "That's it, thank God." He set his tools down and stripped off the gloves.

The Sheriff helped himself to a fresh mug of coffee, then came over to peer down at the Old Soldier. "What's next?"

"Install the keyboard and frame box into the piano, bring the strings up to pitch, then tune them. It's about done."

"And then?"

Paul poured himself some coffee. "Then the baby grand, I think. I start all over again with it. The Lady'll be last." He watched the Sheriff wander to the window. The gray winter half-light was too weak to cast the broad face into much shadow, and he could see the grimness in the set of the jaw.

Paul sank onto a piano bench, twisting his neck to relieve the strain of sore muscles. "And you? What's next for you?"

The Sheriff turned Paul's way and leaned against the sill. "We've pretty much established the order of events. Harrison was killed first, sometime the week after Labor Day. Jason died about the same time. We're theorizing that he was killed second. Next came Obadiah. Then a couple of weeks after that, you arrived on the Island. You kept the killer busy a while, but Walt Gibbons was the one who got it. Then Bobbin three weeks ago and Grace a week ago Friday."

"So Harrison's death definitely started it?"

"The whole chain. Jason was killed to cover that murder up, Obadiah's to cover Jason's, Bobbin's to cover the first three and Grace to cover all of them. All we've got to do is to figure out why Harrison was killed."

"It wouldn't be something weird, would it, like Harrison had some other connection with the Island at some other time?"

The Sheriff swung around, his face glum. "You got something brewing besides coffee around here?"

"No. I'm just doing some wild and wacky thinking."

"What'd you have in mind?"

"How about drugs? Maybe Harrison was running drugs from the Island. The waters around here are open clear up to Canada and on out to sea. And you said he was from San Diego, with the Mexican border right there. Maybe he was in partnership with someone on the Island here."

"We thought of that and ran a thorough, detailed check on Harrison clear back to his birth. The guy was a prude. A nerd. A zip. He disapproved of smoking, snorting and women—though he did have a girlfriend for a short while."

"Maybe he was a thief. He set out to rob the Islanders and was caught in the act."

The Sheriff shook his head. "He doesn't have a rap

sheet. Not even so much as a traffic ticket outstanding. As far as we know, he's clean."

"Well, there has to be some reason he took this job."

"That's easy. Self-flagellation. He was a graduate student in music at San Diego State, broke as a kid's toy, and his girlfriend took off with a working—read, richer—buddy of his. To get away from them, he dropped out of school, looked for the most forlorn, remote, godforsaken area of the country to brood in, and took this job."

"So what you're saying is that Harrison wasn't killed because he was Harrison, he was killed because he was a Piano Man. He's dead because he came here. If he hadn't come here, he wouldn't be dead."

"That's what I'm saying."

"So here we are again, back where we started. You're sure Jason wasn't killed first, then Harrison was killed later because he saw it?"

"I'm sure."

"And you're sure Jason didn't kill Harrison, then someone else killed Jason to stop him from killing others, to put him down like a dog turned vicious?"

"You ever thought of writing mystery books?"

▮

After the Sheriff left, Paul played with the pieces of the puzzle. One Piano Man. Two Piano Men. Each living in a piano coop. Restoring pianos.

Restoring pianos. Slowly he turned and studied the three pianos, massive black hulks now in the gathering darkness. Trancelike, Paul stood among the three.

The upright still lay on its back on the floor, its gaping mouth filled with shimmering wires running like string cheese from upper teeth to lower. He knew every inch of that piano. If it had a secret, he'd have found it.

He turned his attention to the other two. He'd always thought of pianos as instruments of grace and beauty. But these two just sat there, dull and ugly in their coats of dirt and bruises, impassive, uncaring, unyielding.

He kept coming back to the fact that the attacks on him had stopped. Could his ignoring the grands have had something to do with that?

He went back over his first few days on the Island. They'd basically been spent organizing the restorations. He'd checked the soundness of the woods, the condition of the soundboards, the veneer, the keys, the hammers—everything. Then he'd made up a comprehensive list of materials that would be needed and ordered them. Right after that, someone tried to kill him. But once he'd begun working on the upright, the attempts stopped.

He took a slow tour of the grands. Maybe when the killer saw he was working on the upright, he'd backed off. Maybe Harrison hadn't had that kind of luck. Maybe he'd chosen the wrong piano. It made sense. In most grands, there was a small platform at the top of the rear leg, forming a cavity that could be used as a hiding place. Other small hidey-holes were created by the support braces used in the construction of the piano itself. Could something have been hidden in one of them?

Moving swiftly now, he collected some hand tools

within easy reach and began a minute examination of the two grands. Starting with the Lady first, he loosened, poked, probed and pried. Twice, dust got up his nose and made him sneeze. Each time he froze, fearful the raucous sound would wake the dead. Or something worse. And each time he had to gather the shreds of his nerves and stick them back together again. He was jumpier than hammers on the strings.

He didn't find anything, of course. He wasn't surprised. He'd been pretty thorough in his initial examination.

A bump against the outside kitchen wall penetrated his concentration. The door was locked and lights were on all over the Coop. That should've made him feel safe and secure. But with the windows acting as a one-way mirror, he was exposed and vulnerable to any pair of peering eyes that happened to be out in the fog-laden night.

As casually as he could manage, he stood up and brushed the dust off his clothes. If someone was watching, he'd better convince him he was merely examining the grands, getting them ready for their restoration. He began to explore the heavy legs, running skillful hands over the curves and carvings, as if judging the wood for refinishing, hefted the lids a time or two, testing their weight, and examined the hinge screws that would have to come out for removal. Then his imagination deserted him. He could think of nothing more to examine. He replaced his tools and called it a night.

Without appearing to be listening hard, he moved around the studio part of the Coop, turning off all lamps except the soft reading one by his chair. Then he put a kettle of water on to boil for tea. Just an innocent householder going about his nightly routine. But he felt as if his ears had grown a mile. They just about twitched, like a dog's, alert for the slightest sound, the slightest out-of-kilter noise that would indicate a watcher. There was nothing. Only silence.

He had his tea, though he didn't want it, and browsed through a manual on piano parts, though he didn't want to, and when enough time had passed that he felt he'd convinced anyone out there of his ease, he changed into pajamas, turned off the light and went to bed.

Lying stiff on the mattress, hidden by the dark now, he could openly listen. A measure of time passed. Only the intense silence of the winter night surrounded him. Then, in the far distance, he heard the crack of a twig. A few minutes later came a second snap, farther away. Whoever had been out there must've been convinced that Paul was just finishing up a normal workday and had gone away.

Feeling somewhat safer, he rolled over on his side, trying to relax into the mattress, but his mind wouldn't allow it. He had a strong urge to go to Ben Murdock. If something had been hidden in the grands, it would've been placed there twenty years ago, probably by Ilsa. And Ben would be the only person who could possibly help figure out what it might have been.

He tossed and turned for a while, sleep moving further and further away. Finally, he shoved the covers back and got up.

Leaving the lights off, he made a tour of the windows. Nothing but gray blankness and silence out there now. He seemed to be alone. He drew in a deep breath. All right, then, he'd chance it.

Working by feel, he pulled on his clothes and shoes. His sense of time said it was close to midnight. A bit late for a social call, but so be it.

Ben's place was on the opposite side of the Island, directly west of his. He made his way there silently, sticking to the roads when he felt he could, and slipping soundlessly into the trees when he sensed any danger at all. As much of a hindrance as the fog was to him, it cloaked his movements as well. Friend and foe, all at once. Like the killer?

Chapter Thirty-five

Ben's farm was a large, sprawling place at the head of a long sweep of pasture to the sea, lost now in the fog. The house was an old, simple two-story farmhouse, with a wing that jutted off to the side. Diffused light drifted from two of the wing's corner bottom windows. Paul crept up to the side of one pane and cautiously peered in.

Ben was in robe and slippers, sitting in one of a pair of wing chairs in front of a massive fireplace, brandy snifter on a table beside him. A fire had been laid and his eyes were fixed on the flames. He sat so long without blinking that Paul knew he was seeing nothing. Nothing in this world, at least.

Not knowing who else might be in the house, Paul tapped on the window, rather than take the risk of ringing the doorbell. As he did so, he pressed his face close to the glass and waved, so that Ben would know who it was. When he had his attention, he held one finger to his lips for silence.

Ben rose and nodded, and indicated the front door. Paul slipped free of the shrubbery, checked the night silence for any disturbance, then crossed the open lawn area.

Without turning on lights, Ben had the door open and was waiting for him, but he used his body to block the entrance. "What can I do for you, Paul?"

"I need to talk to you, and I don't want anyone seeing me."

Night shadows made it impossible to see the other man's face. Ben weighed the request for a long moment, then finally moved aside, motioning him in.

Ben led him to his study and indicated the vacant wing chair across the side table from his own, then drew the drapes across the window. Without asking, he poured Paul a brandy.

Paul accepted the glass gratefully. Now that he was in a warm room, he realized how deeply the cold, raw air had permeated his body. He took a long sip, stretched legs out towards the fire, and in spite of the time and circumstances, sighed with blissful comfort.

On Ben's face, a small cast of humor inserted itself amidst the heavy lines of sadness. "I must do something about fixing up that Coop one of these days," he murmured.

"I'm sure your future tenants would be most appreciative. I know the current one would be."

Paul looked around at the book-lined walls, the massive walnut desk set facing the room in front of a pair of long windows and the well-worn Oriental carpet laid before the hearth. It was a masculine haven, needing only a baby grand in the far corner to complete his vision of the perfect study. "Was this where your wife kept her piano?" he asked gently.

The sadness returned full force. "Yes. It was where the desk is now. When I had to move the piano out because of Jason, I had the room redone." He stared into his brandy snifter. "I'm not so sure that was a wise decision. Sometimes, if the night and the mood are right, I can still hear her music." He looked up at

Paul. "She was very gifted, you know." Ben lapsed back into a brooding silence.

"Yes, I can imagine she was." Paul waited a long moment, then, reluctantly, knowing he was going to increase this man's pain, he broke the silence. "Ben," he said quietly, "I'm sorry, but I need to know more about Ilsa. I think this whole series of killings is centered around her pianos, and to bring the killer to a halt, we have to figure out what, who and why."

Ben was showing his years now, his face heavily lined, his eyes filled with ancient sorrow. Paul's memory of the youthful, energetic, take-charge executive he'd first met seemed now to be nothing more than a faded snapshot from years before. Ben brooded a moment longer before lifting weary eyes to Paul. "I'm not sure I understand. What could a bitter, unhappy woman of twenty years ago have to do with what's going on today?"

"Harrison was the first man killed. Even before Jason. Every other death that's followed has been to cover up the first. So Harrison's the focal point, the primary target. The Sheriff has run a complete background check on him, and there's nothing there that ordinarily would lead to a violent end. No drugs, no criminal record, no anything. He was simply a lovelorn guy whose girlfriend eloped with a rich buddy. So if there was nothing in his past to make him a target for murder, then it has to be in his present. Prior to his coming to the Island, he had no connection with anyone here. He was a total stranger. He wasn't even in on the Island telegraph. He had no way of learning anything about anyone. Particularly something worth killing him over. Yet he posed a danger to someone, a serious enough danger to have to kill him. The question becomes how and why."

Paul paused a moment to reflect in his brandy glass. "I think I've answered the how. In a grand, there are usually several small chambers formed by the design of the piano, above the rear leg and on top of the brace work. Both of your grands have them. I checked them thoroughly tonight. But the chambers are empty. There's nothing there."

He set his glass down, rose and moved to the fireplace, where he leaned against the mantle. "But supposing, Ben," he continued in a soft voice, "supposing there *had* been something hidden there and Harrison found it and the killer learned he'd found it. That would explain his murder."

Paul came to a halt, seeking the next step in the logical order of events.

Ben waited a moment then said, "Go on."

Paul shook his head. "That's the problem. That's as far as I can take it. I wasn't here when Ilsa was. I didn't know her, and never met her. I can't carry it any further, because if something was hidden in the piano, it's most likely that she put it there. That's where I need your help. I need you to tell me what she might have placed there that would've been important enough to cause a man's death twenty years later."

Silence engulfed them. Ben was lost once again in the past. Paul suspected that when on the Island, he spent a good portion of his time going back there. There's a lesson buried somewhere in there for you, Laddie Boy, he told himself.

Finally Ben reached a decision and his gaze refocused on the present. "You're right, I think. It's the only thing that does make sense. But I'm going to be a disappointment to you, for I don't know everything. In fact, I don't know much. Partly because I never wanted to." Reluctantly, he lifted his gaze up to Paul. "You see, during those last few years with me, Ilsa had a series of love affairs. Mostly in Minneapolis. She didn't think I knew and I never let on I did. As long as she was discreet about them, I tolerated the situation for Jason's sake. He adored her and it would've been tremendously damaging to him to take him away from her, and I wasn't going to leave Ilsa without him." He made a wry face. "The classic stalemate, I'm afraid."

"You said most of them were in Minneapolis. Did she have one here on the Island?"

Ben nodded. "That last summer she was here."

"Who was it?"

"I don't know, Paul. I never made an effort to find out. In all honesty, I didn't want to know, because then I might've been forced to do something about it. Everyone here was a friend of mine. How do you cope with that?"

"Haven't you wondered about it all these years, though?"

"Yes, of course I have. I think that's one reason I've stayed away as much as I have. I used to look at Abner and Bobbin and Calvin and wonder, 'Was it you, my friend? Were you the one?' It was terrible not knowing, I assure you."

"What made you suspect anything at all was going on?"

"I think I explained to you the first day we talked that Ilsa was tremendously unhappy that summer she was here, worse than usual. And I think I described to you the heavy music she played, and the long, solitary walks she'd take. What I didn't mention is that oftentimes she'd take my boat out late at night, ride across the Sound and spend hours on the mainland."

"How do you know?"

"Because I followed her." The admission was made with a degree of shame. "I was worried about her, so I followed her to make sure she'd do nothing—foolish."

"Suicide, you mean."

Ben gave a reluctant nod. "She seemed tormented, tormented by devils. And I'd follow her down to the dock I've got below, always staying out of sight, of course, and then I'd climb up to the bluff and watch the wake of the boat to make sure she made it to shore. Then I'd wait until she was ready to return home and was safely docked back here again. But then, one night, she never came back."

"But she made it to shore."

"Yes. She docked the boat in the marina across the Sound and disappeared forever."

"Did she have anything unusual with her that night? Luggage, for instance?"

"No. Just her purse, and a light jacket against the night chill. It can get cold at night here, even in summertime."

"But she made it across, you're sure."

"If you mean, did she have a boating accident, or jump or fall overboard, I can assure you she didn't. She had the running lights on all the way across, and when she entered the marina, she swung the bow around and backed into the slip."

"That was her usual habit, backing in?"

"Yes."

A sudden thought struck Paul. "But," he began slowly, "if she were planning to run away that night, wouldn't she have guided the boat straight in to the slip? I mean, why would she care if it was in bow-first if she wasn't coming back?"

It took a minute, then the implication hit. Ben's face went white. "Oh, dear God," he whispered. "No! That's impossible! What you're implying is impossible!"

"But it isn't, is it?" Paul said softly.

Ben's shocked eyes were glued to Paul's. "But if she'd been killed, then where would she have been"—he stumbled over the word—"*put*?" he finally selected.

Paul took his seat and leaned forward, arms resting on his thigh. "Tell me what you did after she disappeared."

Ben struggled to regain his thinking. "I waited till dawn, then roused Old Jeb. He took his boat across and found mine, still docked. Then we roused the others and began searching for her. We searched everywhere. We searched the Island here. We combed the shoreline looking for an extra boat she might've used to come back in. And we searched the marina and Steilacoom, in case she'd come to some harm. We searched everywhere we could think of."

"Who's we?"

"Why, Old Jeb, and Abner, and Bobbin and Calvin, and any other man available."

"Then all the men were on the Island when you roused them?"

"Yes."

"But if she was meeting one of them on the mainland . . ."

Ben waved that away. "There are a hundred ways to get here from the mainland without being seen. There are coves and inlets winding in and out all along this shorefront. I didn't rouse anyone until morning, remember."

"And what about the mainland? Did you check on hospitals and morgues and places like that?"

"Of course. We called around, and Abner and Bobbin went into town and toured everything, including the jail. Just in case she'd been picked up on a traffic ticket or something. Then after a couple of days, I hired a private detective from Seattle and he retraced the whole ground again."

"Did he check trains and planes and the bus station?"

Ben nodded. "And taxicabs. She'd disappeared clean. There was no trace of her anywhere. Finally it was decided that she had a car hidden somewhere, and had simply driven off. God knows, I gave her money enough every month to afford a fleet of them, and I never would've known. Hell, I never would've even thought to check."

Paul lowered his gaze to his hands, loosely clasped on his knees. Long, slender fingers, able to span an octave plus two. And strong. Pianists' fingers were unusually limber and strong. Ilsa's probably had been, too. He lifted his head back up. "What about scratches or bruises, Ben? Did you notice anyone scratched or bruised during those days after she disappeared?"

"You mean as if she'd fought to protect herself? No, I'm sorry, I didn't."

"Okay. Let's make the assumption that she didn't just run away, that she was killed instead. And, back to the piano connection, let's assume she'd hidden something incriminating in the baby grand. Do you have any idea what it might've been?"

Ben thought a minute, then slowly shook his head. "Money? Cash to escape with?"

"Ah, but there your thinking's following the old idea of her running away. If she wasn't planning to leave you, why would she stash some getaway funds? No, it wouldn't have been money. More than likely, it would've been something of value to her. A ring, perhaps, an engraved ring given as a gift that she kept hidden. Something with a name on it that would identify the man involved."

"What about a letter? Or letters. Ilsa was lax about everything that summer, except for collecting the mail each day. When it was time for the mailman to drive by, she'd walk down to the end of the driveway and wait for him. Rain or shine, she never missed a day."

Paul thought about it, then nodded. "Love letters. That would make sense. With enough of a signature to identify the sender. Harrison had to have been aware of your position and power on the Island. The Islanders make it pretty apparent from the first step off the ferry boat. Maybe there weren't any dates on the letters and he didn't realize that the letters were written twenty years ago. Then when he discovered them, he put two and two together, thinking the affair was still going on, and he figured your wife's lover wouldn't want you to know about it. He was hard up for money, we know; he'd already lost a girlfriend because of his poverty. So he tried a spot of blackmail, threatening to expose Ilsa's lover if he didn't pay up. The lover, having killed Ilsa, couldn't afford to have the past brought up, so Harrison had to die."

While Paul was speaking, Ben had gradually straightened in his chair. As he'd followed the reasoning, his face took on a firmer, more energetic look. "It makes sense." He nodded. "Yes, it does." Some of the CEO aura returned and his eyes narrowed with sharpness. "Then what about you? Where do you come into this? After all, you didn't find anything, didn't try any blackmail, yet the killer still went after you."

The answer came without thinking. What happened was so clear to Paul now, he could see the whole thing laid out like an opera, each scene leading to the next. "When I first arrived, the killer had to have been in a panic at the thought that he'd eliminated one Piano Man only to have him replaced by a second. So he tried to kill me, too. But then he changed his mind. First of all, I wasn't working on the grands, I was concentrating on the upright instead. And second, he wasn't sure that he'd received all the letters hidden in the pianos. Maybe he could remember writing more of them than he took away from Harrison. He might even have searched the grands before I arrived, trying to make sure he had them all, but chances are, he wouldn't have found the hidden chambers. Few people outside of pianists would know they even exist. So it behooves him to wait until I've taken the grands apart, see what I find, then finish me off if he has to. That way, he knows the threat of exposure is finally dead and buried, that there'll be no unpleasant surprises awaiting him in the future."

"But what about the piano strings, Paul? If Harrison was the first one murdered, how would the killer have gotten hold of one to use as a murder weapon?"

"You know, Ben," Paul said slowly, "the Sheriff asked me once how much work Harrison had done on the pianos before he was killed. At the time, I told him I thought he hadn't touched them at all. But maybe that was unfair. There's a good possibility that the first thing Harrison did was to remove all the strings. If they'd still been in the pianos when I arrived, that's what I'd have done. I'd have taken off every string first so I could have access to the interior of the pianos to check the soundness of the wood. I suspect that's what Harrison did, and they were lying about in plain sight when the murderer showed up. After twenty years, our killer must've been feeling pretty safe, and he might not have come prepared to kill. When the need arose, he simply grabbed the handiest weapon he could find."

Ben rose, vigor in his movements now, and held out his hand for Paul's glass for a refill of brandy. The CEO was definitely back and in charge. "All right," he said briskly, "we're almost home. We've figured out the how and why; now we have to figure out the who. To do that, we've got to unmask the killer somehow. Do you have any thoughts along those lines?"

"Unfortunately." Paul stretched his legs toward the fire and accepted the refill with a murmur of thanks. An image of a goat tethered in a clearing came to mind. He paused for a last second thought, then gave a sad smile. "I guess it's time I took those grands apart."

Chapter Thirty-six

He spent the next day stripping the grands. Keys, hammers, felts and keyboard frames gave up their reluctant place in life. Age had set its mark upon them, melding one into the next, and nothing came out easily. It was long, frustrating work that took him into the early evening hours before the final part came free. He was so tired that he ate a quick supper and fell into bed.

In the morning, he stood long moments under a hot shower, trying to drive the chills of apprehension out of his body with a strong spray. Everything was as organized as it could be. The night at Ben's house, he and Ben had called Tom over to join in a strategy session. Tom would've been only twelve when Ilsa disappeared, too young to be the "other man" in her life. So he was in the clear, as were most of the Pickup Brigade.

The three men had spent the remaining night hours making their plans, with a promise extracted by Paul that at least one member of the Pickup Brigade would guard the store at all times. There were enough uncertainties in the scheme they'd come up with, without having Jenny or Thaddeus led into danger by someone they trusted. And the killer *was* among the trustworthy, Paul thought, as he turned his back to the shower head and let the hot spray pummel aching shoulder muscles.

Calvin, Old Jeb, or Abner. Eliminating everyone not the right age left only those three as suspects. That was it. Finite. No other possibilities existed.

Going over the three men in his mind, Paul subtracted two decades from their ages, trying to come up with a picture of each of them as a sexual male. It was nearly impossible. Old Jeb was an old banty rooster and most likely had been born one. It was hard to picture him even knowing what a hormone was, never mind experiencing one. Except, of course, he must've, for he'd found enough juice within himself to marry his missus.

Abner and Calvin were easier. Subtract twenty years and forty pounds from Abner, and he'd have cut an imposing figure, stately and dignified. The kind of man that just might appeal to an unstable, unhappy woman. And Calvin? Well, turn his hair black again and thicken it up, toss in those deep brooding eyes and chiseled features, and you'd have a man with a primordial appeal for some women. Particularly his muscles. Don't forget the muscles. The man's limbs were as thick as logs. Yes, Paul could see his swarthy presence sending strong primitive signals to a certain kind of woman.

Okay. He'd narrowed it down to two. Abner and Calvin. But which one? Which one would think so little of Ben Murdock that they'd get involved with his wife?

Well, he'd know soon enough.

That thought brought back his apprehension full

force. As he dressed, he roamed the Coop, peering through windows, trying to get a sense of the kind of day it would be. Outside, the fog was a thick mass of gray pressing close against the panes. He couldn't see the shed, nor Bobbin's truck parked next to it. The road below was silent. A good day to stay safe and sound behind a securely locked door, he thought.

He finished dressing, then pulled on his heavy jacket. Fog or no fog, he had to go to the deli. At the back door he hesitated, wanting only to turn around and return to his pianos. He drew in a long, shaky breath, jerked the door open and left the Coop, making sure the door was locked behind him.

The truck headlights cast misty halos a few inches ahead of the hood before dissipating into the murk. He rolled down the window and made it down the driveway, his head stuck out the opening. On the main road, he crept along, looking straight down to where the yellow stripe was barely discernible. The trip took forever.

As he approached the store, fear sent his heart rate skyward. Last chance, Whitman. Last chance to climb on the early ferry to town and keep on going. He imagined an old wooden saloon somewhere in the mountains of Colorado, just waiting for a pianist to show up. Then his chin firmed up and he swung the pickup into the parking lot.

He inched down the line of trucks already parked there, found an open spot and pulled in. He gave quick thought to postponing the whole venture until the weather changed when he tripped over the curb in front of the store because he couldn't distinguish its cement color from the dirty gray of the fog. Except it could be days before the fog cleared, and who knew what the killer was planning next?

As he went through the doorway into the store, bright lights, coffee smells and the loud buzz of voices brought him up short. It was like a time warp, a sudden thrust backward to his first few mornings on the Island. With the discovery of Jason's body, all searches had been halted for good, and with the fog as thick as it was, no outside work could be done, so the Islanders had gathered in the deli.

Thaddeus was at the cash register as usual. Paul nodded, then his eyes sought Jenny. She was peeling potatoes, her head bent over her work, her face flushed from the steam rising from the boiling stock pot. She was dressed in what he'd come to think of as her uniform—dark skirt, white blouse, simple pearl pendant on a gold chain. Her hair fell forward over her cheeks, and he had an impulse to smooth it back from her face.

As if in answer to his whim, she paused for a moment, straightened up and brushed the hair off her forehead with the back of her hand. She caught sight of him then. She started to give him a warm grin of welcome, but as she scanned his face and noted the weariness there, her expression changed to one of concern. He smiled to ease her worry, filled his coffee cup and turned to the tables.

They were all there. Abner, Old Jeb, Calvin, Ben Murdock, Tom and Zeke. Plus assorted other members of the Pickup Brigade. Tom Ross moved his chair over and swung an empty one between himself and Calvin. "Come on over, Piano Man."

"Thanks." He sank into the chair and nodded around the table. "Morning."

"You drive down?" Tom asked.

"Yep. That was a real treat."

Zeke scoffed. "Should'a seen the fogger in 'eighty-six. That was a humdinger. It was so bad you couldn't see your own eyelids."

War stories of previous fogs carried them through a second round of coffee, then Jenny put the last peeled potato on to boil and came over for their breakfast orders.

Before ordering, Paul raised a hand for silence. "Tell you what," he announced, "I could use some help. The upright's ready for tuning. It's on its back and needs righting today. Anyone who'll help, breakfast is on me."

Enthusiasm greeted his request. It was something to do to relieve the boredom of a day idled by the weather. They ordered hearty, ate hearty, scraped the last piece of toast across the egg yolk, drank the last swallow of coffee, then bustled around, pulling on outdoor gear. Only one brawny member of the Pickup Brigade remained seated, settled in for the morning with a full coffeepot nearby. Paul scooped up all the checks, including Jenny's guard's, laid some bills near the cash register and led the way out.

Old Jeb, so familiar with the road he didn't have to see the dips and curves to know they were there, headed the caravan. Even though Paul rode his bumper, he still had trouble seeing the taillights in the fog. The rest were in line behind him, nose to tail like an elephant train.

Once in the Coop, they grouped around the upright. Tom took charge, placing the strongest men at the corners. "All right, on the count of three. One, two, three, hike!"

As easily as a piece of sheet music, the piano was lifted to its feet. Paul inserted the frame box and secured it into place. Then to show them what the finished piano would look like, he replaced the back panels above the pedals, covering the strings.

"Is it playable now?" Tom asked. "We've never heard you, you know."

Paul shook his head. "The strings have to be brought up to pitch and tuned."

Zeke plunked a key. The sound came out a dull clunk. "Gawd, I'll say. That's awful."

They stood back and admired it. Calvin studied it from top to bottom, running his fingertips lightly over the wood, feeling the smoothness, searching the wood for the slightest flaw. Old Jeb watched intently, as if waiting for Calvin's verdict. Abner stood quietly to one side.

Finally, Calvin gave a nod of grudging respect. "Not bad," he muttered. He studied Paul the way he had the piano, as if he might have to revise his opinion of him. Then his gaze moved on to the partly decimated grands. "These next?"

Paul's throat suddenly went dry. "Yep. Believe it or not, they'll end up as magnificent as the Old Soldier. Maybe more so." He wandered over to the grands. "I could use some help here, too. These lids have to come off and they weigh a ton."

The Pickup Brigade gathered around the pianos. They balanced the lids open for Paul so he could get the hinges unscrewed, then they grabbed each slab of ebony and hefted it gently into a corner of the studio, out of the way. Once through, the men peered into the empty piano cases like voyeurs at a gravesite.

"Strange-looking, aren't they, without their innards." Paul gave them a moment to absorb the emptiness, then added, "By the way, if you happen to see the Sheriff, tell him I've got something to show him, something I found."

Like a class of dutiful students, they all nodded. Mission accomplished.

Chapter Thirty-seven

He was working in octaves, bringing the strings up to pitch, when the roar of an engine struggling to come up the rutted drive broke through his concentration. He stood to one side of the back door window, searching for some clue as to the caller's identity. The fog was too thick to see whose vehicle it was. Then a vague outline formed in the mist, coming toward him.

He viewed the Sheriff with a mixture of relief and consternation. On the one hand, he was relieved the killer wasn't there, but on the other, he wasn't thrilled about facing the Sheriff either. He felt like a poacher with illegal traps set and the game warden on his doorstep. But there was no avoiding it, he'd have to let the man in. He'd let him have his visit, tell him nothing, and see him safely on his way. He turned the key in the lock and swung the door open.

The Sheriff's expression as he entered was grumpy. "What a miserable drive that was. Even the birds are walking."

Paul managed a slight grin. "And a good day to you, too. I'm surprised the ferry's running today."

"Only time that thing shuts down is when the barnacles grow barnacles," the Sheriff grumbled. "Or when God wants to trap me here on this godforsaken piece of real estate. Hear tell you got the grands stripped naked."

With a sudden sense of foreboding, Paul recognized a flaw in his scheme. He hadn't figured the Islanders would've bothered mentioning that to the Sheriff. It simply wasn't that important to anyone . . . except the killer, of course. Slowly he nodded.

The Sheriff grunted. "Guess I'd better take a look if I'm to keep up on my restoring lessons."

Paul wanted the Sheriff gone and out of the way; he didn't want to prolong the visit a minute longer than necessary. Yet the man had become so accustomed to being shown everything, Paul didn't dare risk raising any suspicions. He bit back his impatience and led him into the studio.

The Sheriff seemed shocked by the emptiness of the piano shells. Without strings, keyboard, frame boxes or lids, the grands sat like two black, hulking bodies without bone, tissue or teeth. He bent over and looked into, under and around each of the pianos, seeming to search for the pieces.

Finally, he straightened. "Amazing, purely amazing, what they look like this way. Nothing much more than empty harp crates." He studied him a minute. "Calvin says you've found something in one of them when you stripped them down?"

Paul was suddenly exasperated. Flaw number two. When he'd told the Pickup Brigade to tell the Sheriff he'd found something, it had been just a way to get the message to the killer, not the Sheriff. With the fog as thick as it was, Paul figured it would be days before the Islanders would have the opportunity to pass the message on. Now he found himself dancing around a trap of his own making and he couldn't think of a way out. Goddamn it. What else had he overlooked?

He tried to dodge the question. He hemmed and hawed until, uncharacteristically, the Sheriff lost patience.

"Either you found something or you didn't," he snapped. "And if you did, I want to see it."

This was *not* going as planned. Paul cast about one last time for a way out. He either had to admit he'd lied, or he had to produce something. The only thing he could think of was to produce what he would've produced for the killer. It wasn't a great idea. It wasn't even a good one. And there was no time to think the implications through. But it was the only idea he had. Moving slowly, reluctance in every step, he fished out the combination wrench he'd found on the beach weeks before.

Frowning with puzzlement, the Sheriff weighed it in his hands. "Yeah, so?"

"So? So what?"

"This is the great discovery you made?"

Paul said nothing.

"Cat got our tongue today?"

"It's something I found."

"So you've said. So, what's so great about it?"

"I thought it might be important, that's all."

"You thought it might be important." The Sheriff studied him a moment, then sighed. "All right, let's have it, the whole story."

If there was a way out, Paul couldn't find it. The Sheriff waited patiently while he tried, his arms crossed, his gaze glued to his. Trapped, Paul had to tell him about the incident on Lyle Point with the crashing ladder.

The Sheriff listened without interruption, and stayed silent a long moment after Paul had finished. "That's it," he said with flat disbelief. "That's what the big 'find' was."

"That's it."

"Something that you found two months ago, and just remembered having."

Paul nodded.

"And you found nothing in the pianos."

"Nothing."

"Then why spread the word you did?"

"I didn't spread the word I did. While the men were gathered around the pianos, I happened to remember it and said—and I quote myself exactly—'By the way, when you see the Sheriff, tell him I found something.'"

"But the implication was you found the something in the pianos."

"I guess."

"Why?"

His grand scheme was disintegrating with every question. Paul paced back and forth to the window, trying to preserve as much of it as he could. There didn't seem to be a way. Or if there was, he couldn't think of it. Finally, he stopped pacing and stood by the window, staring out at nothing, his voice tired. "It occurred to me that maybe Harrison was killed because he found something hidden in one of the grands, and I thought maybe I'd smoke the killer out if he thought I found it."

"But why did you tell them to tell me?"

Paul's misery was running deep. He turned to face him. "Because I couldn't just announce it. I needed to have a reason to bring it up and that seemed the simplest way. You have official authority. If I *had* found something in the pianos, you'd be the one to be told."

There was a long moment of silence, then the laugh began. It started as a chuckle, born deep in the belly, then swelled into a full-bodied guffaw. Frank enjoyed himself hugely. When at last his mirth died down to a last few chortles, he said, "Amateurs," to no one in particular.

Paul had never felt so stupid.

The Sheriff was relaxed now, his face once more bland and amused. "All right, Piano Man, you better show me this miracle ladder of yours. The one that crashes to pieces, then resurrects itself."

Paul was appalled. "Now?! In this pea soup?!"

"And take a jacket. It's colder'n a glacier out there."

Furious, Paul grabbed up his jacket, his face set with anger.

Nothing was going as planned. *Nothing!*

▮

The Sheriff drove. Creeping through the fog, the noise of the patrol car muffled by the thick, damp air, they headed south, then east, skirting Oro Bay. They took the south fork to Lyle Point, where the cliff and the repaired ladder waited. Paul wondered miserably if Tom, keeping watch, would put the plan into motion even though it was the Sheriff he had gone off with, not one of their suspects. If he did, the whole scheme was beyond salvaging.

The road dead-ended on the high bluff. Still angry, Paul hopped out before the patrol car was quite stopped. He started to stalk off toward the clearing when he realized he had already lost his bearings. Within steps, the fog had swallowed up the car. He hastily retreated until he had visual contact with Frank again. "Guess we ought to stay together," he muttered.

Frank was rummaging in the trunk of the patrol car. He backed out, ropes coiled around his shoulders, flashlights in each hand. He gave one to Paul. "What we're gonna do is tie a rope to the car fender and pay it out as we go. We gotta have some way of gettin' back. When you reach the end of this piece, hitch another section on, and another and another. There's a whole batch more, so you take these." He handed the coils to Paul, then disappeared again.

Paul had the first coil fastened in a double hitch to the bumper and was testing the pull when Frank reappeared beside him. The fog had hidden his movements and Paul started when the other man materialized at his side. "Jesus, Frank, you might as well kill a man as scare him to death."

Smiling, Frank bent down to hitch the end of his rope next to Paul's.

Somewhere in the distance a foghorn blared wearily in the Sound. A few feet out, securely anchored by the umbilical rope, Paul looked back. The patrol car had vanished from sight. He turned around and forged on.

The fog was everywhere. Swirling around the base of the trees, clothing thickets like spun cotton, wrapping itself around branches like bandages. Once in the woods, to keep on the path, he had to shine the flashlight directly in front of his feet. Looking down like that put him at the ruthlessness of every bush, thicket and tree branch reaching out to grab him. He hadn't thought to bring gloves and the thorns were without mercy. Except for the regular lowing of the foghorn, the silence was intense. He felt himself the lone survivor of an earth disaster. Swamped by a sudden desolation, he stopped and called, "Frank, you okay?"

"Okay." The disembodied voice echoed from somewhere behind him. The foghorn blared again as punctuation.

Progress was marked by ropes. One after another after another. His only lifeline in a world of elusive gray. Finally, the path broadened into the clearing.

His first awareness was the lack of whipping from the thickets. Then came a sense of space and level ground. At the higher elevation, the fog thinned considerably and he was able to see vague outlines of trees and shrubs edging the large expanse of space. The air was tangy with salt and carried the smell of mudflats at low tide. The bluff edge was near. His rope, his last rope, was about played out. Only a couple of coils of it remained slung around his shoulder.

He looked behind him. There was no flashlight glow he could see. "Frank?"

"Behind you." The answer drifted through the fog.

"I've reached the Point."

"I'm almost there."

Paul inched forward, a step and a sweep of his

flash at a time. It was a dozen steps before his light showed only mist swirling ahead of his feet. The bluff edge.

He backed up a couple of steps and listened hard. He could just make out the whisper of surf a hundred feet below.

The foghorn lowed like a mournful tuba. The world seemed to hold its breath until it was finished. Holding tight to his rope, he moved back from the bluff edge to safety.

From behind, the Sheriff barked out a gruff command. "Just hold it there, Piano Man. Right there. Don't even twitch."

Paul swung around, then froze. The Sheriff stood a few feet away. In one hand he held a thick, dead tree limb that he was using like a staff, leaning his weight on it in a casual pose. The other hand aimed a gun straight at Paul's chest.

Paul stared. "What the hell are you doing?!"

The Sheriff's blandness was still in place. From the look on his face, he might've been holding a coffee mug instead of a weapon. "Well, now, Piano Man, I'll tell you. You're going to have an unfortunate accident right off the cliff here."

"What the hell are you talking about?!" Paul demanded.

The Sheriff ignored him. "It's too bad in a way. I enjoyed our little game of cat-and-mouse. You made such an intriguing prey. Kinda sad it has to come to an end."

Paul stared at him. "You?" he whispered. *"You?! You did all those killings?!"*

"Me." The usual amusement turned to mockery.

"To think, Piano Man, your trap worked. That's what I found so entertaining back at the Coop. It worked, it surely worked. And you were too stupid to know it." He laughed once again. "That one's going to keep me chuckling the rest of my days."

Paul was still trying to comprehend it all. Protest after protest welled up within him. This couldn't be. The Sheriff wasn't even on his list of suspects. This couldn't be!

Slowly, though, his situation began to sink in. Unbelievable or not, he was here with the killer, on an isolated clifftop, with a gun pointing straight at his heart. He was going to die. The Sheriff was going to kill him. He was going to die.

His mind, sluggish from shock, began to seek a way out. He took stock of his position. Rope still in hand, slack now. Clearing on three sides of him. Nothing near to use as a weapon. Bluff edge two paces behind. *God!* Buy time, he told himself. Buy time. "You'll never get away with this," he said flatly. "Not after Obadiah's fall. The Islanders won't accept another accident happening here."

"Oh, I think I'll be able to persuade them. I've woven enough incriminating evidence into my file on you to convict you—post-mortem, of course—as the killer. You see, the way it'll go is, when you realized I knew you were the guilty one, you tried to get away. I followed you here, and in your haste to escape, you misjudged the edge of the bluff in the fog, and off you went. Poor Piano Man. My file will be reviewed, and guilt pronounced. Case closed. The Islanders will be glad it's over, and relieved—very relieved—it wasn't one of their own. So they'll be happy, and I'll be happy. The perfect ending to a perfect crime."

A branch cracked back in the woods surrounding the clearing. The noise was sharp and loud, like a gunshot. The foghorn lowed again, masking any more sounds. When the mournful note had died away, the woods stood silent once more.

At the snapping sound, the Sheriff's eyes narrowed and he glanced around, trying to penetrate the foggy perimeter of the tree line. He listened hard a minute, then turned his attention back to Paul. His easy relaxed stance was gone now. His face was harsh with impatience. "Time to wrap this up."

Keeping a wary eye on Paul, the Sheriff holstered his gun. He shifted his hold on the dead tree limb, changing it from a staff to a baseball bat. He raised it back over one shoulder, took a long step forward and gave a hefty swing. Paul's head was squarely in the middle of the strike zone.

In the second before impact, Paul dug one foot in against the force coming at him, at the same time throwing himself sideways, grabbing hard at his rope to keep his direction landward. The blow caught his upper left arm and he staggered.

Off-balance now, the Sheriff's body slammed into Paul's and they both crashed to earth. A lifetime of fitness had built muscle and sinew as tough as tree trunks, and the Sheriff scrambled on top of Paul, using his body to pin Paul's chest down.

In a desperate surge of strength, Paul heaved and flung the Sheriff off, rolling frantically towards land. It was a mistake. The rope wound around Paul's chest like a mummy wrap. His upper arms were glued to his sides.

The Sheriff grunted with satisfaction and scrambled on top again. Pinioning Paul's body between his log-like legs, he made a fast adjustment in the top coil of the rope and slipped the loop up around Paul's neck. A yank of the end and it cut across the esophagus like a tight bow tie.

Red rage spread through Paul like a prairie fire. Paul stiffened his neck muscles, trying to get breathing room. That cut off the windpipe further. He clawed at the ropes further down, trying to free his arms. It got him nowhere.

Dimly, through the roaring in his ears, Paul heard a voice snap out, "That's enough, Frank! Let him go!" Ben Murdock loomed over both men.

The noose tightened, cutting off Paul's breath.

"Let him go, Frank! *That's enough, let him go!*"

There were men everywhere now. Several pairs of hands grabbed the Sheriff by the shoulder and yanked him backwards. Frank fought for long seconds before enough men's hands could break him free of the rope. He was dragged off Paul and flung aside.

The rope was quickly unwound. Dazed, Paul sat up. They were all there, Abner, Tom, Old Jeb, Zeke, Calvin, and some of the Pickup Brigade. Wisps of fog cloaked ankles and feet, and they drifted like ghosts as they milled about. Forming a semicircle, Ben at the head, they stared down at the two men still on the ground.

Tom broke the tableau and bent over to give Paul a hand up. "You all right, Piano Man?"

As Paul tried to rise, his legs gave out and he sank onto the tangles of rope around him. Heart hammering, lungs shrunken to walnuts, guts twisted in on themselves, he drew in a ragged breath. "I guess," he croaked, his throat raw.

The Sheriff had regained control of himself. His motions easy now, he stood up, brushed debris off his clothes and turned Ben's way, his face bland and impassive once more. "Sorry, Ben, but I guess I saw red when I think of what this fella's been up to. Kind of glad you came along when you did. Saved me from committing a fearsome act of violence." His voice was amiable, his stance relaxed. "Been meaning to talk to you, Ben, about this Piano Man of yours. Seems like we got a bit of a problem here."

"What would that be, Frank?" Ben said, evenly.

"Looks to me like we've found our killer." He pointed to Paul.

The foghorn lowed again.

Chapter Thirty-eight

The men stood grouped around the two of them, staring from one to the other. Calvin nodded; suspicions confirmed. Abner stroked his beard. Zeke appeared neutral, uninvolved, like Old Jeb. Ben stood quiet, a thoughtful expression on his face.

Tom Ross looked as if he were going to tear the Sheriff apart, limb by limb. He snorted. "If the Piano Man's our killer, then what about the scene we wandered onto here? It took six of us to pull you off of him. How do you explain that?"

"Just a momentary loss of self-control, Tom, that's all it was," the Sheriff said blandly, "just a momentary loss of control. He brought me up here on some wild goose chase of showing me some new evidence, then came at me with a dead branch, trying to knock me off the bluff. I took that real personal, I can tell you." He pointed to the branch laying near the bluff edge. "That's it over there, see it?"

Heads swiveled to check and confirm. Out in the Sound, the foghorn blatted at regular intervals.

For the moment, Paul forced himself to stay put on the tangle of ropes. He wanted to rise up and grab the Sheriff by the throat and squeeze. He wanted to have a piano wire in hand and wrap *that* around the Sheriff's throat the way the man had done to Bobbin and Grace. He wanted to rise and strike out at the

Sheriff and back him all the way to the edge of the bluff, then back him up further. He wanted—

His blood curdled with his wants. His body shook with the force of them. Instead, he reined himself in under tight control. The game was deadly. He could afford no mistakes. There were men staring at him as if he were a venomous specimen in a jar. It wouldn't take much to set them off. And there was the Sheriff with his little game of cat-and-mouse. Now the mouse was under the paw—or so he thought—and one firm push downwards and wham!—splatted mouse. Easy, Whitman, he told himself. Easy now.

Moving cautiously so as not to startle anyone into precipitous action, he slowly rose to his feet.

The Sheriff was speaking, his voice deadly quiet. "You see, Ben, I've run a complete background check on our friend here. He's not quite the innocent he'd like us to think he is. Beggin' your pardon, Ben, but it seems like there was a connection between him and Ilsa that goes way back. Early on, he played a few concerts in Minneapolis and that's where they met. They did a lot of running around together there for a couple of years. Then, that last year Ilsa came out to the Island, the summer she disappeared? Why, our Piano Man cancelled his concerts for the whole of that season and came out here so he could see more of her. They used to meet at night, over on the mainland, Ilsa traveling back and forth in your boat to see him."

"And you know this for a fact," Ben said, quietly.

The Sheriff nodded. "I've built up quite a file on him. I've got evidence of his cancelled tour, and I can come up with a motel clerk or two with a good memory who'd swear he saw them together that summer. I could probably even produce a registration card with his signature on it. Oh, he was here, no doubt about it. None."

Now the Sheriff's face took on a look of deep empathy. "Again, beggin' your pardon, Ben, I know it's going to be painful to hear this, but you see, I don't think Ilsa just disappeared. I think he killed her. I think just seeing her wasn't enough for him. He wanted her with him full time and he planned on taking her away from you. That's why he cancelled his tour to begin with. But despite what the Piano Man here thought was true love, Ilsa was only leading him on. She wasn't about to leave a life of wealth and comfort with you to run away with some two-bit piano player. My guess is that after waiting most of the summer for her to come away with him, Mr. Whitman finally called her bluff. She probably told him exactly what she thought of him, laughing at him the whole while. The humiliation must've been pretty hard to swallow. It turned him into a raging maniac and he killed her on the spot."

The men still stood in a loose semicircle around the Sheriff and Paul, listening closely, watching carefully. Center stage, the Sheriff was calm and composed, as relaxed as if he were discussing the weather over coffee. Paul stood to his right, a couple of paces away from the holstered gun.

Ben studied the Sheriff for a long moment. "But, Frank, even if Ilsa was killed, what would a killing that took place twenty years ago have to do with today? Why the rash of killings now?"

"My best guess, Ben, is—and mind you, it's only

a guess—that there was something incriminating stuck in those pianos. Something Ilsa put there, something that would link our Piano Man here to her disappearance. Harrison must've found it when he started working on the pianos and tried to blackmail him. To keep the link hidden, Harrison had to die."

Ben thought a moment, then shook his head. "I just don't see it, Frank. If he murdered Ilsa as you claim, and there'd been something hidden in the pianos, he had twenty years to find them. Why now? And what would Ilsa have hidden anyway?"

"Well, now, the 'what' part of your question's easy. Probably some trinkets of some kind. For memories and all that. Maybe a picture of the two of them together . . ."

Pictures! Paul suddenly latched on to the thought. Pictures would answer one problem that had troubled him in his theory. Harrison had been antisocial and had had nothing to do with the Islanders. Thus a signature on a letter would have had had no meaning to him. But a signature on a letter combined with a photo? The picture would identify the person and the letter would provide the name. Of course!

"As to the time gap—well, he probably had no idea Ilsa had hidden anything at all. Not until Harrison found them and tried his blackmail scheme. Then he realized they'd been saved." Frank shrugged. "Simple, when you think about it."

The frightening thing was how good he was. He had all the answers, and fielded every question with an easy flow of words designed to reassure and soothe, without once spilling over into the glib. At each point the Sheriff made, the men seemed more and more convinced. The concerts in Milwaukee, the cancelled tour, the motel clerks, the registration cards, Ilsa's known propensity for men, and finally, her complete and utter disappearance, with no trace ever . . . Each item added its weight to the damning whole. More and more of the Island men were nodding agreement. What the Sheriff said made sense to them. The man was beyond belief, Paul thought. Yet they believed. He fought down a sense of panic. He realized with horror that the theory he had outlined to Ben and Tom was being turned onto him. Would they believe the Sheriff, too?

"But there's a problem here, Frank," Ben said, after some thought. "You see, I ran my own check on Mr. Whitman. The concert tour cancelled the summer Ilsa disappeared? It seems he was hospitalized in New York for hepatitis. He wasn't released until after Labor Day. That's a pretty iron-clad alibi. And following the theory you just outlined, that completely eliminates him as a suspect."

For a brief instant, Paul thought the Sheriff was thrown by Ben's statement, but he merely gave a sheepish grin and shrugged. "See how fancy theories can lead you astray? Then the murders don't date back to Ilsa at all. There's a present-day reason for them, and we'll just have to get it out of him."

"But that's another problem, Frank," Ben said, "linking him to the current murders. According to your own information, Grace Duncan was killed between three and five the afternoon we were setting up the Fair. Mr. Whitman here was working under Nellie's nose during that time, either hanging wreaths or washing dishes back in the kitchen. And you know Nellie. When you work for Nellie, you work for Nellie. She doesn't take her eyes off of you for even a second." Ben gave him a chance to absorb that, then continued. "That means one of two things, Frank . . . either he killed all the others and someone else killed Grace—which means there's two killers involved—or he didn't do any of them. And I don't think we're dealing with two different killers here." He shook his head. "No, my guess is that your theory's right. I do think it involved Ilsa and something she hid in the pianos. I think you've explained it as it really did happen. You just picked the wrong man, is all."

The Sheriff was beginning to not like this. His eyes narrowed and his jawline tensed. His voice, though, was as folksy as ever. "Well, now, Ben, just who do you have in mind?"

Paul would never know what Ben would've answered. Determination to best this man was driving him now. This was his chance, and he grabbed it. "You, Frank. You're the killer, the one behind it all."

All was stillness. None of the Islanders moved. Even the foghorn was silent for a long moment.

Before anyone could react, Paul stepped forward in the semicircle and faced the Sheriff, still keeping part of his attention on the gun. Until the Islanders were convinced, he couldn't do anything about it. "It's been you all along, Frank. You weren't a big-shot in the department then, you were only a small-time rookie cop, good enough for Ilsa to play with, but not to be taken seriously. And when she found out you wanted her to leave Ben, she laughed at you. *You* were the one she laughed at, Frank, not me!"

The Sheriff regained his composure and bland amusement. "Nice try, Piano Man, but it won't wash."

Paul stared hard at him. "Once you know that Ilsa was a murder victim, not a runaway, the question then becomes, why didn't Ben and the rest of them suspect Ilsa was dead? Why *did* they so readily believe she'd run away? I'd guess it was the official report from the investigating authorities that convinced them." Keeping his eyes fastened on the Sheriff, he said, "Ben, what did that report state?"

"That there was no evidence of foul play. She was officially listed as a runaway wife."

"And who handled the official investigation into Ilsa's disappearance?"

"Frank did. He was the Island deputy then."

"So in effect, he investigated his own crime and closed the books on it. But then, twenty years later, Harrison comes along and discovers a photo and some letters hidden in a piano, and decides to engage in the little sideline business of blackmail. He *had* to be killed, didn't he, Frank? If anyone knew that you were her lover, they'd question the validity of that report, and the case would be reopened. So Harrison had to die, then Jason, and Obadiah—"

Shaking his head, the Sheriff interrupted Paul. "Obadiah was killed at night, well after the last ferry, and I attended a peace officers meeting that evening. There are twenty people or better who'll swear I wasn't on the Island that night."

"You own a boat, though, don't you?"

"And it's been up on blocks in winter storage since Labor Day." The Sheriff gave him a triumphant look. "If you check the log, you'll see it hasn't been out of the yard since they hauled her out of the water."

"Ah, but there's the missing rowboat, Frank."

"And the fire in the Coop? I flew in by chopper, if you'll recall."

"Then it's back to that missing rowboat, isn't it, Frank," Paul said flatly. "You knew we'd all be at Grace's for dinner, and what time we'd be there. She told you that when she invited you. So you row over, set up a delayed burn and row back to the mainland. It's only four miles across. You'd have plenty of time. Then when you get the call about the fire, you come roaring to the rescue by chopper, acting as surprised and shocked as anyone else. That was a clever piece of business, Frank. With a near-perfect alibi."

The Sheriff shook his head. "Nope, Piano Man, it still won't wash. There's no evidence at all against me."

"Oh, but there is, Frank. Get his key ring, Tom, and hand it to Ben."

As Tom started to move, the Sheriff's hand lunged for the gun in his hip holster.

Paul was ready. He sensed the motion and dived for the man's arm, trapping the gun hand against the leather, half-in, half-out. The two of them struggled for control, performing a bizarre ballet of flexed muscles and grunts.

The Sheriff's left hand raised high to deliver a karate chop on Paul's wrists.

Paul saw it coming. There was nothing he could do to stop it. He was helpless, both hands trapped holding a gun in place. If he let go, they'd all be killed. If he didn't let go, his piano playing days would be over, bones and nerves shattered by the blow. The *bastard!*

"You bastard!"

Paul thought at first he'd yelled the words. But Calvin had cleft the air with a guttural cry and leapt. With a sharp blow, he deflected the karate chop.

The Islanders' paralysis broken by Calvin's war whoop, bodies dived everywhere now. Tom jerked the right hand away from the gun. Zeke yanked the handcuffs free, grabbed the left arm and snapped a cuff in place. Even Old Jeb entered the fray, tackling the Sheriff around the ankles, teeth bared like a terrier ready to gouge a chunk of shin. Paul managed to free the gun from the holster, tossing it to Abner standing on the sidelines, then grabbed the arm once more.

It took five of them to wrestle him to the ground, and five of them to roll him face down in the mist-wet grass, and three to keep his body from lashing out while the other two fought to cuff the second wrist. When the cuff finally trapped the wrist, it clicked home with the grim finality of a prison door clanging shut.

Chests heaving from battle, the Islanders rose and brushed themselves clean. Then one by one, outrage gave way to dismay and dismay gave way to doubt. They formed a dead quiet circle around the fallen man. Was it really true? Was Frank the killer? If he was, what would be done about it? And if he wasn't, did that make the Piano Man the guilty one, in spite of what Ben had said? Was the Piano Man, after all, nothing more than a common killer who'd shrewdly alibied his way through two murders, then tried to place the blame elsewhere?

The men stared at the Sheriff, their senses like tentacles of an octopus, feeling blindly for the answers everywhere. How would they ever determine the truth?

As his breathing returned to normal, Paul became aware of the intensity of the silence surrounding him. The Sheriff was assessing the mood of the men, too. Used to quick readings of uncertain situations, his belligerence eased and a calculating gleam came into his eye. Intuitively, Paul read his thinking. So far, he'd said nothing incriminating. His two mistakes were to try and make a case against a man well-alibied, and going for his gun. Both could be explained. It still was the word of one man against the other.

Growing fearful that at any second the Islanders could be turned against him once more, Paul moved quickly to establish control. "The killer had to have access to the Coop," he said, forcing his voice to remain calm. "He had to have keys to both the old lock and the new one. Especially after the trapdoor was nailed shut. So let's just take a look at the Sheriff's key ring and see what's on it."

The tension eased a bit as the Islanders nodded agreement. The keys would tell the story.

Tom bent down, freed the Sheriff's keys from his belt and handed them to Ben. Paul dug his own keys out, first a key ring, then a single key. These he held out to Ben, too. "This ring holds the old keys to the Coop. The single key is to the new deadbolt put in after the fire. I think if you'll look hard enough, you'll find duplicates to both sets of keys on the Sheriff's ring."

Ben, with Abner and Old Jeb looking on, made first one match, then a second. "Down to the last groove," he said.

At last, the Islanders were convinced. Paul almost collapsed with relief.

"But you realize, Paul," Ben said slowly, "we still don't have enough. A set of duplicate keys won't be enough to convict. And so far, he hasn't said anything incriminating. We need Ilsa's body and enough other proof to bring to a jury. Otherwise, he's certain to get acquitted."

As Ben made it clear that possibly a jury wouldn't see the Sheriff's guilt as clearly as they, the men's anger deepened to barely contained rage. No one actually muttered any threats, but it was there in the tense grooves of their faces and the hardness of their eyes as they stared at the Sheriff.

At last, Calvin stepped forward, his face set in a deep, barely contained fury. "What's wrong with having him walk off the cliff right here and now?" he demanded, pointing to the bluff edge. "Just like he made Obadiah do."

There was dead silence among the men. Kill the man, or watch him walk. Their faces hardened further. The foghorn blatted again.

Paul thought a moment. "Would a confession help?"

At the question, the Sheriff relaxed a little.

"You bet it would," Ben responded. "Especially if it led to the bodies."

Calvin snorted. "Look at him," he growled. "He ain't gonna say nothin' about nothin'."

That was true, Paul thought. A quick probe of the Sheriff's expression confirmed that. The man had played cat-and-mouse for twenty years, and he was too good and too confident to lose the game now through any sudden change in character.

Paul looked down at the ropes, then over at the bluff and began to smile. "Ever seen a piano lowered out of a ten-story window?"

It was gratifying to see the first real fear creep into the Sheriff's eyes.

Epilogue

The Christmas Fair was a boisterous success. In reaction to the end of the siege and tension, the Islanders wore their holiday clothes, laughing as they called out greetings to each other, humming along with the taped Christmas music filling the room. Cigar boxes at the booths overflowed with money, were emptied, then soon overflowed again as the crowds jostled their way from one to another. The holiday spirit was everywhere.

The Sheriff's arrest was the talk of the Island. Over and over, various Islanders came up to the poinsettia booth and asked Paul about it. They were amazed that he'd solved the murders and wanted to know how he'd figured it out.

When Jenny finally joined him, he told her about the questions and the praise, and said in protest, "They're giving me far too much credit. The Sheriff was so far down my list of suspects he didn't even make the cut."

She laughed. "Well, don't let them know that. You're an Island legend now, so you'll just have to learn to like it." Then she turned serious. "Imagine, though, Frank Hall accusing *you* of the murders. Did he really have a file on you?"

"He really did have a file on me."

"And did it show that you were here that summer?"

"Yes."

"How did he do that when New York Hospital proves you were there at the same time?"

"The Sheriff collected favors through the years—he called them markers—from small-time hoods he let off for one reason or another. And he called in a few of those markers. He had them sign affidavits that they'd worked in motels twenty years ago, and they supposedly identified me as the one they'd seen checking in with Ilsa Murdock the summer she disappeared."

Jenny's eyes were wide with indignation. "But they were lying! Wouldn't that have come out at the trial?"

"There wasn't going to be a trial. According to the Sheriff's plan, I was to have a fatal accident off the bluff. I'd be dead; I wouldn't be able to defend myself. So no trial, no attorneys, no cross-examinations. Case closed. Finis."

"Oh, Paul, that was so close. Too close. It almost worked, he almost killed you. And Abner says you stayed calm the whole time up there, though he said a time or two he thought you were going to strangle the Sheriff with your bare hands."

"I gave it serious thought." He smiled at Jenny. "Very serious thought."

A poinsettia customer interrupted them. While Paul watched, Jenny helped them choose a white one as a centerpiece for a red tablecloth. Each time a plant was sold, his thoughts would return to Grace. She should've been here. She should've been *able* to be here, he corrected. His hands clenched into half-fists, as if encircling a throat. The Island was going to miss her. Bobbin, too. They'd added their generous portions of caring, and there was never enough of that in the world. At least, not in the world he'd come from.

Jenny finished the sale and returned to her stool next to his. "Paul, I was thinking of Ilsa being buried on top of Calvin's wife. If only someone had caught on sooner, think of the years of heartache it would've saved Ben."

Paul nodded. "I thought Calvin was going to tear those state troopers limb from limb for having her grave desecrated."

"But whatever made the Sheriff think of hiding bodies in graves anyway?"

"When he killed Ilsa, he needed a place to hide her body where it wouldn't be found. He knew Calvin's wife had gotten sick and died that summer, and once her funeral was over, he simply visited the grave one night and buried Ilsa on top of the coffin. Then, this fall, when the last spate of deaths started, he used the same trick on Jason and Pearson."

"But if he killed Jason first, and Obadiah second, where'd he hide Jason's body until Obadiah was buried?"

"In one of the summer houses already closed up for the winter. Then after Obadiah's funeral, he rowed across at night and buried Jason in the fresh grave. He had to keep Jason's body hidden to keep up the pretense that the boy was behind all the other deaths. He didn't care if Harrison was found. That would be blamed on Jason. And Obadiah? Simply an accident off the cliff. Walt Gibbons, another accident, a drowning. Bobbin and Grace he had to let be found. They couldn't just disappear, the Islanders would've torn the Island out of the Sound looking for them. But Pearson could disappear. In Frank's mind, that added mystery to Grace's death. Remember, Jenny, he had to pick and choose whose body would go where. There simply weren't that many fresh graves available."

She shuddered.

"It was my obsession with humped and unhumped graves that led to finding Jason's body—otherwise we'd still be clearing forests looking for him."

"But why did the Sheriff allow the grave to be dug up? I mean, one thing led to another, and they ended up finding Pearson's body, too."

"He couldn't avoid it, Jen. I cornered him about those graves. I simply wouldn't let it drop, not once my suspicions were aroused, and he knew that."

"But he was the only one you spoke to about it. He could've killed you, hidden your body and gone on his way, instead of digging up the graves."

"Ah, but he still wasn't sure if everything in the pianos had been found. Remember, I hadn't started on the grands yet . . . and he just wasn't positive there wasn't something still hidden there. Besides, by then, he had me picked as his fall guy. So he had to be careful that my death would look like an accident—something that happened while I was attempting to escape."

"And Walt Gibbons? And Grace and Bobbin?"

"Walt Gibbons saw the Sheriff rowing over and recognized him. Bobbin saw the Sheriff on the Island the night Walt Gibbons was drowned, and, according to the confession, Grace had a suspicion about the fire in the Coop. They had to die. His paranoia dictated it."

Jenny mulled it over. "Paul, what about Jason's little Scottie? Did Frank have anything to do with that?"

"Yes. Soon after he killed Ilsa, he brought her body back to the Island and placed it in a temporary grave in the woods until Calvin's wife was buried. Somehow the dog came on the Sheriff while he was doing it, and he had to be killed, too. Otherwise he might've tried to dig it up."

She shuddered. "So many deaths. So many. He deserves whatever's coming to him. Will his confession hold up in court?"

"Absolutely. There are a dozen of us who'll swear that he gave it of his own free will."

She looked a bit skeptical. "He's claiming he was coerced. That he had to admit to something he didn't do in order to save his own life. Something about being dangled over a cliffside."

"Incredibly imaginative, isn't he?" Paul said blandly.

More customers for poinsettias approached. He watched Jenny as she helped them, her eyes warm and caring. There was still the undercurrent of sadness at the loss of her dad and Grace. That would be with her for a long time to come. But for today, her cheeks were flushed a soft pink, her lips were rosy and curved into a happy smile, and the chestnut hair swung like a silken veil over her shoulders.

When the crowds eased, he took her hands in his.

"You know . . . or maybe you don't . . . throughout this thing, I was worried that maybe the killer would think you knew something, and would try to kill you, too."

She smiled. "I can't think of a story I could've been told that would've made me budge from that deli kitchen. I knew it was the one place I was safe."

"Mmmm. What if the Sheriff had brought you a message that I was hurt and needed help?"

"I'd have grabbed Thaddeus to go with me. For a while there, he was the only one I trusted."

"Except me."

A sudden sadness washed over her and she dropped her gaze.

He squeezed her hands in reassurance. "You can trust me, you know."

She stared at her hands folded in her lap.

"Yes, you can," he said, firmly. With a gentle forefinger, he raised her chin up until her eyes met his. He held her gaze until the sadness faded a little and a slow smile began. As her eyes turned warm again, he became lost in the glow now being born, a glow of—

"You here to sell plants or just to stargaze?" The sharp, quavering tones broke the spell. Nellie peered at them from beside her husband.

Paul grinned and hopped off his stool to wait on her.

"I'll take this one, this one and this one. And they need to be carried to the car. After that, you come with me back to the kitchen. It don't take two of you to sell them things and there's a pile of dishes waitin' to be washed. Pay the man, Isaiah."

Isaiah extracted some bills from his wallet and

handed them to Paul. "You ought to develop a limp and take up the cane, young man," he murmured in a voice too low for Nellie to hear. "Takes two hands to wash dishes. And to do a heap of other things, too. A cane only leaves you one."

"I'll give it some serious consideration," Paul murmured back.

Under Nellie's stern eye, Paul caught up on the dishes. When there was absolutely nothing else she could think of for him to do, she released him. "Hummph, hear tell you're playing the pianna today. Hope you play better'n you wash dishes."

Grinning, Paul escaped the kitchen. He browsed among some of the booths and spotted trinkets that Jenny might like in a Christmas stocking. He'd learned from Abner that she had a real gift for art, so her main Christmas present from him would be a roll of canvas, an easel and some oil paints. He'd already placed the order through Thaddeus.

At every booth he was recognized and hailed.

"How's it going, Piano Man?"

"Love to have you at our place for Christmas dinner, Piano Man."

"Hey, Piano Man, I got this old beater of an upright that wants working on . . ."

"Got a kid that needs lessons, Piano Man."

The enthusiastic young minister cornered him by the quilts booth about rehearsal for the Christmas Eve service. "Just give me a time and a list of the carols you want played, and I'll be there," Paul said.

The minister smiled a thank you, then turned serious. "Will you be staying on with us?"

Paul looked out over the throng of Islanders and

spotted Jenny working at the booth. One of Zeke's nephews came up to her and tugged at her jacket, his face filled with excitement. When he had her attention, he held out a beautifully crafted wooden fire engine painted in a glossy red enamel for her to admire. Paul could picture the serene warmth of her eyes as she took the time to examine every inch of the truck. "I wouldn't be surprised."

The minister followed the direction of his gaze, then grinned. "Well, well, think maybe I'll practice my wedding service. Just in case." Chuckling to himself, he bustled off to corral another Islander.

Paul wandered over to the booth selling wooden Christmas decorations, where Tom stood puzzling over a hand-carved Santa in a sleigh filled with dolls, trains and other toys.

Tom looked up when Paul reached his side. "Look at this, Paul." He held up a wooden decoration. "Calvin made it. He made all of them here. But look at this one, doesn't it look to you like it's been carved out of one piece of wood?"

It was a three-dimensional carving of a Santa and a gift-filled sleigh. Paul examined it closely, holding it up this way and that. There were no joinings that he could find. "It must've been a single piece of wood. I can't see any joints." He examined it further. "Nope, I can't see any at all. My God, he's talented."

They turned back to the table and Paul selected an ornament for Jenny. It was an angel with sweet upcurling lips, standing beneath her halo with a songbook in her hands, waiting for the downbeat of some heavenly baton. The one he selected for himself was of an elf working at his workbench carving an elf working at his workbench carving an elf. He paid the eight dollars each, then suggested to Tom, "Let's risk capture by Nellie and have some coffee."

"So you've got Nellie on your trail. Need some lotion for detergent hands?"

"One more session like the last one and I will. She's a dragon, that one."

"You're new. The rest of us, we see her coming, we get real busy. Or look like we are, anyway. It seems to work."

"I'll remember that."

They filled their cups and found a place to lean against the wall. They drank quietly for a few moments, people watching, then Tom spoke up. "Well, Piano Man, our plan worked. Not as we expected, but it worked."

Paul grinned. "With only a mild flaw or two," he agreed. "Like never figuring the Sheriff did it."

Tom looked at him with curiosity. "Who'd you have picked, Abner or Calvin?"

"That's a secret I'll carry to my grave. I guess all in all, it came out all right. Though you came out too soon up on the cliff. He hadn't really said anything concrete yet. Like where he'd buried Ilsa. Would've saved some wear and tear on the arm joints if you'd waited just a bit longer."

Tom grinned. "Yeah, you're right, I apologize. We should've just let him go ahead and strangle you to death. How'd you figure whoever it was would take you there anyway?"

"It was the site of the first attempt on me. I had the story of finding that wrench to lure him there."

Tom thought it over. "Well, fella, for a couple of

amateurs, we didn't do too bad. Next time we'll do better. Practice makes perfect, they say."

"What do you have in mind, the Whitman and Ross Detective Agency?"

"Well, you do have to earn a living. And it would be Ross and Whitman, of course."

"God forbid." Paul was silent a moment. "Ben and I have talked," he said, finally. "I've decided to finish out the year's contract here. He seems pretty sure there's a business to be built up here in the Pacific Northwest, restoring pianos. What do you think?"

"Only problem I see would be the lack of population, getting hold of enough pianos to restore in a remote place like this."

"I'd pick them up on the mainland and bring them to the Island myself. Jenny and Thaddeus have agreed to sell me Bobbin's truck, and Ben said he has the kind of contacts that would give me enough work to get me started and keep me going a while."

"His word's gold, Paul, if that's what you're asking. You can count on him to do what he promises to do."

Paul nodded. "That's kind of what I thought. I've also talked to Abner about Grace's place. In her will, she ordered it sold, with the proceeds going to the Island Historical Society. He thinks I could get it on a land contract. Of course, it's in probate now, so it'd be a while before it can be sold."

Tom glanced Jenny's way and grinned. "Got some special reason you'll be needing a place of your own?"

"Someone's got to grow poinsettias for next year's fair."

Tom chuckled. "You're learnin', Piano Man, you're learnin'."

▮

As the day wore down and full darkness fell outside, Tom shut off the taped music. He and Zeke rolled the club's old upright on stage from the wings. People began drifting towards them in small chattering groups.

Seated on the stool next to Jenny, Paul's heart started hammering and his hands got slick with sweat. He felt shaky all over and his knees had lost control. They plainly knocked. He gave her a woeful smile. "Stage fright. It's the worst part of performing."

She squeezed his hand in reassurance, then felt the slick wetness and pulled a handkerchief from her purse.

Anna would've told him it was nonsense to feel that way. But dear Jenny—if your hands sweat, simply wipe them dry. A practical solution to a practical problem. Bless her.

On stage, Tom towered over the crowd and held up his hands for silence. During the last few weeks, Paul had noticed Tom assuming more and more of a leadership role on the Island. It would be interesting to watch him over the years as Abner gradually relinquished the reins.

The last whisper died away and Tom bellowed out in a ringmaster's voice, "Ladies and gentlemen, the Piano Man!"

Cheers, whistles and hurrahs burst from the crowd. With a grin at Jenny, Paul slid from the stool, moved down the aisle the crowd made for him and hopped up on stage.

He'd worked out the program carefully. He opened with Leroy Anderson's "Sleigh Ride," using the composer's original arrangement. His fingers, dancing over the ivories, were limber and nimble, and the keys had an easy touch. He felt that the sleigh was right up there on stage with him, the bells jingling with every prance of the horses' hooves.

Before the cheers and shouts died away, he swung into "Jingle Bells," motioning for the crowd to sing along. Then he went through all the favorites, the audience belting out the words lustily.

With four songs left in his program, he rose from the piano bench and approached the footlights, raising his hands for silence. "Would all the children come up on stage and help me out with the next two songs, please?"

The children held back, suddenly pulling close to their families.

Paul grinned encouragingly. "It won't hurt, I promise you. It's not like going to see the dentist."

A boy about nine giggled. Paul spotted him and held his hand out. "Good. There's the first one. Now who wants to keep him company?"

Slowly at first, then all in a rush, they clambered up beside him.

"My, you are a swarm," he said. "All right. Three rows. Smallest in front, biggest in the back."

One little girl raised her hand. "Am I a biggest or a smallest?"

Paul cocked his head to one side. "Probably last Christmas you were a smallest. And next Christmas, you'll be a biggest. But I think now you're a middlest."

The Islanders loved it.

Once the children were arranged, Paul bent low and spoke so only they could hear him. "You all know 'Rudolph,' don't you?"

Relief filled their faces as they nodded. He gave them the starting note, then the song began. He carried them through the first few notes, then dampered the piano and let them carry the rest of the song. The voices were a blend of sweet soprano, pleasant tenor and a single cracking croak. Watching them, he thought it might be fun to put together a children's choir. Then they poured their hearts into "Santa Claus Is Coming to Town," as only kids who're desperately trying to be good can do. When the children were through, he led the applause for them.

As he swung into the opening chords of "White Christmas," the Islanders began to sway in rhythm, smiling at family and friends, linking hands as they sang. A falling snowflake would have been a nice touch and he looked up from the keys to glance out the windows beyond the audience. Nothing. Inside he laughed at himself.

He allowed the last notes of the song to drift away. The audience fell silent as he softly began the beautiful bass rhythm for "Ave Maria." He let the body of the music develop slowly, giving the rich chords time to drift and hover before the next chord rose to take its place.

He wasn't sure what he was hearing at first. An angel, perhaps, come to earth on a visit from Heaven above. But as the voice swelled with the piano, he saw her. One of the Island wives had moved to the side of the room and stood with hands clasped simply in front of her, her eyes lost in the wonder of the music as her voice poured forth with clarity and beauty.

He gave her the melody and they met and melded as one—her voice and his piano, her words and his chords, and they soared and swooped and filled the air with musical acrobatics until, at last, they drifted off into silence.

The music lingered in the air. The hush held as the Islanders sat frozen in awe. In that instant's stillness, Paul glanced at Jenny, her face aglow with wonder. Their eyes locked on each other until the sudden crash of applause broke the stillness.

As the cheering and clapping thundered all around him, he sat on at the keyboard of the battered old upright, head bowed, his soul too full for movement yet.

Just the Piano Man.

And he felt strangely blessed.